ANNIE SEATON lives near the beach on the mid-north coast of New South Wales. Her career and studies have spanned the education sector for most of her working life, including a master's degree in education and working as an academic research librarian, a high-school principal and a university tutor until she took early retirement and fulfilled a lifelong dream of a full-time writing career. Each winter, Annie and her husband leave the beach to roam the remote areas of Australia for story ideas and research. She is passionate about preserving the beauty of the Australian landscape and respecting the traditional owners of the land. For those readers who cannot experience this journey personally, Annie seeks to portray the natural beauty of the Australian environment through her stories—the spiritual locations, stunning landscapes and unique wildlife. Annie's books have won several awards. Readers can contact Annie through her website, annieseaton.net, or find her on Facebook, Twitter and Instagram.

Also by Annie Seaton

Whitsunday Dawn
Undara
Osprey Reef

East of Alice

ANNIE SEATON

First Published 2022
First Australian Paperback Edition 2022
ISBN 9781489277817

Published by
HQ Fiction
An imprint of Harlequin Enterprises (Australia) Pty Limited (ABN 47 001 180 918), a subsidiary of HarperCollins Publishers Australia Pty Limited (ABN 36 009 913 517)
Level 13, 201 Elizabeth St
SYDNEY NSW 2000
AUSTRALIA

® and TM (apart from those relating to FSC®) are trademarks of Harlequin Enterprises (Australia) Pty Limited or its corporate affiliates. Trademarks indicated with ® are registered in Australia, New Zealand and in other countries.

A catalogue record for this book is available from the National Library of Australia
www.librariesaustralia.nla.gov.au

Printed and bound in Australia by McPherson's Printing Group

MIX
Paper | Supporting responsible forestry
FSC
www.fsc.org
FSC® C001695

For Ian.
My partner in love and life,
as well as a wonderful research and critique partner!

PROLOGUE

Ethan had asked her to help paint his Land Rover the week before she'd started at Charles Darwin Uni in Alice. He'd used Mum's good vacuum cleaner switched to reverse, reading out the instructions he'd found on YouTube. 'Fit the hose into the blow of the vacuum. Turn on the vacuum, and place your finger on the hole on top of the spray jar to start spraying.'

They'd been weak from laughter by the time the paint job had been finished. Then, when it was dry, Ethan had hand-painted the wheel hubs black with a paintbrush.

He'd surveyed their handiwork. 'Looks bloody shit, doesn't it, Gem?'

Gemma could only nod. Not the best job, by a long shot.

'I won't get lost in Ruby anyway,' he'd said as they'd scrubbed paint off the driveway.

That had been the last time they'd done something together.

By the time Mum had discovered the ruined vacuum, Ethan had headed off, and Gemma had borne the brunt of her temper.

It was another two weeks before they'd started to worry. Ethan had done his own thing in those days, staying away from home a lot because Mum was always on his case about getting a traineeship or going to uni. But he'd always come home eventually.

Until he didn't.

CHAPTER
1

Alice Springs
27 January

Gemma Hayden stood at the front of her new classroom and drew in a deep breath. It didn't matter where the school was or how new it was, that same familiar smell of a primary school classroom always filled her with happy anticipation. The waxy crayons, the rubber of the kickballs in the storeroom, the mustiness of books, and the oddly pleasant smell of glue all combined to create that unique atmosphere. There were only three days before the school year began, and although the fresh and eager faces staring up at her this year would be unfamiliar, the promise of making a difference in those children's lives dispelled any lingering doubts Gemma held about her move back to the Northern Territory.

Home.

Trephina Primary School was on the eastern side of Alice Springs and close to the Ross Highway, which led out to the East MacDonnell Ranges. She was close enough to Ruby Gap to go out and camp on weekends and holidays—if she wanted to. The old house where Dad's great-grandmother had given birth to two boys over a hundred years ago was in ruins, and the land had since been subsumed by National Parks to create a nature park, but Dad had always made sure that she and Ethan knew where their family had come from.

Crossing to the window, Gemma stared across the grey asphalt of the playground to the east, where the range beckoned. The low mountains might look smoky blue from a distance, but she knew that the dramatic ridges and bluffs were a deep ochre and red, broken only by stands of white ghost gums marking dry stream beds. She and Ethan had spent much of their childhood at Ruby Gap, fossicking for gemstones, listening to Dad's yarns and surviving his ordinary camp cooking. Despite his basic cooking skills, he'd taught them both how to survive in the harsh Australian bush, the tricks to finding water, and the bush tucker you could find if you knew where to look.

Gemma opened the equipment cupboard and tried to stop her thoughts being pulled down into the dark past. She had clung to hope for a long time, and maybe it was time to accept her brother was not coming back. Maybe her mother was right; maybe she shouldn't have come back to the Territory.

She shook her head; her happy mood had evaporated. She'd come back to the school tomorrow and finish her inventory. She closed the cupboard, resting her head against the doors. 'Where are you, Ethan?' she whispered.

'Who are you?' Gemma jumped at the gruff voice and turned to see a woman with tightly permed grey hair framing an unfriendly face furrowed with deep wrinkles.

'I'm the new Year Two teacher. Gemma Hayden.' She crossed the room to stand beside the newcomer and tried not to wrinkle her nose at the strong smell of smoke emanating from her clothes. 'Can I help you?'

The woman nodded and looked her up and down, unsmiling. 'You're a bit early for term, aren't you? I'm Pat Turner, the head cleaner. I don't let the teachers come in this week. How did you get the key?'

She doesn't let *them?* Gemma raised her eyebrows and stared back. 'Jeff gave it to me. The principal. Along with *his* permission to come in this week.' As soon as she justified her presence in the school, she was angry with herself that she'd found it necessary.

'I know who Jeff Thompson is.'

'I imagine you do.' Gemma couldn't help the coolness in her voice. If there was one thing she wouldn't tolerate, it was bullying and this woman was trying it on.

'So, are you going now?'

Even though Gemma had been about to leave, there was no way this woman was going to harass her out of her own classroom. 'No, I have a few more things to do. I'll be here a while yet.'

Pat folded her arms and sat on the edge of one of the low tables. 'I'll wait here until you're done. We're going to polish the floors in these rooms this afternoon. There's a mess of paint on the floor in the wet room. I hope you've got more control over the kids than the last one.'

'There's no need for you to wait.' The pursing of the woman's mouth reminded Gemma of her mother and that made her all the more determined not to be bullied. The days of being cajoled into doing what everyone else wanted were long gone. She held her gaze steady. 'I'll let you know when I'm finished.'

The woman shook her head. 'Jeff had no right to give you a key. You don't officially start until Monday.'

A great start to my time at Trephina. Then common sense kicked in; there was no point pushing the issue. If there was one thing Gemma had learned about the politics of schools over the past three years, it was the importance of keeping the cleaners on side.

'Okay. I'll get out of your way.' Gemma forced a smile, keeping her voice sweet. 'My preparation will have to wait. It was good to meet you, Pat.'

The woman's eyes widened as she stood. 'Hang on … Gemma *Hayden*? You related to Ethan Hayden?'

A tremble ran through Gemma and she lifted her chin. 'Why do you ask?'

'He was good mates with my Jed.' For the first time Pat's face lost its belligerence. 'You're his sister? You look like him. Twins, weren't you?'

'Yes, we *are*.' Gemma's interest quickened. 'I didn't know Ethan had a mate called Jed. Did the police talk to him back then?'

Pat shook her head. 'I don't know. Jed—the boys called him Screw—had already gone to work on a cattle station in the East Kimberley when I heard Ethan went missing.'

'Oh, I remember Screw!' Ethan, Screw and Saul Pearce had been tight from their first day at high school. They used to do everything together, and Gemma had been terribly jealous. They were allowed to go bush and she hadn't been allowed to tag along. Her dad had allowed Ethan to go because Saul was a couple of years older, but Gemma had long suspected he hadn't wanted his little girl camping in the outback. 'How is he?'

'He hung around for a while when you all left school, then took off to Roselyon.'

'Where's Roselyon?'

'Some bloody huge cattle station near Lake Argyle. You know, that bugger hasn't been home once since he left. But that's kids for you.' Pat's tone was friendlier. 'So, you're a local girl, hey? The school community'll like that.'

'I am. It's good to be home.'

'Come outside with me, love. We can chat while I have a smoke.'

Gemma picked up her bag and followed Pat outside. 'Where are you living? Your parents aren't here anymore, are they?'

'No. Dad lives in Darwin. I moved to the east coast with Mum when they split up, and I finished my teaching degree there. I've got an apartment out near the university now.'

Once they settled on one of the box seats surrounding a pretty garden with a small lemon tree in the middle, Pat lit up. 'Move further up so the smoke won't bother you.' She waved to the far end of the wooden bench.

'No, it's okay.' Gemma didn't care how much smoke there was if Pat wanted to talk about Ethan. 'So, the police didn't talk to Screw, I mean, Jed, back then?'

'I don't know. I'll be honest with you, we had a blue before he left, and we haven't talked since then. Maybe they did contact him, who knows?'

'So, is he still there?'

'I got a Christmas card from him the second year he was gone, from a cattle station up in the Gulf. Who knows where he is now? Bloody kids. Don't even have his phone number. Never hear much from his sister either. She lives in Cairns. Haven't even met my first grandchild yet.' Pat shrugged.

Gemma gave a sympathetic murmur. 'Do you think Jed might have known something? Did he leave home before Ethan went?'

The woman puffed a cloud of smoke. 'Listen, love, I can't remember what I had for breakfast most days, so I sure as hell ain't going to remember the date he took off. What was it? Five years ago?'

'Six.' Gemma tried to contain her frustration. 'Do you remember my brother? He went to Screw's house—I mean, to your place—a lot when they were at school.'

'Of course I do. The three of them used to hit the fridge like a plague of locusts. When I'd had enough of them, I'd hunt them off to the Pearce place.'

'I didn't know they went there too. Ethan never said.' Gemma knew her voice was dull. She'd managed to put Saul Pearce out of her mind after he'd left her without a word. *Don't think about it now.*

Pat nodded. 'Ethan was a good kid. Always polite and knew his pleases and thank-yous.'

'He spent a lot of time away after we turned eighteen, but he always texted me and stayed in touch. Mum used to get really angry with him because he didn't enrol in uni when we left high school. You might remember she was principal at St Mary's.'

'Yeah, I remember your mum,' Pat said, her tone indicating they were not friendly memories.

'I thought he'd gone away to keep the peace, but when he didn't come home and we couldn't contact him, we knew something was wrong,' Gemma blurted, unable to stop herself. 'Even after three months the police refused to list him as officially missing. "Ninety-eight per cent of missing persons turn up, and if they don't, there's a good chance they don't want to be found," they said.' Gemma's voice shook. It was still hard to talk about it. She and Mum rarely did. As for Dad . . .

'Slack bastards.' Pat put her head back and blew out a stream of smoke.

'They just didn't seem to care. They told Mum he was just another young guy who wanted to get away from home and was probably off working somewhere.' Gemma swallowed and sat up straight. 'I knew there was something wrong. It wasn't like him. Even though he and

Mum fought, Eth was thoughtful. He'd never take off without telling us. Dad spent weeks driving around and putting up posters of him and his red Land Rover at every rest stop from here to Western Australia, then Queensland. Not one person ever contacted us.' It had broken Dad, waiting for Ethan to come home.

'I wondered where your dad had gone,' Pat said thoughtfully. 'I used to see Tony at the Gidgeewalla pub. I worked there for years before I got the job here at the school.'

'Mum said she knew Ethan was dead and that he wouldn't come back. That's when Dad took off.' Gemma closed her eyes as she remembered the massive fight she'd had with her mother when Mum had announced they were moving to New South Wales. She'd dragged eighteen-year-old Gemma with her, away from her university course. 'I knew . . . I mean, I know . . . I know Ethan's not dead. I'd feel something if he was.' Wouldn't she? He was her twin, after all. Gemma was determined not to give up hope. The sooner she could get out to Ruby Gap, the happier she would be. Her only regret was that she had left it for so long to go back out there.

Pat pushed her cigarette butt into the dirt before leaning down to retrieve it and pop it in her pocket. 'I'm sorry you've been through the wringer, love,' she said kindly. 'Anyway, I'd better get back to work. And listen, if there's anything you need here at the school, you ask me. Okay?'

'Thank you, Pat.' Gemma pulled out her phone. 'Can you tell me the name of the cattle property Jed's at now?'

Pat shrugged. 'The only one I ever knew was the first place he went to. Roselyon.'

Gemma nodded, making a note in her phone. 'Okay, thanks.'

It was a start; she'd see if she could contact the property, and maybe they'd know where Screw had gone. She was not going to give up until she found Ethan.

CHAPTER
2

Berkshire, England
10 May 1886

'Don't listen to her, Rosie.' Amelia Ashenden tugged on her sister's arm.

'What do you have to say to that, girlie?' Aunt Eloisa leaned forward with her ear trumpet.

'To what, Aunt?' Rose deliberately yelled into the flange.

Their aunt jumped back with a frown. 'I said, "marry in May and rue the day".' Aunt Eloisa had repeated the old proverb at every dinner and afternoon tea of Rose's bridal tour, and while it played on Rose's mind, she refused to look bothered by the warning.

'Mr Lindsay has recently requested that William join him in September,' Rose explained for the thousandth time. 'That means our wedding must be in May, so we can travel to Venice for our honeymoon before he departs for the Antipodes.'

'Foolish. But at least you are marrying on a Wednesday.' With that, Aunt Eloisa lost interest and moved on to her next victim.

Seventeen-year-old Amelia giggled and led her sister to the table where an array of cakes and dainty sandwiches were displayed. 'Where's William anyway? He should have been here by now. He's always late. Father is looking quite cross.'

'He'll be here very soon. He promised. Mr Lindsay's representative requested to speak with him, so he was meeting him for lunch at the club.'

'This Mr Lindsay you are always talking about, is he an eligible bachelor?'

'Amelia, he is in Australia. William knows him purely by their correspondence. Mr Lindsay was made a fellow of the Royal Geographical Society, and William wrote to him.'

'But is he a *bachelor*?'

Rose laughed. 'You are incorrigible, and too young to be thinking of marriage,' she told her sister primly. 'And no, he is married. William told me that when Mr Lindsay made his famous discovery, he named the gorge Glen Annie, after his wife.'

'What famous discovery?'

'The rubies. The reason William and—I mean the reason William is going to Australia. After he assists Mr Lindsay on the surveying expedition, he is going to make our fortune.'

Amelia's mouth opened in a large O. 'What did you mean to say? William and …? William and who? You are not going to go to the colonies, are you, Rosie?' Amelia's voice was shrill, and a couple of the guests looked over.

'Shh. Keep your voice down.'

'Tell me you are not going!'

Rose smiled brightly for the onlookers. 'If that is what my husband decides, I will travel there and join him in a couple of years.'
Privately, she hoped it would be sooner, but Rose knew if she
conveyed her hopes to her sister, there would be a scene. Being
brought up by a succession of governesses and housekeepers since
Mother's passing had left Amelia wilful, and cast Rose in the role
of peacekeeper.

Amelia stamped her foot, but her words were whispered. 'No, I
will not allow it. Nor will Father. That is the most ridiculous thing
I have ever heard. And you know I don't like William. Are you
really sure you want to marry him?'

Rose frowned. Her sister's words echoed closely some of her
own thoughts in the dark of night. Perhaps she had been too hasty
in accepting William's unromantic proposal … but Rose dreamed
of being the mistress of her own home, and as each season passed,
the risk of being left on the shelf became all too real.

They had met by chance at Reading Library when Rose had
dropped her books in the foyer. To her surprise, the gentleman who
helped her had invited her for tea in the adjacent tea room, and she
had been feeling very bold. William's stories of travelling to the
Antipodes had fascinated her. When he had met with Father to ask
for her hand a scant twelve weeks later, Father had, by all accounts,
been very pleased to agree, despite their short acquaintance.

'The proper role of a wife is to love, honour and obey her husband, and when I make my marriage vows in two weeks, that is
what I shall then do. When you grow up, Amelia, you will learn
that too.'

'Well, I don't want to grow up if I have to do what some man
tells me!' Amelia folded her arms. 'And I shall be telling that very
same thing to William Woodford when he arrives.'

Later that night, although Rose was disappointed that William did not arrive to attend the afternoon tea for her aunts, she was equally pleased that Amelia was not able to waylay him and deliver her threatened directive.

Rose lay on her bed and opened her diary. Privately, she hoped that William *would* request that she accompany him to the colonies. The content of Mr Lindsay's expedition report fascinated her, and the land sounded beautiful. How exciting would it be to experience it for herself! She ran her finger down the words that she had copied from the letter William had sent from London, where he had heard a member of the Royal Geographical Society repeat the report Mr Lindsay had given in Port Adelaide.

We travelled north along the Overland Telegraph line in February 1886. Even though the season was poor compared to previous years, at times, the vegetation was over our heads as we sat upon the camels' backs. The air was alive with the music of many birds: magpies, parrots of various sorts, pigeons, doves, diamond sparrows, and many others.

Three days further on took us to the Hale River, another of those sandy rivers peculiar to Central Australia. We followed it downstream until it entered a gorge, where we made camp on the afternoon of 8 March. At that point, we came across a bar of granite completely studded with garnets. Just above this point, when scratching for water under a rocky cliff, I found a quantity of beautiful gem sand containing many garnets and some red stones of great brilliancy which, after careful examination, I believe to be rubies.

Rose shivered with excitement. Oh, to be there, to explore new lands, and see such sights and riches! She lay back and held her diary to her chest, dreaming of exploring that magical place. She could indulge her love of plants and create a beautiful garden of her own design.

It was only when she drifted off to sleep that she realised she hadn't missed William terribly much this afternoon.

★

To Rose's surprise, Father was still in the breakfast room when she made her way downstairs the following morning. She had slept late after lying awake until the early hours, thinking of her new life, dreaming of the freedom it would bring. She would build her own household, create a home where she would have a say, and would no longer face the dreaded fate of spinsterhood.

'Good morning, Father. Are you quite well?'

Her father looked tired, and for the first time, she took notice of how he was ageing. When Mama had been alive, they had been such a happy family, but these days, Father rarely smiled.

He nodded. 'I was about to send Mrs Connell up to get you. I hope you do not continue these bad habits once you are Mr Woodford's wife. I have done my best in the absence of your mother, and lying abed when you are not ill is not to be tolerated.'

'No, Father.'

'You are required to supervise your sister's lessons until the new companion arrives.'

'Yes, Father.'

'And I wish to speak to you about Mr Woodford.'

'Yes, Father.'

'It was your mother's wish that both you and Amelia would be provided for in future years. I am pleased that you are marrying, as it makes the inheritance matter much easier. Now that you will have a husband, as the eldest daughter, on my demise, this estate will go to him. I have also set up a trust for you.'

'There is no need to do that, Father. I do not expect it.'

Nor do I want it. A new life beckoned, away from the sadness and cloying suffocation of living under Father's grief.

'This is the way it shall be,' he said. 'Please do me the courtesy of listening.'

Rose suppressed a sigh. 'Yes, Father.'

CHAPTER
3

**Parks and Wildlife office, Alice Springs
27 January**

'Saul. Gotta job for you, mate.'

Saul Pearce saved the file he was working on and quickly left his desk to join his boss on the other side of the office. The possibility of getting out of the office was very welcome.

'If you want it, that is.' Terry O'Neil was standing in front of the large map that covered the side wall. 'You been out to the East MacDonnells yet?'

'Not since I started here, but I spent a lot of time out there when I was a kid.'

'In the East MacDonnells?' Terry frowned.

'Yeah,' Saul said. 'Out at Ruby Gap.'

'I thought you were a blow-in. Didn't know you grew up out here.' Terry hitched his pants up, and Saul avoided looking at the huge beer gut that hung over his boss's trousers.

'Yeah, Alice is home.' The Darwin office was in a suburban shopping precinct, but here in Alice, they were on the south side of his hometown, on the site of the Arid Zone Research Institute. Saul hadn't spent much time out in the field yet because of the intense heat. National Parks had bloody rules about being out in the field in high temperatures that made Saul laugh; for him, the heat and the brilliant clear blue of the sky were signs of home.

Terry pointed to the right-hand side of the map. 'I want you to go out to Arltunga sometime this week. Check the signs, check the buildings, and put some new brochures out. While you're out there, swing by Ruby Gap. A couple of hikers were out there last week, and they called in a dumped vehicle when they got back to town. Silly idiots should have had more sense than hiking out there in this heat. The police have passed it on to us. If they chased up every bloody abandoned car, they'd have no time for anything else. Because it's on our patch, it's our job. It'll be another one from the community a bit north of the Gap.'

'Which community?' The only one he knew out that way was on the Hale River, just off the Binns Track.

'On the way to the Plenty Highway. We've had a few of the cars already in the park. The young Arrente kids drive 'em until they break down then walk away.'

Saul frowned. Even though it had been a few years, the last time he'd been out near the Plenty Highway to see his mate, Danno, there was only a small community with few vehicles.

'The police won't waste manpower going out there, so it's up to us to do their bloody work for them. As if we don't have enough to do.'

Saul refrained from commenting. He hadn't seen much evidence of overwork in the three weeks since he'd transferred from head office. Everything Max, his boss, had warned him about before he'd left the Darwin office was right. Max was a great mentor and Saul trusted him.

'I'm pleased you want to transfer back to your home town, Saul,' he'd said. 'You're going to find it very different but I want you to do some work on the quiet for me while you're there.'

'What sort of work?' Saul had asked.

'Terry O'Neil's been running Parks down there for a long time, and for some reason, he focuses all of the attention on the west of town,' Max had said. 'A lot of money's been allocated over the years to get the east side developed, but it never happens. He always has reasonable justification in his reports, but I'd like you to see what's actually happening in the east. What do you think?'

Saul had nodded. 'I'm happy to take a look around and keep in touch.'

Now he frowned at Terry as he traced a route on the map to the far eastern edge of the nature park. 'Glen Annie Gorge?' He frowned. 'How the hell did a car get out there? We couldn't even get our bikes up the riverbed, even in the dry.'

'I'm just passing on what was reported.' Terry shook his head. 'There's an old track in from that settlement to the north of Ruby Gap Nature Park. Comes off the Binns Track and bypasses Hale River Homestead. They've come in that way, broken down and abandoned their car, then it washed down when the Hale was running,' Terry said. 'Don't waste time out there. Just have a look at it, take a note of the numberplate, and we can call it in.'

'Must be a new road,' Saul mused. 'There never used to be one out there.'

Terry huffed. 'Look, don't stress about it, mate. There's a good chance there's not even a car out there, but we'll cooperate and take a look, but don't bother going any further than Glen Annie.'

'Not out to Fox's Grave?'

'Mate, I've never been out further than Arltunga. Deskbound for the past ten years, and it's showing.' Terry patted his beer belly. 'Would you believe I was a cop before I got this job? Life got cushy and that's the way I like it.'

Saul shook his head. 'If they ever expect me to stay at a desk, I'll be out of here quick,' he said.

'No sights set on promotion?'

Saul grinned. 'What, and end up with a gut like that?' They both laughed. 'Nah, I'm in it for the outdoor side of the job. Staying stuck at the computer for the past three weeks has just about done my head in.'

'I've noticed. Never seen a bloke play so much Solitaire on the computer.'

'Well, there's been nothing else to do.'

'Don't get your undies in a twist, I'm not having a go at you. At least you make an effort. You've done all the work you've been given, not like your predecessor. Had to give him the flick after he brought his own laptop in and spent the summer playing games on the office network.'

Saul shrugged; to him, that was more an indication of poor supervision. There'd always been plenty to keep him occupied in the Darwin office and out in the national parks. He'd started to wonder if his dream job being back in Alice Springs was going to be what he'd hoped, but he'd remembered what Max had said. Maybe he could make a difference.

'So, you're sweet to go out there and take a look?'

'Of course.'

'Great. You can take Dazza with you. He's spent the last three weeks washing the cars for the Arid Zone blokes. He'll be pleased to have a break.'

'Right. You want us to go today?'

'Whenever it suits you.'

Saul glanced at his watch. The lack of direction didn't bother him; he was beginning to think Max was right. 'There's enough time to get out there and back before dark.'

'Goodo. Darren's down in the car park. Take the newest Land-Cruiser, it's got a satphone mounted on the dash, and we've just restocked.' As well as a fridge that plugged into a second battery, all Parks vehicles carried water, dried food, a pop-up tent, fire blankets and a comprehensive first-aid kit. 'Let me know what it is when—if—you find it.'

'Will do.' Saul knew his grin was wide. 'It'll be good to be outside.'

'If you're so antsy about being in the office, I can get you painting the facilities at Ormiston Gorge.' He shot Saul a sideways look. 'I didn't ask because I thought you'd turn your nose up at that sort of work.'

'Shit, no. Anything's better than being stuck in the office.'

'You can go out to Ormiston Gorge next week. You know, I might have read you wrong.' Terry looked at him thoughtfully. 'Welcome to the team.'

★

Just under an hour later, Saul turned left before the resort that was at the end of the sealed road—the resort hadn't been there last time he'd been out here.

'A resort in the bush, for Christ's sake,' he muttered.

'What's up?' Darren looked at him curiously. Saul had noticed Darren lose motivation over the weeks he'd been back in Alice. He couldn't blame the young bloke; washing cars was not the sort of work to inspire a love of the job. He'd jumped at the chance to get out with Saul today.

'Nothing, just talking to myself.'

Even though there was no service, Darren turned back to his phone and Saul focused on the road. The sealed section went longer than it used to, so maybe Terry was right and there were some new roads at the back of Ruby Gap. You never knew with mining companies all over the place. You'd often come across a surveyor, an exploration geologist, or a bloody truck with wheels that were two metres high. He'd discovered that in his years in Darwin. Uranium, zinc-lead, bauxite, gold, phosphate and manganese, and now rare earth, were all mined in the Territory, and probably more he'd never heard of. Wherever you went these days, you were likely to come across a slash in the landscape, and all that mining pissed Saul off, big time.

The days of camping in the wilderness were long gone. He owed a lot to those days of camping with Ethan and Screw in the wilds at the back of Ruby Gap, where the pristine environment had given him a deep respect for this country. Ethan and Screw had searched for their fortune, while Saul had wandered around, appreciating the solitude and the majestic beauty of the East Mac-Donnell Ranges.

He pulled up the satnav, zoomed in on their location, and slowed down.

'Are we there?' Darren looked up.

'No, we're not even halfway yet, but the road looks to be badly corrugated from here. I'll let the tyres down in a bit.'

'It's pretty rocky from here to Arltunga. It'll slow us down.'

'What about from Arltunga out to Ruby Gap?'

Darren put his phone in his shirt pocket and shook his head. 'I haven't been past Arltunga.'

'So if Terry doesn't go out there and you haven't, who keeps an eye on the nature park?'

'The guy you replaced. Rick O'Connell. But he got the boot. Left the service. Works on boats out of Darwin now.'

'Terry said he was slack.'

Darren's eyes widened. 'You know about it? You mean, it got all the way to head office? Terry said it was all hush-hush. Between you and me, I think Terry got a bit of a kickback from the mine guys to put the skids under Rick.'

'The mine guys?' He frowned. 'What mine? I thought he got the sack for playing computer games.' As soon as he spoke, Saul regretted opening his mouth. If there was one rule he followed, it was keeping his mouth shut in the workplace. He'd learned at a very young age not to trust, and that had stood him in good stead in his years at the Darwin office. He knew he had a reputation as a loner and it didn't bother him. After Screw and Ethan, Saul had decided to make his way through life on his own, doing what he wanted when he wanted and not depending on anyone else. Sometimes he got lonely, and he'd wander into the local pub for a beer and a bit of a yarn, but most of the time, he and Attila, his bull-mastiff cross, got on just fine by themselves.

'Jeez, no. But hey, forget I said that,' Darren said urgently. 'Don't tell Terry I was talking about it, okay?'

'No problem. I know nothing.' Saul knew when to shut up. Looked like Max was right.

Money was always changing hands in the Territory. The influence of money in politics was continuing to undermine integrity across all areas of government, and from Max's suspicions and what Darren had said, it seemed the local office of the Parks service wasn't immune.

Lip service was paid to anti-corruption efforts across the country, but Saul was cynical about the implementation of it. He and the boss he'd had before Max had fought against the building of a caravan park in one of the protected areas on the coast west of Darwin, but a government minister had stepped in and approved it, despite the fragility of the mangroves there. A kickback there too, all swept under the carpet.

One thing he'd admired about Max when he'd taken over was his integrity, and Saul vowed to work the same way.

'So, you know this place we're going to?' Darren asked.

'Yeah. I used to camp out there when I was at high school. A couple of mates were keen fossickers, and we'd come out on our bush bikes as far as we could.' He couldn't help a smile at the memory. 'We'd leave all our gear out here in the ruins of the old homestead between visits, but I don't know if it's there anymore. It was a long time ago.'

'Your mates don't come out here these days?'

Saul stared at the dirt road ahead rutted with corrugations, angled rock veins running across to each side.

'No, they moved on too,' he said briefly.

Saul had already moved to Darwin when he heard about Ethan's disappearance, and he'd called Mrs Hayden to see if he could help. He couldn't get any sense out of her, and he didn't ask to speak to Gemma. He doubted if she would have talked to him anyway. He knew that Screw had gone west; he hadn't heard from him since Screw's dad had dropped Saul off in Katherine. He'd hitched the rest of the way to Darwin.

'It'll be interesting to see if your old house is there and your stuff's still in it. Like a blast from the past. What were you looking for out there? Gold?' Darren sounded keen. 'I've heard there's still gold out here.'

'Not gold.' Saul's laugh was short. 'Rubies. My mate Ethan had this theory that there were some big rubies out here, just waiting for him to find. All we ever got were little garnets, but you couldn't sway him.'

As they hit the worst of the road, Saul slowed the LandCruiser again then pulled off to the side. 'It looks as though a grader hasn't been out this far.'

The road was lined with untidy green scrub, the leaves dull from the red dust. As they got out of the car, a huge flock of budgerigars rose from behind the trees.

'Jeez, will you look at that.' Darren ducked as the flock swooped over them, chattering and chirping, the movement of their wings disturbing the air as they flew past. 'I didn't know there was any waterholes out here.'

'There's not. Not until you get to the Hale River, but that's a long way from here. There's permanent water out at Annie's Gorge,' Saul said as he crouched down at the front wheel. 'They've adapted. If there's no standing water around, they drink the early morning dew and "bathe" in wet grass.'

Saul could feel Darren's stare. 'How'd you know that?' he asked.

'Growing up out here taught me a lot.' Saul didn't say he'd been to uni and done an environmental science degree before he started work with Parks and Wildlife; he didn't like talking about himself. He still felt like a fraud at times; it was hard to let go of that kid from the wrong side of the tracks. But even when he was that kid, he'd learned all about the bush. Dad had been a bushie, he'd just liked the grog more than he'd liked work. He'd died just after Saul had left for Darwin.

That year had been a shit year—Dad, Gemma, and then Ethan.

It didn't take long to lower the tyre pressure, and after they'd each grabbed a bottle of water from the camp fridge, they headed east. They stopped at Arltunga to check the signage and top up the brochures, and Saul glanced across at the old settlement. The old gold mining area fascinated him. First settled in 1887, Arltunga was officially Central Australia's first colonial town and had once been a thriving community. His forbears on his father's side had run the combination store and pub until the mining boom came to an end, according to what his dad had been able to remember. One day, when he had more time, he'd come back and have a good look around. Terry had mentioned ranger-guided walks in the winter, and Saul was keen to take them up.

They'd never stopped here on their bikes on the way out to Ruby Gap; Ethan had always been in a gut-busting hurry to fossick in the dry riverbed of the Hale River. It had been easy to see why he was so keen. The riverbed glowed red in the sunlight, where the hundreds of small pink garnets were caught on the rocks, and in the shingle left from the flow of the water. One night, as they'd sat around the campfire, he'd told them the story of his dad's great-grandfather, William Woodford, and his involvement in the discovery of a rich ruby seam. Ethan had been determined to find it and make his fortune. He'd been good for Saul. Even though he knew Ethan's dreams were just that, his optimism had rubbed off on Saul and he'd even started to believe in himself.

Saul stared at the rough road ahead as they turned onto the track that led to Ruby Gap.

Those days were long gone.

CHAPTER
4

**Berkshire, England,
25 May 1886**

Rose's wedding day dawned bright and clear. She'd awoken early and gone to sit in the window seat, looking out over the expanse of emerald-green lawn as the early sunlight crept in from the east. Pressing her fingers to the cool glass of the window, she stared out over the gardens surrounding Ashenden House. The glass was latticed with diamond panels of soft lead and framed the exquisite view of the lawn and colourful flowers. The roses were fat with early buds; it had been a very warm and dry spring, and already the hollyhocks had reached the top of the wall next to the stairs that led to Rose's favourite part of the garden. She closed her eyes, imagining the sweet perfume of the garden surrounding her. It would be hard to leave behind, but she would soon have her own house and gardens at William's family home in Stoke Newington.

Her young sister flew through the door without knocking, flopping on the end of her bed and folding her arms with an exaggerated sniff. 'I don't want to think of you leaving today. I cried all night, Rosie.'

Rose raised her eyebrows. 'You look very well rested to me, Amelia.'

'Well, I shed a tear for a minute or two before I went to sleep,' Amelia confessed, pouting. 'I don't want you to get married. I don't want you to leave home and live in London with William. Why does everything have to change?'

Rose moved to sit next to her sister on the bed. 'Because we grow up,' she said simply, clasping her sister's hand. 'You will one day marry and have your own home away from Ashenden House. Please be happy for me on my wedding day.'

'Oh, I am, dearest,' Amelia sniffled. 'It's just that I worry that I will barely see you.'

'You can come and visit. William has a house in Stoke Newington, and I am looking forward to being mistress of my own household.'

'Does his house have a garden like ours, or is it in the middle of the city?'

'William assures me that I will be very happy with the house. It has a small back garden, and I have asked that he hire a gardener to help me.'

'There is no gardener?' Amelia looked horrified. 'What household staff will you have?'

'I will find out all of that when we stay there for the week before we leave for the Continent.'

Amelia hmphed. 'I hope the generous dowry Father agreed to is not being used to fund his journey.'

'Amelia!'

'Well, I'm not wrong to worry. William told Father this week that he will be away in Australia for many months. I don't understand why you have to move to London at all if your husband won't be there.'

Rose had privately had the same thoughts, but fearful of sounding snobbish, had not spoken of them. The last thing she wanted was for William to change his mind; he would make a suitable husband. He was a professional, middle-class man and a well-respected surveyor. To her understanding, the house at Stoke Newington was the family house that he had inherited on his parents' deaths. And as his wife, it was her home too.

When Father had spoken to her of the trust he had set up for her, she had wondered why he had found it necessary. Although Rose sensed his relief in her finding a husband, she wondered if Father had doubts too. Pushing the cloud of doubts away, Rose smiled, trying to look happy. It was her wedding day, after all. 'You can come and visit me, and I will be able to tell you about our honeymoon. I am so excited to be travelling to the Continent.'

Amelia looked at her from beneath her lashes. 'Will you tell me *all* about your honeymoon? Are you worried about your wedding night?'

Rose blushed. 'Dear sister, there are some things that ladies do *not* discuss.' Her sister spent too much time unsupervised, and Rose wondered where she had learned about such things. In the absence of a mother, after the engagement was announced, Aunt Eloisa, her late mother's sister, had taken it upon herself to take Rose aside and provide detailed advice that still made Rose uncomfortable.

Amelia pulled a face and flounced off the bed with a parting shot. 'I hope William's not late to the church.'

★

'Are you ready to leave, my dear?' William, now her husband, leaned across to Rose five hours later. The wedding breakfast was over and the guests were waiting for the cake to be boxed.

Rose nodded, her eyes stinging. It was only the sweet smell of the orange blossom in the coronet holding her veil that had tears pricking her eyes, and had nothing to do with the fact that William had barely spoken to her during their wedding breakfast. He had left her side as soon as they had eaten and spent the remainder of the time talking to his two friends from the Royal Geographic Society. He had not commented on her appearance, or the beautiful wedding gown Father had ordered from the House of Worth. William had made his vows then waited a less than polite time after the breakfast before asking if she was ready to leave.

Rose fiddled with her kid gloves and glanced down at the wedding ring that now bound her to her husband. Perhaps he was nervous, or shy. 'Yes, it is time.'

Her husband stood and did not offer his hand to help her rise. 'We will break our journey at Hillingdon. It is too late to travel all the way to London. It was very kind of your father to let us take the barouche.'

Rose stood and gestured to her father that they were leaving. She fought tears as Amelia clung to her.

'Write to me from Venice. I will come to stay with you when you return.' Amelia glanced at William, who stood back while Rose made her farewells. 'As soon as William leaves for the Antipodes.'

The road to London was unfamiliar; Rose had travelled no further east than Reading and she took great interest in the countryside and the large towns they passed through.

They broke their journey at the Red Lion Inn at Hillingdon, and Rose's expectations of marriage took a further blow when the consummation of their marriage was unpleasant but brief. William departed immediately after, not saying where he was going.

Rose saved her hope and tears for her diary.

I will be a good wife. Our marriage will improve as we learn to love each other, and I will be a good mother.

CHAPTER

5

Ruby Gap
28 February

Saul drove the LandCruiser through rock-strewn, tussocky gullies and crossed several dry creek beds as they headed out to Ruby Gap, as well as one flowing creek where the water came up to the running board. Each creek had the inevitable gnarled white ghost gums lining its banks, the white bark contrasting against the rich red of the quartzite cliffs. Contentment filled him as they moved deeper into the remote wilderness and closer to their destination.

The narrow, winding road was much as he remembered, but he was surprised to see several new gates between Arltunga and Ruby Gap with signs declaring private property, and a couple of big *Keep Out* signs, complete with warnings that trespassers would be shot.

'What's all that about?' Saul asked when they passed the third sign. This one had huge letters painted in white over a black background with a skull and crossbones on the bottom. 'Not exactly conducive to getting tourists out here.'

'That's why Terry puts all our manpower into the west.'

Saul's interest flared. 'Why? Because of those signs?'

'That, and the distance from town. Plus, the bad road. Only hearsay too, but there's supposed to be a few crims out here,' Darren said earnestly. 'Not a place you want tourists. Did you hear about those blokes that carked it in the desert out near the Finke River a couple of years back?'

'Yeah, I did.'

'Coroner's report said they'd buried a stash of meth and heroin in PVC containers. When they went out to get it, they got bogged and didn't have any survival gear or water with them.'

'Yeah, I heard that. Shit way to go.'

'Bloody forty-degree-plus heat and barely any water between them. Idiots.'

'So, you reckon that's what's out here now?'

'Who knows? I wouldn't be a bit surprised.' Darren pointed at the next gate, with another hand-painted warning sign. 'I wouldn't be game enough to go through any of those gates, though. You'd probably never come out.'

Saul shrugged. 'Could be people who just wanted to drop out and live off the grid.'

'Could be, but jeez, mate, I could never do that. What a boring life. Could you?' Darren shook his head.

'Easily. It'd be a great way to live.' Saul was thoughtful as they approached the nature park. Maybe Ethan had gone into one of those properties. Maybe he'd seen something he shouldn't have. Surely the police would have investigated out here? Then again, maybe not.

Bloody hell, he wished he knew what had happened to Ethan. He wondered how Gemma was coping, and what she was doing now. Six years had passed since they'd all left Alice, and Saul was the only one who'd come home. He was a couple of years older than the rest of them; his dad hadn't sent him to school until he was six, then Ethan's mother had made him repeat a year before he'd gone to high school. Mrs Hayden had never liked him, and the feeling had been mutual.

He and Ethan had been good mates until they'd fallen out over Saul seeing Gemma. Saul knew Ethan would never have got involved—intentionally, anyway—with anything criminal. He'd been obsessed with his bloody rubies and nothing else.

'Here we go, mate. There's the sign ahead.' Darren undid his seatbelt as Saul pulled up on the side of the dirt road beside the *Ruby Gap Nature Park* sign. 'I guess we're hoofing it from here. How far is it out to the gorge, d'you reckon?'

'It's only about three ks out to Glen Annie. We used to drive along the riverbed as far as the waterhole, but I don't know it well enough these days. Could be water under the sand. We'll walk in, it won't take long.'

'I'll grab the fly nets out of the back.'

'Thanks. There's been a lot of rain this year, they'll be worse than ever.' Every paradise had to have a bad side, and the 'fly in the ointment' was literally that in the Red Centre; small black flies that sought moisture in any orifice they could find.

'Yeah, there's millions of the little black bastards this summer.'

While Darren went around to the back of the vehicle, Saul took the satellite phone from the case on the dashboard, and his hat from the back seat. Once they were kitted up with two bottles of water each and a couple of packets of trail mix, they set off down the rocky slope that led to the wide riverbed.

'Good to see no one's camping out here.' Saul looked ahead as the coarse sand of the riverbed crunched beneath their boots.

'Yeah, we get a lot of enquiries about camping out here in the dry season. Mainly rock climbers and fossickers.'

'Do we run *any* tours out here? Out to Fox's Grave?' For the life of him, Saul couldn't understand why this end of the East MacDonnells had been ignored. He'd discuss that with Max.

'Nah. Haven't heard of that, what is it?'

'An historic site. I'm surprised Parks aren't doing tours and walks out to it,' Saul commented.

'Nah. The guided tours stop at Arltunga. Like I said before, most of our manpower goes out to the West MacDonnells, although Terry has talked about it. Between you and me, apparently, he hasn't changed anything in the years he's been boss. Rick suggested getting some tours out here once, but he reckoned it didn't happen because Terry's too lazy to change anything. Says there's no spare money for the east.' Darren tapped his nose through the fly net. 'But I didn't tell you that.'

Saul gave a noncommittal nod; Darren obviously liked to give his opinion. He was way too chatty for Saul, but some of the information he'd dropped was interesting. They didn't speak again until they reached the point where the Hale River looped to the south.

Saul drew a deep breath and drank in the landscape that brought so many memories. Good and bad, happy and sad.

'What's all that red in the sand? I haven't seen that before. The sand is white in the waterholes over at the West MacDonnells.' Darren slowed his pace.

'Tiny garnets. Pick up one of those big flat rocks and have a look underneath.' Saul waited while Darren stopped and picked up a rock. He put it to the side and reached down again and picked up a handful of shingle.

'Bloody hell, it's almost pure red! Are they worth anything?'

'The tsavorite and demantoid varieties are the rarest and most expensive varieties of garnet, but they're hard to come by.'

'Jeez, you know your stuff.'

'Yeah, I had a mate who was an expert.' Saul shook his head. 'I could tell you enough scientific stuff to bore you to tears. But to answer your question, no, generally garnets are not a valuable gem.'

'Reckon I've got any of that sort you said here?' Darren peered at the red, pink and brown shingle on his palm.

Saul chuckled. 'No. Those rare varieties are green.'

'So, no rubies out here then, even though it's called Ruby Gap?' Darren let the shingle fall through his fingers then wiped his hand on the side of his pants. 'I can see how people get addicted to fossicking. Maybe that's what they're doing on those properties. Digging claims?'

'I doubt it. You need good waterways where the gems wash down.'

'Come on, let's go find this car.'

'If there is one.' Saul strode out ahead. 'I don't reckon there's anywhere up here a vehicle could drive in. The only thing that could have got in would be an ex-Vietnam army truck like a Dodge M37 or a Mac 125.'

'How do you know all this shit?' Darren asked as he puffed along beside Saul, trying to keep up with his pace. 'Budgies, garnets, trucks. You're a bloody walking encyclopedia, mate!'

Saul shrugged. 'I like to read.'

'You must be a good guide. I stick to the patter on the brochure. Rick was like you, he knew heaps of stuff. I liked working with him.'

'Read a bit and it's not hard to come up with some interesting facts.'

Darren shook his head. 'I hate it when the tourists ask questions. It puts me on the spot and I get stuck.'

Saul grinned. 'Make it up, then go back and research it, then you'll learn. It's rare that you get pulled up.' He stared at the red quartzite cliffs, thinking back to the days when he'd camped out here with the boys. They weren't far along from the ruins; it was only a couple of kilometres in from the river and around the next bend. If they had time, he'd go for a wander and take a look. Turning his gaze to the narrow neck of the gorge, Saul followed the direction Darren was pointing in. It was just before the bend where the river turned back to the east, not far from the spot where they'd done most of the fossicking. Ethan had always said it was where the rubies would be, but he'd never found any.

'Is that what you—hey look at that. Is that the vehicle, d'you reckon?' Darren pointed to the far end of the gorge.

Saul put his hand up to shade his eyes from the relentless sun. 'You're right. There's something there. Come on, let's go check it out.'

The vehicle was buried up to the doors in the damp shingle on the north side of the riverbed. From as much as they could see in the shade from the dark cliffs above, it looked as though the front of the vehicle was smashed.

'It's an old Land Rover,' Saul said. The sun glinted on the bare aluminium.

'Most of the paint's oxidised,' Darren said.

'Must have been here a while.'

'How the bloody hell did it get here?'

'No idea,' Saul replied, his mind working. 'The river flows from the east so it had to wash down from upstream. You had a lot of rain out here around Christmas, didn't you?'

Darren nodded. 'Yeah, it pissed down.'

'And there's no road at the top of the gorge, so no vehicle could have got into the bush there,' Saul said as they paced closer. 'That is, there was never a road coming in that way before, and this Rover looks like an old one.'

'With that much paint oxidisation, it's been here a long time.' Darren looked proud as they reached the vehicle. 'I used to be a panelbeater before I joined the Parks. But I got sick of the smell of paint.'

'Look, there's some flakes of red just above the wheel arch.' Saul stepped back and looked around. 'I reckon it could have been here for a while. Look.' He pointed to the cliff face at the back of the vehicle. 'You can see where those two big gums have sheared off when the water was flowing. Probably this year. The trunks and the foliage would have hidden it from view while the trees were there. Plus, being on the north side of the gully, it would have been in the shade because the sun would have been behind that cliff for most of the day.' He stepped back further and turned around. 'And there's a couple of big rocks between the edge and the main channel of the river, and they would have blocked it from the view of anyone walking past.'

'So unless you were looking for it, you wouldn't spot it.'

'I'd say not.'

'I just hope there was no one in it when it came down,' Darren said. 'They wouldn't have had a chance, going nose first like that.'

'What do you mean came down?' Saul followed him around to the front of the Land Rover. 'Came down with the river flow?'

'No, it hasn't come down the river. I'd say it's come off the cliff-top there, hit the river and gone headfirst into those trees and the cliff.' Darren leaned over the front to the vehicle and ran his hand over the bonnet. 'See how it's all pushed in at the front grill?'

Saul examined the smashed grill. 'But how did it get up there?'

'I guess we won't know until we find out who owned it.' Darren looked up at the towering cliffs. 'Looking at the pattern of oxidisation, I'd say it started off here, nose down, and the movement of the river this summer moved it.'

Saul stepped back and followed Darren's gaze. 'Do we ever bring the Parks chopper out here?'

'Not that I remember. There's not much out here to maintain. We've only got Trephina Gorge and Ruby Gap Nature Park out here in the East MacDonnells, but in the West MacDonnells, there's two big national parks. There's only a couple of walking tracks this side, and the one guided tour at Arltunga.'

'I'm going to suggest to Terry that we start some guided walks out here,' Saul said. 'We can come out in the chopper and see if there's a road up top.'

'Good luck with that, mate.' Darren pulled a face and shot a glance at Saul. 'The boss doesn't like change. Or suggestions. Rick was full of them.'

Saul shrugged. 'Whatever. Come on, let's see if there's any ID or rego papers or anything so we can call it in to the police.'

'Doubt it. The windscreen's gone and water would've poured in through the body and the window edges too.' Darren peered through the window. 'The interior's cracked and rotten, and there's mud right up to the seats and covering the floor. But the dashboard and glove box look pretty much intact.'

Saul went around to the side and looked at the passenger-side door. The bottom twenty centimetres was buried. He began to scoop out the loose shingle with his hands. Darren moved past him and started digging on the other side, and it wasn't long before the base of the door was exposed.

'It must have been here a while,' Saul said.

Darren leaned forward, frowning. 'That's a strange paint job.' He bent and ran his hand over the door and looked down at the paint that came off on his hands. 'It's not the original paint. It's not a genuine Land Rover colour . . . and it's not automotive paint.'

Saul reached out to the door handle. 'Hopefully it's not locked.' He pressed the handle and grunted with satisfaction when the door moved slightly. 'The door mechanism's still working but there's a bit of shingle left on the right side. You clear that away and I'll pull the door open.'

As Darren dug and Saul pulled, the door finally opened with a grinding screech that set Saul's teeth on edge. The hinges were full of shingle, and the floor was covered in dark sediment.

'I think it's a write-off,' Darren said with a grin.

'No doubt about that.' Saul pulled a face at the mouldy, wet-dirt smell as he climbed into the cab. 'There's nothing left in the front. I think you're right about it having been nose down. You can see the line on the firewall above the pedals where it was buried up to.' He reached over and tried to open the glove box, but it refused to budge. 'Glove box is locked. There might be something in there.' He frowned as he stared at the metal dashboard. If he didn't know better, he'd have sworn that was a bullet hole punched in the centre.

'Could be.' Darren peered in through the open door. 'God, it stinks. I sure hope there's not a body buried in there. I'll climb in and look in the back. You never know, there might be a jack or something stuck in that mud. It wouldn't float out.'

'You stay there. No point both of us getting dirty. I'm half in already and you're right, it stinks.' Saul carefully climbed over between the front seats and kneeled on the semi-intact back seat, looking over into the rear of the Land Rover.

'Yeah, we're in luck. There's a few tools sticking out through the mud,' he yelled back to Darren.

'As long as that's all that's in there. Do you need a hand?'

'I should be right.' Saul leaned over the back seat and reached for the square piece of rusted metal that was sitting at an angle in the mud. Bracing his knees, he reached across and dug around it. His hands were soon red and brown from the sediment and rust. Once he'd dug down a bit, it gave way a little. He could feel more solid items in the mud under his hands, but Darren's suggestion that there could be a body in there made him uneasy.

'I've found something,' he called out. His scalp was prickling strangely. The sooner he got out of here the better.

'What is it?'

'Almost got it . . . it's sharp, whatever it is,' Saul said. He tugged again, and the metal came out as he pulled. 'It's an axe.' His breath caught as he stared down at the broad-head axe and despite the heat, a shiver ran down his back. 'Can you reach in and take it from me, please?'

Goosebumps rose on his arms as he passed the axe across to Darren then clambered out of the Land Rover.

'That should do the trick,' Darren said. 'It won't matter if you destroy the dashboard, as long as you can get enough leverage to get it open.'

Saul took a deep breath as he stood next to the young ranger and held his hand out for the axe. 'I just need to do something first.' He looked around. There was water at the base of the cliff about fifty metres up the river. Taking the axe, he strode towards the waterhole.

'Please let me be wrong,' he muttered to himself. It couldn't be. Everyone who camped out here would have an axe.

Saul crouched at the edge of the shallow waterhole and sub-merged the axe in the brown water. Even as he ran his hands over the handle to remove the sediment, he knew it wasn't good. He could feel the initials carved into the top end of the handle, just below the blade.

Lifting the axe carefully, he didn't want see what was there in front of him.

W.W.

He was holding Ethan's prized axe; the broad-head axe that had been in Ethan's family since his dad's great-grandfather, William Woodford, had come to the area in the late 1800s. The ancestor whose supposed ruby discovery had driven Ethan his entire life.

Saul walked slowly back to the Land Rover. Darren looked at him curiously.

'What's wrong?'

'We need to keep digging in the mud, in case there's a body.'

CHAPTER

6

London, England
May 1887

Rose Woodford spent her first year as a married woman trying to be content in William's home at Stoke Newington. The long months were difficult; Mrs Best, the long-serving housekeeper—who William spoke most highly of—kept to herself and continued to tend to the house as she had always done. Any suggestions that Rose made were ignored. In this middle-class household, there were no maids and Rose learned to look after her own needs. The garden was non-existent, and all attempts by Rose to start a small flower garden were unsuccessful and met by the housekeeper with a sniff.

What sort of man was William to leave her in this lonely household? Did he care at all for her happiness? The one time she had expressed her doubts to him on the eve of his departure, he had been impatient and dismissive of her concern. Sometimes, Rose wondered if she had made a mistake, and whether perhaps life as a spinster, working in the family gardens, would have been a happier choice, but she always pulled herself to task and tried to stay positive. Her spirits were lifted by constant letters, and one precious visit, from Amelia.

William's letters also reassured her and made her hopeful. Communication from the Antipodes was sporadic, but his letters described a world she was keen to see. His descriptions of rolling green grass plains, jewelled seas, colourful trees and flowers and luscious fruits such as she would never see at home enticed her. His letters were much more communicative than he had been in the two weeks they had spent in Venice, and it was obvious that he wanted her to join him and begin a proper married life together.

She shivered as she sat in the parlour rereading the most recent letter from William. Despite Rose's request that the fire be lit each morning, it had not been done once. Pulling her wool wrap around her shoulders, she smiled as she again read William's news. The letter had arrived a week after their first wedding anniversary, and had filled her with excitement.

My dear Rose,

I have booked a passage for you on the *Oceanien*, departing Plymouth on 28 August. I look forward to you joining me. The journey will take approximately one hundred days, and I shall be waiting in Port Adelaide with great anticipation.

We shall travel to Ruby Gap, in the far north of the colony of South Australia, where I have been allocated a claim and forty acres, and we shall make our home there as I seek our fortune. The discovery of Oriental rubies in the creek beds flowing south from Hart's Range—the area I surveyed with Mr Lindsay—will be most beneficial for our future. The area is growing quickly as miners arrive in the gorges. There are currently over two hundred people working here. By the time you arrive, our house shall be built and I am sure there will be company here for you. I anticipate a small township will develop in this area. At the moment, our supplies come from the town of Stuart, including a monthly mail service.

'No!'

Rose jumped and hurried to the window as a woman's scream rent the air outside. She lifted the drapes and stared through the glass as a ruckus began outside. A small crowd soon gathered, but she was not tempted to go outside. A few moments later, the woman climbed into a hansom cab and the crowd dispersed. Used to her country life in Berkshire, she found the city overwhelming, and often felt unsafe. She had not ventured far from the house in Stoke Newington, and had made no new acquaintances in the year she had lived there. The prospect of her imminent departure filled her with excitement.

Rose nodded as Mrs Best walked in quietly and placed a morning tea tray on the table. She left the window and came to a quick decision.

'Mrs Best?'

'Yes, madam?'

'I have heard from Mr Woodford. I shall be departing in August. I shall spend the next two months in Berkshire with my family before I embark on my journey.'

'Very well, madam.'

The dour woman nodded and left the room. Rose turned back to her letter. She wouldn't mention going home to Ashenden House to William. With the distance and the monthly mail service, she would probably arrive before any letter.

Did they need to maintain a house here? A housekeeper and a cook seemed to be a great waste of money. No wonder William had dismissed her suggestion of a gardener. Perhaps when she got to know him better, she could suggest that they sell this cold and lonely mausoleum at Stoke Newington.

Ruby Gap! The name alone conjured up beautiful images. She would be the mistress of her own household with no horrid housekeeper to deal with. The first thing she would request was that William employ a gardener so they could begin to beautify the grounds. Forty acres! Imagine the gardens she could create.

Rose put her head back and began to make a mental list of the seeds she would gather from the garden at Ashenden House to take with her to South Australia.

Oceanien, *29 August*

It saddened me to take leave of Father and Amelia at Plymouth, knowing it will be a very long time before I see them again. Amelia was distraught and though it saddened me to see Father's eyes glisten, it made me happy to know he will miss me. His arms were tight around me as he bid me farewell before I boarded the ship that will be my home for the next three months. My last sight of Father and Amelia as the vessel made its way from the dock will stay with me forever.

Tears will not help me in my new life with William. On this long voyage, I will turn my attention to the seeds that Mr Marley, Father's groundskeeper, packed carefully for me, and I will spend the journey transcribing the brief notes I wrote as he instructed me in their care and planting. As they grow in my new home, the plants will be a connection to all I have left behind, and those I love.

CHAPTER

7

Trephina Primary School, Alice Springs
Tuesday 1 March, 10 am

'Ms Hayden?'

Gemma looked up as Sylvie Ross, one of the casual relief staff, tapped on the open door of the classroom.

The first four weeks of term in her new school had flown by and she'd settled in well. The majority of the other teachers were young too, and she'd already joined in a few social outings, and was looking forward to the Friday-afternoon drinks and pizza at the pub tonight. Fledging friendships had been forged, but strangely, it was Pat Turner who seemed to be looking out for her. Pat had invited her over for a baked dinner last Sunday, and Gemma had met Rob, her retired husband. It had been a pleasant evening and had further cemented Gemma's conviction that Alice Springs was where she would make her home.

Gemma gestured for Sylvie to enter, but turned back to listen to the second-last pupil as he took his turn for show and tell. Friday morning was one of Gemma's favourite parts of the week, as it gave the students a moment in the sun to show off what was important or interesting to them. She learned more about their young personalities as they showed off their treasures each week.

Jordy Smith, the smallest boy in the class, proudly pulled out his lunch bag. 'These are my wild pig sandwiches,' Jordy announced. 'Why they are important to me is because my dad and I went shooting last weekend and we brought down a friggin' huge sow, miss,' he said, his dark eyes wide and earnest. 'It was a bugger, though. She had a few babies and we had to leave them in the mud.'

'Thank you, Jordy.' Gemma hid a smile as she made a mental note to talk to him later about appropriate language. She turned as Sylvie walked across to stand beside her. 'Just one more show and tell, and then I'll be with you, Ms Ross.'

Lauren Hepplewhite, one of the brightest children in the class, skipped to the front of the room and held up a plastic bag containing a lump of what looked like brown mud.

'Maybe she was out with the pigs like Jordy,' Sylvie muttered.

'Shh.' Gemma smiled brightly at the little girl. 'What do you have there, Lauren?'

'This is important to me because I like learning about medical things. I'm going to be a nurse when I grow up.' Lauren's smile was wide as she opened the bag and held it away from her.

Gemma frowned as a sour, pungent odour emanated from the bag.

'This morning when our dog Stinky did a poo, I was really interested to see it had bits of carrot and corn in it, and it was still the same colour as it was when Mummy cooked our dinner last night. The interesting thing is that the colour stays even when it turns into poo.'

'Thank you, Lauren.' Gemma met Sylvie's eyes over the top of the little girl's head, and it was hard to keep a straight face. 'That *is* very interesting. Now, close up the bag, and I'll get you to put that bag outside the door. Then you go and scrub your hands with soap over at the sink.'

The little girl nodded gravely. 'Yes, I know all about germs too.'

'I'll look after Lauren, Ms Hayden,' Sylvie said, still smiling. 'Mr Thompson asked me to mind your class while you go to the office.'

'Oh? Okay.' Gemma turned to the class. 'Class, everyone back to your tables, please. Ms Ross is going to be supervising you for a little while.' The chorus of chattering provided Gemma cover to ask, 'Is there a problem?'

Sylvie shrugged. 'He didn't say, but he said it might be for the whole day.'

Gemma frowned. 'The whole day?'

'That's what he said, but take care. Pat's there with him. She probably got wind of the dog poo show and tell.'

Gemma chuckled. 'I'm sure that's not why. Besides, Pat's okay.'

'You'd be the only one on staff not scared of her,' Sylvie said darkly.

'Okay, I'll go and report in. From now until recess, the class can each choose a book from the shelves at the side and have some quiet reading time. I'll get back as quickly as I can.'

'It's fine. I've got a quiet day. Grab your coffee first.'

Gemma took a quick look around the room. Lauren was scrubbing her hands, and the rest of the class chatted and giggled as they waited for their reading time. A surge of affection filled her; they were the best bunch of kids she'd ever taught, very different to what her mother had predicted.

When Gemma had finally told her mother that she had accepted a new position in Alice Springs, her objections had been swift. And loud. And constant. 'I have no idea why you would want to go back there, Gemma. There's a huge teacher shortage here in New South Wales.'

Gemma had dug her heels in, refusing to be swayed. 'I'm going home.'

'Home! The Territory isn't your home,' she'd scoffed. 'You haven't lived there for almost six years. You can get a job *here*. It's about time you looked for a permanent one anyway. You'll never get a promotion if you stay casual.'

'I have a permanent job at Trephina Primary School.'

'You'll regret it. The children there truly *are* more difficult.'

'What do you mean difficult?' Gemma had not been able to stop her temper flaring up. When her mother hadn't replied, Gemma had added coldly, 'As an educator, you should know you can't stereotype children by race.' Gemma's fingers had hovered over the disconnect button on her iPhone as the audible sigh sounded at the other end.

'Gemma. Just because your—'

'Don't go there, Mum. I've accepted the position, and I'm quite happy being a classroom teacher. I'm starting at the end of January. Subject closed. I'll see you on Christmas Eve.'

Now, Gemma shook her head as she walked up the side corridor leading to the administration block. She supposed she'd better call home and report in this weekend.

A quick *call.*

Despite the hundreds of little footsteps that had walked and run the corridor every day, the lino floor still gleamed from the polish Pat and her crew had sealed it with four weeks earlier. The maintenance was top-notch; the playground was clean and, despite the heat of summer, the gardens were green and lush. Jeff ran a good school, and he was a good man. Gemma had come in to work a couple of weekends ago and had been surprised to see Jeff on the ride-on mower on the school oval. Trephina was the best school she'd taught in, and the strategies for Indigenous education were not just given lip service, but were at the forefront of all school activities. She'd love her mother to see the things that happened here on a daily basis.

Linda, the school office manager, was talking to a guy in a khaki uniform. She looked up and gestured for Gemma to go straight into Jeff's office. With a quick smile, Gemma walked over and tapped on the door. Jeff opened the door straight away.

'Gemma. Thanks for coming across.'

'Is there a problem?' Her gaze slid to Pat, sitting at the meeting table at the side of the office, staring at her hands folded in her lap. 'Have I done something wrong?'

'No, not at all,' Jeff said hurriedly, closing the door behind her. 'There's been some news, and I know you and Pat are friends, and she might help as a sort of . . . um . . . support person.'

Gemma's blood chilled as Pat looked up at her. 'My mother? My father?'

'No, no, they're fine. Please sit down, Gemma. Your mother has called and asked that we pass some news on to you, but I'll leave that to Saul.'

Saul?

Jeff opened the door again as Gemma sat beside Pat. When Pat reached out and took her hand, Gemma's stomach churned.

What the heck was Saul Pearce doing here?

Sure enough, when Jeff came back into the room followed by the man who had been in the foyer, Gemma looked into the eyes of the man she had fallen in love with when she was sixteen.

★

Saul tried to keep his expression bland as he walked across to Gemma and held out his hand. It was probably inappropriate to lean down and kiss her cheek in the principal's office. Or anywhere else, really, after the way he'd left town, and her.

'Hello, Gemma. It's been a long time.'

Her cheeked flushed as she looked up at him. 'Hello, Saul.' Her gaze dropped to the Parks and Wildlife logo on his shirt and he saw the moment that she realised why he was here, and she pulled her hand with a jerk. She drew in a sharp breath. 'Ethan?'

He nodded. 'Your mum asked me to talk to you.'

'Mum?' Gemma looked around the room, confusion clear on her face.

Jeff gestured to a chair on the other side of the small round table. 'Sit down, please, Saul. I believe you know Pat Turner?'

Saul nodded. 'Hello, Mrs Turner.'

'Hello, Saul. It's been a long time.'

Jeff moved to the door. 'I'll go and get some coffee organised. Coffee alright with you all, or would you rather tea?'

Saul and Pat both nodded, but Gemma didn't answer, not taking her eyes from Saul. The door closed quietly behind Jeff, and she continued to stare.

'Why are you here?'

'Take it slow, love. Just listen.' Pat glanced at Saul.

'Why are you here, Saul?' Gemma repeated, her voice getting louder. 'Why did Mum call you? Why did *you* have to come and see me?' The 'you of all people' was not spoken aloud, but it was there.

Saul took it slowly. '*I* called your mum a couple of hours ago. She told me you were out here at this school, and she asked me to tell you what's been found.' He moved the other chair so he was sitting beside Gemma.

'Why did you call her?'

'Because I didn't know you were back here, or I would have come to see you last night. It took me a while to track your mum down. We still haven't located your father.'

Gemma's voice was terse, and he remembered her well enough to know how tightly she was holding her emotions in check. The flamboyant, loud teenager he'd adored had grown into a quiet, serious woman.

'Just tell me. Have you found Ethan? Or … or his body?' Her voice broke on the last word.

'No. Neither.'

'Thank God.' She put one hand on her chest, and as the tears spilled over, Gemma's voice was fierce. 'He's not dead. If Ethan was dead, I'd know.'

Pat moved closer. 'Of course you would, love.'

Gemma nodded through her tears. 'I want to know what's going on. So why did you ring Mum? Have you heard from him?'

Pat reached over to the tissue box in the middle of the table and passed a tissue to Gemma, who dabbed at her eyes.

Saul leaned forward. 'I work with Parks and Wildlife, and we were asked to go out to Ruby Gap yesterday to see if the report of a vehicle wreck out there was correct. We went out to Annie's Gorge and we found Ethan's Land Rover.'

'You found Ruby? Are you sure it was?'

'I'd never seen his vehicle, but the rego papers and documents we found in a bag in the glove box indicated that Ethan was the owner.'

Gemma drew in a shaking breath. 'Why didn't you recognise it?'

'Because he didn't have it when I left town.'

Their eyes met briefly.

She doesn't even remember when I left.

'How old were the papers?'

Good question, Saul thought. After they'd jemmied open the glove box and found the rego papers dry and intact in a ziplock bag, he'd been too busy worrying whether they'd find Ethan's remains in the car. He hadn't even considered looking at the date until Darren had suggested it.

'The rego was dated almost seven years ago,' he said.

Gemma shook her head from side to side. 'So, what does that mean? Ruby's been out there all the time? It couldn't have been. We searched out there a couple of months after he disappeared. Where was it exactly?'

'It was at the base of Annie's Gorge, and by what paint was left on it, it looked like the vehicle had been there a long time.'

'No, that's not right. It wasn't there. Dad and I looked.'

'The matter has been handed over to the police. I'm sure they'll be talking to you.' Saul was bloody hating every minute of this. The official tone he had to take, and the distance he was trying to put in place. It wasn't the way he wanted to meet up with Gemma again. As her lip quivered, all he wanted to do was take her in his arms, like he'd had the right to once. Like he had no right to anymore.

'Can you promise me absolutely he wasn't in it? I don't want to hear that from the police.'

'I can.' There was no need to tell Gemma how he and Darren had frantically dug the wet shingle out with their bare hands, looking for any sign of Ethan's remains. It had been one of the hardest things Saul had ever done.

Before Gemma could respond, the principal came back in, carrying a tray of coffee mugs. The room was quiet as he sat down at the table.

Saul stared at Gemma, wondering whether it was the right time to tell her what else they'd found before deciding it was best to share it with her in private. When he'd seen the envelope with Gemma's name on it, he'd slipped it into his pocket before Darren noticed it. Maybe he should have given it to the police with the rest of the papers, but something had told him it was private. It was addressed to her, and she should be the one to decide if the police needed to see it.

CHAPTER

8

Port Adelaide
December 1888

Port Adelaide was a bustling place, and reminded Rose of the docks at Plymouth where she had embarked on her journey thirteen weeks ago. Steamers and sailing ships jostled for space in the small harbour, and there was a constant stream of workers coming and going as they loaded and unloaded the vessels. She stood on the deck, clutching her small bag as she worried that William would not be there. The other passengers had all disembarked, and Rose stood there biting her lip, wondering what to do. If he was late and she went elsewhere, he may not find her in these large crowds.

'We did arrive three hours earlier than expected, Mrs Woodford.' Captain Ellis stood beside her. 'I am sure your husband will be here soon.' Captain Ellis—Richard, as he had requested she call him about a third of the way through the voyage—had been kind to her over the long journey. They had discovered a common interest in plants, and some afternoons he had stood beside her on the deck, telling her of the exotic jungles he had visited in his travels. Rose told him of her plans to create a beautiful garden like that of Ashenden House when she and William settled on their acreage.

'Where is it located?' he had asked one day.

'A place called Ruby Gap.'

Richard had frowned. 'I have heard of the excitement of the ruby discovery there. That is a very, very long way north of Port Adelaide.' He looked out over the water. The seas had been calm for most of the journey, and the captain had spent much time ensuring that the passengers were comfortable and happy.

'I am not sure how far it is. I wonder how we shall travel there?'

'I'm sure you are aware that it will be very different to home. The railways are slowly moving to the north, and although the Overland Telegraph line has been completed to the north of the continent, Ruby Gap is a very remote location.'

'William assured me that a township is developing,' Rose said confidently. 'I have seeds in my luggage to begin my garden.'

'I'm not sure how far north the railway has progressed, but hopefully you won't have too far to travel overland.' The captain had turned and leaned his elbows on the railing at the edge of the deck. 'I don't want to discourage you, but I do hope you won't be disappointed, Mrs Woodford. I believe the country has been in the grip of a drought for some years. It will be very different to what you are used to. It is also close to the December equinox, and the heat in the desert may be . . . unpleasant.' Captain Ellis lifted his hand. 'I believe that may be your husband coming along the wharf now?'

Nervous excitement roiled in Rose's stomach as she watched the man walk through the crowd. His stride was confident, and his neck and face were tanned to a nut brown. For a moment, she thought the captain was mistaken but then he looked up and smiled, and she knew it was William.

He seemed taller and straighter as he ran up the walkway, and Rose was quite taken aback when her husband pulled her into his arms and kissed her soundly, not caring who was watching.

'Oh Rose, I am so happy you have finally arrived.'

*

Four weeks later, Rose recalled the captain's words as she and William spent their first night beneath a roof at Dalhousie Springs homestead one hundred miles north of a place called Oodnadatta.

It was the first opportunity she had had to write in her diary, as the unending days had been spent travelling in scorching heat, and the nights endured sleeping under a canvas tent, trying to keep cool. William was taking port with George Bagot, the son of the pastoralist who had established the homestead, and had reportedly died recently on another property. As George and his wife Ellen had greeted them, Rose's head had been aching, and she'd found it hard to follow the conversation. Ellen had taken one look at Rose, and immediately ushered her into a small brick building, where she had soon filled a hip tub with warm water piped from the springs, and brought in fresh towels and soap, and a large pitcher of cool water.

'My dear, you must stay out of the sun. You look to me like you have heat stroke. I shall tell your husband you both must stay here for a few days to allow you to recover.'

She had thanked Ellen, even as she knew there would be no possibility of William agreeing to a delay. After the luxurious bath,

Rose had excused herself from dinner and gone to the room they had been given for the night.

She climbed into the soft bed, and pulled out her diary for the first time in weeks, making the most of the time alone. For all the time they spent together, she didn't feel she knew William any better. All he talked about was getting to his claim. Rose's questions about the house and garden only received vague responses that gave her no picture of her new home.

She looked around the well-proportioned room, part of a sprawling homestead with wide verandas and many outhouses and, best of all, surrounded by watercourses and lush green grass. Rose's spirits had revived greatly when she had seen this cool, green landscape in the middle of the parched desert.

Maybe this was the end of the desert and the landscape would improve from here. Perhaps their house at Ruby Gap could become a fine homestead like Dalhousie Springs.

Rose dipped her fountain pen into her precious glass inkwell, and began to write.

William was late arriving at the harbour to collect me from the Ocean-ien, but he seemed very pleased to see me, and took me in his arms in front of Captain Ellis. Our reunion was very pleasant. He apologised profusely for his tardiness, telling me he had been organising our camel train and supplies for our new home. It sounded very exotic. A camel train!

We had a very pleasant dinner, and a mutually satisfying night in a hotel called the New Central. My hope to soon be with child now has foundation. We set out for our new home in the East MacDonnell Ranges from the railhead at Hargett Springs, on camels! The outback is too dry for teams of horses or bullocks, so we had three camels: one that we rode together, and two pack camels, assisted by three cameleers.

I learned on the journey that Hergott Springs was the hub of camel cartage, servicing virtually the whole of the desert.

The first ten days of our journey were trying—the heat, the dust and the smell. The spectacular thunderstorms were like nothing I have ever imagined in my worst nightmares. This hard and vast land frightens me, and I long for William to take me back to the soft, green fields of home. The sun burns my skin and I have taken to wearing a hat fashioned out of a piece of canvas. Sher Dadleh, the youngest of the cameleers, made it for me when he saw me placing my handkerchief on my head two days ago. I do not care that it smells of camel dung, but it was thoughtful of him. He and his father and uncle set up camp close to the camels a distance away from our tent, but Sher often talks to me in the evenings in his broken English. He told me they have left their family to come to this country, as I have.

The hard landscape frightens me and I try to hide my distress, but one night, William came upon me crying in the tent after a close encounter with a deadly snake. He promises me that all will be well when we reach our new home at Ruby Gap. He told me that our new house is small, but well-built. He described the extra two rooms that he plans to put on in the winter. I am learning more about my husband each day. He is apparently a man of many skills.

After two weeks of travelling, the rain set in and has made the roads boggy and caused the creeks to flood, making them impassable, and his impatience as we were delayed for three days and nights showed me a side of William I had not seen since England. He was impatient with my distress, and angry with the cameleers as our progress slowed. I was very pleased when we reached this homestead and they had a place of their own to sleep away from William's endless scrutiny.

However, my demeanour has greatly improved after a hot bath this evening. I dug into my bag to find a cotton nightgown trimmed with

lace, and hope that William will soon join me. Despite his bad mood
in the flood, he has been mostly considerate and kind to me since we
left Port Adelaide, and my doubts about the wisdom of such a marriage
have gone.

CHAPTER
9

**Trephina Primary School, Alice Springs,
1 March, 11 am**

Jeff insisted that Gemma take the rest of the day off and go home, but the last thing she wanted to do was sit around her apartment by herself, worrying. An idea began to take hold as Pat walked her to the car park. She glanced at her watch; there *might* be time.

'Do you want to come over to our place, love? I've got a hot lunch on for Rob. He'll be home from bowls soon,' Pat said. 'Not good for you to be home by yourself, thinking about things.'

Gemma shook her head. 'I'm okay, thanks. It was a shock, but it's a positive. At least something's been found. I've got some things to do that'll keep me occupied, and I'll have to ring Mum. Plus, I'll have to see if I can get onto Dad if Mum hasn't yet. He needs to know too.'

They reached Gemma's car, and Pat put a reassuring hand on her arm. 'It's a tough time for you. You call me if you want to talk.'

'I will. Thank you, Pat.'

'Just looking out for you, love. Your brother was a good kid.'

'He *is* a good person,' Gemma insisted. Pat's expression was kind but sceptical. 'I mean it, Pat. You might think I'm holding false hope, but Ethan is not dead. We were so close, I'd know. It would be as though a part of me was gone. And I've never felt that. Wherever he is, and for whatever reason, Ethan is somewhere. But he is alive.'

Pat squeezed her arm. 'If that helps you, Gemma, it's a good thought to hold onto.'

'Do you want a lift home?'

'No, I'll walk, but thanks.'

Gemma nodded briefly and opened her car door. 'I'll see you on Monday morning.'

Pat turned towards the road where she and Rob lived a couple of streets from the school, and walked away. Gemma stood there for a moment, looking out over the distant mountains as she pondered what to do, and whether she'd have time today or if she was better to leave it until early tomorrow.

A clue about Ethan, after all these years. She still missed him every day. They shared the same DNA, even though they were fraternal twins and looked nothing alike. Ethan had always called her 'Short Stuff'. Ethan reached a hundred and eighty centimetres before their sixteenth birthday; he took after their dad. Gemma was petite, a good thirty centimetres shorter than her twin. They shared olive green eyes, but Ethan was fair-skinned and fair-haired like their mother, and Gemma had inherited Dad's dark hair and complexion. When they were at primary school, a lot of kids refused to believe they were twins.

But like she'd told Pat, they had been close. So very, very, close. From a very young age, they could communicate without talking. Each of them knew what the other was thinking and feeling. It wasn't magic or some kind of telepathy, but Gemma truly believed it was a part of being in the womb together. They used to finish each other's sentences, and when they were about eight, around Harry Potter times, they'd developed a coded print language.

Like she'd told Pat, if Ethan was dead, a part of her would know.

'Gemma!'

Saul was walking across the concrete driveway. For the first time since she'd heard what he'd come to tell her, she took a good look at him. In Jeff's office, she'd been too stunned to take much notice of him. It was hard to think straight while all sorts of possibilities circled her thoughts.

Saul's uniform shirt stretched across broad shoulders, and his work pants moulded solid thighs. He'd always been a tall and lanky teenager—when he'd held her in his arms when they were seeing each other, Gemma used to have to tip her head back to look at him—but he'd filled out and grown into his height as he'd matured.

The sun burned down on her bare head as she waited for Saul to reach her. His hair was shorter than it had been in his teens, but he obviously spent a lot of time outside these days as his light brown hair was now tipped blond at the ends.

Unless it was dyed? Gemma quickly discounted that thought. That wouldn't have been the Saul she had fallen in love with. He'd been rough around the edges back in those days, and that had been part of his wild-boy appeal. She straightened her shoulders as a dull pang of hurt settled beneath her breastbone. *Dumped her without a word and taken off.* She quickly dismissed it; teenage heartbreak, and she was long over it. She'd had a lot more to worry about when Ethan had gone. Plus, she'd had to deal with Mum and Dad splitting, then Mum dragging her to the east coast. Saul had been relegated to a distant place in her heart, but his behaviour had left her wary of men, and he had been her last steady relationship.

When Saul reached her, he didn't speak immediately, just stood in front of her, so close she could smell the freshly laundered scent of his work clothes. Gemma took a step back so she could see his face, but his eyes were hooded, his mouth set in a tight line.

'I need to talk to you,' he said quietly. 'Somewhere private.'

Shock rippled through her as she stared at him. 'My place. Follow me, it's not far.'

Why did he need to speak to her privately? Was there bad news?

Gemma's hands were shaking as she started the car and pulled out of the driveway with the Parks LandCruiser following her closely along the highway until they turned right, crossed the Todd River and passed the casino, following the route to her apartment near the university.

Instead of going into the underground car park, Gemma parked her small hatchback in the visitors' car park so Saul could park beside her. Quickly climbing out and locking the door, she waited while he parked and came over.

'This way,' she said shortly.

Her apartment was on the second floor, and she was aware of his footsteps on the concrete behind her as they walked up the steps to the foyer. Gemma swiped her security card and he followed her across to the lift. Her apartment was at the far end of the complex and not one word had been spoken by either of them as the lift ascended and they walked to her apartment. Once upon a time, Gemma wouldn't have been able to put up with the silence, but she'd changed since Ethan had been gone.

As she flicked her security card over the electronic lock, the door unlocked with a loud click and Gemma pushed it open. 'Come in.'

The air inside was cool and pleasant after being in the sun, and the smell of the sandalwood candle she'd had burning last night lingered. Gemma crossed to the living area and gestured to the single chair.

'Sit down, please.' Her voice was husky and she cleared her throat. 'Do you want a glass of water? I need one.'

'I'm all good, thanks.'

After quickly reaching into the cupboard for a clean glass and filling it with filtered water from the fridge, she joined Saul in the living room, sitting on the double sofa. After taking a few sips, she placed her drink on the low coffee table and turned to him. 'So, what couldn't you tell me back there?'

Saul held her gaze with his as he reached into his shirt pocket and pulled out a long white envelope. He flicked it open with his thumb and pulled out another envelope, this one yellowed, and handed it over to her. 'I found this in the glove box of the Land Rover, in the bag with the rego papers. Because it had your name on it, I decided—maybe I was right, maybe not—not to give it to the police. Before I knew you were home, I was going to find out where you were and come and find you. I was really surprised when your mum said you were here.'

Gemma drew in her breath in a loud gasp, and reached out, her hand shaking as she took the faded envelope.

*

Saul's phone buzzed as Gemma stared at the envelope; he ignored it. Whoever it was could wait. He wanted to focus his attention on Gemma when she read whatever was in that envelope. Her cheeks were pink and she picked up her glass and drank again.

'Are you sure you wouldn't like a cold drink?' she asked, nervously pushing a stray strand of fine hair away from her face.

'No, I'm fine.'

She took a deep breath, and as she looked down at the envelope in her hand, Saul let his eyes roam over her face. She had barely changed, except maybe to get more beautiful.

Saul had fallen for Gemma when he was eighteen years old, but he'd known even then he couldn't—shouldn't—do anything about the way he felt. It was okay to be mates with Ethan and knock around with him, but the Haydens were a family from the good side of town, and as their daughter, Gemma was way out of his reach.

Saul came from the wrong side of town, living in a rundown old house with his alcoholic old man. Christ, her mother had been the principal at St Mary's Primary School. He'd spent more time in her office than he had in the classroom. He'd wondered whether Mrs Hayden—he would always think of her as that, even though she'd remarried and went by a different name these days—would remember who he was when he'd called, but she'd recognised his name straight away.

He'd been stunned to learn that Gemma was back in Alice Springs. As he stared at her now, he remembered that first afternoon at the movies when he'd found the courage to hold her hand, and then put his arms around her and kiss her. Seven years later, he could still remember how pretty she'd looked that afternoon. What she'd worn—a pale blue T-shirt tucked into short denim shorts—and how her hair had been pulled back into a high ponytail.

It had been the year Gemma had turned sixteen, their last year at high school. The feeling that had settled in Saul's heart that night had been like nothing he'd ever felt before. There'd been no love shown in his house, and he was unsure of how to show Gemma how he felt.

Not that he'd ever intended to, but he spent a lot of time dreaming and wishing.

And taken every opportunity to be where she was.

Saul had hidden his feelings for almost two years, knowing Ethan wouldn't be happy Saul was interested in his twin. That afternoon in the cinema, he'd been unable to resist when she'd turned and held his gaze. Her skin had been so soft when he'd brushed his fingers over her cheek, before they'd kissed. He'd been so happy in those months they'd been together. After they had shared their first kiss in the cinema, Saul and Gemma had been in their own world, even though no one else had known they were seeing each other. She had been the catalyst for him deciding to make something of his life, and over the years that had passed he'd often wondered if he'd see her again one day.

He hadn't even known where Gemma had gone after he'd left for Darwin, and when he'd let his thoughts linger on her, he'd imagined her married with a couple of kids, living in a flash house with a rich husband somewhere.

And here she was in a small apartment on the outskirts of Alice Springs, in the last place Saul had expected to find her.

His phone buzzed again and Gemma looked up, the envelope still in her hand, unopened.

'Take your call. It's okay.'

Saul read the missed call number—it was only Mick, the mate he played squash with every weekend—and shook his head. 'No, it's not important. Open the letter.'

She stared at him and he wondered if she'd share what was inside.

'I can't seem to, Saul,' she said finally. 'I'm scared of what might be in there.'

Saul went to move, to sit next to her, but checked himself. 'Do you want me to look?'

Gemma closed her eyes and her shoulders lifted as she took another deep breath, releasing it slowly. 'Would you?'

'Of course.'

Their fingers brushed as she handed the envelope to him, and it was like a jolt of electricity running up his arm. Maybe the past wasn't as far away as he would have liked.

Aware of her tension and Gemma's eyes fixed on his hands, Saul carefully lifted the flap of the envelope. The glue had dried out over the years and it lifted easily. The paper crackled beneath his fingers as he slowly drew out one folded page. Carefully unfolding the stiff paper, he frowned as his eyes skimmed over the text.

'Tell me, Saul. Please.' Her voice rasped, and she picked up the glass of water again.

'It's a letter to you with a drawing around it.'

Her eyes widened. 'Can you read it, please?'

He nodded then cleared his throat. Seeing Ethan's writing and reading his words was hard. As he began to read, Saul frowned.

Dear Gem,

Miss you heaps. Hope Mum isn't giving you too much flack with me not there to stick up for you. Screw and I are in a bit of trouble so we're lying low.

Saul's gone. Screw's off to the Gulf. And I'm going to go too, when I can.

'Lying low?' Gemma stared at him, her eyes wide and her mouth set in a straight line. 'You were with them?'

Saul shook his head. 'No, I wasn't.'

'So why would he say you'd gone?' Her voice held suspicion and that hurt.

Saul stared down at the letter, trying to make sense of it. He lifted his eyes to meet Gemma's stormy gaze.

'How dare you not tell us you and Screw were with him!' she spat. 'Did you tell the police? That he just took off with you and Screw without telling any of us at home? Is that why they were happy to let it go?'

'Do you really believe I'd do anything to hurt you or Ethan?' Saul put the letter aside on the arm of the sofa and leaned forward, his hands clenched. 'Gemma, listen to me. I haven't seen Ethan since after I saw you the night before I left town.'

'Left town?' She scoffed. 'The night you left *me*.'

'Yes, that night.'

She looked away from him, and there was an awkward silence. Finally, Gemma reached over and took the letter, and began to read the rest of it.

> I'll write to you when I get where I'm going. Not safe here. I doubt there'll be phone service. No service anywhere out here. Just like Ruby Gap. A man could get lost out here and never be able to call for help.
>
> Talk soon,
>
> Love, Eth.

Her eyes were cold when she looked up at him. 'Don't lie to me, Saul.'

'Gemma, I haven't seen Ethan since that night. He and Screw were talking about going out to Ruby Gap, one last trip before Screw left. He asked me to come, but Ethan and I had a blue and I left.' Gemma didn't know what that fight was about, and he wasn't about to tell her. 'Look, I can prove it. I started work in Darwin as soon as I got up there. You can check the dates with the people I worked for, they looked out for me and I worked part-time in their service station the whole time I was at uni. I'm still in touch with them.'

'You went to uni?' Her voice softened a little bit. 'What did you do there?'

'Yes, I went to uni, but that's not important now. We need to understand this letter.'

Gemma glanced down at the letter, rereading it silently. 'It doesn't sound like him, does it?' she said eventually. 'It doesn't make sense. Something was wrong when he wrote that.'

Saul caught her hand as she put the letter down. 'Gemma, are you sure it's even Ethan's handwriting?'

'Yes, it is. Our writing is almost identical.' Her head moved slowly from side to side and she looked at him suspiciously. 'Why wouldn't he tell me he was going to leave, if he really planned to?'

'Maybe he had a reason. Maybe he was in some sort of trouble.' Saul kept hold of her hand; her fingers were icy-cold. 'And don't you think it's strange his letter was in a ziplock bag in a locked glove box? If you'd written a letter, wouldn't you address it and put it out, ready to post?'

'And only my first name is on the envelope. It's as though he knew it wasn't going to be posted and would somehow be given to me.' Gemma let out a big sigh then, glancing down at their joined hands, she pulled away from his grasp.

'The glove box was locked, too.' Saul stared at her. 'I find that strange.'

Gemma shook her head. 'That last night . . . did he seem happy to you? What did you argue about?'

'It's not important now.' This wasn't the time to go there. 'He was just Ethan. Obsessed with his blasted rubies. I packed up and was going to hitch to Darwin, but Screw was getting a lift with his old man to Katherine the next morning, to be interviewed for a job on a station in the East Kimberley. They drove me as far as Katherine, then I hitched. I didn't go anywhere with Ethan, and by the time he left, Screw was out of town too.'

'I don't understand. Why would he say Screw was with him if he wasn't?' Gemma looked down at the letter, running her fingers over the words, then the fancy border drawn around the edge of the page. Her eyes widened and she drew in a sharp breath.

'What?' Saul leaned forward. 'What is it?'

CHAPTER
10

Ruby Gap
May 1888

Rose stood in the doorway of the two-roomed wattle and daub hut that had been her home for the past four months. She put her hand to her stomach and wondered if she would ever feel right again. After leaving Dalhousie Springs—a night that now seemed like a dream—the camel train had travelled another twenty-one days before reaching Ruby Gap. The closer they had drawn to their destination, the quieter William had become, and Rose's trepidation had grown. The heat had been unrelenting. Some days, she'd closed her eyes and imagined herself to be in hell. Ten days into the second leg of the journey, she began to feel ill. The smell of the camel's breath made her gag each morning, as did the pungent smell that emanated from their legs throughout the day.

One evening, as one of the Afghan cameleers was hobbling the camels for the night, Rose went for a walk to stretch her aching buttocks and lower back after sitting on the ungainly beast all day. Sher nodded at her as she watched him. Rose wrinkled her nose as the familiar smell drifted across to her.

'Sher?' She pointed to the camel, pulled a face and covered her nose. With a combination of hand gestures and English words, she finally managed to get her question across to the young man. His comprehension was improving from their daily conversations.

'Ah.' He nodded. 'It is the camel piss. On the legs, to keep them cool.'

Rose put her hand over her mouth and ran back to the tent.

As they had reached the Hale River, her hopes lifted; spirals of smoke filled the blue sky ahead and she waited to encounter a village or a township of some sort. As the camels wound through a sandy riverbed between red perpendicular cliffs, she saw that the smoke was from cooking fires scattered through small camps on the edge of the wide river.

A river that held no water.

A river that held no township.

William leaned forward, his voice full of excitement. 'We are almost there, Rose. Three more miles between the cliffs and you will see our beautiful gorge, and the house I have prepared for you.'

Rose leaned her head back on her husband's shoulder. 'That will be nice, William. It will be good to see our home. I just wish I felt better.'

'You can rest as soon as I get the men to unload the bed I bought for you in Port Adelaide. And a feather mattress. My homecoming gift to you.'

My feather mattress is the one thing I like about my new home. It is the one thing that makes life in this hellhole bearable. Diary, I also include William in that.

He is now focused on the mine workings, and the potential of rubies. He has already buried two bags of stones beneath the front steps of the hut. Yes, a hut! Nothing better than a dwelling the poorest villager would have lived in near Father's estate in Berkshire. Sometimes I feel guilty, because William was so excited to bring me to our home. But a home? The home and acreage that I envisaged turning into beautiful gardens? The seeds I brought from England are still wrapped away. I know that if I put them in this hot earth, they would shrivel and die.

Some nights, when I lie listening to William snore beside me, I wonder if that is what will happen to me out here in this desolate wilderness.

Yes, I feel guilty. William was like an excited child when he pulled me from the main room to our sleeping quarters then showed me where he had pegged out the area where the two new rooms will be added. At times, I wonder why he brought me here and if he doubts that there is a fortune to be made. Showing me our home then taking my hand and leading me through the bush to the perpetual waterhole in our bend of the river reassured me that he wanted me here with him. I am his wife and I will make the best of it.

Our waterhole is the one spot that brightens this place, and I spend many hours sitting in the shade of the cliff, watching the wind on the water. The colours of this land are so bright, they hurt my eyes and I long for the soft colours of the English summer.

Today, William came to me as I sat listening to the birds.

'Rose?'

Rose lifted her head and looked at her husband. Over his head in the distance, she could see the men working in the riverbed. More than eight hundred claims had now been made for the land along the Hale River, and a small hamlet was developing.

Food was plentiful, and they wanted for nothing. Occasionally, two local Aranda men would bring kangaroo and emu meat to the settlement. A couple of the white men who had lived out here for a while could speak their language. William told her that in other places there was resistance, but the local people were very generous to the new settlers. Rose was surprised to find that some of the miners lived as husband and wife with Aboriginal women.

A Chinese gardener travelled out from Stuart town every couple of weeks with vegetables. Once a month a camel train would arrive, stocked with kegs of wine, cases of beer and staple provisions such as flour and salt and tea.

Rose switched her gaze back to William. His clothes were stained and his beard was matted; he bore no resemblance to the man who had asked her father for her hand in marriage two years ago. 'Yes, William?'

'I wanted to ask how you were feeling today,' he said. 'You were asleep when I left this morning.'

Rose put her hand to her stomach. 'I am feeling better, thank you.'

'I also have some news for you. I think it will please you.'

Rose stared at him. The only news that would make her happy would be to hear that they were going back to England. Even the home at Stoke Newington and Mrs Best would be better than Ruby Gap. 'What news do you have?'

'You have met Mr Pearson? The gentleman who has the claim three miles upriver from us?'

She nodded. 'I have.' He was a cultured gentleman who had always treated her with respect.

'His wife is arriving tomorrow. She will be good company for you. It will be good for you to have another woman with you when the baby is born. I worry about you, Rose.' He reached out and took her hand with his rough, work-stained fingers. 'I know it is different and very hard for you now, but once the child is born, and when I have enough rubies to sell, we can build our fine home, and life will be much easier for you. Mr Pearson told me that when he was in Adelaide, the first lot of rubies sent to England received a very good price per ounce. It puts paid to the scandalous suggestion by that Bond Street jeweller in London.'

William's words managed to penetrate the fog that seemed to always be in Rose's head. 'What scandalous suggestion?'

'He is warning investors against our rubies. He claims they are only garnets, but he is a lessee of the ruby mines in Burma, so he does not want his own investment to be threatened. If he'd known what was out here, I am sure he would have invested in Ruby Gap.'

Rose's heart beat a little faster. 'If they did turn out to be garnets, would we go home to England?'

William's eyes widened then he frowned. 'No, of course not. There is no chance of that. I have seen the stones, and I had the first batch assayed in Adelaide. They are rubies, I have no doubt of that. Please be patient, Rose. There will be a town here soon.' He gestured to the men working up the river. 'Every day, more men arrive, and I have heard that the storekeeper from Paddy's Rock-hole is going to set up another store at the head of the Gorge.'

His enthusiasm and certainty lifted her spirits, and she reached out and took William's hand. 'Mr Pearson's news is certainly reas-suring. And it will be wonderful to have a new friend close by.'

CHAPTER
11

Alice Springs
1 March, noon

Gemma's hands shook as she stared at the border around Ethan's letter. She couldn't take her eyes from the hand-drawn border. She took a deep breath and tried to steady her hands.

'Gemma? What's wrong?' When she didn't answer him, Saul stood and came over to sit beside her. 'You're as white as a ghost.' He leaned closer, his breath brushing her cheek as he examined the drawing.

She moved away slightly, ignoring the pleasant tingling that ran down her arm where he leaned near to her. 'It's code,' she whispered, pointing to the blocked squares that edged the letter.

She turned to Saul and his face was close to hers as he frowned. 'Code?'

'Yes, Ethan's code. Look at the squares around the edge.'

As he examined the page, he nodded. 'They're all different.'

'When we were kids, Ethan created a code we could use. A sort of twin thing. We used it for about three years. It used to drive Mum crazy.' Gemma smiled at the memory. 'When Ethan read it out, he used to make stupid clicking noises.' Gemma stared at the squares. 'He made it up and I had to learn it, so he knew it a lot better than I did.'

'So, what does it say?'

'That's the problem.' She blinked as she looked at Saul. 'I've forgotten most of it. We grew out of it when we went to high school. But I know he's trying to tell me something.'

'Keep looking at it, and see if you can remember anything.' Saul spoke quickly, his voice holding suppressed excitement.

Gemma traced her finger over the top left-hand corner. 'Those three squares are my name. I remember that much.' The wrinkled paper crackled beneath her finger as she touched each square. 'I remember there was no logic to it for me, but Ethan was—is—so mathematical, it came naturally.'

Saul put his hand carefully on hers. 'Stop for a minute. Before we go any further, I think we need to take a copy of this. Now that we know it's from Ethan, I'd hate for the paper to tear, or worse.'

'Don't worry. I won't be losing it. I need to figure out what he wrote, and why he wrote it.' Gemma gritted her teeth as she stared at the squares until they ran together. 'It's for me, because no one else even knew what we did. There's something here that he wanted me to know, and nobody else.'

'Nevertheless,' Saul pulled his phone out of his shirt pocket, 'let's take a photo of it.'

Gemma looked at him, wondering if she could trust him. Was he being truthful with her, or did he have some other motive for turning up here?

'It's been a long time since I knew you, Gemma, but I can still see what you're thinking.' Saul held the phone up and waited for her agreement. 'You can trust me.'

Trust him? After Saul had left, Gemma had lost her ability to trust. Up until that dreadful year, she'd been wide-eyed and innocent and taken everyone at face value, and seen the best in every situation. A real Pollyanna. She'd soon learned what life could serve up.

She nodded briefly and Saul took two photos of the letter then sat back. 'What's your mobile number? I'll send them to you then delete them from my phone.'

She told him her number, adding, 'I don't mind you keeping them. It'll be a second backup.'

Saul flicked her a surprised look. 'Okay,' he said, putting his phone away. He moved away from her and leaned back on the sofa. 'Do you think you can remember the key to the code?'

'Some, maybe, but the more I look at it, all the squares run together. To be honest, I'm finding it a bit hard to focus. When I look at it now, I can't see the differences I know are there.' She gave a huff of frustration. 'When we were in year six, Ethan wrote a key to the code and he gave it to me on the promise of death if I showed anyone. You know, a "cross your heart and spit to death" type promise. Problem is, I don't have a copy of the key here. Maybe it got thrown out when we moved. I wasn't thinking straight back then.'

'I didn't know you'd moved away until I came back for a visit after I heard Ethan was missing,' Saul said softly. 'I came back to see you, Gemma. I knew how much you'd be hurting. But you were gone.'

Pain tore through Gemma's throat and for a moment she couldn't speak. 'Three months after Ethan disappeared, Mum made me leave uni and go to New South Wales with her. I did my teaching degree at Coffs Harbour.'

'Why did she want to leave here?'

Gemma knew her voice was cold. 'She got a better job offer. She and Dad had split by then.'

'When I called and discovered you'd left, I asked your father to tell you I was thinking of you, but I doubt he even heard me.'

Regret ran through Gemma as she folded her arms across her chest and straightened her shoulders. She didn't know how she would have reacted if Dad had passed that on. 'Dad was a mess then. He still is, Mum says. And that's another reason we have to get this sorted before we tell him that Ethan left a letter in the glove box.'

Saul looked at her thoughtfully. 'Okay, to figure out this code, what do you have to do?'

'It's too far to go to get something I don't even know still exists. I'll just have to try to remember. I could ring Mum and ask, but I don't want her to know about the letter yet.' As Gemma stood her knee knocked the empty glass. Rolling off the coffee table, it hit the white-tiled floor and smashed into jagged shards. She bent to retrieve it the same time as Saul, and their hands tangled and their heads bumped. Gemma jumped back, embarrassment at her clumsiness heating her cheeks. 'I'll get the dustpan.'

Saul straightened and his voice was low and calm. 'Gemma, keep calm. It's okay. Look, whatever you need to do, I'll help you. It's Friday afternoon and I've got the whole weekend off. You sit down and I'll get that glass cleaned up.'

Gemma sat back down, rested her head on the back of the sofa and closed her eyes. Random images filled her thoughts as she tried to plan a course of action. Ethan walking through the gate the last time she saw him. Ethan chuckling with her as they painted Ruby. Ethan with his head close as he held his hand over hers, tracing the squares when he taught her the code—his code.

He'd been so proud of what he'd done. 'Told you I was the smartest, Gem,' he'd bragged as she'd struggled to memorise it.

Gemma focused on her breathing until her heart rate got back to normal, and the fuzzy, light-headed feeling eased. She was scarcely aware of Saul at her feet, sweeping up the glass, and then all was quiet for a minute.

Her thoughts cleared as her breathing evened out. She began to make a list in her head. She knew what she had to do.

Until Saul had turned up with the letter and the drawing addressed to her, she'd had every intention of getting some gear together and heading out to Ruby Gap to see where Ethan's Land Rover had been found. But now that she'd seen this letter, she had to get that code book from Mum without telling her what had been found. She decided she wasn't going to let Saul know that. It was best if she only relied on herself.

'Thanks, Saul,' she said when he came back from the kitchen.

'Least I could do, Gemma. Clean up a bit of glass.'

'No, I owe you for bringing me that envelope. You could have quite easily handed it over to the police.'

His steady gaze pinned hers. 'It was a no-brainer. It had your name on it. It belongs to you.'

'Thank you,' she said, unable to meet his eyes any longer and looking down at her hands. 'Anyway, I guess I need to get going.'

She stood, running her damp hands down the front of her skirt. 'Where do you live? Still in the old place? Or?'—Gemma widened her eyes as embarrassment surged back— 'It's been a long time. Are you married? Kids? A house somewhere?'

Saul shook his head. 'None of the above, except a yes for the old place. I live out there by myself these days. I don't know if you knew my father died.'

No wife. No partner. No family. Life had obviously taught him he didn't need any of that. The same lesson Gemma had learned.

She knew about Saul's difficult family background so she didn't ask any more questions.

'What are you going to do?' he asked.

'I've got my head sorted a bit now. Today has been full of shocks, but I know I have things to do.' She lifted her head, holding his gaze this time. 'I want to go out to Ruby Gap and see Ruby—his Land Rover—before it's moved. I want to see where it is and how it got there.'

'Any way I can help, you just have to ask.'

The way he spoke, with such resolution and kindness, made Gemma make a split-second decision that surprised even her. 'Would you come out to Ruby Gap with me, Saul?'

CHAPTER
12

**Ruby Gap
October 1888**

Dear Amelia,

By the time you receive this letter, our little Rufus will be five months old. It is hard to believe that we've had him in our life for eight weeks already. I have written to Father in a separate letter to let him know he has become the grandfather of a beautiful little boy, but I also wanted to write to you and tell you of the joy and the love that this child has brought to our lives.

I was very fortunate that Mrs Pearson, my dear neighbour, was experienced in the ways of childbirth and she assisted me when my time came. Little Rufus arrived in a rush, and William barely had time to ride over and summon Betty—yes, we now have two horses—and when she arrived, Rufus was ready to be born. The pain was over very quickly, and all the frightening stories of childbirth that I had heard did not come to fruition. Rufus is a good little baby and he looks just like William.

Life is progressing well here at Ruby Gap. I have started to develop my garden and take every opportunity when Rufus is asleep to go outside and tend my plants. The winter season has allowed me to raise many flowers from seed. I have a pretty spring garden around the house and that gives me such pleasure. We don't have a gardener yet, and perhaps never will. Life is very different in Australia.

William has built two more rooms onto our small house. There is an abundance of timber, and he has proven very competent at building furniture for us. We have created a happy little home and I look forward to bringing up our family here. Would you believe I have my own chicken coop! And I have learned how to bake bread! It is certainly not the life I imagined, and I would much rather be gardening, but I have learned to love this place.

Rose lifted her pen and smiled.

Don't look so horrified, Amelia. I can imagine the look on your face. I do wish you could see where we live. I am sitting on our front porch in my rocking chair—William built it before Rufus was born—while William sits on the step. He is carving his initials into an axe handle that he made last week. He has developed a new skill and has a small blacksmithing forge in a shed behind our house, and he has been overwhelmed with requests to do work for the miners who have settled either side of our bend in the river. The sky is so blue it hurts your eyes. The cliffs behind our house are a brilliant red, and contrast with the verdant green of the winter bush. The golden balls of the wattle trees are in full bloom, and I can hear the bush bees buzzing in their hive and making the wild honey.

I pray one day that we can come back to England and visit, although I think William intends to make our home in Australia for the rest of our lives. We may have enough money saved to journey to England before Rufus is two or three years old. The ruby prospecting is going well, and keeps William busy. He will go to Port Adelaide in two months to get a second batch assayed and valued. The news that is being spread by the jeweller in London is unsettling, although I doubt it would be newsworthy in Berkshire.

Please write to me as soon as you can and tell me all of the news at home. Describe the gardens to me so I don't forget their beauty. (I forgot to tell you I am also growing our own vegetables.)

I do hope you are happy, and I look forward to hearing of news of a proposal from your Mr Oldham. I miss you greatly, Amelia. My life would be complete if I had my sister here close to me.

Your loving sister,
Rose Woodford

CHAPTER
13

Alice Springs
2 March, 9.00 am

'Morning, Mum. I didn't get you out of bed, did I?'

'Heavens no. I have the school fete this morning. How are you coping, sweetheart? Are you taking any time off school?'

'No, but I did come home early yesterday. Jeff, my principal, insisted.' How could Mum be so calm?

Her mother made a disapproving noise. 'That wasn't wise. When Saul rang yesterday, all I could think about was you being out there by yourself when you heard the news. I wanted someone with you when you were told. You need to be with people so you don't go into your usual shell,' she said; it was a lecture Gemma had heard a thousand times. 'He didn't have much to tell me, just that the car had been found. I was really surprised to hear that he's a park ranger these days. I never thought that boy would make much of himself.'

They never seemed to be able to talk about anything without Mum being critical of something or someone. *A great attitude for an educator.* What about empathy for Saul's awful situation? The way he'd lived growing up, fending for himself and looking after his alcoholic father, had been dreadful. Saul had never complained or talked about it, but Ethan had made sure that he always brought him home around mealtimes. That was one of the reasons they'd kept quiet about seeing each other, knowing that Mum would go off.

Gemma ran a hand over her hair, trying to dispel the dark feeling that talking to Mum always brought. The phone was on speaker; she was sitting at the small dining table and had taken several deep calming breaths before she'd made the call, but her calm was rapidly disintegrating.

'I'm pleased you're not taking time off, Gemma. You need people around you, so you can't dwell on it.'

I've been dwelling on my brother's disappearance for six years.

She pushed the darkness away, and swallowed. 'What about you? Are you all right, Mum?'

The voice stayed firm and brisk. 'Of course I am. I'll admit, it was a shock to get the call, but it's going to let us finally have closure.'

Gemma felt a flash of frustration. 'Finding Ruby doesn't prove anything, Mum. He could have left it there before it was wrecked.' Gemma swallowed. 'Ethan's not dead, Mum.'

'Sweetie, please don't harp on that twin thing. You have to be realistic. If he was alive, he would have let us know,' her mother reasoned. 'Do you want me to fly over there? Or better still, why don't you take some family leave and come home for a while?'

'No, I have commitments here.' Gemma closed her eyes; she'd known that Mum would use this to try to get her back to the east coast. 'I haven't been able to reach Dad yet. Have you?'

'I've left a message at the fishing lodge.'

'What fishing lodge?' Surprise rocketed through Gemma. Her parents had barely spoken since the divorce, or so she thought.

'The Barra Lodge, up at the Cobourg Peninsula. Tony was going out there last week. I thought he'd be back by now.'

Her mother knew an awful lot about her dad's life. 'What? Are you and Dad talking again? Why didn't you tell me?'

'Yes, we keep in touch.'

The idea of her parents talking again was surprising, and Gemma wondered what had caused it. She'd always thought that Mum hadn't tried hard enough when Ethan had gone missing. It was easy for her to make a judgement, but maybe their marriage would have survived if Mum and Dad shared their grief instead of letting it pull them apart. Then again, she'd often thought that Mum hadn't tried hard enough in so many things.

'Gemma? Are you there?'

'Yes.'

'Look, I have to go in now and help set up for the fete. You take care of yourself, and make sure you stay in touch. If you won't come home now, think about coming home for the school holidays. They're only six weeks away.'

'I'll see. Oh, Mum before you go, I need a favour. I need something from one of the boxes I left in your garage. Could you find a book of mine, and take some photos and text them to me?'

'Photos of what?'

Gemma crossed her fingers. 'I'm doing a literacy unit with my class and we're doing some fun activities with code. Remember when Ethan and I had that coded language when we were kids? I thought I'd use that as an example for them rather than making something up.'

'Vaguely. What am I looking for?'

'There's one box there marked books on top with a black texta. All our Harry Potter books should be there. I'm pretty sure there's an exercise book where we wrote it all up. It should be in there too.' Despite what she'd told Saul, Gemma knew it had been in there when she'd stored the box. 'It's got a red cover. Can you photograph the first six pages and text them to me? I need it today to write up the unit of work over the weekend.'

'I can't promise, I'm running late, but I'll get Colin onto it if he has time. He's playing golf today.'

Gemma rolled her eyes. 'Thanks Mum.' Colin jumped through every one of Mum's hoops, something that Dad had never done. 'Does he have my mobile number?'

'I'll give it to him now. Bye, sweetheart. I'll have a look at flights home for you in the holidays.'

The call disconnected before Gemma could reply.

She walked into the bedroom to gather some clothes and toiletries together. Saul was picking her up at nine-thirty. They'd planned to be out at Ruby Gap by lunchtime and stay out there until tomorrow afternoon, but he'd said not to bother bringing anything apart from clothes, boots and a hat.

'I can throw in a swag for you and my camping gear is always in the back of my ute. Don't worry about a fly net, I've got a few.'

'What about food?' she'd asked.

Saul had shaken his head. 'It's fine. You just bring yourself, and make sure you have some solid walking boots. I'll pack food and plenty of water. I want to walk to the top of the bluff while we're out there to see if we can find how his car might have ended up in the river.'

Gemma put Ethan's letter in her bag, and checked her phone, hoping that Colin would send that text soon. The last time she'd been out on the Ross Highway, phone service had dropped out not far from town.

She'd stared at the coded border late into the night before giving up in frustration, but apart from being able to recognise her name and Ethan's she could make no sense of the rest of it. Her focus on Ethan and the strange message he seemed to have left for her had consumed her and led to a sleepless night but, in a way, it had helped her face the weekend ahead. Going out there was going to be hard, but being in Saul's company was going to be even more difficult. The biggest problem was her lack of trust. Until she had proof that Saul hadn't been with Ethan before he disappeared, she was going to be very careful. Maybe she was foolish to have invited him to go to Ruby Gap with her . . . and probably even more foolish when no one knew he was taking her out there.

Gemma quickly pulled Pat's contact up on her phone and sent her a message.

Thanks for being so kind yesterday. I'm good today. Going out to Ruby Gap to check out the car with Saul Pearce until Sunday night.

When she'd sent it, she scrolled through her messages and pulled a face when there was still no text from Colin. She hoisted her backpack onto her shoulder and grabbed her hat before taking a breath and releasing it slowly. Time to go see Ruby.

★

Saul whistled for Attila, grinning as his huge brown dog bounded across to the passenger side of the ute, his tongue lolling as he looked up at Saul hopefully.

'No mate, we have a passenger, and I'm sure she wouldn't appreciate you slobbering all over her.'

Attila sat and waited by the door, but Saul ignored him and walked around to the back of the ute. 'Come on, you're on the back.' He didn't add that Attila was only going as far as his mate Rodney's place a bit further along the Ross Highway.

Attila slunk around the side of the ute and whimpered, knowing where he was supposed to be.

'No way, mate. I'm not lifting you up there.' Saul tapped on his leg to call Attila back, and gave him a pat when the dog obeyed. 'Good boy. Now get up there, you great galumph.' He pointed to the tray and with a short bark, Attila ran towards the ute and jumped, scrabbling for purchase with his front paws when his back legs hung over the back.

'I hate to say it, boy, but you need to go on a diet.' Saul lifted Attila's rump onto the ute and received a wet lick on his cheek for his efforts. 'And I'll have to have a word with Rodney. Too many treats last week, methinks.'

Once he'd tied Attila to the grilled mesh at the back of the cab, ignoring the dirty looks being sent his way, Saul loaded the esky, the water and the box of food, as well as the swag and his bedroll, and secured them too. Saul had stopped off at the supermarket in town late last night to make sure they had everything they would need for the trip. Gemma had enough on her mind.

He'd been a bit surprised when Gemma had asked him to go out to Ruby Gap with her. He could understand her not wanting to go out there by herself, but he thought he would have been the last person she would have asked to go with her. Ethan's letter had cast suspicion on him. It made no sense to Saul. The letter said that Screw had been with him and they were in trouble. As far as Saul knew, Screw had gone to Katherine. Maybe he hadn't got the job and had gone back to Alice for a while? He made a mental note to ask Pat about that next time he was in town. Saul had been so pissed off when he'd left for Darwin, he hadn't contacted anyone back at home. Not until he'd heard Ethan was missing about three months later.

Like Gemma obviously did, Saul had thought Ethan was alive until he and Darren had confirmed it was Ethan's Land Rover in the Hale River. For the millionth time since he'd heard that Ethan had disappeared, Saul wondered what the hell had happened to his mate. Ethan had always been a straight shooter and would never have got mixed up in anything dishonest, but that was the only thing Saul could think of to explain his disappearance now, with the discovery of his Land Rover. And now from that letter, it seemed that Screw had been with him too.

Unless he'd met with foul play, Ethan must have had a good reason to disappear. Maybe this coded stuff would give them some idea about what had happened, if Gemma could figure it out. Finding the wreck of Ethan's Land Rover in the river wasn't a good sign, and for the first time, Saul considered that he might not have taken off. Maybe he was dead.

At least if the news was bad, he'd be there for Gemma.

It wasn't far from Saul's place back to Gemma's apartment, where she was waiting by the entry to the car park. She didn't look up from her phone as he drove past and did a U-turn. He pulled up beside her and was pleased to see her tentative smile as she walked over towards the ute. She was dressed for the outback: cargo shorts, lace-up boots and a khaki shirt. A small backpack was over her shoulder, and she held a wide-brimmed hat in one hand, her phone in the other.

'Good morning,' she said through the open window. She looked back at Attila, her smile widening. 'And good morning to you too, lovely boy.'

Saul leaned over and opened the passenger door from the inside. 'Bring your bag in here. There's room behind the seat. Don't pay Attila too much attention. He won't leave you alone if you do.'

Gemma climbed up and put her bag where Saul had directed. 'He's a big dog.'

Saul nodded. 'He is. And he's a pretty useless one. He loves anyone who comes to visit, so he's a hopeless guard dog. And the few times I've tried to take him on a long walk in the scrub, he's jacked up and refused to go more than a kilometre or two.'

'But you love him. I can tell.'

Sean grinned. 'He's good company. Most of the time.'

'I didn't think we could take a dog out to Ruby Gap? It's still a national park, isn't it?'

'It's a nature park, but dogs aren't allowed out there. I'm dropping him off at a mate's place just up the road a bit.' Saul rolled his eyes. 'I can leave him home during the day, but if I leave him too long at night, he frets. He might look mean and tough, but he's a big sook. Plus, if I leave him, he chews up anything he can get to.'

'Have you had him long?'

He knew she was digging for more about why he was back in Alice Springs. Saul could still read Gemma well; they'd been very close in the six months they had been in a relationship. Was that a sign that she was interested, or was she just being polite? Or was she trying to work out if she could trust him?

Saul started the ute and looked behind them before he pulled out onto the highway. 'No, only since just before I came back home. I was in Darwin for a long time. Attila was a rescue dog. He'd been pretty badly knocked around, so I go pretty easy on him.'

'You always loved your dogs, didn't you?' Gemma said. 'More than you liked people, if I remember correctly.'

Maybe she could still read him well too. 'Still do. Most people reckon it's because we feed them and give them shelter, but I disagree. There's nothing like the loyalty of a dog. But Attila is too dependent on me, so I take him out to Rod's when I need him minded so he can learn to be a bit independent.' He forced a smile even though the conversation was a bit too close to home. 'Problem is, I think he's feeding him too much when he's out there, even though I've asked him not to. He's turning into a big lazy lump.'

Saul relaxed as they continued to chat until they reached the turn-off to Rodney's place. It was good to be with Gemma. They'd always been good mates. When that had segued into a relationship, they'd kept it quiet. Maybe if they hadn't, Ethan wouldn't have lost it with him. Maybe things would have turned out differently. Maybe he wouldn't have gone to Darwin. Or maybe if he had waited, Gemma would have moved with him and transferred her teaching degree there.

As it turned out, Ethan had done him a favour and stopped him making a stupid mistake. So he would play things the same way she was. No mention of a 'them'. The hardest part was going to be surviving the weekend in her company. The instant he'd seen her at the school yesterday, Saul knew even though six years had passed, he still felt the same way about Gemma.

And that is not on.

Despite a few casual relationships over the past few years, he'd never found anyone that he'd wanted to spend his life with. Not even a weekend. He'd never even taken a woman home to his place, and that had nothing to do with it being half-renovated. Saul had gutted the old building over the years. Every year, he'd spent his holidays working on the old place.

It was finally starting to look like a house, and it wouldn't be much longer before he could move out of the caravan he'd put onsite a couple of years back.

Once the house was finished, he'd start travelling in his holidays. He glanced across at Gemma. How good would it be to have company? He pushed the thought away.

Three dogs came running out to meet them as they approached the yard gate. Attila stood on the back of the ute and his fearsome bark reverberated through the cabin.

Gemma jumped and when Saul turned to reassure her, she was studying his face with a frown. She looked down and a faint blush tinged her skin.

'He sounds ferocious but that's all,' he said. 'Don't let him worry you.'

'I'm not. I'll wait in the car. I've got a text to send before we lose service.'

'Yeah, service'll drop out just past Trephina Gorge, then we won't have any until we come back in. I've got a satphone in the glove box for emergencies.' He put his hand into his pocket and pulled out the small yellow PLB attached to his belt. 'You don't have to worry about accidents or anything out here. If we were unlucky enough for something to happen, or to break down, we're covered with the satphone and the PLB.'

'PLB?' She frowned at him.

'Personal Locator Beacon. Essential out here where there's no phone service. It pinpoints our location to emergency services if we set it off.'

'That's good to know.'

'And as the crow flies, we're not that far from town. It's only the road that's shit. In an emergency, a chopper can get out here quickly. That being said, the only deaths out here were an elderly German couple at Trephina Gorge a few years ago. There was a proposal after that to get the phone coverage expanded. Out here with all the sunshine, elevated hills for antennae and the Sky Muster satellite, it wouldn't take much to improve the coverage.'

'But it's not happening?'

'Apparently not.' Saul had bought the satellite phone as soon as he could afford it after he'd moved to Darwin. In the break between uni semesters, he'd done a lot of travelling around the Territory, and Ethan's disappearance had made him cautious. He'd travelled as far as the East Kimberley one summer to catch up with Screw, but had missed him when he'd headed up to the Gulf a few weeks earlier, the head stockman had told him.

He'd enjoyed driving through the west of the Territory, and had put the west down as one of his preferences when he'd filled in the application, in case he didn't get the transfer to Alice Springs he'd wanted. Maybe he wouldn't have been so keen if he'd known Gemma was coming home too.

Saul frowned as he untied the rope from Attila's collar. Ethan must have known that Screw was heading to the Gulf because he'd mentioned that in the letter he'd left for Gemma. That sort of dated it because Screw had been in Western Australia at Roselyon, though they'd never caught up for the first couple of years that Saul had been at uni. So the letter must have been written a bit later, and that meant that Ethan *had* dropped off the radar for a couple of years.

Attila bounded into the yard, and Rodney came around from the front of the house. 'G'day Saul.'

'Hey mate. Thanks for this. I've fed him, so he won't need anything until tomorrow morning.'

'No prob. You'll collect him tomorrow afternoon? I'm flying out on Monday and our three are enough for Julie.'

'Yeah, not a problem. Thanks, mate. Owe you one.'

'How's the house coming along?' That's how he'd met Rodney. Before he'd started his FIFO work at the mine, Rodney worked at the local metal fabrication business where Saul had bought the new roofing for his house. 'Looks good from the outside.'

'The kitchen has to be installed, then I have to paint through. Then I'll be able to move in.'

'Good stuff. If you need a hand with the painting, I haven't got a lot on after this ten-day shift.'

'Thanks, I'll keep you to that, mate.' Rodney shot a curious glance over at the ute, but Saul didn't comment on Gemma's presence. It would be around town soon enough that Ethan's car had been found at Ruby Gap.

'See you tomorrow, mid-afternoon.' Saul lifted his hand in a wave and headed back to the ute. By the time he opened his door, Rod and Attila had disappeared around to the back of the house. Gemma's head was down and she was focused on her phone.

She looked up. 'How long will it take us to get out there?'

'Nothing's changed. Road's still the same as it always was, so about two hours. Two and a half, tops.'

Her attention was still focused on her phone, and her expression was closed.

'What's up? A problem?'

'No. Before the road gets too bad, I just want to read something.'

'Sure. Don't feel as though we have to chat all the way out. It's a long way out to Ruby Gap.'

'I know. I do remember.' She sounded irritated.

'You sure everything's okay?'

She nodded but wouldn't meet his gaze. Her cheeks were pinker than before and her eyes were downcast. 'Yes. I just want to read Ethan's letter again.'

'Gemma?' he said softly as a wave of regret rose in his chest.

This time she lifted her eyes to meet his. 'Yes?'

'You can trust me, you know.'

'Can I, Saul?' Her voice was quiet.

He turned his attention back to the road without answering.

CHAPTER
14

Arltunga
Saturday, 10.30 am

The ute bounced over the corrugations and Gemma's phone slid to
the floor as she grabbed for the Jesus bar above the passenger door.

'You going okay over there?' Saul's voice broke into Gemma's
thoughts.

'Yes, I'm good.' She reached down and retrieved her phone. 'Are
we almost there?'

'Sorry, we're not even to Arltunga yet. The road is the worst I've
ever seen it.'

'Okay. No prob. I'll do some reading. Tell me when we get
close.'

Gemma tried to hide her satisfaction from Saul when she opened
the text from Colin. She felt like jumping and cheering.

Here you go love. Six pages for you. Hope you are going along okay. Your mother worries about you, and so do I. Don't work too hard. Looking forward to seeing you home in the holidays. Love Colin.

Despite her satisfaction at receiving the code key, she shivered. She couldn't stand her mother's partner, and preferred to see him as little as possible. Colin was an absolute sleaze, and she'd always made sure when she lived with them for a short while that if Mum was out, so was she. She wouldn't trust him as far as she could spit. Luckily, she'd had some friends she could spend a night or a weekend with at short notice. Why the hell Mum couldn't see what he was like was beyond her. Colin couldn't be more different to Dad if you placed an order for an exact opposite. Flashy with his gold chains and white shoes, he fitted the stereotype of a real estate agent on the east coast. That's what he'd been before he'd made his fortune and retired in his late fifties. Mum had taken up with him within a few months of them moving to the coast.

Sleazebag, she mouthed to herself before she opened the attached photos.

Yes! The code was what she needed to decipher Ethan's squared message. All she had to do was memorise which letter or combination of letters that each filled square stood for. Her name and his name were what she'd remembered. A circle with a small cross underneath, the female symbol, had represented her name, and Ethan's was the male symbol with the arrow pointing to two o'clock. She worked her way through each of the codes.

Gemma shot a sideways glance at Saul. She wanted to pull out Ethan's letter without appearing obvious but it was hard; she wasn't keen on letting Saul know she had the code until she read what Ethan had to say, but in the end, she pulled her backpack onto her lap, opened it and pulled out the ziplock bag holding the letter.

The LandCruiser ute bumped across the corrugated road, and occasionally Gemma had to grasp her phone more tightly and lean to the left and the right as she read the letter then checked the cipher. The vehicle slewed from side to side. Saul had barely spoken—apart from checking she was okay—since she had responded to his statement about trusting him. She should have kept her mouth shut and focused on getting on with him. They were going to be alone together for two days.

'That rain the day before yesterday has stuffed the road a bit,' Saul finally said as he gripped the wheel when the front of the ute bounced across a wide corrugation. Gemma nodded and didn't speak as she memorised the code before she went back to Ethan's drawing. Her mind was going nineteen to the dozen as she went over and over the squares. The more she looked at each one, the more the logic of the pattern came back to her. Even at ten years old, Ethan had had a logical mind, and the code made perfect sense.

Keeping the code in her head, she moved from the top left-hand corner across the top of the border. She had already deciphered her name, and focused on the paragraph that began with it. Glancing back at the screen, she confirmed the code and what the letters spelled out. As she read, she fought not to react or gasp even as her blood ran cold. She put the pages and the phone down on her lap, and stared ahead, trying to breathe evenly as ice ran through her veins.

Gemma. Repeated: *Gemma. Do not trust anyone.*

She risked another sideways glance at Saul, but he was still focused on the road ahead. His brow was furrowed and even with the air-conditioning on, perspiration ran down the side of his face. The vehicle bumped again and slowed, and she glanced down at Saul's hand near her knee as he changed down through the gears.

'I thought we might stop for a break at Arltunga, if you don't mind. This road is worse than it was on Thursday.' He looked across at her and she lifted her gaze from his hand. She used to love holding hands with Saul. Even back then, his hands had been calloused and work-hardened. He'd never complained, and even though she'd never visited where he lived, Ethan had told her it was barely live-able. She wondered if Saul had done much to it since he'd come home, or if he still lived in the same conditions. Even though she thought she'd known him well, she wondered if the blinkers of first love had blinded her to the true Saul.

Do not trust anyone. The words pounded through her head.

Mum had always said Saul had a wild streak, and that his father had been in and out of jail. Gemma had always thought she was being unfair. There'd been no mention of his mother, and she'd never found the courage to bring it up.

Gemma had to put their relationship behind her, and remember Saul had been a good mate to Ethan, plus he'd readily agreed to bring her out to Ruby Gap this weekend. Was he the good guy Ethan had always said he was? Was he the kind and caring guy that she'd fallen for? Or had it all been an act? Was it a coincidence that he was the one who found the wreck of Ethan's Land Rover? Or was he involved somehow?

Do not trust anyone.

Does that include Saul and Screw? Or even Pat?

Gemma closed her eyes, not knowing what to think. The con-fusion, combined with getting close to seeing Ruby and the small niggle of fear about being out here alone with Saul, made her feel sick.

'Gemma?'

She jumped and stared at him. 'Sorry, what did you say?'

'I asked if you're okay with stopping for a break. Cold drink? Cuppa? I've got a thermos of hot water in the camp stuff.'

'Yes. That'd be good,' she agreed. 'To be honest, I'm a bit carsick.'

'You've been glued to your phone.' He didn't mention the letter on her lap.

'Yes, I was reading.'

Saul let the turbo run down before he switched the ignition off.

'Funny the things that stay in your head, isn't it?' Gemma said, striving for normal conversation. 'I haven't been in a four-wheel drive since we moved to the coast, and yet the sound of it running down was familiar to me, and I knew exactly what you were doing. Ethan taught me how to do that when I was learning to drive. He got his licence first and he taught me in Ruby.' She opened the door and jumped down from the ute cabin. The road was dry and dusty, and the light wind blew away the red dust her boots had stirred.

Saul went around to the back of the ute and the only sound was the esky sliding along the tray for a few seconds. Gemma closed her eyes and tipped her head back. Total and absolute quiet. The encompassing silence of the outback cocooned her; she was home in the place she loved. The only sounds that broke the unique silence were natural: the rustling of the dry grass, the thud of a wallaroo hopping across the ground, the occasional raucous call of a bird. Here, despite her earlier fear, she felt safe.

Saul came back around carrying a thermos and a box, and they walked up the slight rise to a dead stump beside a tree about thirty metres into the scrub. The hill overlooked the historical settlement of Arltunga. Gemma took her phone from her pocket and checked if there was any service.

'Nope, not even SOS,' she said, putting her phone away.

'No point looking here. There's never any service.'

'It always used to worry me when we were out here, what we would have done in an accident. Maybe that's why Ethan couldn't contact us before he left.'

Saul held up an enamel cup. 'Tea, coffee or a cold drink?'

'Tea, please.'

She stood back and watched as he poured the boiling water into the cup and dropped a teabag in.

'I always feel as though I'm breaking the real bushie tradition when I use a teabag out here.'

'Quick and convenient,' Gemma said with a shrug.

'True. Have you seen the old settlement here since they've re-created the village?' He held out the tea. His face had changed in the six years she'd been gone. Slight wrinkles fanned out around his eyes, and his face was tanned from his outside occupation, she guessed. He'd been a good-looking teenager, but he had grown into a very attractive man. Slim and wiry, but he'd broadened in the shoulders, and there was a toughness about him that reassured her.

'Gemma?'

She blinked, realising she was still staring. 'Um, no. I haven't.' She took the cup. Black, how she liked it. 'Thanks. Did you know they discovered the rubies out at Ruby Gap a few months before the gold rush here at Arltunga?'

'I knew a bit of the history. I must admit that I used to switch off when Ethan was talking about it. He was like a walking tour-ist brochure.' Saul grinned at her and it chipped away at a little of her distrust. 'Do you want something to eat? I've got apples and biscuits.'

'Maybe an apple when we get back in the car.'

'I'll put some water bottles in the car too. It's going to be a forty-degree day, I think, although it should be cooler in the gorge. There's plenty of shade at Ruby Gap, and there's still water in the river.'

Gemma looked at the familiar bush surrounding them. 'It's good to be back,' she said.

Saul nodded, draining his cup. He placed it back in the bag and turned to her. 'I know what you mean. I was surprised when I got posted back here, but really happy to be home.'

'Are you here to stay, or could you be transferred to another park?'

He shook his head. 'Only if I decide I want to move. What about you?'

'Same.' She looked down as the silence stretched again. When she looked up, Saul was looking at her and her heartbeat kicked a little.

'I'm pleased,' he said. 'Maybe . . . we could spend some time together, re-establish a friendship.' His eyes were intense and she couldn't look away. 'We were good mates back in the day, Gem,' he added softly.

'We were. Back in the day,' she echoed. That was one way to put it; Saul had been the first person she'd had a sexual relationship with.

'Done?' he asked, holding his hand out for her mug.

'Yes, thank you.' A pang of regret for the easy relationship they'd once had rippled through her. Saul's fingers brushed hers as Gemma handed the mug back and she turned away. Until the mystery with Ethan was sorted, she couldn't afford to trust Saul.

As soon as they set up camp, she'd be back into the letter and code to work out the mysterious message left by her twin.

CHAPTER
15

Ruby Gap Road
Saturday, noon

'I love those ghost gums,' Gemma said as they crossed yet another dry creek bed. 'The white bark, and the way the green leaves contrast against that smooth bark.' They'd been travelling for over two hours and were getting close to Ruby Gap. The cool and shady valleys they'd passed through were a pleasant change from the hot sun beating down from the cloudless sky.

'There's plenty of them,' Saul commented, changing back a gear as they approached a steep rise. 'Have you ever been out to Hermannsburg?'

'We did. When I was in Year Eleven, we went on an art excursion to the museum and the Namatjira Gallery. Weren't you on it?'

Saul shook his head. 'Nope. I never went on any excursions. The old man refused to cough up.' It hadn't bothered him. He'd liked having the day off school. Dad was usually at the pub by midmorning, and it gave Saul the freedom to do what he wanted. He thought back to those days. Most of the time, Ethan and Screw would wag school and come out to his place, and they'd go bike riding on the old bush bikes that his old man seemed to find the time to keep going. They had been good days.

Gemma put her head back down and seemed to be scrolling through messages on her phone. She'd been quiet since they'd had morning tea, and he wondered how the weekend was going to pan out. He'd just take it easy, show her the car then see what she wanted to do out there. He was going to hike to the top of the gorge and see if there were any car tracks up on the bluff. But the car could have been in the riverbed for years, so he didn't hold out much hope of discovering anything.

Small rocks dotted the centre of the narrow road and he moved across to the right. As they neared the crest, a huge cloud of red dust appeared ahead warning of an oncoming vehicle and he pulled over to the right side of the road where there was more room, next to one of the gates he and Darren had commented on when they were out here.

As they waited, a motorbike roared over the hill in front of them, narrowly missing the front of the ute. It slowed to a stop across the front of the ute and the rider climbed off and strode over to them. He didn't remove his helmet or lift the visor as he stood beside the ute and gestured for Saul to get out of the vehicle. His long grey beard reached the centre of his chest.

Saul frowned and unwound his window. 'Is there a problem, mate?'

'I'll give you a fucking problem. What the hell are you doing at my gate?'

Saul went to open the door, and was surprised when Gemma's hand tentatively touched his thigh.

'Don't get out, please.' Her voice shook, and he hesitated. A rifle was strapped to the back of the bike.

Biting down his immediate reaction to the belligerence of the guy standing beside the car, Saul kept his voice calm and civil. 'I pulled over when I saw your dust. Not a good place to have a head-on, mate.'

The guy stood there for a while then turned away sharply without speaking. He opened the gate with a key, climbed back on the bike, roared through and swung the gate closed while still on his bike, and locked it behind him.

He sat on the bike and gestured jerkily for them to go. Saul shrugged and put the ute into gear and took off up the hill.

'What was that all about?' Gemma asked. 'Do you know him?'

'No. Just a landholder who thought we were trying to get onto his land, I guess. Darren—my offsider—and I were talking about that the other day when we were out here. The area's changed a fair bit since we all used to come out here. If I was a parent, I wouldn't be keen to let my kids camp out here.'

'Is it safe for us?' Her voice was hesitant, and Saul kicked himself for saying too much.

'Of course. We're sensible. We know the risks and how to keep safe, and we're not coming out here to get drunk and play up.' He would have taken the words back if he could. Shit, they were coming out here for Gemma to see her missing—probably dead—brother's car. Her next words surprised him.

'Ethan never came out here to play up, but you and I did once, if my memory is correct.'

Saul widened his eyes and stared at the road ahead.

It was the first time Gemma had referred to their past relationship.

He didn't reply for a while, then he swallowed, choosing his words carefully. 'They were good days, weren't they? Coming out here with the boys—and you—it was an escape to normality for me. I was always happy then, but it was twice as hard to go home after we'd been out to the Gap.'

'You never used to say much about your home life, but I knew it wasn't very good.'

'Ethan told you?'

She nodded.

'I'll never forget the day he turned up uninvited, and walked into the hovel that I lived in. I can still see the look on his face. Dad was passed out on the floor, and I was cleaning up the spew around him. Ethan turned around and walked out and said he'd wait outside for me to finish. He wanted me to pack up and come back to your place, but I knew your mother wouldn't want me there.'

'What about your mother?' Gemma asked.

Saul stared ahead at the road. 'She died when I was about five, I think.'

'You think?'

'That's what my old man used to tell me,' he said, keeping his voice steady. 'But when I was staying at my aunt's place at Tennant Creek when he got locked up for a few months the last year we were in primary school, she told me that my mum had taken off. So, who knows?' Saul tried to hide his angst with a casual shrug. He hated talking about family.

'Oh, Saul, that's awful. I'm so sorry to hear that.'

He hated the pity in her voice. 'It is what it is. I've been renovating the house since I started at Parks. I'm living in a caravan while I make it liveable.'

'You are? Or someone is building it for you?

'I am. I learned a few skills when I was in Darwin.'

'Good on you.' For the first time since he'd had to break the news to Gemma about finding Ethan's car, here was some animation in her expression, and genuine emotion in her voice. 'I'd like to see it one day.'

He shrugged again; when it was perfect, he would show her. If she still wanted to see it. 'Not a lot to see yet.'

'Fair enough.' She turned away to look through the window. 'We're almost there, aren't we?'

Saul was impressed she remembered. 'One more bend, then down the hill and we'll be in the riverbed. Even though the area was gazetted as a nature park well before we used to come out here, they've done a bit of work lately. A new sign and a map of the park just above the river course.'

'Can we still drive in like we used to?'

'Yep, but not as far as we used to go on the motorbikes.' A memory of Gemma on the back of his bike clinging to his back sent a shaft of warmth rushing through Saul. His voice was gruff when he continued. 'After the gravel road in to the park boundary, we drive up the sandy riverbed. Do you remember how the track drops immediately into the riverbed at the park entrance? There's an occasional detour onto land where some big rocks now block the riverbed track.'

'They weren't there before?'

'No.' He glanced across at her. 'They were exposed after the rain last year.'

'And you think that's what happened with Ethan's car?'

'Possibly. Probably.' Saul slowed the speed as they crested the last hill, then negotiated their way down a slope over huge boulders. 'I think it was there all the time but when the river went down, it exposed it.'

Gemma leaned forward as the wide *Ruby Gap* timber sign sitting on four posts came into view. Saul looked at the recent improvements with fresh eyes. A small construction with a green Colorbond roof sat at the edge of the track between the riverbank and the nature park sign.

'Do you want to stop and look at the map? It's as good a place as any, because I have to let the tyres down some more.'

'Sounds like a good idea. I'd like to reacquaint myself with the river and the track to Glen Annie.'

Saul pulled up and Gemma was out of the car before he'd opened his door. He sat there and watched as she strode across to the small building and stood there, staring at the map. She'd barely changed in the last six years. She was still tiny and slim and wore her hair the same way she had when she'd been at school. She could still be the eighteen-year-old that he had spent an incredible weekend with at Ormiston Gorge the week before he had left for Darwin. The same week that he had realised once and for all he'd been kidding himself he was good enough for Gemma Hayden.

Longing filled him, but Saul gripped the steering wheel hard. He was dreaming.

Hadn't been then, and wasn't now.

CHAPTER
16

Ruby Gap
November 1890

'Rufus, you come inside and wash your hands for dinner.' Rose jiggled the baby on one hip and stirred the pot of beef stew on the stove with her spare hand. She could hear Rufus playing outside, making no move to obey.

'I'll get the little rascal, Rose,' William called from the porch. By the time a very dirty Rufus and his cross father came in, it was almost dark, and the baby had been fed and was asleep in his crib.

'Where were you?' Rose frowned.

'He ran away again.' William held the wriggling Rufus tightly. 'And then he hid from me. At least he can't get underneath the house since I filled it with dirt.'

Rose held her arms out for her grubby child. 'Well, my boy, you've missed out on lovely warm bath water, and you will have to have a cold wash. Then your dinner, then straight to your bed.'

'Story too, Mumma.'

William shook his head. 'No story tonight, Rufie. You ran away.'

Rose rolled her eyes as the howling began. 'Don't you dare wake Bennett up.'

An hour later, both children were asleep and William and Rose sat at the table enjoying the beef stew and the first quiet time of the day.

'I've organised with Tom Pearson for us to share a beast, and Rolly Edmunds is going to build that extra room while I am away. I've done so much blacksmithing for him, he said he will not charge us the full rate.' William put his hand out and took Rose's fingers in his. She looked at their joined hands with a grimace. Her hands were brown and rough, and she was ashamed to see dirt beneath her short fingernails.

'Gone are the soft white hands from the days when I wore gloves to bed with glycerine to soften my skin,' she said regretfully.

William lifted her hand and raised it to his lips. 'I see the hand of a wonderful woman who works very hard to make a good life for her husband and children.' His eyes were intent on hers. 'Rose, I beg you to please reconsider. I want you and the boys to travel to Port Adelaide and stay in lodgings there while I go to England after Christmas. We can afford it now.'

Rose sat straight. 'No, William. We will stay. I could not abide doing that trip from here to the railhead at Hergott Springs while the children are so small. It was bad enough when it was just you and I. Not with a baby and a little boy.' She leaned forward and held his gaze, knowing he would see her intent. For the first two years of their acquaintance and marriage, they had not known each other well, but over the past year, Rose had realised what a fine and upstanding man her husband was, and that he had seen her strength grow as they had endured hardship together. William was quiet and focused, but a very kind man. Not only to her and the children, but to their neighbours. 'Do you really have to travel to England? Can't we just continue the way we are? We have a good life, and now there is a store and a post office at Arltunga, life is so much easier. Does it matter what they say of the rubies?'

'It does. It is a deliberate ploy to make the rich richer, and stymie the work of all those who have worked so hard out here,' William said firmly. 'It is not honest. I cannot in good conscience allow this deceit to continue, my dear. It is not fair to us, and it's not fair to those around us who work so hard.'

Rose suppressed a sigh; her husband's kindness and sense of fairness extended to all, and he would not be dissuaded. 'Then if you must go, I will be safe here. Our friends are close by, and they will ensure that Rufus, Bennett and I are safe and well.'

'It will make a difference to the rest of our lives. We shall be comfortable.' William's sad expression broke her heart. 'But by the Lord, Rose, my love, I will miss you and our boys every minute of every day I am away from you all.'

Rose stood and began to unlace the back of her apron. 'Perhaps it is time we went to our bed too, my heart?'

William's smile was wide as he stood and slipped his hand beneath her blouse. 'I think that is a fine idea. And we must be quick, before one of the children decides he needs your attention more than his father does.'

★

Rose fed Bennett just after midnight and as his little eyes drooped shut, she ran a gentle finger along his soft, downy cheek. Both of their boys looked like their father, and she knew that would help her in the long months that William was absent.

Once Bennett was settled in the crib, she stood there, her mind working, and she knew she would not sleep. Walking to the small desk in the dining room, Rose pulled out her paper and her fountain pen.

Dear Amelia,

William is travelling home on business, and I have instructed him to contact you as soon as he disembarks. With some luck, he will be able to attend your wedding, and come back and describe your happy day to me. Rufus and Bennett are growing like weeds. The next time my dear husband travels home, we will accompany him, I promise!

How strange it is to still call England home. I do love our new life and home at Ruby Gap, and it is where our boys were born. I do want to bring them home to see their heritage, but they are too young as yet.

I hope this letter finds you well and happy, and that Father is in good health too.

Your loving sister,

Rose Woodford

★

Ruby Gap
July 1891

Rose waited until the children were asleep before she opened the mail. Two letters had arrived from England in the monthly mail bag from Arltunga, and she had savoured the prospect of reading them since Tom Pearson had ridden in with them at noon.

The boys were snug in their bed. Now that Bennett had grown, he shared a bed with his brother and the crib was stored in the new shed behind William's blacksmithing workshop. Thoughts of William brought tears pricking to Rose's eyes. She missed him so much; the day of his departure had been extremely hard, but she knew he was determined to go. Rose had put on a bright face and a cheery voice, but she knew William understood as she clung to him before he climbed onto the horse. He was picking up a camel train at Arltunga and then travelling back to England, coincidentally on the same clipper she had travelled in all those years ago.

'I am a man of few words, my dear, but I do hope you know that I love you and our boys.' His beard had been rough against her face as he'd rested his cheek against hers.

'And I you, William.' Rose had lifted her face for his kiss. When he had lifted his head, she had held his gaze, reaching one hand up to his face. She had changed into a clean pinny for his departure and taken more trouble than usual with her unruly hair. 'You stay safe and come back to us quickly.'

'I will. You make sure that these two rascals don't run you ragged. Betty has said she is more than willing to help.'

Rose and the boys walked down to the rock shelf at the bend of their river and watched until William and his horse were out of sight.

Now, she stoked the fire and quickly read Amelia's letter first, but with only half her attention as she anticipated her husband's letter. Skimming over the pages, she took note of the words that were important to her.

Father is well.

William will be in time for the wedding. Mr Oldham is looking forward to meeting his brother-in-law-to-be.

I miss you, dear sister.

She skimmed the parts about the wedding breakfast and the wedding dress, and how handsome Amelia's soon-to-be husband was. Putting the letter aside with a whispered apology, she reached for William's letter. His handwriting was clear and precise, and there were no ink stains on his letter, as there always were on her lengthy epistles.

My dearest Rose,

I hope this finds you and the boys well. The weather should be clear and cool by the time you receive this, and I am sure your garden will be beautiful. As I travelled to Port Adelaide, I heard of the late summer rains in the north, and I gave thanks. I hope Rufus is being obedient, and that Bennett's teething pain has eased.

I am so proud of our family, and my loving wife.

I have visited Berkshire, and am pleased to write that your father is in good health. Amelia's fiancé appears to be a good man, and cares for her. As the wedding is in London, I shall have time to attend before I embark for home in three weeks.

I have excellent news. I have taken the rubies to the assayers and the report is favourable, as I was certain it would be. The gems I have brought with me are valued at fifty shillings per carat, and the hardness has been confirmed as the same as the Oriental gems. I have also requested a chemical examination of the specimens I have brought with me as that seems to be the major point of contention, and I have a meeting with Mr Nock tomorrow. I have no doubt that the gems from Ruby Gap are indeed rubies, and not worthless garnets as is the story many seem to be perpetuating. I have met with a hostile reception from some quarters here, and I fear there

is subterfuge afoot. It is the only explanation for the varying
results. I am keeping my own counsel now.

Take care, dearest, and be wary of strangers.

Your ever-loving husband,

William Woodford

CHAPTER
17

**Ruby Gap Nature Park
Saturday, 11.30 am**

Gemma stared at the map of the Ruby Gap Nature Park that sat behind a perspex cover. Saul was slow getting out of the ute and she glanced around to see if he was coming over, but he was crouched down beside the back wheel, holding a tyre pressure gauge.

Dad had often taken her and Ethan out on four-wheel-driving adventures. Mum had more often than not come up with an excuse not to come with them—school meetings, reports to file, or simply that she was exhausted from a big week at work and said she'd appreciate the peace and quiet of an empty house. Maybe the writing for their split had been on the wall back then, and she and Ethan had been having too much fun to notice. Dad had taught her all the skills he said she'd need living close to the desert: how to change a tyre, how to check the tyre pressure and how to use the compressor.

'You've got more nous than your brother will ever have, Gem.'

Ethan had pulled a face at her whenever Dad had said that, on their camping trip out to Ellery Big Hole. It was the second-last trip before their final exams, and the last trip with Dad before her whole world went to shit.

They'd sat their exams, and gone out to Ruby Gap with Saul and Screw the weekend before the Year Twelve formal. They had a flat tyre on the way, and Saul and Screw were ahead on their motorbikes so Gemma changed the flat while Ethan passed her the wheel brace and the jack. 'See? I didn't need to learn what Dad tried to teach us,' Ethan had laughed. 'You'll be with me, Gem, and you can do all the dirty work.'

When they hadn't been out somewhere in the western ranges with Dad, they were out at Ruby Gap with Saul and Screw, looking for Ethan's elusive rubies. Gemma had finally been allowed to go once she was sixteen.

She lifted her hand and traced the route to the old house at Glen Annie Gorge with her finger. The memories flooded back now that she was back out here. The familiar smells and the absolute silence tore at her heart. Blinking back tears, she stared at the map of the river, where Saul had described finding Ethan's Ruby, then read the new instructions on the board that laid out the rules that hadn't been there when they were kids. Everything they'd known and had taken for granted in their teens was now outlined in detail on the map in front of her.

Walking: Much of the park's terrain is extremely rugged and is only suitable for the experienced walker. There are no marked trails. Visitors can follow the riverbed and tracks upstream.

Allow four kilometres and two hours return to Glen Annie Gorge.

Allow eight kilometres and four hours return to Fox's Grave via Glen Annie Gorge.

Driving: Do not enter the Hale River if the sand is soft and wet after recent heavy rain. In the event of mishap or breakdown, stay with your vehicle. Do not attempt to walk back to Arltunga.

'As if anyone would.' Gemma shook her head and traced the map again. The only thing missing from the map of the river and the gorges was the site of their ancestor's house, that he had built before word came back from England that the stones were worthless. She wondered if it was still there or if the Parks service had removed it, considering it unsafe in a nature park.

Sadly, according to family lore, William Woodford had abandoned his wife and children and gone searching for gold, never to return.

Never to return. Like Ethan.

A surge of frustration hit her, and she pounded the palms of both hands on the map in anger, the perspex cover rattling.

'Gemma?'

She jumped; she hadn't heard Saul come up behind her.

'That stupid, bloody story of Dad's great-grandfather fascinated Ethan ever since he was little. He was always asking Dad about him. If it hadn't been for Dad sharing the family history, Ethan would never have been obsessed with finding rubies, and he'd still be here.' Her voice broke and she reached up to brush away the hot tears coursing down her cheeks. Embarrassment flooded through her and she turned away. 'I'm sorry. Being here and knowing I'm going to see Ruby but not Ethan . . . it's hard.'

Taking a deep shuddering breath to try and compose herself, Gemma stiffened when Saul's hands came down on her shoulders.

His voice was low as he leaned forward and his breath brushed her ear. 'I swear to you, Gemma. No matter what it takes, we'll find out what happened. I'll be here for you if you need to vent or talk, or just cry. Just let it out. You've held this in for a long time.'

Gemma turned and Saul's arms went around her. Relieved, and knowing she was safe in his arms, she buried her face in the soft cotton of his khaki shirt and cried for the first time in many months. Sobs racked her body, and he held her close as she let it all out. 'I'm scared he is dead, and I didn't know. I should know but I'm scared I'm just kidding myself.'

'We'll solve this together, Gem. Whatever it takes. Trust me.'

Do. Not. Trust. Anyone.

Gemma pulled away and took a step back. 'Thanks, Saul,' she said shortly, moving back to the ute. Until she had deciphered the code—and she intended doing that as soon as they set up camp—she could not freely give her trust to anyone, not even Saul.

*

After driving down the dry sandy riverbed as far as they could, Saul pulled up on a grassy patch halfway along to Annie's Gorge.

'We're on foot from here,' he said, as he parked beneath the western side of the sheer cliff face, behind two large leafy trees. Even though it was the Red Centre and thought of as only desert, this area around the Hale River had surprising pockets of green. The deep-rooted buffel grass grew profusely near the sandy river. 'We'll do one trip across together, then I'll come back for the swag.'

'Do we pass Ethan's vehicle on the way to where we'll be camping?'

'No, it's further on. Up around the bed on the way to Fox's Grave. We'll go up there as soon as we've set up the camp site.'

Gemma walked around to the back of his ute. 'I can handle the box of food and the esky. If you can carry the stove and the swag, we can do it in one trip.'

'Okay, but if it gets too much, we can leave it halfway and I'll come back.'

'It's only another couple of kilometres, isn't it?' Gemma pulled a face at him as she took her small pack from behind the seat and slipped it on her back. She put her phone in her shirt pocket and buttoned the flap down, then put her hat on her head. 'Righto, load me up,' she said as she tightened the string of the hat beneath her chin.

Saul picked up the box of food and tested the weight, then lifted the esky that held the water and the meat he'd bought for dinner. Putting them both down, he removed a four-litre bottle of water from the esky and transferred some of the food from the box into the esky. 'Now it's balanced.'

'Can we afford to leave that water here?' Gemma screwed her forehead up in a frown.

Saul shook his head. 'Trust me, I've learned a few tricks since I've been with Parks.'

He hoisted the swag off the ute, and scrabbled in the tool box for an ockie strap. He looped it through the swag and secured the water bottle to it, as well as his bedroll. 'Okay, see how you go with the esky and the box.' He waited while Gemma reached down and picked them both up, holding the esky by the handle and the box beneath her other arm.

'They're fine.'

'Have you got all your stuff out of the ute?'

When she nodded, Saul locked it and picked up the swag and stove. 'Okay, let's go find a camp site.' He'd lead the way and stay on the solid ground on the right-hand side of the riverbed as much as possible. In the places where the cliff face came too close to the riverbed, he waited for Gemma to walk across the damp sand ahead of him, making sure that she was okay with her load.

Progress was slow because Saul insisted on stopping every couple of hundred metres to rehydrate. Perspiration trickled down his neck and soaked his shirt, but Gemma seemed to be coping with the heat. He shook his head the next time they stopped for a drink. 'Not far now. You haven't even got a sweat up.'

'I cope with this dry heat much better than the humidity on the coast.'

'That's pretty obvious.' Saul was pleased when she smiled back at him; it was the first genuine smile he'd seen. 'I might have to spend some time on the coast and see if it works. I still can't cope with the heat out here at this time of the—' He stopped and cocked his head to the side. 'That's strange. There's a chopper coming. I wonder who it is.'

'Tourists?'

He shook his head. 'They don't run any tours out here in the summer. The tourist season kicks off in late March.'

They were close to the bottom of the cliff face, and a large rock was ahead of them. 'You might think I'm being overly cautious, but come over between this rock and the cliff while it goes over.'

'Why?' Gemma looked uneasy and he understood her fear. He had an uneasy feeling in the pit of his stomach that something wasn't right.

'Because it's just the two of us out here and until we know what's happening, I'd prefer to keep a low profile.' Gemma's eyes widened as he hurried her into the shadow cast between the cliff and the large quartzite boulder at the base. 'We can have a break and another drink while it goes over. Then I'll take you to the part of the gorge where his car is.'

'Won't they see your ute?'

'No, I parked it in the shadow and between those two trees deliberately.'

'You're scaring me, Saul,' Gemma said as she moved quickly. 'After that bloke on the motorbike with the gun strapped to the back, I'm wondering what's going on out here.'

He frowned. 'I didn't want to mention the rifle in case you hadn't seen it.'

'What's happening out here?' she demanded. 'Do you think it had something to do with Ethan's disappearance?'

'Honestly? No, I don't. He went missing before all these private signs and skulls and crossbones went up on the gates out here.' Saul put the swag down on top of the bright blue esky and the cardboard box and took Gemma's hand. He led her further into the shadows as the noise of the approaching helicopter reverberated off the cliff walls. 'Apparently, over the past few years, there's been quite a few of those signs on gates like the one we saw today. Rumour has it there's a bit of a drug trade going on out here, and we certainly don't want anyone to think that we're encroaching on their business.'

'But it's a nature park, for God's sake! Surely there's tourists and fossickers out here all the time, like there used to be when we were kids.'

'Yes, but not in the heat. We never came out in the summer, remember? It's always pretty isolated at this time of the year.'

She shrugged. 'It was such a long time ago. I don't remember when we came.'

Plus, we had other things on our minds back then. Saul suppressed a smile at the thought.

He gestured for her to get closer to the boulder as the noise of the helicopter filled the gorge. Gemma closed her eyes and put her hands over her ears as the downdraft whipped up sand around them. He covered his eyes with one hand and looked up, checking they were out of sight.

When it had gone, they stood away from the rock, brushing the sand from their clothes. 'That was pleasant. What do you think it was doing?'

Saul stared in the direction the helicopter had taken. 'I was just thinking about that. There are a few mines out here. They mined mica and beryllium at the old Leprechaun site but it's closed now, but I think the Tourmaline uranium mine is still going. It's a bit further away.'

'How far?'

'Just beyond the south-eastern boundary of the park. There's no access roads out that way, so it probably was a mine helicopter.'

He knew she needed reassurance, but he was yet to be convinced there was a working mine out there.

Two hours after he had held Gemma in his arms and comforted her, Saul looked around the camp they had set up in the small clearing at the western end of Annie's Gorge. It would have been foolhardy to start a fire with the hot wind that had come in from the north, which was why he'd brought along the butane stove. The weather was not conducive to being outside; even though it was the weekend, they hadn't passed one other vehicle or hiker. No one was camping or fossicking, and not for the first time Saul wondered at the wisdom of being out here. Then again, if he hadn't agreed to come with Gemma, she was likely to have come alone.

She was quiet, sitting in the swag Saul had set up in the lush grass beneath an overhang of the cliff. He'd put his bedroll a few metres away.

The helicopter had headed east, and he was keeping an ear out in case it came back. He hoped where he'd put their stuff was out of sight. He walked back to the edge of the water and stared across at their camp site. The dark brown of the swag blended in with the cliff face, and unless you knew it was there, you'd never spot it against the variegated rocks. The esky was a different matter; it stood out like a sore thumb. He crouched down at the water's edge and dug a hole in the soft shingle with his hands. The small garnets stuck to his hands, glistening in the afternoon sunlight.

He thought about Ethan as he walked back over for the esky and ockie strap. No wonder he'd been so certain he was going to find something out here when they were kids. If garnets were worth anything, he would have made his fortune.

Saul made sure the lid of the esky was secure, looped the ockie strap around the handle, and secured it to a small branch that was hanging over the water, before covering the esky with the damp shingle.

His scalp tingled as he stood, and he put his hand to his eyes and scanned the cliffs that rose dramatically on each side of the gorge. But there was nothing to see apart from the never-ending red of the cliffs. The shadows were growing longer but the sun still burned deep red on the eastern side, and the sand glimmered with the 'rubies' that gave the gorge its name.

A lone wedge-tailed eagle wheeled in the clear blue sky high above him. Saul turned back towards the camp, constant unease tugging at him.

CHAPTER
18

Ruby Gap Nature Park
Saturday, 2.00 pm

'I'm just going to take five and have a bit of a rest.' Gemma crouched next to the swag.

'Good idea. Five long enough?' Saul stared at her, his expression serious.

She returned his gaze steadily. 'Yes,' she said, trying not to sound defensive. 'I just need to catch my breath.'

'Look, we've got plenty of time. Take a half-hour break while I'll go up the cliff and see if there's a road up there.'

Gemma crawled into the swag for a few minutes to herself, away from Saul's watchful eye. Trusting him was hard. Not being able to trust him hurt. She reminded herself that she had asked him to come out to Ruby Gap with her, and her heart told her she should trust him, but his actions had forced logic to come in. His reactions seemed to be exaggerated, and it made her wonder. Saul had been quiet and on edge, and even though he tried not to make it obvious, his eyes had constantly scanned the cliffs ahead as they'd trekked along the riverbed to the camp site.

She sat with her legs tucked beneath her, trying to breathe evenly and calm down. The helicopter—or more so Saul's reaction—had scared her. The aircraft had swooped down low along the riverbed, but Saul had been determined that they stay out of sight. The fact that he felt it necessary for them to hide frightened her, even though he'd said it was probably only a mine helicopter. She listened for its return. Damn it, Saul's paranoia was rubbing off on her, or maybe just knowing she was so close to Ethan's Ruby was adding to her stress.

What was she going to discover? Maybe it had been a stupid idea to come out here. Six years had passed, why had Ruby only been found now? Was it a coincidence that the vehicle turned up when she'd come home to Alice Springs?

And what were the chances of Saul being the one to be sent out to investigate it?

Questions circled around Gemma's mind like the whistling kites soaring in the sky above, and she vowed she would find the answers; this was the first time there had been any chance of discovering where Ethan was, and she would not give up.

Taking deep even breaths, Gemma closed her eyes, knowing she wouldn't be able to focus on deciphering the code if she let stress and fear take over. After five minutes of concentrating on her breathing, she felt a bit better. Closing her eyes, she lay on her back for another fifteen minutes, thinking about the letter. The fact that Ethan felt it necessary to revert to the code signalled that something was very wrong, and she was worried about what she would discover in his message. She sat up and took the letter from her backpack but her hands were still trembling. Staring at the border, she knew there was something in there . . .

Her stomach grumbled and Gemma glanced at her watch; it was heading for two-thirty, and all she'd eaten today was an apple. The lack of food wouldn't be helping her shakiness. She'd have to leave the letter for later; she'd had a half-hour rest.

Crawling out of the swag, she looked around for Saul. He was crouched down at the edge of the water and as she watched, he stood and looked around again, shading his eyes with one hand as he scanned along the cliffs in both directions.

What is he looking for?

She waited while he walked back to the camp site.

'Feeling a bit better now?' he asked.

'Yes. Why are you being so careful out here, Saul? What do you know? What are you worried about?'

He shook his head. 'Nothing in particular. I always stay aware of my surroundings when I'm out bush. There's always danger and this time of the year, if there's rain, you have to get out of the riverbed quickly.'

Gemma looked up at the clear sky. 'Doesn't look much like rain to me.' Her stomach grumbled loudly and she put her hand against it. 'Excuse me.'

'Hungry? I bought some readymade sandwiches at the bakery in town before I picked you up. I took them out of the esky before I buried it. They're over there in the shade.' He gestured to where his bedroll was set up at the other end of the overhang of the cliff.

'I *am* hungry,' she said. 'Saul? Why did you bury the esky?'

'To keep it cool.' He looked past her as he answered, and she wondered if he was being truthful. When he'd opened the esky to lighten it for her to carry, she'd seen the ice in there. All that was in there now was the meat for dinner tonight, and then there was nothing left to be kept cool.

So why bury it?

Gemma shook herself mentally. God, she was being stupid. Being suspicious of every little thing.

Saul walked past her, calling over his shoulder, 'A sandwich and a bottle of water okay? Or do you want a cuppa?'

'Water is fine. What will we do then? Will we go to look at Ruby?'

He picked up two brown paper bags. She hadn't noticed them over on the bedroll. He'd left a couple of bottles of water outside the swag for her.

'We'll let the sun get a bit lower, then we'll hike up the gorge.' He passed her one of the sandwich bags. 'You look a bit pale. Are you okay? The heat's not getting to you too much?'

'Just hungry. I'm keen to get going.'

'I'm sure you are. The river's still got a fair bit of water in some of the narrow parts, so we'll have to do a bit of rock climbing.'

'Did you go to the top of the cliff?'

'Yep.' He nodded but didn't elaborate.

'And? Did you see anything?'

After a moment he met her eye, but she knew him well enough to know when he was being evasive. 'Not really.'

He unwrapped his sandwich and looked up at the cliff as he ate silently. A frisson of nerves sent a shiver down Gemma's back.

Ten minutes later, she watched Saul put the rubbish into the food box and top up their empty water bottles from the four-litre container. He turned to her with a smile.

'Good to see a bit of colour back in your face. Right to head out now?'

'Yes, please.' Gemma hesitated and looked back at the swag where she'd left her gear. 'I'll just grab my phone.'

'No service out here.'

'I know, but I want to take some photos of Ruby to send to Mum and Dad.'

'Fair enough.'

They set off together, the trek much easier now that they had set up camp and weren't carrying anything apart from a bottle of water each, plus Saul had put two more bottles in a small nylon backpack. Mentioning her parents had made Gemma think of her father, and she wondered if Mum had been able to get in touch with him to tell him about Ruby being found. Hearing that they'd been in touch had really surprised her, and she hoped that things were a bit better between them now. Each of their lives had changed when Ethan had disappeared.

Saul gestured to his backpack. 'Do you want a fly net?'

She shook her head. 'No, I'm fine. They don't seem too bad today.'

He nodded. 'Yes, the slight breeze keeps them away. They were shocking out here on Friday.'

Gemma grinned as a memory popped into her thoughts. 'Remember the day Ethan swallowed a fly?'

'I do. He sure put on a performance.' Their eyes met and Gemma felt the tension between them ease just slightly.

'We didn't wear fly nets back then. I don't even remember having them.'

'No.' Saul's smile was wide and Gemma ignored the warm flutter in her stomach. 'We were too cool back then to wear them.'

The only sound was the crunching of the shingle under their boots, and as the riverbed flashed red in the afternoon sun, Gemma tried to stay composed as they got closer to the gorge where her brother's vehicle was waiting. She was determined not to break when they got there. It was only a car; it wasn't Ethan. She had to remember that. But the memories of driving with him in Ruby were making her throat ache as they trudged along the soft riverbed.

Saul slowed his pace as they approached a narrow part of the gorge, where the water had backed up and almost reached to the cliffs on each side. 'There's actually more water here today than there was last week. They must have had more rain out here last night than we had in town.'

'Is that going to be a problem? For seeing the car, I mean?'

Saul stepped up onto a large rock at the base of the cliff and held one hand out to Gemma. 'I don't think so. It was completely out of the water on Thursday. Just buried in the shingle.'

She took his hand. His grip was warm and firm as he helped her up onto the flat wide rock. Another gust of wind ruffled the water and a strange sound came from ahead of them. Gemma froze.

Saul's voice was calm. 'Stay completely still. They won't touch you.'

Gemma stopped dead as a huge dark mass filled the wide gap of the gorge ahead of them, expanding and contracting as she stared.

'What is it?' she whispered, her voice shaking. 'It's like when the air moved in that movie Ethan used to watch all the time. The alien in *Predator*.'

'Don't worry. It's a natural phenomenon—a murmuration. A massive flock of budgies. Bloody hell, look at them. I've never seen a flock that size.' As Saul spoke, the sound of wingbeats from the approaching flock surrounded them. The air shimmered green and gold as the birds flew towards them. The shrill chattering was deafening and soon they were engulfed in a sea of colour and shrill noise as thousands of the small birds flew past them. The little wings created a cool breeze and Gemma's hair flew around her head in a halo.

She put her hands to her mouth as the flock disappeared towards their camp and silence descended again. 'Oh my God, that was amazing.' She looked down, surprised to see that Saul was still holding her hand. She flushed as he let go, but suddenly the tension that had been between them seemed to have eased even more.

'It was pretty special,' he said quietly, holding her eyes with his. Gemma found it hard to look away. 'Right to keep going?'

She nodded as the present came swooping back. The magical sight of the birds had made her forget what was ahead, and she had just enjoyed being part of the landscape. 'Yes. Let's go.'

★

Gemma's reaction when they reached Ethan's Land Rover surprised Saul. She stood beside the car staring at it, her face devoid of any expression.

'It's just a car, isn't it?' she said quietly. 'It doesn't even look like Ethan's, with all the paint off it. I thought it would upset me, but . . . it's just a car.'

'Yes, it is just a car.' He moved closer to it. 'Darren and I got everything out of it.'

'Thank you. I'm pleased it was you who found it, Saul. If it had been anyone else, I mightn't have seen that envelope.'

He frowned as he stared at the car. 'Actually, there was something else. Once we got the glove box open, I forgot about it.'

'What else was there?' Gemma moved closer to the Land Rover.

'Hang on. It should still be on the floor in the front.' Saul couldn't believe that he'd left the axe there, but when they'd found the papers in the glove box, it had thrown him and he'd forgotten all about it. All he'd wanted to do was let Ethan's family know that his vehicle had turned up.

He climbed in and retrieved it. When he was back out again, he handed it to Gemma.

She frowned. 'What is it? Was it Ethan's?'

'Yes, he found it in the ruins of the old house the last time we were out there. He said they were your ancestor's initials. Didn't he tell you about it?'

'He mentioned an old axe and I forgot about it. I've never seen it before.' She turned it over and looked at the initials carved into the handle. 'His name was William Woodford, so it could be.'

'Ethan always left it out there. He was mucking around that night when we were playing cards and started digging around a bit of wood that was sticking out of the dirt floor. When he dug it out, he was really excited.'

'Where did you find it?'

He gestured to the back of the vehicle that was still buried in the shingle. 'We dug it out of the back.'

'Was that all you found? Nothing else?'

'That was all. Anything else would have been washed away when the river was flowing. It was jammed against the wheel arch.'

'I'd like to take it home. Dad would probably be interested to see it.' Her voice was quiet, but steady.

'Do you want to walk up to the ruins in the morning? It's not a bad walk from here. We'll have time before we head back.'

'Are they still there? It's been a few years.' Gemma's eyes brightened. 'Did you go out there when you found Ruby?'

'No, we went straight back to town and reported what we'd found. I imagine it will still be there. It was a pretty solid construction.'

'We might find something else. Maybe Ethan's been back here since Dad came out to look there when he went missing? Maybe that's how Ruby turned up here.'

'Worth a look,' Saul said. The hope in her eyes sent pity spiralling through him. Maybe he shouldn't have suggested going to the site of her forbears' house. He'd been preoccupied with what he'd seen when he was up on the cliff. There had been a track of sorts, and about half a kilometre away, a metal shed was situated in a fenced enclosure. He'd walked along the clifftop until he could see upriver and he'd been surprised to see some timber platforms and earthworks at the edge of the river below Fox's Grave. Darren had said that there were no plans to do tourist walks up here, but he was obviously wrong. He'd follow it up with Terry next week.

Gemma nodded and moved away from the car, still partially buried at the side of the river. The shadows were lengthening and Saul turned and gestured downriver. 'Come on, let's go back to the camp site.'

It was about an hour before sunset, and the sinister shadows at the base of the cliff brought another prickle to the back of Saul's neck. He didn't know what was making him feel so unsettled. Probably just the fact that somewhere out here was the clue to Ethan's disappearance.

Gemma set a brisk pace, her boots crunching in the shingle, obviously keen to get away from Ethan's vehicle. He strode out and caught up to her. 'How long do you think it'll be before you can get that code stuff?'

Gemma's pace slowed and she turned to look at him. 'I already have it,' she said after a long moment. 'That's what I was looking at on my phone on the way out.'

'Christ, you should have said.' Exasperation surged. 'You still don't trust me, do you, Gemma?'

'I asked you to bring me out here, didn't I?' Her eyes were dark.

'I guess you did.' Disappointment vied with frustration. 'Look Gemma, even though we parted on bad terms, I'm still the same person you knew six years ago, and I want to find out what happened to Ethan as much as you do. You *can* trust me.'

'Don't take it so personally, Saul,' she said coolly. 'I don't trust anyone these days. I've been let down by too many people. Ethan was the only person I could trust. Mum never cared for anything except for her school, and Dad can't bear to be with me since Ethan went. *I* look after me these days. And we've all changed. You're not the same person I . . . I knew back then. None of us stay the same.'

The relationship they'd once had remained unspoken, and the fact that she still didn't trust him hurt, even as he knew that he was partly responsible for her inability to trust.

'Sounds like you've had a rough time of it,' he said finally.

'Yep.' She was tight-lipped as she strode ahead again. 'You could say that.'

Saul caught up to her and reached out and held her arm. As Gemma turned to him, the uncertainty in her eyes broke his heart. Those beautiful green eyes that had once looked at him with humour and caring were flat and cold.

He held her gaze steadily. 'When we get back to camp, will you please trust me to help you with the code? Seeing as you've got it now, there might be a clue to something out here. And I know this park like the back of my hand.'

'As long as I can trust you to be truthful with me. Like why did you bury an almost empty esky?'

He held her gaze steadily. 'To keep it cool . . . and so it didn't stand out to anyone flying over.'

★

Gemma didn't know how to react as Saul held her arm, his eyes intent on hers, and that stupid fluttering came back to her stomach.

He was very keen to find out what was in that border around Ethan's letter. Did he know that there would be something there to incriminate him?

Does he not want me to read it?

No, that was stupid. He would simply have destroyed the two pages and not given them to her in the first place. And he'd been truthful with her about the esky.

'Okay.' Her head was spinning and as she looked up, the cliffs receded in a blur. She stumbled and Saul's grip tightened. He put his other arm around her waist and led her over to a flat rock in the shade. 'You're dehydrated. You've been walking too hard and fast.' Pulling a bottle of water from his backpack, he unscrewed the lid and handed to her. 'Small sips to start.'

She sat on the warm rock and his hand stayed on her shoulder. She closed her eyes and sipped, trying to ignore the nausea that had crept up on her. Gradually, it eased and the lightheaded feeling passed. She pushed herself up to her feet.

'Rest a little while longer,' Saul said.

Gemma shook her head so fast, her head began to spin again. 'No, I'm feeling okay now. I want to go back to the camp. We can look at the code together.'

A relieved sigh escaped Saul's lips and Gemma looked up at him. He'd always had a beautiful mouth. It was one of the first things she'd noticed when she had become aware of him as more than Ethan's mate. Those lips had lived up to her imagination two years later when he'd kissed her the first time in the back row of the cinema. Why had everything gone wrong between them? Why had Saul taken off without telling her?

Should she follow her heart and trust him? Or would Saul let her down like everyone else had? Since Ethan had gone, Gemma had withdrawn into herself. Avoiding relationships, keeping her distance from her parents. If she didn't get close to anyone, she couldn't be hurt when she lost them.

Taking a deep breath, she came to a decision. She would trust Saul and let him help her, but she would keep him at a distance. It was the safest thing to do.

CHAPTER
19

Ruby Gap
April 1892

Tom Pearson called in one afternoon with a sack of potatoes.

Rose ushered him inside to the warmth, where the fire was crackling, and the boys were sitting playing on the rug. 'You are just in time for a cup of tea, and I have just this minute taken a pound cake from the oven.'

Tom nodded and put his hat on the table before crouching down beside Rufus and Bennett. 'Hello, you pair. Have you been well behaved for your mother?'

Rose glanced over as she made the pot of tea and saw Rufus looking at her. He quickly dropped his eyes, and she knew he was wondering if she would tell Tom what a naughty child he had been.

It was in the past now, and there was no need to mention it. Rose knew that Rufus had given himself a fright when he'd got stuck halfway up the cliff two days earlier, and she knew he would stay close to home for a while. At just over four years of age, he was a strong-willed child who would not do as he was told.

No punishment seemed to make a difference, and Rose was looking forward to William coming home. For a moment, she was tempted to ask Tom to play father figure, then had second thoughts.

That would not be fair.

The boys ate their cake and went back to playing quietly on the mat in front of the fire.

Tom sat back and lifted the enamel cup of tea. 'Thank you, Rose. 'Tis a fine cake.'

They sipped the hot liquid quietly until Tom spoke again. 'I wanted to show you a story I read in the *Port Adelaide Advertiser* when I was in Arltunga last week. The newspaper is over two months old, but the content is concerning.'

Rose leaned forward. 'I do hope William's journey hasn't been in vain. All that time away. He will barely recognise the boys. Please read it to me, Tom.'

Tom reached into his pocket and put his spectacles on the end of his nose. He cleared his throat and began to read.

'While the early rubies from the Hale River district initially brought excellent prices in London, one hundred times more than gold, buyers have become wary as the results of recent assays have been made public. The quality of the gems is questionable. Two years ago, the *Adelaide Observer* carried a report by the well-respected jeweller, PL Nock and Son of Leadenhall Street, London. They had commissioned a laboratory analysis by Smythe and Stoddard to determine the quality of the rubies coming out of Hale River. The report was published on 29 May 1890.' Tom shook his head. 'It appears that the results of the analysis by Smythe and Stoddard were not encouraging. The percentage of alumina is only a quarter of the whole gem.'

Rose frowned. 'I'm sorry, Tom, what does that mean?'

'They are saying we are wasting our time if we think we have valuable rubies here. The word has got around and many of the miners in the gorge have gone to Arltunga in search of gold instead. I have heard of one suicide too. They tell me that a man by the name of Fox took his own life when he was told his gems were worthless.'

'Oh, how sad. What will *we* do? There is no reason to live out here without our claims, is there?' Rose asked. 'William will be so disillusioned.'

'I know what William will say and I trust him. He is an intelligent man, and a good man, and he would not make accusations like that lightly. He believes that the testing and the reports are a conspiracy to stop the mining rush here, and that in a time to come, those who know the true value will come in and reap the benefits.'

Rose widened her eyes. 'If he states his case publicly, will he be safe, Tom?'

The look on Tom's face frightened her. 'I will be pleased to see him home, Rose.'

'As will we. May I read the paper, please?'

Tom handed the broadsheet over to her.

It can't all be for nothing.

Rose was unaware of the children playing and Tom sitting there as she concentrated on the words.

Despite their brilliant appearance, the report showed that the rubies sent for analysis contain only a quarter of the crystallised alumina that make up a quality ruby. It is reported that some of the stones are garnets, but garnets have no aluminium oxide.

She shook her head. 'I don't understand this. I much prefer working with my seeds.'

Tom stood and reached for his hat. 'Don't worry yourself, lass. William will be home before you know it, and I'm sure his calm reason will make a difference over there.'

Despite his words, Rose found it difficult to sleep that night.

Where was William? And why was he taking so long to come home? He should have arrived home months ago.

Doubt and loneliness overwhelmed Rose in the early hours, and she pressed her face into the pillow to soak up the hot tears spilling from her eyes. Was that why William had wanted her to go to Port Adelaide?

Had he never intended to return?

CHAPTER
20

Ruby Gap Nature Park
Saturday, 6.30 pm

By the time Gemma and Saul reached the campsite, the sky was still blue and clear above them, but there was no sunlight at the bottom of the gorge. The cliffs towered high above them and where the setting sun hit the top of the eastern side, the cliffs glittered a sinister red.

'Eat first, then we'll look at the code. Is that okay with you?' Saul had been quiet as they'd walked back along the river.

'Yes,' she said, even though she didn't feel hungry.

Within minutes, Saul had retrieved the steak from the esky and lit the butane stove. Gemma sat on the bedroll and watched as he deftly sliced a potato into thin rounds, then an onion, and added them to the pan. Soon, the aromatic fragrance of frying onions had her mouth watering.

The sky darkened as Saul cooked their meal. He left the stove and pulled out a small torch, shining it onto the box at the end of the bedroll. 'There's two enamel plates and cutlery in there.'

Gemma nodded. She retrieved the plates and held them as Saul dished up, and once he'd turned the stove off, he sat beside her on the bedroll.

Her stomach was churning again, and she nibbled at the steak and potato on her plate. This was the closest she'd been in six years to finding out what had happened to her twin, and she was sick with apprehension.

'Come on, Gemma. I carried that stove all the way in to cook you a meal and you're looking at it as though that eye fillet steak is a piece of tough old camel.' His white teeth flashed in the torchlight. 'It's wagyu beef, I'll have you know.'

She laughed and, with an effort, cleared her plate, and actually did feel better for it. While Saul packed up the stove, Gemma walked down to the river to wash the plates and pan. It reminded her of when she'd camped out here with the boys. Back in those days, she'd always been given wash-up duty but she hadn't minded; she'd enjoyed the solitude of the walk down to the water while the boys played cards under the large tarp they'd rigged up to the posts that still stood on the four corners of the old ruins.

The old house had been set well back from the river. As well as the side posts, the brick chimney of the fireplace still stood as a sentinel. It was easy to see the layout of the four-room dwelling. Gemma had wondered what it would have been like to live out there in the olden days, so far away from everywhere. Even these days, it was a remote and isolated location, a long way from Alice Springs. In those days, Alice Springs had been called Stuart, Dad had told them. Arltunga, where the gold rush had followed the ruby rush, had been Central Australia's first official town, once supporting up to three thousand people. Maybe living out here wouldn't have been so bad.

Sadness filled Gemma now as she walked slowly to the edge of the water. The moon had risen and was close to full, and the smooth water gleamed in the soft light. It was a beautiful night to camp, even though it was the middle of summer. Occasionally, a cooling breeze ruffled the surface and the sounds of the bush drifted across to her. As Gemma stood there, the grass rustled and she waited, still and quiet. The moonlight reflected on the pale fur of a cute little bilby as it emerged from the long grass and cautiously made its way down to the water's edge. Watching the small creature made her smile, and she didn't move as it scratched in the shingle. When it had finished and hopped back towards the crevice in the cliff, she scooped some water into her hands and wet her face and hair to freshen up.

Gemma turned to go back to the camp, ready to face whatever was in the words she—they—were about to decipher. She put the dishes back in the food box and carried the pan over to where Saul was sitting on his bedroll. He had the torch propped up on his thighs. 'I thought we could sit out here. It'll be a bit cooler.'

'I'll get my phone and the letter.' Gemma put the pan back on the stove then crawled into the swag. She ran her fingers through her damp hair. Her feet were hot and sweaty, but she knew it was unwise to take her boots off and go barefoot in the soft green grass. Even though it was inviting, there could be snakes lurking near the water. She'd be safe in the swag tonight because the fly net could be zipped up.

She frowned as she went back to Saul. 'Are you going to be okay out here just on your bedroll? What about snakes?'

'I've camped out in the bush heaps of times over the past six years, Gemma. I've never had a problem. If you leave the wildlife alone, they'll do the same.'

She sat beside him and carefully laid out the letter, and took her phone from her pocket.

'I turned it off to save the battery,' she said as she pushed the button on the side.

'Wise move. It'll use up the power quickly searching for a network.'

Opening up the text messages, she clicked on the photo of the first page that Colin had sent to her and it filled the screen. Beneath three columns of boxes Ethan's loopy writing provided the key for the letter each different square represented.

'He sure did a detailed code.' Saul's breath was warm on her neck as he leaned over her shoulder.

'He did.' Gemma swallowed, ignoring the warmth his proximity brought. 'Can you direct the torch onto the page, and I'll look at the photos and see if I can match any of the letters to the squares on the first page.'

Saul did as she asked, but before she could look down at the border of the page, he turned the torch off.

There was enough light from her phone for Gemma to be aware of his frown when she turned to Saul. 'What—'

'Turn your phone off. Now,' he said quickly as the low thud of a helicopter reached her ears. 'Now.'

'The same one, do you think?' she asked nervously once she'd turned the screen off.

'I'd say so. Probably the one from before going back to Alice. It must be a mine helicopter.' There was something in his tone that made her uneasy.

They waited, listening as the helicopter approached.

'What's it doing?' Gemma asked nervously.

Saul got up to his feet and looked upriver. 'It sounds like it's around the bend, where the Land Rover is.'

'What do you think it's doing?' Gemma put her phone down on the bedroll and stood. 'Is it landing?'

'No, it's just the noise being funnelled up by the shape of the cliffs.' He turned to face her, but she couldn't see his expression in the darkness. 'I thought a mine helicopter would have gone back a lot earlier.'

'What are you worried about, Saul?'

He didn't answer for a moment. 'Look, I'll be honest with you, Gem.' She held her breath, ignoring the diminutive of her name. Saul had always called her Gem, before. 'It might sound stupid, and I can't pinpoint why, but I've had a feeling that we've been watched today. I haven't seen anyone, and there's been no sign that there's anyone around, except for that helicopter. I know it sounds stupid, but if there's someone around, why don't they show themselves? And then that helicopter coming back at this time of night doesn't feel right. Maybe it has been to the mine, but it's late coming back.' Saul walked towards the river and Gemma followed him. 'Also, the Tourmaline mine is to the south,' Saul said as they stood next to the water. 'That chopper came in from the northeast. There's nothing out that way but desert. The closest settlement is the Atitjere community at the base of the Hart Ranges. It's a long way from here by road, but only about seventy ks as the crow flies. I've got no idea what a helicopter would be doing out here, and at this time of night. There aren't even any remote cattle stations out that way. It's pretty much desert.'

Gemma stared at the chopper, snaking its way up the gorge. 'Should we be worried?'

Saul reached out and took her hand. 'Sorry, I don't mean to worry you. We're fine here. We're out of sight, and if they are up to anything dodgy, I don't think they'd have seen my ute when they came through earlier.'

Gemma tensed as the throb intensified. 'Here it comes.'

Saul grabbed her hand and headed closer to the cliff. 'Come on, we'll stand beneath that ledge near the swag. No need to draw attention to ourselves.'

They reached the ledge and Saul turned her around so that her back was to the river. He stood close behind her, his arms around her. Suddenly, the gorge around them lit up.

'What are they doing?' she asked nervously. She put a hand to her chest as her heart began to race.

'Maybe they saw Ethan's vehicle and they're checking that there's no one wandering around hurt. But I'd prefer they don't see us.'

'Won't they see the swag and the bedroll?'

'No. They're dark and tucked in enough to stay in the shadows.' Gemma could tell from the tone of Saul's voice that he wasn't convinced. 'Just keep turned that way, in case the light reaches under here.'

*

Gemma pressed closer to him and a surge of protectiveness filled Saul as he held her in his arms.

'There's nowhere it could land even if they saw us, is there?' Gemma asked, fear in her voice.

'No, the river is close to the escarpment here,' he replied. 'There's nowhere for it to put down along here. Don't stress. It'll be gone soon. I'm probably overreacting.' He knew he wasn't overreacting, but he didn't want to scare Gemma any further.

'Don't stress? All I can think of is that guy on the motorbike who bailed you up this morning,' Gemma said crossly. 'And you said you feel like we're being watched. Who knows who else is lurking out here in the bush?'

The chopper lifted above the clifftop, and the light disappeared as it made its way west. Saul's mind raced as he stood still for a moment longer to make sure it didn't come back. Helicopters going to and from where? Buildings in the middle of a remote area?

What the hell is happening out here?

He finally released Gemma and stepped away, trying to inject some positivity into his tone. 'Right, now the excitement is over for the night, let's go and decipher this code.'

★

'We make a good team,' Gemma said an hour later, her excitement growing. The more she focused on transcribing the cipher, the more her worry about the helicopter disappeared. Her interaction with Saul had been easier as they'd both concentrated, and a couple of times their eyes had met and held in the dim light.

As they had worked out each square, Gemma noted down which letter was represented in the small notebook that Saul had taken from his pocket along with a stubby lead pencil. At first, she'd typed the cipher into the notes of her phone, but switching between the message screen, the photo and the notes screens had slowed them down. When Saul had pointed out that the battery life was down to less than twenty per cent and reminded her that they had no way of charging her phone until they headed back in his ute tomorrow, Gemma had willingly accepted the offer of the paper and pencil.

'Okay, that's it.' She sat back and rubbed her eyes. They were dry and gritty from concentrating on the screen in the torchlight. 'Are we ready to crack it?'

Saul was sitting close to her and his leg rested against hers. 'Let's go. Are you going to start from the top or down each side? There's two rows of squares on the top and bottom of the border and three down each side.'

Gemma bit her lip. 'I'll start at the left and try going clockwise. If that doesn't make sense, I'll move the start point around.'

'Do you want me to write it down while you read each word?'

She nodded, tore a page from the notebook and handed over the pencil. 'Yes, please. To see if it makes sense. Let's go.'

She put her finger on the top left square and read out the letters. She paused as Saul carefully wrote them down.

'I, then a space. I remember that. The triangle in the square means a space between words.'

'Good. That'll make it easier. W . . . A . . . S. *Space*.'

'I was,' Saul said.

'Yes. R . . . I . . .G . . .H . . . T.'

'Right,' they both said at the same time.

'I was right?' Gemma said. 'He was right about what?'

'Keep going,' Saul said.

As Gemma got used to checking from the code to the border, she got faster at reading the squares. 'About the rubies, the rest of the line says. Write that all down, Saul.'

'I was right about the rubies,' Saul repeated.

'Yes, and then he says, "Gemma".' She stopped reading and glanced across at Saul, but he was intent on the paper he had rested on his lap.

Should she be honest and read it all to him? Could she trust him, even though the next words in the border filled her with doubt?

Finally, he looked up. 'What's wrong. What's next? Can't you figure it out?'

She nodded slowly and came to a decision. As she spoke, she kept her eyes on his face. 'He says next, "don't trust anyone. No police".'

Saul looked up and met her eye. 'I can see why you hesitated.'

She nodded, not sure what to say.

Saul shook his head. 'I told you before, Gem. You can trust me. I swear to you, I knew nothing about any of this. I was gone by the time Ethan disappeared.'

Go with your gut. Gemma kept her voice soft. 'I do trust you, Saul. I always did. Even though you let me down.'

'I've regretted that every day since.' His quiet reply sent warmth spiralling through her chest.

'Every day?' She needed to hear it again.

'Yes. Now, keep on with that.'

Gemma put her finger back on the last square and kept reading slowly. 'S . . . C . . . R . . . E . . . W . . . Screw. Screw and I found it.' Her voice broke. 'Found what? This is leading us on a wild goose chase and not telling us anything.'

'Calm down. Don't get frustrated until we get to the end.'

Gemma blinked back tears. *We.* For the first time since Ethan had gone missing, she knew someone was on her side. Her voice shook again when she read out the next letters.

'Find Saul. Tell Saul. Trust Saul.' She lifted her face to his and smiled. 'But you found me.'

'Yes, it was lucky that Terry sent me out here to check out the wreck.'

'Otherwise, it might have gone to the police and Ethan says don't trust the police,' Gemma said. Why couldn't they trust the police? What was Ethan mixed up in?

'Exactly.' Saul nodded. 'Now keep going.'

It took almost an hour to transcribe the six columns, and Gemma's phone was down to three per cent battery when she read the last four squares out to Saul.

His eyes were wide and his mouth set grimly as she watched him read over what he'd written down.

'Read it all out. Let me try and make sense of it, Saul.'

She closed her eyes as Saul read the words.

'*I was right about the rubies. Gemma, don't trust anyone. No police. Screw and I found it. Find Saul. Tell Saul. Trust Saul. Screw came back. Gone now. Not safe. I'll go too. Can't come back. Saul's gone too. Can't tell him what we found. Find him, tell him, get them.*'

Gemma interrupted. 'He sounds desperate. Scared. Almost as though he was sick or something. He repeats himself.'

Saul nodded. 'You're right. It doesn't sound like Ethan's usual happy-go-lucky self.'

'Keep going. I'm trying to make sense of what he's saying.'

'Okay.' Saul cleared his throat and kept reading. '*Found GGG's letter in tin. WW. In the ruins. Under stone east corner. Still there. Don't tell anyone else. Don't trust. Told you it was real. Love you, Gem. Eth xxx.*'

'Well, we're definitely going out to the ruins tomorrow,' she said. 'There's another letter out there.'

'But we'll be very careful,' Saul said. 'There's something still going on. I don't know what, but we need to be careful.'

Gemma nodded, blinking tears away. 'But he's alive. I *knew* it.'

Saul put the paper down and the pencil on top. He reached over and took Gemma's hands between his. 'You have to be realistic, Gem. It's been six years. If he was alive, Ethan would have come back. He would have contacted you.'

'I know, and the police kept asking me if I'd heard from him. When I said no, they said he obviously wanted nothing to do with the family anymore.' Her voice was fierce and she pulled her hands from his. 'Please don't doubt me, Saul. I know he's alive, and if he is and he hasn't come back, there's a damn good reason for it. Ethan sounds scared in that message.'

'I'll agree with that.'

'I'm not going to give up hope. I want to go out tomorrow and search for that tin he talks about.' This time, her voice broke. 'I just hope to God that it's still there.'

CHAPTER
21

Ruby Gap
1892

'Rufus! Come back inside immediately. I will not chase you.' At four years of age, her eldest son was inquisitive and had no awareness of the dangers around them. Only the other day, Rose had found him climbing a tree, trying to catch one of the huge sand lizards that had scurried up there.

Rufus was cunning and would pick his time to slip quietly out the door and off into the bush before she could catch him. Rose had constant nightmares of him drowning in the river, but Rufus was more interested in the bush and the creatures that inhabited it.

'I'm getting some wood for the fire, Mumma.'

'Thank you. You be careful, though. Bring the kindling in and we'll light the fire for your bath.' Rufus had been allowed to use William's axe for the past three months, and had shown he could be careful.

Rose could hear him just outside the door and turned back to the letter from William that had arrived that morning.

I have had great success in my meetings with Mr Nock, the jeweller in Leadbetter Street. He agreed to have the two large stones that I brought with me tested by a different assayer as I insisted. I do not trust the results from Smythe and Stoddart, and I made this quite clear to Mr Nock.

Rose, I was right. Imagine his surprise when our rubies were definitively proved to be genuine. In addition, a further test was carried out, and our rubies were tested at a high temperature, and they took on the green hue of a genuine stone then regained their original colour on cooling. Mr Nock and I attended the testing, and he turned to me, and shook my hand. He was delighted that I persisted in my quest and came to England to pursue the truth. He has advised me to not speak to anyone of the findings, and I request that you do not share this news. I will tell Tom Pearson on my return.

Amelia and Edwin's wedding went very well, and your father sends his best regards. My luggage will be very heavy on the return voyage, and I think I will need a whole camel train to bring back the presents that have been sent to you and the boys. I

Rose's blood ran cold as a terrified scream pierced the quiet. She dropped the letter to the table and hurried outside. 'Rufus, what is it? Where are you?'

'Snake, Mumma!' Rufus was in the corner next to the woodpile, the axe in his hand as he leaned against the timber wall behind him. A huge broad-headed mulga reared up in front of him, only two feet away. It flattened its neck and swayed from side to side.

Rose grabbed the shovel next to the door and ran down the steps. 'Stay still, baby. Don't move.'

Rufus's whimpers echoed around the small dirt yard as he obeyed, but the snake moved closer, its head still swaying as it coiled the rest of its length into an S-shape.

Rose kept her eyes on Rufus, barely able to inhale as fear closed her throat. 'You're doing well, sweetheart. Stay perfectly still and Mumma will kill the snake. Don't breathe, and don't move one finger. Pretend you are a statue like that game we play.'

Rufus stood perfectly still, his eyes wide and his face white. Rose stepped quietly towards the back of the snake, its attention still on her little boy. She bit back a sob as fear slammed through her; if she moved too slowly, the mulga snake would attack him without hesitation. Too fast and she could miss it and it could attack Rufus and then turn back on her.

As she stood there, willing Rufus to stay still, a noise came from behind.

Bennett came down the steps and tugged on her apron. 'Mumma, I hungry.'

In one endless second, Rufus screamed as the snake reared, striking him high on his left arm. As Rose dashed forward, it struck twice more before she slammed the shovel into the snake's back over and over again, screaming with each thrust.

Rufus slid down the timber wall, his bare brown legs stretching out over the snake's mangled body.

Rose threw the shovel, scooped her little boy into her arms and ran for the door, ushering Bennett inside before them. She slammed the door shut and lay Rufus on the horsehair couch in the corner.

'Mumma, it hurts.' Already, he was turning blue around the lips.

'I know, baby.'

Rose grabbed the knife from the kitchen table as Rufus gagged and vomited. There was no time to sterilise the knife; it would take too long to strike a flint.

'Bennett, get Mumma a cup of water. Now.'

Rose took a deep breath and leaned over Rufus. His little body was limp, his eyes closed as the venom raced to his heart. She took the knife and cut the wound where the fangs had marked his skin, and bent down and sucked as hard as she could. After every suck she turned and spat the bitter-tasting venom to the floor. On the third attempt to get the venom out, when she turned to spit, Bennett held out the cup of water.

'Thank you.' Her voice was hoarse. Rose rinsed her mouth and kept sucking at the wound. Tears rolled down her face as Rufus convulsed and she prayed she wasn't too late, hoping she had taken enough of the venom from his little body.

CHAPTER
22

Ruby Gap Nature Park
Sunday, 9.00 am

Saul and Gemma set off the next morning after having a quick breakfast and packing up the camp.

'That way, we can pick up the gear quickly on the way back to my ute,' Saul said.

To her surprise, Gemma had slept soundly and woken just after dawn to the sound of Saul's footsteps crunching on the shingle. There was no tension between them as they headed away from the camp site. Ethan's letter and her phone were stored safely in her backpack; she wouldn't let the letter out of her sight.

They didn't speak much as they walked along the riverbed but today, the silence was comfortable. The rocky path was rough and overgrown, and Gemma stumbled a couple of times before they stopped for their water break. After they took a break, Saul filled their water bottles from the spring-fed waterhole. When he'd put the bottles in their backpacks, he held out his hand to Gemma.

'It's pretty narrow from here on. Remember?' he asked.

Of course I remember. This part of the river was full of memories.

Gemma hesitated then took the offered hand. She ignored the rush of the past as his fingers curled over hers. They were at the part of the Hale River where a long, narrow shelf of rock jutted into the water and he was right, the rock did slope unevenly into the deep waterhole. At the top of the slope, the track to the ruins headed away into the bush.

It had been a rough walk in when they'd camped out here; the bikes had been left under the cliff where she and Saul had camped. The boys had carried the water and food, but even before she and Saul got together, he'd always insisted on helping her with her backpack. His quiet and kind demeanour had been the opposite of Screw and Ethan's rowdiness, and Gemma had always appreciated his thoughtfulness.

Dad had told them that his great-grandfather had chosen the site because there was always water in this part of the Hale River. Even in the driest season, the spring-fed waterhole on the bend held pure, cool water. They used to come down and swim after the boys had spent the morning fossicking, but Gemma would come down every morning and have an early wash before she'd light the fire and cook the boys' breakfast.

When she and Saul had been together, he'd follow her down and they'd have some time alone together before the day began. Ethan had been too focused on the fossicking to notice.

Despite being close to the river, William Woodford had built the original wattle and daub hut on a slight rise a few hundred metres back into the bush, so that it would stay high and dry in the occasional floods. Gemma wondered what it would have been like to live out here in those hard days. Ethan and Dad had been the family history experts—Ethan was always reading the old journals that their grandmother had left to Dad, but she'd been too focused on Saul and their fledging romance to be interested. Gemma wondered where the journals were now.

Dad had been pleased when Ethan had shown an interest in the family history and had begun to delve into more records at the library. He and Dad had spent so much time together, Gemma had felt a bit left out. Like his obsession with the rubies, Ethan's obsession with their family and the past had meant a lot of time spent looking at the microfiche journals of the explorers and early settlers held in the Alice Springs Library. When he'd discovered Trove, the online resource at the National Library, Ethan had been ecstatic. He'd always been reading out snippets to her. If only she could go back. If she'd shown some interest, maybe he would have shared his plans with her.

'Come on, not far to go now.' The pressure of Saul's fingers squeezing hers pulled Gemma back to the present. She loved the feel of his hand, and it was hard to block the memories of those past happier days.

'Are you okay?' he asked as they reached the top of the rocky incline.

'I'm fine. I was just thinking how hard it must have been to live and survive out here. And with a family.'

'It would have been a hard and frugal life. My forebears ran the store at Arltunga at the same time.'

Gemma turned to him, but his eyes were hooded before he turned towards the track ahead. 'Did they? I never knew that. I thought you only moved to Alice Springs when you were young.'

Saul didn't answer as he led her into the bush. The silence deepened and pressed around them. He seemed to withdraw into himself, and she wondered if she'd said the wrong thing. As soon as they left the rocks, he let go of her hand, and she felt the loss, sure she'd upset him somehow.

As she followed him along a barely discernible track into the bush, it was obvious it hadn't been used for a long time. The scrub had thickened and the occasional fallen tree slowed their progress. About five hundred metres in, they came to a wide sandy creek bed filled with dry logs and dead foliage.

'Looks like the river came through here this year.' Saul finally spoke as they stopped beneath the ghost gums for another drink break. 'The floods have hollowed out this bank and created a new creek.'

Gemma nodded, intent on her surroundings as she sipped at the water bottle. The air had stilled as they'd moved away from the breeze that ran down the gorge near the river. And that meant the black flies were back.

'Are you sure we've followed the right track? It all looks so different.' She jumped as there was a rustling in the bush ahead of them. Saul stepped forward as a metre-long perentie lizard ran across the track ahead. 'Oh my God, I'd forgotten those sand goannas. They look so ungainly until they take off and then they run so fast.'

'Come on, he won't hurt us. We're almost there.' His voice soothed her. 'We'll have to get a move on, so we get back to Alice before dark.'

Further along, the early-morning sunlight filtered through the leaves of four big ghost gums at the top of a small hill, where the track turned east to the site of the old homestead.

'I remember those trees. This *is* the right way!'

'Were you doubting me, Gem?' he asked playfully.

She shook her head and hurried past the white trunks of the river gums, their leaves already wilting in the morning heat. 'Come on, it's just through here.'

'I reckon old William planted them,' Ethan had said once. 'Sort of like a front gate to their property.'

Even though she hadn't been as interested as Ethan, Gemma knew some of the family history and how they'd moved to Ruby Gap. Their great-great-grandparents had lived out here with their children at the end of the nineteenth century. Ethan had started asking Dad questions about their life and how they would have lived when he was in primary school.

As they walked closer to the ruins, Gemma realised how much she'd blocked those memories since Ethan had disappeared. A light breeze sprang up and the temperature cooled slightly as she stared ahead, looking for the old structure nestled in the trees. How hard it must have been in those days. Even driving out from Alice Springs these days took a few hours. Back in the days when they relied on horses and camels, it must have been an arduous trip.

As her eyes scanned the bush, she let her memory kick back to the first time she'd been allowed to come out and camp with the boys. Ethan had been sitting on the top step, staring into the bush, Screw had been sitting on the step below him, sharpening his knife, and Saul had been smiling at her; that wide open smile that she'd fallen in love with.

That had been the trip when she'd stumbled on the small grave at the top of the hill. It was a small rectangle of rocks with a cairn at the head. Ethan had already known about it.

She'd gone running down to the river to tell him what she'd found.

'Yeah, I know,' he'd said. 'One of their kids died.'

'How?'

He'd shrugged. 'Dad didn't know. We don't know a lot of the small details about them. Just that Rose and William got married in England, and she followed him out. They had two kids but one died. Apparently, he took off and left her then she moved to Arltunga and worked in the general store.'

Gemma frowned as they followed the old track through the trees to the clearing. Once, there had only been buffel grass from the ghost gums to the old chimney. Now, low scrubby trees had seeded and grown where there had been a clearing only a few years earlier. A large tree had come down halfway in and Saul helped her over the wide trunk as they both kept a close eye out for snakes. In the heat, they'd be out looking for water. King browns, death adders and curl snakes—all of them were deadly.

Once they'd climbed over the trunk, Gemma looked around and frowned. It was hard to see where the track ended, and there was no sign of the clearing that Ethan had kept trimmed and tidy when they'd camped out here.

'Look.' Saul pointed ahead to the distinctive ghost gum with the forked trunk. 'That's the tree that was behind the chimney.'

Her eyes widened as she stared at the familiar tree. The ruins of the homestead that her great-great-grandfather had built almost one hundred and fifty years earlier were gone.

★

Gemma stopped dead in front of Saul as they both realised at the same moment that everything had gone. Saul put his hands on Gemma's shoulders. She held them rigid and he could feel the tension radiating through her slight frame.

'It's all gone,' she whispered. 'How can it be gone now, when it had lasted all those years? Even the chimney. Even though it was so old, it was still sturdy.' Her voice shook.

'Come on. We'll go and see what we can find.' He was also sad to see it destroyed; the site held many memories for him.

Saul took her hand again and led her through the low, scrubby bush to where the ruins had been. 'Look, you can still see the outline where the stumps were driven into the ground.'

'What do you think happened?' Gemma let go of his hand, and her hands went to her hips. 'Do you think someone knocked it down?'

'I'm not sure. Maybe the Parks service took it out.'

'It's criminal if they did,' she said vehemently.

'I don't think that's what happened,' he said as they stopped where the front right corner of the small homestead had once been. He slipped the backpack from his shoulders and put it on the ground beside them. 'Look. At a guess, I'd say that new creek we saw flooded through here in the big flood before Christmas. Look at the dry spinifex wrapped against that log.' He moved closer. 'It's not a log, it's one of the original posts.'

'So it's only just gone?' Gemma's voice was ragged, and it rose in pitch. 'What about the tin Ethan said he'd buried here? Will that have washed away too? What if we can't find it?'

'Gem, calm down.' Saul's hands went back to her shoulders; for the life of him, he didn't want to touch her, but he couldn't help himself. To his surprise, she turned in his hold and gripped the front of his shirt with her fingers.

Her breath hitched as she stared at him, her eyes wide. 'I thought I could do this, Saul, but it's so hard. Knowing that Ethan was out here after the last time I saw him. Knowing that something happened to scare him senseless. If it wasn't his writing, I would have said someone else wrote it. And now we've come out here and it was all for nothing.'

Saul put his arms around her and held her close, and when she turned her face into his shoulder, he rested his chin on the top of her head. They stood there quietly and he didn't move, trying to give Gemma comfort. The last time he'd held her out here had been six years ago after Ethan told her the grave she'd seen had belonged to a child. It had really upset her.

'It's not all for nothing,' he murmured quietly as she clung to him, his khaki shirt bunched in her fists. 'We've come this far, Gem. And we won't give up until we search every bit of this ground. If that tin's here, we'll find it.' As she began to relax in his arms, Saul looked around the site. 'There's a log caught against those two trees, and the soil's banked up on this side and made a bit of a barrier. You can see where the water has pushed over to one side and made a channel on the other side of where the posts were. It looks like there was enough pressure to take them down on that side. I think the actual floor stayed dry, because the soil was built up to the floor, two steps high.'

'To keep the snakes from under the house, Dad used to say,' Gemma said quietly. She let go of Saul's shirt and moved back away from him. Strangely he felt bereft; having Gemma in his arms felt good. Too good.

For a few seconds, he stood there before coming to a quick decision.

'Come on. It'll be easy to find the corner he described in the code.' He turned her around and guided her away from the small rise on the northern side of the house.

'In the ruins. Under stone, east corner.' Gemma repeated the words she had memorised last night, plus Saul had the pages of the notebook in his pocket.

Saul picked up the backpack and took out the small folding camp shovel he'd taken from the survival kit in his ute.

'Come on, you start digging. I need a minute in the bush.' He waited until she was crouching on the site where the homestead had stood for over a hundred and thirty years. When she took the shovel, Saul slipped between the trees until he reached a secluded spot out of Gemma's sight.

A moment later, when he zipped up his fly, his attention was caught by a cleared spot over on a small rise between two large ghost gums, where the child's grave that had upset Gemma was located.

He walked over and his blood chilled. A second grave was on the top of the hill, a couple of metres away from the small cairn. Crouching down, he looked at the small wooden cross at the head of the grave. His lips moved soundlessly as he read the initials carved into the white cross.

He closed his eyes. *Sweet Jesus.*

*

Gemma grinned up at Saul as he crouched in the dirt opposite her.

She'd lifted the flat stone in the corner and started digging but the ground was hard and she hadn't made much progress. He'd taken the shovel from her and it wasn't long before it hit something solid with a metallic clink. Saul reached down and pulled out a strangely shaped tin and passed it to Gemma.

She turned the rough and dirty tin over in her hands and tried to brush the red dirt off it, but it was encrusted firmly. 'I really feel as though we're getting somewhere now. It was exactly where he said it would be. Let's open it, and see what's in there. Maybe he's told us where he's gone.'

Saul shook his head. Even though he'd looked pleased when the shovel had hit the tin, he had been quiet. Ever since he'd held her in his arms and comforted her. Maybe he was worried she'd read too much into him holding her.

'I'd like to look inside.' She knew her tone was petulant, but she wanted to know what Ethan had put in there. 'Now.'

He shook his head. 'We need to get back to town, and we've got a long walk back to the ute. And we don't know what's in there. We'll put the tin in your backpack, and I promise as soon as we get to town, we'll open it and check out what's in there.'

Gemma stood and held the tin to her chest. She could see now it was a hexagonal shape. 'I've never seen a tin that shape before,' she said turning it over. 'Look, it's narrow at the bottom and it widens at the top. The top's a strange shape too. It looks like an antique. I wonder—'

Saul cut her off. 'Gem, there's no point hanging around out here speculating. Ethan's not here.' His tone was tense, and she frowned at him.

'You're worried about something, aren't you? I wish you'd be honest with me, Saul. It's that helicopter, isn't it? Ethan said to trust you, but how can I when you won't be honest with me?' Gemma glared at him as he stood and dusted his hands on the front of his shorts.

He took the tin from her and slipped it into her backpack without answering.

'What do you know about that helicopter?' She tensed when he reached over and put his hands on her shoulders.

'I don't know anything about it. Like I said, I just felt like someone was watching us. I was probably imagining things.'

'So, what's wrong now?' As she held his gaze, she watched his expression change.

'I wasn't going to say anything because I didn't want you to panic.'

'Panic about what?'

'We need to get back to Alice—'

'Yes, and see what's in the tin.'

His fingers tightened on her shoulders. 'No. We need to go to the police. Gemma . . .' Saul swallowed and her neck prickled.

'Why?'

'I think there's another grave in the scrub.'

'A what?' Her blood chilled as Saul gestured to the bush behind them. 'What grave? Yes, there is. Remember, I told you about that when we were out here camping?'

'Yes. I remember that one. Another one.'

Gemma pulled away from him and stepped back, her muscles tensing with shock. *No, no, no. He's wrong. It can't be right, it can't be true.*

'Show me.' Her voice was calm as cold ran through her body. 'It's not Ethan. He's not dead. And don't you look at me like everyone else does.'

Saul sighed. 'I'm not looking at you in any way.'

'Then show me what you're talking about.'

Gemma clenched her hands as he turned and walked up the gentle rise where she had once strung the washing between two big gum trees. As soon as she looked ahead, she could see what Saul had seen. The top of the hill had always looked as though it had been sliced off by nature's hand, with a perfectly square flat area at the top of the rise. They'd often sat up there in the evening while one of the boys cooked dinner. Ethan and Screw had rigged up a tripod and in the cooler weather, they'd sat around the fire after they'd eaten.

Gemma's eyes burned with unshed tears as the memories rolled in. If she closed her eyes, she could almost hear Ethan's teasing voice. 'Gemma forgot the marshmallows again.'

Stopping beside Saul, she stared at the raised mound next to the small grave of years ago. 'Maybe an animal has been digging something and changed the shape of the hill.'

'Maybe.' He sounded like he was trying to reassure her.

Gemma gasped. 'Look. Look at the other end of it.'

Saul took her hand before she could rush forward. 'Wait.'

'Oh, God, no.' Her voice broke. 'It's a cross, with something written on it.'

Gemma pulled away from Saul's grip and took two long strides to where the cross was buried in the hard dirt. She dropped to her knees beside it and leaned forward.

Her breath came out in an anguished cry and tears rolled down her cheeks as her fingers traced the two letters on the two pieces of white gum bound together with a strip of narrow brown leather.

After a moment, Saul pulled her to her feet and put his arms around her and she sobbed into his shoulder. Finally, she lifted her face and looked into Saul's eyes. Her grief was echoed in his expression.

'I was wrong, Saul. So very wrong,' she whispered. 'Ethan's been dead all that time, hasn't he?' Her eyes held his as reality hit. 'Who buried him, and why didn't we know? Why didn't they tell us he was out here?'

CHAPTER
23

Annie's Gorge, Ruby Gap Nature Park
Six years ago

'Come on, Eth, I'm ready to head back. I've gotta get packed. I'm leaving the day after tomorrow, and I've got things to do.'

Ethan had one more section of the dig he'd marked out for the afternoon in the shingle at the edge of the river, and didn't want to leave before he'd finished that part of his grid, so he used one of his dad's old tricks.

'Did I ever tell you the yarn about Fox's Grave, mate?'

'Probably.' Screw picked up a rock and pegged it across the river, where it landed in the deep waterhole with a loud splash. A flock of pink galahs rose screeching as the noise disturbed them. 'What is it?'

Ethan stood and sweat ran down his face as he pushed his Akubra back. Half a dozen flies immediately honed into his eyes with the precision of fighter pilots. He took his hat off and waved it around. 'Little black bastards are biting more every season.'

'Okay, finish your story. What's this grave?'

'Well, you know about the gold rush over at Arltunga?'

'Yeah, after the rubies were discovered to be duds here, someone discovered gold at Arltunga. There was a town there back in the day.'

'Well, there was one guy who was determined to stay and find the rubies. He was called Fredrick Fox. He reckoned the rubies were real.'

'Well, holy shit, Eth, you're not the only one. Was he a relation?'

'Ha ha.' Ethan put his hat back on and wiped his face with the back of his hand. 'Nah, poor old Fred carked it up here in Annie's Gorge about the time the ruby boom ended, and all the others took off to Arltunga, chasing their fortune.' He looked up at the cliff and pointed to the north-east. 'I've never been that far up the gorge, but Dad said his grave is at the top of a small knoll up there. There's a big headstone carved out of river rock, and someone engraved it in fancy writing.'

'Who would of bothered to do that way out here in the middle of nowhere?'

'Who would *have*,' Ethan automatically corrected him.

'Oh, la-de-dah,' Screw scoffed. 'Principal's son.'

'Can't help myself.'

Screw grinned back at him. 'Who would *have* done a gravestone way out here?'

'That's part of the mystery. No one knows.'

'What's the rest of the mystery?'

'How he died.'

'Murder?' Screw put on an evil cackle.

Ethan shrugged. 'Dad always said there was a few theories. One is he got sick and died. Another is he played up with a married woman and her husband came looking. Someone else told Dad he took his own life.'

'So how far up there?'

'Up where that bit of rock sticks out, I think. Where the river bends. Never been up there.' Ethan turned back to his dig and bent down as the sand glinted red.

'Okay, finish your grid and we'll go for a climb. Who knows when I'll ever be back here?'

Ethan sighed. 'I'll miss you, mate. It's bad enough with Saul gone. What'll I do without my mates here?'

Screw laughed. 'What you do now. Spend your weekends digging for rubies that don't exist.'

'One day I'll prove you all wrong, you know, and you'll all be sorry you took off and left me.' He had no intention of telling Screw what he'd found yesterday.

'Did you and Saul sort out your problems before he left? We gave him a lift as far as Katherine when I had my interview. That was a good shiner you gave him.'

Guilt rippled through Ethan. 'No. I was waiting to calm down before I went to apologise but when I went out to his place, his old man said he'd already left.'

'How's Gemma?'

Ethan shrugged. 'I'm keeping a low profile. Keeps the peace. She doesn't know it was me that put the skids under him. She still thinks he pissed off.'

'Wimp. Are you going to tell her?'

'Maybe one day. But no matter how much of a good bloke he is, Saul's not the right one for her,' Ethan said. 'She's going to go to uni and his old man said he got a job working in a garage up in Darwin.'

'Shit you're a snooty bastard, Ethan,' Screw said. 'We can't all have a mother with money and a career. There's nothing wrong with manual work.'

Ethan's hackles rose. 'I didn't say there was.'

'You don't need to. You live it.'

Ethan threw his shovel down and it bounced on the hard ground. He was over being judged. The words he'd had with Saul had been harsh, and he'd felt bad when he'd seen the acceptance in Saul's expression. But no matter what he and Screw thought of Ethan, he still didn't think that Saul was good enough for his twin sister. His old man was a drunk, and he'd grown up in a very different environment to them. Ethan tried to convince himself he'd done the right thing, but the hollow look in Saul's eyes wouldn't leave him. He hadn't even retaliated when Ethan had clocked him when he'd admitted to taking Gemma out to Ormiston Gorge for the night.

'Come on, let's go climb this cliff and then we'll go back to town. I've had enough for today.'

Screw looked at him sideways. 'Enough digging or enough home truths?'

Ethan ignored him as he strode back towards the ruins. He didn't want to fall out with both his best mates in the same week.

'What are you going that way for?' Screw hurried up the sloping rock shelf behind him. 'I thought we were walking up to the grave?'

'You've got to get back to town, so it'll be quicker if we take our gear back to Ruby then drive up.'

'Drive up?' Screw frowned as he gestured to the red cliffs towering over the water on the other side of the river. 'There's no bloody road up there.'

'There is, you know. Last time I drove up to the Atitjere community at the base of the Hart Range, Danno from soccer told me about a short cut down here to Ruby Gap. It's not used much, but apparently there's a new track almost as far as the gravesite.'

Screw shrugged. 'Sounds good to me. The less climbing involved, the better.'

Ethan quickly packed up his swag and put it beside the esky. Screw looked at his. 'I've got a new one to take away with me. I might as well leave the old swag out here. That okay?'

'Yeah.'

'What about your old axe?' Screw bent down and pulled it from the log beside the step.

'Might as well take it. Who knows how long it'll be before I get back out here?'

'I promised the old lady I'd get some firewood and take it home. Remind me to look for some up on the cliffs.'

'I'll get some too. Might get me back in Mum's good books.'

An hour later, they'd packed up the gear at the ruins and trekked along the riverbed to where Ruby was parked at the western end of the nature park.

'You gonna keep coming out here once I'm gone, Eth?' Screw asked as he climbed up into the passenger seat.

'What do you reckon?'

Screw chuckled. 'Stupid question, I suppose. What about a job? Saul's in Darwin. I've got my start at Roselyon, and Gemma's going to uni.'

'Yeah.' Ethan started the engine and the rattle of the old diesel shook the vehicle. 'That's what I was doing out at the community. Danno said there's a job going out there in the store, driving the truck to Alice three times a week to get fresh stock, and working in the store for two days.'

'I thought your mum wanted you to go to uni.'

Ethan shrugged. 'She does, but uni's not for me. I want to spend my time out here. Working out at the community still gives me two days a week at the gorge.'

'Look, mate, don't you get pissed with me, but don't you think you're wasting your time?' Screw said. 'I mean, we've had a blast camping out here when we were at school, but you know there's only garnets out there. Nothing of any value. If you're after your fortune, go somewhere where they find good stones. Up on the Plenty Highway or at the Gemfields in Queensland.'

'They're for tourists. And I *know* there's rubies here,' Ethan said obstinately. 'That's the reason I want to check out this road that's supposed to be there. I can drive down the other side of the river *if* there is a road over there, and then all I'll have to do is climb down the cliff and it'll be a much shorter walk across to the camp.'

'So why didn't we do that before?'

'Because I only heard about the road last week.' Ethan's voice was tight and he bit down on the anger that rose in his chest. 'Plus, I've been reading some of my Dad's great-grandfather's journals. I think I've been working at the wrong bend in the river.'

'Fair enough.' Screw looked doubtful, and for the first time, Ethan wondered if he was doing the right thing. He'd had a huge fight with Mum last weekend when she'd heard he was going out for the interview. And then the stoush with Saul had left him cranky, plus he'd avoided Gemma the past few days. At least Screw was a good and reliable mate.

'Anyway, it might just be talk. But we'll go have a look.' He glanced across at Screw. 'Things are changing, aren't they? I guess this is what growing up is like.'

'Why don't you come to Roselyon with me? Good money.'

'Maybe,' Ethan said. 'Worth thinking about. I've heard there's diamonds out that way.' He chuckled when Screw rolled his eyes.

'You're bloody obsessed, mate.'

CHAPTER
24

Ruby Gap Nature Park
Sunday, 11.00 am

Saul held Gemma close, his hands on her shaking shoulders. Her keening cry when she'd read the initials on the roughhewn cross had broken his heart, and he found it impossible to speak. He stood there, gently rubbing her shoulders as she sat straight and stiff beside the grave.

Her brother's grave. Next to the child's grave that had upset her so much when they had camped out here. The one she had always put wildflowers on.

EH. There was no doubt: Ethan was dead.

Finally, Gemma stepped back, her head shaking from side to side. Saul stood beside her quietly, letting her talk out her grief.

'We'll have to report it, you know.'

'I know.' When she lifted her red-rimmed eyes, they were full of pain as tears coursed down her cheeks. 'I still don't understand it.

I never felt as though he was dead.' She grabbed at his hand. 'I still don't believe it. I won't believe it until they dig up the grave'—her voice broke again— 'and they prove it's Ethan.'

'Come on, we'll head back now,' he said softly. 'But first, we'll finish off the water that's left and refill the bottles at the river. It's going to be a hot walk back to the ute. Are you right to walk back?'

'I have to be, don't I? And then when we get back, we'll have to report it, and I'll have to ring Mum.'

'Yes. It's going to be a long day, Gem.'

Gemma nodded with a sigh. 'Before we leave, Saul, I need to . . . um . . . go.' Colour stained her cheeks and he understood what she meant.

'Okay, you go down to the river and I'll have a bit more of a look around here.'

'I'll have a wash while I'm down there too.'

'Okay, I'll give you ten, and then I'll come down and fill the bottles. Is that enough time?'

Gemma nodded. Saul was surprised when she reached up and cupped his cheek with one hand. 'Thank you, Saul. If anyone had to be with me for. . . for that, I'm glad it was you.'

'I'm sorry that you had to see it.' He put his hand over hers and her smile was sad as his eyes met hers. 'Now go and do what you have to. And watch out for snakes.'

'I know. I grew up out here, remember?'

Saul watched as she headed towards the track, and soon she disappeared from his sight and all he could hear was her steps as she walked through the dry scrub.

*

Gemma stood in the blinding sun at the edge of the river, the cool water lapping over her bare feet. Once she'd relieved herself in the bush behind a log, she'd taken off her boots and socks and left them on the rock platform before heading to the little sandy bay where they'd swum when they'd camped at the old homestead site. Her head had spun and her eyes ached as she'd made her way along the track. She couldn't bear to think about what Saul had found back there; her whole world tilted as grief consumed her. It was a physical pain throughout her body; her limbs ached and nausea roiled in her stomach. Gemma put one hand to her eyes as she breathed in and out; the sun was so bright it was making strange patterns in her vision.

Not once in the past six years had she considered that Ethan was dead. She had imagined him alive and knew that he would return, one day. Now cold and harsh reality had hit. Of course he was dead; if he'd been alive, he would have been in touch with her somehow. Six years of refusing to accept the truth had kept grief away. Mum had been right all along, but Dad was like her; he'd gone into his own world, refusing to accept the reality that Ethan was gone. For the first time in many months, Gemma longed for her father. Fragments of memories of being out here with him when they were kids drifted in and out of her mind. She had no idea how she was going to learn to live in a world without Ethan, her twin.

Leaving her shirt on the grass, she waded into the cool water, not caring about getting her shorts and singlet wet; they'd soon dry on the trek back to the camp site. Floating on her back, she stared up at the clear sky and the red cliffs, trying to process the fact that her vibrant, funny brother was lying cold in his grave. She dipped her head beneath the water and when she surfaced and headed for the sand, tears mingled with the water on her cheeks.

★

Saul stood at the side of the grave and stared at the cross. He'd kept his thoughts to himself as he'd comforted Gemma. If it was Ethan in this grave, and the rough cross seemed to indicate it was, someone had buried him and made the cross. If Ethan had died in an accident, someone would have reported it. The more Saul thought about it, the more it appeared that Ethan had met with foul play. Someone knew what had happened and had taken care of him, and there was only one person who would have done that.

No matter how long it took, Saul would find out the truth for Gemma. He walked back across to the site, wondering how it had been destroyed. It seemed strange that the structure had stood there for well over a hundred years and survived previous floods and fires then had gone around the same time that Ethan had disappeared. Was it a flood, or had something happened out here? He shook himself as suspicion tainted his thoughts.

He reached out and ran his fingers over the smooth white timber of the cross. 'I promise you, Ethan. I'll find out the truth.'

Screw was the key, and he was going to search until he found him.

Reaching down, Saul picked up Gemma's backpack and drank the last of the water before checking his watch. She'd been gone almost fifteen minutes. He'd fill the water bottles and try to make good time as they got back to the campsite and then headed back to the ute. As he slipped the light pack over his shoulders, the corners of the tin dug into his back.

It didn't take long to get to the river. Saul frowned as he scanned the rock platform and the waterhole; there was no sign of Gemma, only her boots and socks at the edge of the rock. Hurrying down to the edge, his eyes scanning the waterhole, panic gripped him.

Where the hell has she gone?

Relief flooded through Saul when a splash came from upriver. Gemma had walked upstream and entered the water where long buffel grass edged a small sandy inlet. She was waist-deep in the water, wading in towards the sand. Her shirt was draped over the long grass in the sun, and she'd gone into the water in the rest of her clothes. Her hair was wet, and slicked back from her forehead and as he watched, she stopped in the shallows and tipped her face up to the sun. She bent down, filled her hat with water and tipped it over her head. Her singlet was wet, clinging lovingly to her body. She was fit and lithe and curved in all the right places.

Not for you.

Saul looked away as she ran quickly over the hot sand to retrieve her shirt. He walked over to where her boots were and as he bent to pick them up, a movement in the long grass caught his peripheral vision.

He froze as a massive black speary-horned scrubber bull stopped at the edge of the long grass, his head held high, his rheumy eyes intent on Gemma. From where he stood, Saul could see the aggressive intent of the thick-necked beast, and he knew what harm those huge, curled horns could do. The animal bellowed, and Saul saw the exact moment that Gemma spotted it.

'Gemma, stop! Don't move,' he yelled.

Her eyes widened and she stopped dead in the middle of the hot sand. The beast lowered its head, ready to charge. Then, ignoring his instruction, Gemma ran up the shingly creek bed. Saul flung the backpack off, and it landed on the rock with a tinny clang. He had to get between Gemma and the bull.

The beast swung its head sideways and observed Saul, but immediately turned back to Gemma, back arched, head down, pawing at the ground. Saul leaped off the rock and took off at a run with a yell.

'Hey, scrubber! Over here!' Making as much noise as he could, he yanked his shirt off and waved it in the air. The bull hesitated, looking from Gemma to Saul, who was still about fifty metres away, undecided.

'Head back for the water, Gemma. Zigzag, move as fast as you can,' he yelled, quickly closing the distance. 'Hey, you lump of lard, come and get me!'

At the last minute, the bull turned for Saul. The snorting beast filled his vision and he feinted to the left, but the bull was smart enough to anticipate his move. It lowered its head just as Saul moved again to the right, whipping his shirt through the air. 'Get in the water, Gemma.'

Her scream rent the air as the bull charged, and Saul knew he was in big trouble. The jagged horn caught him a glancing blow on his right hip, but it was enough to send him tumbling through the air like a ragdoll. The old bull swerved then stopped, staring at him.

Saul pushed his fists into the loose shingle and tried to get to his feet, but the pain in his leg was excruciating and he knew it wouldn't take his weight.

He lay there, fear holding him rigid as the bull snorted and pawed the ground only metres away. His vision blurred as he stared at the beast and an unfamiliar cold feeling settled in his chest.

Saul closed his eyes as the bull charged . . . when the crack of a gunshot echoed around the gorge. He opened them again, forcing himself to stay conscious as pain gripped him. Gemma was at the edge of the water, her eyes wide and her face pale.

The old bull stopped and snorted, spooked by the shot.

'Get away, you bastard,' Saul yelled.

The bull shook his head, a cloud of flies buzzing around him. His tongue flicked at his nostrils as he sniffed the air for danger. All was quiet and the beast lowered its head again, pawing at the shingle. Another shot echoed, and a cloud of gravel and shingle flew up between its front legs. Snorting, it turned and slowly lumbered away into the scrub.

Gemma was beside Saul in an instant, dropping to her knees in the sand. 'Saul, where are you hurt?' She used her shirt to try to stem the blood that was seeping from a large, ragged gash along his side.

'My hip and my ankle,' he managed to get out between gritted teeth. His vision was blurring again, and he began to shake. As he looked up at her, fear filled her expression. 'The satphone, Gem. And the PLB. Set it off.'

*

Fear held Gemma stiff as she crouched beside Saul, staring at the bearded man who sauntered out of the bush, a rifle tucked beneath his arm.

'Cranky old bugger, that bull,' he growled.

Gemma looked down as Saul tried to push himself up on his elbows, but he flopped back down onto the shingle with a groan. 'Who is it?'

'Better have a look at the damage.' The man ignored Gemma and kneeled beside Saul, putting the gun aside. As she met the man's gaze, Gemma realised it was the man with the long grey beard they'd seen on the motorbike yesterday. 'He's bleeding pretty bad. I think something is broken from the way his leg is bent.'

'I need to call for help,' she said, mostly to remind herself. *And the PLB.*

'You got a satphone, love?'

She nodded. 'Saul, where's the backpack?'

'Over at the edge of the rocks.' His voice was ragged and sweat covered his face.

'Can you watch him, please, while I find it?' She looked at the man warily, her gaze dropping to the rifle beside him.

'Don't worry, love, I won't hurt you,' the man said. 'Go and find that phone and when you get onto emergency, tell them you think he's bleeding internally.'

She nodded. 'Do you know how to set the personal beacon off? It's in the pocket of his shorts.'

Leaving the stranger with Saul, Gemma ran over to where the track came down from the ruins. As soon as she retrieved the backpack, she pulled the phone out, turned it on, and focused on staying calm as she made the emergency call, described his injuries and gave their location.

'Stay calm and keep him cool and in the shade, if it's possible. We'll get a medical team to you as quickly as we can. No liquids though, until the paramedics check him out.'

Hurrying back to Saul, Gemma dropped to a crouch beside the man.

'On their way?' His dark eyes bore into hers.

'Yes.'

Saul's eyes fluttered open. He tried to sit up again but his face crumpled with pain.

'Stay there, mate,' the stranger said gruffly. 'You're better off not to move.'

'They said to keep him in the shade. We haven't got anything here to use.' Gemma looked up. The sun was a burning white sphere in a cloudless sky. Saul's face was white, perspiration dotting his brow.

'Yeah, we'll have to risk moving him. If we leave him in the sun, he's got no hope. He'll dehydrate fast.'

Between them, Gemma and the man managed to get Saul up. He groaned as he put his right foot on the ground but they were able to support him across the short distance to the shaded area beneath the cliff. Blood ran down his leg into his boot as they settled him on the soft grass.

'Did you set the beacon off?' Saul croaked.

'Yeah.' The man's voice was guarded. 'What first-aid gear have you got at your camp?'

'Just a snake-bite kit.' Saul lay back in the shade, his face contorted with pain as he looked up at the stranger. 'But there's a full first-aid pack in the ute.'

The man stood and looked at Gemma. 'I'll go. My bike's over there and I know where your ute is. You stay here and keep pressure on that wound, it's a pretty deep gash.'

She wondered how he knew where Saul's ute was, and why he'd been up here at the gorge. It was a long way from his gate.

'I will.' She moved closer to Saul and checked that her shirt was still tied tight around his leg. The bottom of his work shirt was sodden with blood, and she wondered how long he would stay conscious. Her mouth dried as fear gripped her, and she leaned over and placed pressure on the wound.

Saul barely reacted; only his eyelids fluttered.

The man stood and lifted his rifle. 'You ever used one of these?'

She nodded. 'Yes, my dad taught me.'

'It's a .270. If that bull comes back, aim to one side of his head. Hold the thing tight, though. It'll kick pretty hard if you need to use it.' Before Gemma could reply, he disappeared into the bush.

She looked around warily, making sure there was no sign of the scrubber bull.

'Lucky he was here.' Saul's breathing sounded thready. 'Did he take the ute keys?'

'No, I didn't think of that,' Gemma said.

Saul closed his eyes, and she stared down at him. A rush of love hit her firmly in the chest. His mouth was tight and occasionally his forehead would wrinkle as he flinched.

Keeping one hand on the leg wound, she pulled a tissue from her pocket and wiped the perspiration from his brow. She should have thought to get some water to keep him cool but she couldn't move and risk taking the pressure off his leg.

He'll be okay. He will. Please, Saul, hang in there.

Gemma promised herself that when Saul was safe and recovering, she would make her peace with him, and then she would examine the feelings she still held for him. The feelings that were as strong as they were six years ago.

*

Fifteen minutes later, the sound of a bike at full-throttle came up the river. Relief flooded through Gemma as the stranger approached, the first-aid kit tucked under his arm. As he slid to a stop, he threw the pack to her. 'Here get out some bandages, something clean to cover that gash as quick as you can.'

'Do you think I should wash it with the saline first?'

'Has it been opened? It'll be better than river water. No chance of infection that way.'

Gemma pulled her blood-soaked shirt away, relieved to see the bleeding had slowed considerably. It was easy to see the gash as the bull's horns had ripped Saul's shorts from the waist to the bottom of the hem. Nausea threatened as she realised how close he'd got to a torso injury. She dug in the pack until her fingers closed around a small bottle of saline solution.

She shook her head as she unscrewed the cap. 'No, it's sealed.'

'Jesus, Gemma!' Saul grimaced as she applied it liberally to his leg.

The man watched without speaking as she applied cotton pads to the cleansed wound. Finally, she looked up at him. 'Thank you. We owe you.'

He looked down at Saul. 'Had to bust the driver's window of your ute, mate. Sorry, forgot the keys.' His taciturn face split in a grin, and Gemma noticed two of his front teeth were missing. 'But I guess that's the least of your worries, hey?'

It was well past midday before the welcome sound of a helicopter came up the gorge. As it hovered over the gully, the down draught sent shingle flying. Gemma could barely hold in her worry as the machine seemed to take ages to come down on the rock platform not far from where Saul lay in the shade. She let out the breath when the paramedic jumped clear, covered the short distance and examined him, asking questions as he checked his vital signs.

'Broken ankle and a gash that will need stitching plus possible internal bleeding. We need to get him back to Alice, ASAP.' He signalled to the pilot and it was only moments before they had Saul settled on a stretcher, a drip in his arm.

'You be careful going back to the ute, Gem. Watch out for that rogue bull,' Saul said.

'Don't worry, mate, I'll see she gets there safely.' The man stepped back as Gemma squeezed Saul's hand before they lifted the stretcher from the ground.

'As soon as I get back to town, I'll come to the hospital,' she said.

'Are you okay, Gemma?' His eyes held hers, and she knew he was referring to what they'd found at the old homestead.

'We'll talk about all that later.' Gemma couldn't help herself. She leaned over and brushed her lips over Saul's cheek. 'You just hang in there until they get you patched up.'

'I'm tough. I'll see you. Be careful. Drive safe.' Saul's eyes closed with pain as they loaded the stretcher.

The helicopter lifted off, and Gemma drew a deep breath. Her legs shook as she realised how close Saul had been to a more serious injury. How close she had been to the bull too. She wouldn't let herself think about the grave they'd found.

Or the fact that she was now alone in the bush with a stranger. A stranger who was watching her and had picked up his rifle.

A stranger who helped us.

She turned to him. 'I'm Gemma.' She extended her hand to him hesitantly. 'Thank you for helping us.'

'Mike.' The man's hand was rough and calloused as he held hers. 'Come on, I'll help you pack up camp and get you back to your ute.'

He walked across to his bike and secured the rifle to the side before gesturing for her to get on behind him. Gemma climbed on and gripped the sides of the seat tightly as the bike followed a track through the scrub along the edge of the river. After they reached the camp site, it didn't take long to collect the swag and the bedroll. Mike carried the heavier stuff, and she carried her backpack and the small stove in the esky. When the last of the gear was on the back of the ute, she turned to Mike.

'Thank you again. I don't know what I would have done without your help, Mike.'

'Are you going to drive back to Alice? Or do you want to camp out here? It'll be dark before you get back. I'll stay with you if you want to wait till morning to head back,' he said. 'It's not safe out here for a woman on her own.' There was something in the way he was staring at her that Gemma didn't like.

'I want to get back tonight, but thank you.'

He nodded, taking a step closer and lowering his voice. 'It's best to mind your own business, that's what you need to do,' he said. 'Just forget anything you seen out here. That's what I do.'

What does that mean?

Gemma just nodded, anxious to get away.

'Wait here while I go back and get my bike. I'll take you as far as my gate, then you should be right after that.'

'Thank you. I know the road well.'

'You used to come out here when you were kids, didn't you?'

Gemma nodded, wondering how he knew that.

Mike gestured to the ute. 'Wait in the ute and turn the air on. It's bloody hot now, with that sun high. It'll be dark before you get onto the tar if we don't hurry.'

Gemma climbed into the unfamiliar ute and started the engine with the keys she'd pulled out of Saul's backpack, stored safely on the floor of the passenger side. It was only a short while before Mike appeared over the rocky crest on the bike; he must have run back to get it. He gestured for her to pull out onto the track and follow him.

The track out was rough, and avoiding the corrugations and navigating over the dry rocky creek beds kept Gemma's dark thoughts at bay. She was running on adrenaline and had managed to keep her emotions in check. A half-hour passed before Mike pulled up at the gate where they'd first encountered him yesterday morning.

Mike climbed off his bike, checked the rifle was secure and walked over to the window. He put his hand on the bottom of the window, and Gemma looked down at his dirty, calloused fingers resting on the shards of broken glass in the window cavity.

'Thank you for helping us out today. I couldn't have got back here without you.'

'You would've been right. It's amazing what a person can do when there's trouble.' He cleared his throat and looked away from her, but he kept talking. 'I want you to listen to me. And take notice of what I say.'

He was quiet as the wind picked up and a willy-willy of red dust swirled in front of them. A crow squawked above and Gemma waited for him to continue. Finally, Mike turned to face her, both hands now gripping the window cavity. 'I know what you and your bloke found out there today. I've been watching you. I'm gonna give you a piece of advice. I know you're upset, but forget what you saw.'

Gemma was shocked, and started to reply but Mike rushed on. 'Trust me, love, if you stir the pot out here, it could be deadly. No, it *will* be deadly. You can't trust anyone around here, the coppers, no one.'

Do not trust anyone. Ethan's warning, now Mike's too. What was going on out at Ruby Gap?

'Just go home, see your bloke, and tell him I said to stay away and let things lie.'

'Why?' Her voice broke as she pictured that grave in the bush. 'You know what we found?'

Ethan. His name screamed through her head and for a moment, Gemma thought she'd said it aloud.

Mike stared at her, his expression unsmiling, and he didn't answer her question. 'No questions. Just trust a bloke who's been out here a bloody long time. Don't come back here. Stay away from Ruby Gap.'

'What do you know?' Her voice broke as the emotional toll of the day combined with memories of Ethan.

He didn't answer, turning and striding over to the bike. Within seconds, the gate was locked behind him and Gemma was left staring at a cloud of red dust.

CHAPTER
25

Ruby Gap
1892

When Tom Pearson knocked at the door of the Woodford homestead just before sunset, Rose was sitting on the sofa, cradling her two boys. It was a while before she could summon the energy to answer.

'We're in here, Tom.' Her throat was ragged from crying and she could barely get the words out.

'I have to talk to you, Rose.' Tom walked over to her and his eyes widened as he looked at the two small boys in her arms. Bennett had cried himself to sleep and his warm little body was pressed hard against hers. Rufus was cold and stiff in her arms.

Tom broke down, his face stricken. 'Oh, lass. Oh, sweet Lord, no.'

Rose's shoulders were aching and her fingers were numb, and she moaned as Rufus slipped from her arms into Tom's. She didn't have the strength to hold him any longer.

She buried her face in Bennett's hair, but there were no more tears. Rose felt nothing. The grief had leached her of emotion, and she found it hard to listen to Tom when he spoke.

'What happened, Rose?' His voice came from a long way away and as she tried to respond, Bennett stirred in her arms.

Her son climbed down from her lap, and Rose bent double as a tremendous ache ripped through her.

'A snake bited Rufie, and Mumma hit it with the shovel. Mumma said he's gone to sleep forever.'

★

Tom took them back to the Pearsons' small house, and Betty tended to Bennett until they buried Rufus on the hill near the Woodford homestead two days later. That was how long it took Tom to fashion a small coffin. Betty washed Rufus and dressed him, and placed wildflowers around the edge of the coffin. Rose sat on the chair in their kitchen for two days and didn't sleep.

She shed no tears, and held herself straight as Tom filled in the grave. She looked up at the clear blue sky where an eagle wheeled above. The chatter of the birds and the sound of the winter wind provided a backdrop to Tom's prayers.

They all kneeled as he prayed. 'Father of all, we pray to you for Rufus Woodford. Grant to him eternal rest. Let light perpetual shine upon him. May his soul, through the mercy of God, rest in peace. Amen.'

As Tom's voice broke, Rose stared at the sky. 'I want William to come home and take us from this place.'

Tom and Betty looked at each other, and Betty gripped her husband's hand.

*

A week after Rufus was buried, Rose stood at the door of their homestead. She was torn, but had not been able to talk to Betty about it. Leaving Rufus here alone in his grave was heart-wrenching, but she could not face the danger of losing another child to this wilderness. Paddy's Rockhole Hotel at Arltunga took in boarders—several of the wives and children of the prospectors stayed there. Rose had decided to go there and await William's return.

As she turned to pack the last of their clothes and some provisions to take on the half-day journey, Tom and Betty walked up the track to the front porch. They were accompanying Rose and Bennett to Arltunga, and making sure they were settled at the hotel.

'Mr and Mrs Pearce will look after you and see you don't want for anything,' Tom assured her.

'They are good people, and they run the hotel and the store,' Betty said. Betty had stayed in the house with them each night. Tom and Betty had both been quiet over the past week, and Rose knew they were grieving almost as much as she was.

As they rode along the river, Rose found it hard to imagine Arltunga with a store and a population of three hundred people. She had not left their home at Ruby Gap since she had arrived with William four and a half years earlier.

Mrs Pearce showed Rose the room that had been set aside for her and Bennett. Rose carried Bennett to the sitting room to say goodbye to Tom and Betty. They were returning to Ruby Gap that afternoon. Tom was holding a letter, and his face was set.

'Tom?' she said quietly. 'What is it?'

Betty's eyes filled with tears, and she squeezed Rose's hand before she picked Bennett up and took him outside.

'Tom?' Rose's hands began to shake.

'Be strong, Rose dear. I'm so sorry.' Tom handed her the letter and stayed close to her. 'I was bringing you this letter the day . . . the day Rufus . . . I could not give it to you then. It was addressed to me to read and then to bring to you. To stay with you.'

Dread pooled in Rose's stomach as she reached for the letter, expecting it to be from William, but it was from her father. Her breath caught as she began to read.

My dearest daughter,

It is with a heavy heart that I put pen to paper to write to you. There is no gentle way to tell you that William was involved in an accident two days ago. He was taken to St Bartholomew's Hospital where he did not regain consciousness before he passed away.

Rose dropped the letter and bent double. She held her stomach, and a long drawn-out keen came from her lips.

CHAPTER
26

Annie's Gorge
Six years ago

'Come on, Screw. We can't let them know we've seen their stash.'
Ethan's voice was low and urgent as they moved away from the
river on the western side of Fox's Grave. In all the times he'd been
out here, he'd never come this far up the gorge past Ruby Gap and
he wished he never had.

'Do you think they saw us?' Screw gripped the old axe as they
ran along the track to where they'd left Ruby.

'I'm pretty sure they did. I saw the glint of a pair of binoculars
when we were on the edge of the cliff.'

'We'll be right. We'll be long gone before they can get up here.
They won't even see Ruby.' Screw stumbled and swore.

'What's wrong?'

'I've got a bloody rock in my boot. It's worked its way down under my sole. Here, take the axe.' He sat on a stump at the side of the track and quickly unlaced his boot.

'For frig's sake, Screw, hurry up! There had to be thousands of dollars' worth of stuff in there. Probably more.' Ethan gripped the axe and looked around nervously.

'What do you think it was?' Screw took off his boot and shook it and then pulled it back on.

'Meth, I reckon. I know there's a big problem with it in town and it's trickling out to the settlements. There's been a few busts written up in the paper. Come *on*.'

They ran together. 'What do you think they were doing down at the river?'

Relief filled Ethan as the sun glinted off Ruby's shiny paintwork fifty metres ahead. 'It looked like they were fossicking on a big scale. The way they had the dig area set out in grids, it looked like a professional outfit.'

'But isn't it a national park? There'd be no company out here mining, would there?'

'A nature park and yes, that's the way it's supposed to be. Just recreational fossicking.'

'Maybe they have nothing to do with the stash up top. Maybe it's just a storage shed.'

'Strange place to stash it, and I'm not going to risk it.' As they got closer to Ruby, Ethan cocked his head. 'Shit, I can hear bikes.'

Screw swore. 'How'd they get up here so quickly?'

'They must have someone up here guarding the other end of the track. They wouldn't have expected anyone to come up the back way we did. They saw us on cameras, or we set off some sort of alarm.'

The throaty roar of three four-stroke off-road bikes drowned out Ethan's words as the machines sped towards them. The bikes slewed around, kicking up red dust and almost knocking Screw off his feet before they pulled up on the track, one bike in front and two behind them.

'Hey. Watch it,' Screw yelled, spitting dust out of his mouth.

'What are you blokes doing up here?' the bloke on the front bike demanded.

Ethan straightened his stance, gripped the axe in front of him and despite his dry mouth, he spoke politely. 'We hiked over to Fox's Grave to have a look at the site. We're just heading back to town now.'

'That's Ethan Hayden,' one of the blokes behind them yelled. 'The crazy bastard who's been trying to find his fortune down in the river. What's with the axe?'

'We were going to get some firewood.'

'So where is it?' The guy in front wore no helmet and his face was unshaven and dirty. A red and black bandanna was wrapped around his forehead. Ethan stared in disbelief at the hand gun he lifted.

There was a distinctive click from behind and Ethan turned to see the barrel of a rifle pointing at him. His blood chilled. The guy's shirt had a logo on the front, but he lifted the rifle before Ethan could take a good look at it.

Ethan raised his hands and took a step back, glancing at Screw who stood there, eyes wide. 'Hey, mate,' he said quietly. 'We're not after any trouble. Like I said, we were looking at the grave and then getting some firewood. Come on, Screw. We'll head home now.'

'No, boys. You're both coming back to our shed. I hear you've already had a good look around it. Now, get moving, back the way you came.'

Ethan took another step back and was shocked when Screw lunged at the guy with the hand gun. A shot fired into the air as the man fell backwards over the bike, landing on the track with the bike on top of him.

'You little bastard!' he roared. 'Shoot him, Ant.'

The guy with the rifle stepped forward. 'He's the one who pocketed some. You've always been into the junk, haven't you, you bastard?'

Shit, who are these guys?

Ethan's mouth dried as the guy pointed the rifle at Screw. Without thought, Ethan lifted the axe, swinging it from side to side. 'Put the fucking rifle down.'

The guy laughed and turned it on Ethan. 'You're dead, little boy.'

'Run, Screw,' Ethan yelled, running at the bike then feinting to the left as he swung the axe on front of him. The axe came back in a wide arc, hitting the guy with the rifle square in the forehead, splitting it open like a melon.

Ethan dropped the axe in disbelief as blood spurted out, splattering him. Blood ran into the guy's eyes as he stared at Ethan, the rifle falling from his hand as he pitched forward onto the front of the bike.

'Jesus, Ethan, you've killed him! Run!' Screw took off and Ethan bent down and retrieved the axe.

'You bastards! You're dead.' The other guy was back on his feet and reaching for the hand gun lying on the ground.

Ethan had never run so fast in his life.

Reaching Ruby, he flung the door open, chucking the axe over the back, bloody pleased he'd left the keys in the ignition. He didn't even wait for the diesel glow plug to do its stuff. He started the engine and dropped the clutch as Screw slammed the passenger door shut.

'Jesus, Ethan, *move* it! The bastards are gaining on us already.' Screw turned around, and the sound of bikes followed them as Ethan planted the accelerator to the floor. He glanced in the rear-vision mirror. Black smoke billowed from the exhaust, but the bikes were quickly gaining on them.

As the Land Rover finally gained some speed, Ethan gripped the wheel and pushed the truck hard along the unfamiliar track. His heart was hammering and his chest ached. The guy had a split forehead. There's no way he could be dead.

He couldn't.

But it was the image of the wide, lifeless eyes covered in blood that Ethan couldn't forget. Screw was bouncing in the seat as Ruby slewed from side to side on the rutted track.

'What did he mean you pocketed some?' Ethan yelled above the roar of the engine and Screw's panicked yells.

'Plant it, Eth. He's gaining on us and he's got a rifle. He's gonna shoot.'

'What did he mean, Screw?'

'I didn't think they'd miss one bag,' Screw bleated. 'It's worth a fortune in town. I could do with a bit of extra dosh.'

'Jesus, Screw. Didn't you see the bloody cameras?' Ethan had taken one look around at the drug stash and gone straight outside. No wonder he hadn't seen Screw helping himself. 'That's why they're after us.'

'No.' Screw swivelled around, putting his arm along the back of the seat as something smacked into the passenger side of the vehicle. 'Christ, he's shooting!'

'Put your head down.' Ethan slipped down in the seat as a bullet whistled past like an angry bee, but had to keep his head high enough to see where they were going. On the way up, the track had gone very close to the edge of the cliff. Too close to take it safely at this speed, but there was no way he was slowing down. The window behind them shattered, and another bullet whistled through the cab between them and whacked into the dash.

'Shit, man. He nearly got me,' Screw screamed. 'And you know who that bloke you killed fucking was? The copper who chatted me when I got caught with weed at school.'

'What, he's police?' Panic kicked in harder.

'He's as crooked as they come,' Screw yelled. 'He let me off as long as I gave him my stash and all my money. Two thousand bucks, it was.'

'Don't worry, they can't ride and aim at the same time,' Ethan said, hoping it was true.

'I don't want to risk it, I'm getting—' Screw howled in fright as another bullet whistled past the window. 'Jesus, he nearly got us. Fuck, Ethan, go faster!'

Ethan glanced over at Screw, but jerked as something slammed into the side of his head. He put his hand up and it came away covered in blood. His head spun and he gagged, almost spewing.

'Shit, Eth, he got you. You're bleeding. Ethan?'

Blood ran down Ethan's neck and soaked his T-shirt. Searing pain ripped through the side of his face. He pressed one hand against his head and gripped the steering wheel with the other, but it was impossible to steer one-handed.

'Help me steer, mate.'

'No, I'm not leaning over. He'll see me.'

Terrified and fighting the urge to throw up, Ethan looked into the rear-vision mirror, gritting his teeth as another shot came. The Land Rover suddenly skewed left, and Ethan knew a tyre had been hit. He wrenched at the steering wheel as the car headed bush, but they were going so fast, he was unable to control the vehicle.

'Shit! No. Hang on!' Ethan yelled as Ruby headed towards the edge of the cliff.

CHAPTER
27

Alice Springs
Sunday, 7.00 pm

On the way back into town, even though emotional and physical exhaustion had well and truly settled in, Gemma stopped by Saul's mate's place where they'd dropped his dog off yesterday morning—it felt more like a week—to introduce herself and explain the situation.

'Is he okay?' Rodney met her at the gate. Attila bounded over, standing on his back legs before howling. 'Will you see him tonight?'

'I'm just calling in at home on the way, and then, yes, I'll go and see him.' Gemma had to speak loudly to be heard over the racket the dog was making. 'I'll know more then.'

'Oh, for God's sake, Attila, shut it.' Rodney looped his arm around the large dog's top half. 'What a bummer for him. How long do you reckon he'll be in there?'

'I'm not sure.'

'Well, I've got to leave in the morning and Julie—my wife—
can't look after Attila. Do you want me to organise something? Be
happy to.'

'I'll take him,' Gemma said, biting her lip. 'I can come and pick
him up about seven. Is that too early?'

'That'd be good. Has Saul told you what a pest he can be? You
don't want to ever leave this mutt by himself.' Despite his words,
Rodney leaned down and ruffled the dog's head. 'He's the most
lovable dog you'll ever meet, but he sure likes to chew things up.
He's a shocker. Do you think Saul'll be home or will you take
Attila back to your place tomorrow?' Rodney looked at her curiously. 'Good to see Saul have company. He's usually a bit of a
loner.'

'Oh, we're just old friends.' Gemma waved a dismissive hand.
'I'm just seeing to Attila for him. I live in an apartment and didn't
want to leave him by himself at Saul's tonight. Hopefully he'll be
home tomorrow.'

'Okay, call in early and I'll help you get him on the ute.'

Attila was still howling as she backed out of the driveway.

Tomorrow could be interesting.

Gemma quickly called in to her apartment, took a brief shower
and changed her clothes before getting back in Saul's ute and heading to the hospital.

'Hello?' Gemma called tentatively when she reached the nurses'
station on the ground floor of Alice Springs Hospital.

'Yes?' A sister in a blue uniform came out from the glass-fronted
office.

'A friend of mine was brought into emergency in the helicopter,
and I was hoping I could see him.'

'What's his name?' The woman spoke briskly as she looked up from the clipboard in her hand.

'Saul Pearce. He was brought in by helicopter around lunchtime.'

The woman crossed to the computer and tapped the keyboard. 'A friend, you said?' She frowned.

'Girlfriend.' Gemma crossed her fingers behind her back. She had been once, so it was only a little white lie.

The nurse nodded. 'Mr Pearce is out of surgery and still in recovery. He should be back in the ward before visiting hours are over. He's in Ward 26A on the first floor. If you go and wait in the visitors' room outside the ward, he should be back there soon.'

'Thank you.'

Thank God. If Saul was going back to a normal ward, he must be okay. Exhaustion slowed her pace as Gemma walked out to the corridor with the dull brown lino floor before the sister could change her mind. It was almost eight o'clock; she hadn't been sure she'd make the hospital before visiting hours ended. She'd not been sure if she had the energy to keep going.

She made her way upstairs to the post-surgical ward, hands by her side. Mum had always had a phobia about germs, and sixteen years of being told not to touch communal stair railings and never to go into the first cubicle in public toilets had instilled the same habits into Gemma.

Gemma glanced into the ward on the way to the waiting room. Only one of the four beds had a patient in it—an elderly guy who appeared to be asleep. She continued on to the waiting room and sat on a hard plastic chair. She fought back a yawn; her whole body was weary.

The air-conditioning was turned up high and she shivered. The only sounds breaking the silence were the ticking of the large clock on the bare white wall and the hum of a machine in the corridor.

Gemma sat there, ill at ease and wondering if she should have called first. She didn't know anything about Saul these days apart from where he worked and that he owned a dog. Maybe he was seeing someone; someone who had a right to be waiting here in the hospital for him. Her previous determination to talk to him about their past faded as each moment passed. With a deep breath, Gemma chastised herself silently. She owed Saul; if he hadn't distracted that bull, she could have died.

Long minutes passed and there was still no sign of him coming; the corridor was silent. Her worry grew. Maybe he'd taken a turn for the worse? Maybe he had internal injuries? Maybe the sister had looked up the wrong person and Saul was still in surgery or intensive care?

Where the heck is he?

With a glance at her phone to check the time, Gemma decided to give him another ten minutes before she'd leave a message at the desk to say she'd been and gone home. Tomorrow was Monday and she was due back at school; she hadn't given any thought to the program for the day. Getting her head back to schoolwork, kids and classrooms was going to be impossible. Maybe she should take a bit more time off.

Gemma nervously bit her bottom lip. Mike's warning had frightened her, and she was just holding back the grief that had brought a permanent dull ache to her chest. Talking to Saul would give her a focus; she needed to discuss it all with him before she made any calls.

Just as she was about to give up waiting, the lift dinged and a wardsman pushed a bed along the corridor. Gemma jumped up and stepped out of the waiting room as the bed was wheeled into the ward opposite, followed by a nurse. She caught a glimpse of Saul's sun-tipped hair and pale face before the curtains closed around the bed. Relief flowed through her and she relaxed her tense shoulders as she waited for them to get him settled.

It wasn't long before the wardsman came out. He nodded at her as he walked past. She hovered in the doorway until the nurse opened the curtains and walked across the ward.

'Hello. Have you been waiting for Mr Pearce?'

'I have. Is it okay to go in? The sister told me I could come up.'

'You must be Gemma.' The dark-haired young nurse smiled, her cheeks rosy.

'I am.' Gemma frowned. 'How did you—'

'Your gorgeous man thought I was you when he was in recovery,' the nurse said. 'He wouldn't let go of my hand. He begged me not to leave him, so you'd better get in there quick and hold his hand. You're a lucky girl.'

'Lucky?'

The nurse's short dark curls bobbed around her face as she nodded. 'If I had a man love me half as much, I'd be a very happy woman.' She lowered her voice. 'You can stay with him until just before nine. That's when they lock the front doors.'

Gemma's face flamed. 'Thank you.' The nurse smiled again and Gemma paused. 'Is he okay? I mean, the operation or whatever they had to do?'

'You'll have to wait to talk to the doctor tomorrow, but he wouldn't be in the general ward if he wasn't, so don't worry yourself,' she said kindly. 'He's still very sleepy, so he'll probably doze on and off, but enjoy your hour with him.'

Gemma stood in the door and looked across at the bed as the nurse left her. Saul was on his back, his eyes closed, his dark lashes fanning onto his cheeks. He looked peaceful, and she took a hesitant step towards the bed. She jumped when he opened his eyes and stared at her.

'Gem. Please don't go.'

She moved closer to the bed and stood beside him. His right arm
was hooked up to a drip, and she glanced at the monitor that was
recording his vital signs.

'Promise me you won't go. Please. Promise.' His breath started
coming in quick short pants and she reached for his hand.

'It's okay, Saul. I'm still here. I'll stay with you.'

Gemma pulled the vinyl padded chair out from the wall with her
other hand so she didn't let go of the hand that was gripping hers
tightly. 'I can stay for just a little while, Saul. How are you feeling?'

'Stay.' His eyes closed again and his breathing settled.

Gemma sat there, enjoying the warmth of Saul's fingers wrapped
around hers. For the first time since this morning, a measure of
calm descended and she let herself relax. After a few minutes, his
eyes fluttered open again and Saul turned his head to look at her.

Gemma spoke quietly. 'I hope it was okay. I called in to tell
Rodney you were here. Attila is fine and I'm picking him up in the
morning.'

'You'll have to take my ute,' he murmured, eyes closing again,
but she was pleased he was coherent now.

'I will. On the way to school.'

'Can you pass me the water please?'

He opened his eyes again as she looked around and saw the plastic cup and straw on the table on the other side of the bed. She let
go of his hand and reached across and then held the straw to his
mouth.

'Thank you, that's good.' Saul nodded when he'd had enough
and she put the cup closer this time. 'There's a bone for Attila in
the freezer in the annexe of my caravan. It'll keep him occupied.
Make sure you lock the front gate with the chain.' Saul was quiet
for a while and his breathing was even. The white sheet covered

him to his waist so Gemma couldn't see if his leg was in plaster or not. 'I missed you, Gem. I came back the other day but your mum said you didn't want to talk to me,' he rambled.

She realised he was only half in the present. 'That's okay. I'm sorry.'

'I had to tell you . . . why I have to go.' His breathing quickened and his hand gripped hers. 'But your mum said no. But you have to come with me, Gem.'

'It's okay. We're all good now.' *He wanted me? He didn't want to leave without me?*

'I have to go. You're right. But come with me. Go to uni in Darwin . . . will you come with me?' He let go of her hand and put his hand to his head.

'Are you okay? Is your head hurting?'

'I deserved this,' he mumbled. 'Ethan's right. She's right. You'd better stay here.'

'Deserved what?' Gemma frowned, looking at his face.

'The shiner. Ethan gave it to me.' He tried to lift his arm to his face but the drip tube caught on the edge of the bed, and Gemma gently pushed his hand back to the bed. 'And I know now why you can't come. You were right. Not good for you.'

Tears blurred Gemma's eyes as she remembered her harsh words to Saul that night. The last time she'd seen him before he'd gone away and left her. The night she'd told him he had to make something of himself and not carry a chip on his shoulder for the rest of his life. She'd never meant he wasn't good enough for her.

When he recovered, she vowed she would set him straight; Saul had carried the wrong impression of what she'd thought for six years. And she'd had no idea that Ethan had apparently given him a black eye. And now she couldn't even ask Ethan why.

Her eyes welled again and she dug for a tissue in her pocket, dabbing at her eyes as Saul lay sleeping. His breathing was even and his eyes stayed closed; he'd fallen into a deeper sleep. She looked up at the clock near the door. It was only eight-thirty, but she'd go now. She took his phone from her bag and put it in the drawer of the cabinet beside the bed.

The legs of the chair scraped on the lino as she pushed it back, and his eyes flew open.

'Where're you going?'

Gemma leaned over and spoke quietly. 'I have to go home. I brought your phone from the car. It's in the drawer there.' She gestured to the drawer beside the bed. 'It's the same as mine, so I've charged it for you. I hope that was all right. I'll give you a call in the morning and see how you're feeling.'

'Promise?'

'Yes. I'll call you.'

Saul lifted his hand and touched his cheek. 'I'll sleep better if you kiss me goodbye.'

Gemma smiled and looked down at him; his eyes were clearer now. Slowly, she bent down and brushed her lips over his. 'I'll see you tomorrow. Sleep well, Saul.'

CHAPTER
28

Alice Springs
Monday, 7.00 am

'Another couple of centimetres and it would have had a very different outcome, Mr Pearce.' Dr Hemmings stood beside the bed and Saul blinked as he tried to focus on the man's face.

'What do you mean?' He was still feeling groggy. His tongue seemed to be stuck to the roof of his dry mouth and his leg was aching like a bastard. Rolling his lips, he tried to get some moisture into his mouth and looked up, surprised when the doctor picked up the small plastic cup with the straw that was on the cupboard next to the hospital bed and passed it to him. He'd barely been awake when the doctor had appeared at his bedside. Through the night, he'd woken several times when the nurse had come to check on him; she'd told him some painkilling stuff was going through his drip, but it didn't seem to be doing much.

'The injury was very close to your femoral artery.'

'In my leg?' Saul sucked through the straw and the water was cool on his tongue. He finished the drink and the surgeon took the cup from him. 'Thank you.'

'The femoral artery is the large artery in your thigh, the main arterial supply to both the thigh and leg. If the wound had been any closer, you would have bled out.'

Saul closed his eyes. 'I was lucky.' He didn't feel lucky.

'Very. Having an injury like that in such an isolated location would have given you little chance.'

'So, what's the damage?' It was easier to speak now that his mouth had some moisture.

'First off, we stitched up that wound at the top of your thigh. You'll have a decent scar, but the good news is there was no injury to the muscle; it'll just take time for the wound to heal.'

'How long?'

Dr Hemmings picked up the chart at the end of the bed and flicked though a couple of pages. 'You're a healthy man by the look of things, and with proper care you should heal fairly quickly. Plus, the break to your ankle is a clean break. It's called a medial malleolus fracture.'

Saul had reached down and tried to feel his right leg a couple of times through the night but there was some sort of frame around it. 'Is my leg in plaster?'

'No, there's a frame around your leg to support it. We'll plaster it this morning.'

'For how long? When can I go back to work?'

'Mr Pearce.' The doctor shook his head. 'You'll be spending at least three days, maybe four, right where you are. You'll stay on the antibiotic drip for another thirty-six hours and then we'll see how you're going.'

Saul stared at him. 'I can't stay here any longer than that. There's things I have to do.' Even though he'd been out of it after the chopper had picked him up, Saul hadn't forgotten what they'd found out at the ruins. 'And I have a dog.'

'At least three days,' Dr Hemmings repeated. 'Plus, it will be about six weeks before you're walking normally again. You've got some slight tissue damage. Ligaments and tendons often take longer to heal than the bones themselves. What sort of work do you do?'

'I'm a National Parks ranger.'

'You'll be off for a while, then.' The surgeon shook his head. 'That break shows you the force that bull hit you with.'

'Yeah, I went up in the air and came down hard on my foot.'

'Like I said, you're a very lucky man.'

'So I can't go to work this week? I need to call in sick.'

'Not this week. You can go back to light office duties after ten days or so, but it will be at least six weeks before you can do anything too strenuous.'

Saul could already feel the claustrophobia setting in at being forced back to desk duty.

Dr Hemmings continued. 'Is there someone to look after you at home? You'll need to get that sorted. I'll be back to see you tomorrow, Mr Pearce.'

Saul stared at the door for a long time after the surgeon left. No, there was no one to look after him at home.

What an absolute bummer. He'd go stir-crazy.

He flopped back on the pillow and closed his eyes. He had to think of the positives; if he hadn't distracted that bloody scrubber, Gemma could have died. *He* could have died out there. Saul frowned and opened his eyes again; he had a vague memory of Gemma talking to him last night. Something about his phone? Maybe he'd dreamed it.

Saul looked over at the cupboard beside the bed, but there was only a box of tissues next to the water jug. He reached for the drawer and pulled it open, and the memory returned as he spotted his phone.

Gemma had been here with him when he'd woken up, and as it all came back, Saul smiled. She'd told him she'd brought his phone in, then she'd kissed him before she'd left.

And it hadn't been on his cheek.

He lifted his head at the rattle of a trolley coming into the ward. 'Good morning, gentlemen.'

Saul glanced over at the bed in the opposite corner; the old guy there still hadn't stirred.

'Mr Pearce, here's your breakfast. It was late when you came back from theatre, so you've got the standard choice. Would you like a cup of tea or coffee to go with your Weet-Bix and eggs?'

'Tea, please.'

By the time his breakfast was placed on his tray, his tea was poured and the woman had lowered the trapeze above the bed so he could pull himself up to a sitting position, Saul's thoughts were firmly back on his present dilemma. It was only seven am, so he had a couple of hours before he had to call in sick. It would give him time to think of what he'd say. He needed to talk to Gemma first to see who else knew where he'd had his accident. The content of Ethan's coded message made him wary, reinforced by what he'd seen out at Ruby Gap. He'd prefer to keep that to himself for the time being. He had a vague recollection of Gemma saying she'd call him this morning. He'd wait to talk to her before he called Terry.

Saul gave the unappetising-looking breakfast a chance and tried to eat. If there was one thing he hated, it was bloody Weet-Bix. The number of times he'd had to eat that for his dinner when he was a kid had never left him. But he forced himself to eat it. He had to get his strength up so he could heal quickly. The sooner he got better, the sooner he could go home. The rubbery scrambled eggs stuck in his throat before he gave up and pushed the plate away.

As he lifted the tea cup and sipped the steaming liquid, his phone buzzed on the cupboard next to him. He reached over and picked it up and looked at the screen.

'Hi, Gemma.'

'Saul, it's good to hear you talking. How are you feeling this morning? I hope I didn't wake you up.'

'No, I've been awake a while. The doc's already been to see me and I've had breakfast. I'm a bit sore and sorry, but I'll live.'

'Oh, thank goodness. I was so worried about you until I got to the hospital last night,' she said. 'Driving into Alice not knowing how you were was pretty stressful.'

While he didn't want to stress her, Saul couldn't help but feel pleased at her concern. 'I'm okay, so you can stop worrying. I can barely remember you being here last night, but thanks for coming in. How are you today? How did you go with the drive back to town?'

'I'm fine. Slept surprisingly well,' she added. 'Listen, Saul, I have to be quick. I'm in the car and about to go into school, but I wanted to ask you something before I spoke to anyone.'

'Yeah, I wanted to talk to you before I ring in sick too. Have you told anyone I'm in hospital?'

'Only your friend, Rodney. I called in there.'

'I remember now. You told me that last night.'

'Until I come and see you later, can you please not mention to anyone what . . . what we saw out at Ruby Gap?'

'Of course, I agree,' he replied. 'I'd prefer it if we could keep quiet about where we were over the weekend too. We need to work out a few things first.'

'We do. And yes, that's not a problem. I won't say anything. Do you think you'll be home today? Do you need picking up from the hospital?'

'No. The doctor's been around already, and it looks like I'll be here around three days. I'll give Rodney a call and let him know that Attila will have to stay out there for a while longer.'

'Um, don't worry about that. I've got Attila sorted.'

Saul hesitated. 'Okay . . . thanks.'

'Look, I've got to go.' Gemma spoke quickly. 'I'll come and see you after school today. Is that okay?'

'Of course it is. I'll look forward to it.'

Saul closed his eyes as the call disconnected. Having Gemma back in his life was so good, even under such shit circumstances. Whatever happened, he was determined to solve the mystery of Ethan. How he'd died, and who had buried him. It was the only way Gemma and her family could move on.

And then he could focus on restoring a relationship with Gemma.

*

Monday, 7.00 am

Rod had opened the gate so Gemma could drive the ute in just before seven. Attila bounded over to the vehicle, and Gemma could have sworn there was disappointment in his big brown eyes when she climbed down from the cabin. The huge dog sat and put his head back, giving a mournful howl before running over to her. She patted him and he sat beside her, leaning his head against her leg.

'Your dad's doing well. And he told me to give you a big bone when we get you home.' She grimaced as a big dollop of slobber ran down her grey trousers.

'How's Saul?' Rodney smiled at her as he walked across from the gate.

'He's a bit knocked around. He may be in hospital for a couple of days.'

'What happened? I didn't like to ask too much yesterday. You seemed a bit upset.'

Gemma rubbed at the wet patch on her trousers. 'We were out bush, and Saul had a bit of a run-in with a scrubber bull.'

Rodney's dark eyes widened. 'Jesus, that's not good. Where were you?'

'Just out Arltunga way.' Gemma waved in a vague easterly direction.

'Where's he hurt?'

'His leg. But he'll be home soon.' Gemma forced brightness into her voice. Until she talked to Saul, she didn't want to let on too much. 'Anyway, I have to drop this boy off and get to work.'

'No worries. Whereabouts do you work, Gemma?'

'I'm a teacher at Trephina Primary School.'

'That's where our two kids go.' Rod stared at her. 'You're not Ms Hayden, the new teacher, are you?'

Gemma nodded and Rod looked embarrassed.

'I owe you an apology. I heard what Lauren took to school for show and tell last week.'

Gemma chuckled and for a brief moment, the emotional load that had filled her since Friday lightened. 'Ah, Lauren Hepplewhite is your daughter. She's a very bright young lady.'

'She is.' Rod's grin was wide. 'Julie was mortified when Loz came home and told us. There's going to be a bag check every morning now.'

'She's a sweet kid.'

'Listen, when Saul's recovered and I'm home from this stint, how about you both come out for a barbecue? Julie would love to meet you. We were both working the day of the school welcome afternoon.'

'That's kind of you.' Gemma nodded slowly. 'That would be nice.'

Once Rod had secured Attila to the back of Saul's ute, it was only a few kilometres back towards Alice to Saul's place. Gemma knew exactly where he'd lived, even though Saul had never taken her there. The front gate was open and once she'd driven through, she stopped the ute and shut the gate. The last thing she needed was for Attila to escape. The driveway was smooth and edged by small saplings, and black irrigation hoses ran the length of the gardens on each side.

Attila began barking as they traversed the rest of the drive and climbed a small hill. Gemma's breath caught as she slowed the vehicle. A new timber house with a dark green Colorbond roof sat on the crest of the hill. A caravan sat at the left-hand side of the house beside two large water tanks the same colour as the roof. The house was surrounded by newly dug gardens full of saplings; each garden was edged with an irrigation hose. To the right of the caravan was an area fenced off by a timber fence, high enough that she couldn't see what was there. Maybe it was a dog yard, or a veggie patch?

Curiosity replaced her surprise as she climbed out of the ute. Saul's place was nothing like she'd expected. Nothing like Ethan had described when he'd come out here occasionally when they'd been in their teens.

She stood by the ute and stared to the west. The mountains of the West MacDonnells still held the bluish hues of early morning as the first rays of the sun touched the top of the rocky outcrops. The vista was magnificent, and she reluctantly pulled her gaze away to untie Attila's lead, holding it firmly as he jumped off the back of the ute. He was a big, strong dog, but he stopped pulling when she spoke.

'Come on, you. You can show me where you live.' She picked up the pace as Attila almost dragged her to the high wooden fence. She stood at the gate and her mouth dropped open as she peered over.

★

Monday 8.30 am

The school car park was almost full as Gemma grabbed her bag from the back of her car and locked the door. She'd moved her car to the front of the apartment block this morning and parked Saul's ute in her car space in the basement after she'd come back from collecting Attila. Once she'd left Saul's property, she'd looked down and realised a change of clothes was needed.

Pat was standing at the edge of the car park smoking, and she put it out quickly as Gemma walked over to her. 'I know, I know. I shouldn't be having a quickie in the car park, but Jeff's in a staff meeting.' Her gravelly voice was apologetic.

'Oh no, I forgot all about the Monday morning muster.' Gemma frowned and Pat looked at her curiously.

'You okay, love? Guess that's a stupid question after Friday, isn't it?'

'I'm okay,' Gemma said quietly. 'But thanks for asking.'

'It's not like you to be this late. And if you don't mind me saying, you look like shit. I'm actually surprised you're here. I thought you'd take a few days off.'

'No, I'd rather be busy.' Which was true.

'How did you go on the weekend? Did you go out to Ruby Gap?'

Gemma bit her lip, regretting that she'd told Pat they were going out there. She decided to play it low-key. 'Yes, but it was just Ruby. I guess I was getting my hopes up. Wrecked and rusted, and had been there a long time by the look of things.' She sighed. 'Anyway, I'd better get into the meeting. I'll see you later.'

'Bye, love. Take it easy.'

As Gemma crossed the playground, she decided to give the meeting a miss. She'd catch up with Jeff later and apologise. As she pushed the door open, exhaustion rolled over her. Pausing in the doorway, she leaned on the doorframe looking at the empty desks. With a sigh, she closed her eyes. She admitted to herself that she didn't want to be here. So much had happened, it seemed like weeks since she'd been called into Jeff's office on Friday.

The bell rang as she sat in her chair. The room swam before her eyes as they stung with threatening tears. She took a deep breath, and forced herself to look up with a smile as the sound of happy voices and little footsteps came from the corridor.

'Gemma! What are you doing here?' Sylvie stood in the doorway, her arms full of books. She turned to the children in the corridor. 'Line up quietly please, and put your hats into your bags.'

Gemma stood and held onto the desk as the room tilted. 'Hello, Sylvie. I missed the muster, but I'm here now.'

Confusion crossed Sylvie's face as she came to the desk and unloaded her books. 'Jeff said you were taking some time off. I'm rostered on your class for the whole week.'

'Oh.' Gemma felt a rush of relief, but stood up straight. She didn't need help; she could do this. 'I guess I forgot to ring him to tell him I was coming back today. He must have assumed I wasn't. I'll go and see him now.'

She began to cross the room, but Sylvie's gentle hand on her arm stopped her. 'Gemma, I'm so sorry. Jeff told us what happened. About your brother.'

The sympathy in her voice brought the whole mix of emotion that had been building in Gemma to a crescendo. The threatening tears spilled over onto her cheeks, and she put her hands up to her face. 'I'm sorry,' she gulped. 'I think you're right. I do need to take some time.'

'It's okay,' Sylvie said softly. 'We've got you.'

Gemma sniffed. 'I'll go and see Jeff now.'

The children barely took any notice as Gemma rushed out the door and down to the principal's office. Jeff ushered her inside and closed the door to his office. 'Sit down, Gemma,' he said kindly. 'I'm surprised to see you here. How are you?'

'I'm fine. I should be working,' she blurted. 'I don't want to let my class down. Or the school.'

'You're not letting anyone down, Gemma,' Jeff said. 'Sylvie is an above establishment staff member, so it doesn't cost the school anything in casual relief.'

'Oh. Okay, maybe just a day—'

'Maybe play it by ear? If you don't feel ready to come back in a couple of weeks, just give me a call,' Jeff said firmly. 'Just see your doctor and get a certificate before you come back, so all the paper-work's in order.'

'But . . .' She looked down at her hands clenched in her lap.

'Gemma. Sometimes, you have to make sure you look after yourself.' He lowered his voice. 'I know what happened over the weekend, and I know how hard that would have been for you.'

Her head flew up. 'What do you mean, what happened?'

'I know about the accident. My wife is an RN in emergency and she was at the hospital when the helicopter came in.' Gemma's panic must have shown on her face, because he added, 'Don't worry, it won't go any further. Carissa was telling me about the accident last night and I put two and two together, and realised it was Saul, and that you'd probably gone out with him to see the wreck. I didn't even tell her the connection. I tried to call you, but there was no answer.'

Gemma lifted a shaking hand to her face. 'It was pretty scary. The worst part was driving back to town after the helicopter took Saul out, not knowing how he was.'

'And how is he?'

'I was talking to him earlier and he said he's okay.'

Jeff nodded. 'That's good. Now, you need to look after yourself, and make sure you're okay too.'

The phone on Jeff's desk buzzed and Gemma stood. Her head had settled, but she felt teary. Maybe everyone was right. Maybe she needed to take some time. Being focused on Attila this morning had kept her mind away from Ethan, and now it was all coming back.

She put her head down, barely holding herself together as she headed out of the office. 'Thank you, Jeff. I'll keep in touch.'

CHAPTER

29

Alice Springs
Monday, 2.00 pm

Saul sat up straight and ran his hand over his hair when Gemma walked into the ward just after two o'clock. 'This is a surprise. I wasn't expecting to see you until after school.'

'I ended up taking some time off.' Despite her smile and bright voice, her face was pale and dark circles shadowed her eyes. 'I thought I'd come in and see if there was anything you needed, so I'd have time to come back later if you did.'

'You look tired, Gem.' Saul gestured to the chair beside the bed. 'Pull up a pew.'

'Would you believe after I called into school, I went home and slept for three hours? Even after I crashed last night. I never sleep in the daytime.' She shook her head.

'Understandable. It was a pretty stressful weekend.' He lowered his voice, although there was no one close by to hear. The old guy had been discharged just before lunch and Saul had the ward to himself. 'Before you leave—and yes, I do need a few things, thank you—we need to talk about what we're going to do—and say. And who to tell about the . . . about what we found.'

'Ethan's grave.' Gemma sighed. 'Yes, I've been doing a lot of thinking about that. I still can't believe it. What do you think we should do?'

'If it wasn't for this blasted broken ankle, I'd be heading north, looking for Screw. I think he's the first person we should talk to.'

'We have to find him first.' Gemma pulled a face. 'And there's something else I have to tell you.'

Saul held her eyes with his and she was the first to look away. 'What? Has something else happened?'

'No. It's what Mike said when I left there yesterday. He warned me to stay away. Or warned us. He said to tell you too.'

'Tell me what?' Rage simmered at the thought of Gemma being threatened.

'To stay away from Ruby Gap, or there'd be deadly consequences.' Gemma paused. 'Saul, what is going on out there?'

'I don't know.' Saul shook his head. 'I'm sorry you were left out there with him. I was bloody relieved to know you were back safely last night.'

She stared at him. 'I owe *you* my life, Saul. If you hadn't distracted that huge bull—'

'Let it go, Gem,' Saul said firmly. 'What's happened has happened. We're both okay. We can't change anything, just like we can't change what happened to Ethan. We'll just tell everyone we went out there so you could see Ethan's car.'

'Well, we did.'

'But we don't mention anything else. With a bit of luck, no one will know exactly where we were when that bull fronted us. And really, no one except for me and Darren knew exactly where the Land Rover is. But there's something not right out there, and it's wise to stay away for a while.'

'What do you mean by not right?'

'I saw something out there.'

'When you climbed the cliff to look for that road while I had a rest?'

'Yes,' he admitted.

'I knew you were being evasive about something!' His eyes snagged hers again and this time she didn't look away.

'You know me too well, Gem. I thought you had enough to worry about.'

'What did you see?'

'There was a road, and further along the gorge, around the bend, there's something happening at the edge of the river.'

'Happening like what?'

'It looked like some type of construction work. It's all national park land out there, so I even wondered if it was the beginning of a new tourist facility. Like a boardwalk or a proper track up to Fox's Grave.'

'Could it be?'

'That's the strange thing. There's no plans in the works to develop the nature park that far out. The ranger who's been there longer than me was telling me that when we were out there look-ing for Ruby. Apparently, the powers that be think it's too far off the beaten track. I'll do a bit of quiet investigating when I go back to work. The other thing I wondered—and I couldn't get enough of a look at where it was—was whether it was some sort of mining. That helicopter headed up that way, remember?'

'Is that allowed in a nature park? Mining, I mean.'

'No, not legally, but it's happened before. It's hard to police when you've got such vast tracts of land, not to mention the remoteness of some of our parks.'

Gemma's hands were clenched in her lap, and Saul reached over and took the hand closest to him. He smoothed his fingers over her soft skin. 'The other thing we have to keep in mind is what Ethan's message said.'

'Not to trust anyone?'

'Yes. And you said that Mike guy said it too. I think we need to keep everything to ourselves for a while.'

Gemma nodded slowly, and Saul smiled when she curled her fingers around his and squeezed gently. 'I was thinking that when I woke up before. As far as we know, Ethan's been out there for six years now, so there's no tearing rush to tell the police. I don't think we should tell my parents yet. I want to know more about what happened. Get it all over and done with when we know. Then we'll have a funeral and give him a proper send-off.' Her voice broke and he held her hand tightly.

'It's going to be hard. I just wish I wasn't in this damn hospital bed.' Frustration laced his words. All he wanted to do was take Gemma in his arms and comfort her, but he wasn't going to say that. He had no right to. 'I worry about you, Gem. How are you coping?'

'I'm okay.' Saul could tell she was lying but didn't say anything. 'It'll be good to be done with all this and try and get back to a normal life again. I've managed to get through the last six years pretty much alone. I can look after myself.'

'I hope you trust that I'll help you find out the truth of what happened.'

She nodded. 'I know you will now, and I appreciate it.'

They sat in comfortable silence, each lost in their thoughts.

A trolley rattled down the hall and the buzzer went.

'Afternoon tea and end of visiting hours,' Gemma said. 'How long do you think you'll have to stay here?'

'Three days at most, so I'm hoping for Wednesday.' He downplayed his injury and didn't tell her how bloody painful the gash in his thigh was.

'Can you walk?'

Saul pulled a face. 'They've already had me up and walking this morning.' He'd wondered how he was going to cope in the caravan by himself, but there was no way he was going to stay in hospital once the doctor was happy to discharge him. 'I'll be right.'

'Anything I can do to help out, let me know. And you'd better tell me what you need brought in.' Gemma hesitated and a slight blush stained her cheeks. 'Saul?'

'What is it?'

'Um, I just want to know . . . if I'm stepping on anyone's toes.' She blushed. 'I mean, is there someone else who should know you're in here? Or someone else who should be looking out for you?'

Saul's smile was slow. 'No, Gem. It's just me and Attilla.'

'Good,' she said briskly. Pulling her hand away, she pushed herself to her feet and took out her phone. 'Now, tell me what you need.'

*

Gemma was greeted by a strange noise—a cross between a human groan and a loud yawn—as Attila ambled over to the gate of the yard, making that horrendous noise every time he stretched. He spotted her and she could have sworn he smiled as he picked up the pace and came over to her. Gemma dropped to her knees and put her arms around his neck, not worrying about the slobber this time. 'Oh, Atty boy, you're such a mess!' she murmured. 'Come on, we'll go and get your master's stuff.' Attila followed her closely as she walked over to the caravan. Surprised to see it was a new, modern van, Gemma pulled down the zip of the annexe at the end near the house.

'Are you allowed in here?' She put her hands on her hips, but Attila had flopped to the ground and stretched out his front legs. He lowered his head onto his paws and his soulful brown eyes followed her. 'Okay, I guess you know the rules.' She stepped into the annexe and found the brass key Saul had described. She slipped it into the door of the van, but Attila's short bark reminded her to get his bone first.

A small table, two chairs and a reclining leisure chair sat on an orange and black mat that covered the entire floor; the whole area was neat and tidy. A chest freezer hummed in the far corner, and she walked over and opened the lid. A huge bone wrapped in plastic sat in the top basket. She unwrapped it and put the plastic into the metal pedal bin in the corner before going back outside and dropping the bone on the dry grass next to Attila. His eyes flicked sideways, but he didn't touch it.

'Too cold? It won't take long to thaw out in this heat.' Gemma smiled. It was a long time since she'd talked to a dog. She crouched down beside him and ran her fingers through his short fur. With an ecstatic groan, he rolled over onto his back and presented his tummy.

'You're a big sook, Atty.' Another groan. 'And you're a lucky boy having a master like Saul, you know.' She kept scratching. 'He's a good man. Don't tell him, but I still care about him. Maybe it's only sympathy and thanks because he saved my life, and now he's hurt and in the hospital. Do you think that's why?'

Attila stretched his head back and licked her arm.

Gemma shook her head. 'I'm kidding myself, aren't I, Atty? The minute I saw him at the school last Friday, I knew. Nothing's changed. He was always the one for me, but he didn't want me. I mean, he doesn't want me.' With a sigh, she stood up. 'So that's our secret. Now, enjoy that bone.'

It was strange being at Saul's place without him, but there was a real sense of his presence. She stood in the annexe and looked around. An Akubra hat hung on a hook and a pair of highly polished boots was underneath the step. A fishing magazine sat on the table, next to a packet of plastic lures. There was so much about the Saul of these days she didn't know, and Gemma was unsure of how to deal with her feelings; she didn't want to appear needy and embarrass him. It was as though the last six years—her uni life and her teaching career—had disappeared, and she hadn't ever left Alice Springs. But she knew she had changed so much, and as much as Saul was being kind and helping her out, he didn't know the person she was now.

She was much more wary of people and very hesitant to trust; too many people had let her down. It was safer to rely on yourself, and no one else.

Gemma knew she had to be realistic. Saul had left her, and he was being kind to her because of the circumstances. He'd said he'd help her, but then she knew they'd go back to their own lives.

And that was how she'd deal with it.

CHAPTER
30

Alice Springs
Monday, 3.00 pm

'G'day mate.'

Saul looked up from his phone, quickly closing the screen he'd been reading as his boss walked into the ward. He put his phone on the table beside the bed and hoisted himself up on the pillows.

'Hey, Terry.' He pulled a face and gestured to his leg. 'Sorry about this.'

'No wuckers, mate. At least you're off in the quiet time,' Terry said, seating himself by the bed. 'How long do ya reckon you'll be off?'

Saul shook his head, wondering how Terry had found out he was in hospital. 'Not sure yet. Hopefully not too long.' He'd been vague when he'd rung the Parks office this morning and left a message at the office. All he'd said was he'd had an accident and wouldn't be in for the week. He looked at Terry curiously. 'How did you know I was in here?'

'Alice might be a big town, mate, but word gets around. Heard you got choppered in yesterday,' he said, leaning forward. 'What were you doing out at Ruby Gap on the weekend anyway? Didn't you and Daz get out there Thursday?'

'Haven't you talked to him today?' They'd called in the number-plate of the car on Thursday when they'd got back to the satphone, but Terry had already knocked off for the day, and had been on an RDO on Friday. 'Read the report?'

'Nuh, I haven't. *You* tell me what happened and why you were out there again on the weekend.' Saul didn't like Terry's tone, and he remembered how his predecessor had lost his job. But weekends were his own time, and it was none of Terry's business that he and Gemma had gone out there.

'You were right,' he said carefully. 'The car had been washed down the river.'

'So why'd you go back out there after you'd done your job?'

Saul stared at his boss, surprised that he didn't want to know more about the vehicle.

'I'd forgotten what a great spot it was, so I took my friend out for a drive,' he lied. He wasn't about to tell Terry about Gemma; the fewer details he knew, the better.

'And fell over and broke your leg?'

'Yes, my ankle.'

Terry nodded thoughtfully. 'Bad luck, hey?'

'I guess you could say that,' Saul said. 'It's a nice spot out there. I'm surprised it hasn't been developed more.'

Terry seemed to relax. 'Too far out, mate. Most of the tourists want to go west anyway. More out there to see and do. No idea why they ever gazetted it as a nature park. All it ever does is cause us trouble.'

'Trouble?'

'Hikers getting lost, bloody fossickers leaving their mess out there. And now you breaking your leg. It shouldn't be under our jurisdiction. Too much trouble for no return.'

'Didn't you tell me you'd never been there?'

'Spot on. But I see all the bloody reports that cross my desk from the police and the rescue helicopter.' Terry folded his hands over his substantial belly. 'So, that vehicle was the usual? A wreck from the settlement that's been dumped?'

'No, we found the rego papers in the glove box and it belongs to a bloke who went missing a few years back. It's all in my report, and Darren said he'd lodge a report with the police on Friday morning.'

Terry stared at him. 'No need for me to read it if the cops have taken it over,' he said finally. 'So, not long off work, you say?'

'I'll let you know as soon as the doc says I can go back. Maybe a week.'

Terry shook his head. 'No point coming back if you can't get about. I checked your file and you've got plenty of sick leave. Take a few weeks.'

Saul shrugged. 'I can do desk duties. It's pretty much all I've done since I arrived anyway.'

'Mate, you'll do what I say,' Terry said. His voice had taken an edge. 'The tourist season will be here before we know it and then we'll be overrun with grey nomies and bloody tourists.' Terry cleared his throat. 'We want you well and back on deck at a hundred per cent, so take the time off. Six, eight weeks. Whatever it takes.'

'Okay, if that suits you best.'

'And a word of advice, mate?'

'Yeah?' Saul waited.

'You want to keep your job, don't go mixing business with pleasure. Okay?' Terry rose, hitching up his shorts. 'We'll see you when
you're fighting fit again. Look after yourself, mate.'

'Sure. Thanks for the visit.' Saul looked after him thoughtfully as
Terry lumbered into the corridor.

Business with pleasure?

He picked up his phone and maximised the report he'd been
reading about a proposed park development out at Ruby Gap
Nature Park. It was time to call Max.

*

By the time Gemma visited later that afternoon, Saul had finished
reading the reports and was ready for company. Gemma looked
happier as she put a plastic bag on the end of the bed. 'Got all your
stuff.'

'Thanks, Gem. You didn't have any problems out there?'

She pulled the chair away from the wall and sat down beside
him. 'No.'

'How's Attila? Is he behaving?'

Her lips tilted in a smile. 'No. But he's a beautiful dog. I'm going
to go back out there again before dark because he stood at the gate
and howled when I left.'

'He hates being by himself.' He shook his head. 'Once I left work
and got back home in the middle of the day, and he was still crying
at the gate. I'd only been gone the morning.'

'Poor baby,' Gemma said. 'I think he's probably still howling
now. Once I was around the bend, I stopped the car and wound the
window down and I could hear him. He broke my heart.'

'Yeah, I hate him being upset too. I guess I'm a softie. That's why I want to get out of here as quick as I can.'

'It's a shame I can't take him home.' Gemma's brow wrinkled as she stared at him. 'It's the first time I've lived in an apartment.'

'Did you live with your mum on the east coast?'

'Oh, hell no. I rented a house in a small coastal town not far from the border. I picked up all my teaching work in a couple of schools. There's no way I could have lived with Mum. Plus, I can't stand her new partner.'

'Is that why you came back?'

She shrugged and shook her head. 'No, I always wanted to come home. Alice is home.'

Saul tipped his head to the side as an idea struck him. 'Maybe you could do me another favour.'

'What would that be?' Gemma sat up straighter.

'Would you feel comfortable staying out at the van for a few days until I'm discharged?' He rushed on. 'I mean, you don't have to. It's just a suggestion. You'd probably find it a bit lonely out there.'

'No lonelier than in a small apartment.' Gemma looked back at him. 'If you don't mind me staying in your van?'

'It's probably a bit cramped for you.'

'I'd be happy to. And Attila will be good company. He makes me laugh, he's such a character.' She looked past him to the door and he wondered what else was on her mind. 'I guess I should leave you in peace.'

'You don't have to,' he said hurriedly. 'It's bloody boring here.'

'How's your leg?'

'Since they took the drip out, the aching's ramped up a bit but I'll live. I'm due for some more painkillers soon.'

'I put your book in the bag so you'll have something to read.'

'Thank you. I've been doing some googling on the nature park. There was a development mooted a couple of years back but nothing came of it. And my boss called in before to visit me. He doesn't want me back until I can go back to full duties.'

Gemma looked down at his leg encased in plaster. 'That might be a while.'

'Yeah, but it'll give us time to do some investigating. Especially with you off work too.'

Gemma turned back to him; her face was pale. 'Don't you think we're wasting our time? Should I just accept that Ethan is dead, tell Mum and Dad, and move on?'

'Could you?' he asked quietly. 'I'm pretty sure I know you well enough, Gem, to know that you couldn't.'

'I'm not the same naive young girl I was back then, Saul.' He was surprised by the harshness in her voice.

'Maybe not, but some things don't change, and you'll want to know why and how, and see justice run its course. And I'm the same,' he said. 'If there was any foul play out there—and you have to remember that someone knows what happened—the police will need to be involved.'

Her hands twisted in her lap, and he wished she was closer to the bed so he could hold her hand again. 'But Ethan said not to trust anyone. Maybe we should talk to Mike again.'

'Do you think he'd tell us anything? And don't you even think about going out there by yourself,' he added. The thought of Gemma, out there alone . . .

'I wouldn't, Saul. I know how dangerous it is, and how all those things worried you. And no, probably not. He told me to stay away.'

'When I get out of here, we'll sit down and work out what we're going to do. In the meantime, you get yourself settled at the van—there's clean sheets in the top cupboard in the bathroom—and look after that mutt of mine. Make sure you padlock the gate too.'

Gemma didn't stay much longer and Saul was restless once she'd gone. He wasn't worried about Attila getting out, but if Gemma was out there by herself, he felt better knowing that the main gate was padlocked.

CHAPTER
31

Alice Springs
Wednesday, 10.00 am

While he was waiting to be discharged on Wednesday morning,
Saul called Max in Darwin and brought him up to speed with what
was going on. He told him what he'd seen out on the river and
about the shed in an enclosure in the middle of the park.

'Thanks. I'll keep an eye on things while you're off. And I'll look
into that helicopter activity. Take care of yourself, Saul.'

'Thanks, Max. I'll keep in touch.'

Saul could have jumped for joy—he probably would have if he
hadn't been on crutches—when he limped out of the hospital an
hour later, and spotted Gemma getting out of her small red sedan
in the pick-up area. There had been some discussion about which
vehicle she'd pick him up in. He was getting around fairly well; he

was surprised how quickly he'd got the hang of the crutches, but determination was a great motivator, and Saul was determined to heal as quickly as he could. He had to come back early next week and hopefully could move from crutches to a moon boot.

'Morning,' he said as Gemma walked around the back of the car and met him. He was pleased to see her smile was as wide as his.

'It's good to see you mobile.' She reached out and took the plastic bag he had looped over his arm.

'It's good to be outside, and on my feet—or one foot, anyway,' he said with a laugh. 'I think I would have gone stir-crazy if the doctor had made me stay in that bed one more day.'

Even though the hospital stay had been arduous, Gemma's daily visits had brought them closer. She'd taken his clothes and washed them, swapped his book over when he'd finished it, and kept him company for a couple of hours each afternoon. The awkwardness and hesitation had disappeared from their conversations, and the old lightness had come back into their relationship.

Not a relationship. They were friends. Even though he'd like to take it further, this wasn't the right time, but who knew what could happen down the track?

'It's good see you outside. I know someone else is pleased to see you.'

A loud bark had Saul turning back to the car, and he chuckled when Attila's head poked above the top of the slightly open back window.

'God, Gem, how did you ever get that hulking brute into the back of your little car?'

'He's not a brute, he's a big softie and he does everything I ask,' Gemma replied primly. 'He's been very well behaved while I've been at your place.'

Saul balanced on one crutch as he reached out and patted the top of Atilla's head. He looked down at the window with a grin. 'There's slobber on your window.'

She shrugged. 'It'll wash. He likes being in my car. We've had a few outings.'

'You should've taken my ute.'

She shook her head. 'It's easier to get him in the back seat of mine than up on the tray of your ute. I've tried, trust me. Now to get you in the car.'

By moving the front seat as far back as it would go, Saul was able to back into the front and swing his legs into the car one at a time. By the time Gemma was in the driver's side, he was settled and had his seatbelt on, and he was sweating and shaking. The broken ankle wasn't aching as much now he was in plaster, but the wound at the top of his thigh pulled like a bastard whenever he moved his leg.

Gemma looked at him with a frown. 'Are you sure you're well enough to come home? You're pale again.'

'Too bloody right I am. That's the last time I want to see that place for a while.'

'Don't you have to come back for physical therapy?' she asked as she started the car.

'No, the physio is in town. She gave me her details. Hopefully I'll get a moon boot next week. And I have to see the surgeon in his rooms in town about the wound and the stitches.'

'Good.'

'You look happy. I hope it's because I'm coming home.'

'I'm pleased you're better, and I'm pleased you're coming home. But I also have news.' Her fingers were tapping on the steering wheel with suppressed excitement.

'Good news?'

'I hope so. I haven't done anything about it because I wanted to see what you thought. It came from a friend who sort of did the wrong thing and I don't want to get her into trouble. Although I can't see how she will. And even though it might be a chance of finding the truth about Ethan's death, I feel good about having the lead. What do you think?'

Saul turned in his seat. Gemma's cheeks were pink and her eyes were glowing. 'Um, if I knew what you were excited about, I might be able to comment.'

'Oh, sorry. Atty, sit down,' she yelled over the back as she turned into the roundabout.

Saul couldn't help the chuckle that escaped as he looked into the back seat. 'Atty?'

'Yes. Attila's not a nice name for such a softie. And don't worry, he's secure, and strapped in. I made a harness, but he's such a lump, you can't see it. It's around his neck and one of his back legs. I hope you don't mind but I found some ties and clips in your shed.'

'I'm impressed. And of course, I don't mind. I told you to make yourself at home.'

'Don't worry, he can stand up, but he can't get in the front.'

'That's a relief. Now are you going to tell me this news?'

'It's confidential. Okay? My source, that is.'

'Not a problem. So tell me.' It was good to see her pink cheeks and hear the animation in her voice.

'My friend works in a government department in Darwin. She knows about Ethan—about him going missing, I mean—and I called her the other night, and asked her about any clues about how to find out where Screw could be. And she did better than that. She works on a database for itinerant workers, and would you believe he was on it? So she didn't have to hack into anything that would be tracked. It was a place she was allowed to be. Her own work files!'

'And?' Saul prompted.

'And she had two property addresses for him. One was as recent as last Christmas. Isn't that great?'

'Keep your eyes on the road,' Saul said as she looked at him to get his reaction. 'That light's about to turn red. And yes, it's good news. Very good. What will we do about it?'

'We?'

'Yes, we. Don't go getting any ideas about taking off by yourself. Until we know what happened, no one can be trusted. Remember what you decoded.'

Gemma nodded as she slowed to a stop. 'Yes. I've looked at it a dozen times since Mandy gave me the property names. What Ethan said about Screw doesn't make sense, does it?'

'I can't remember the exact words. Refresh my memory. Jesus, Gemma!' Saul grabbed the dash as Gemma planted the accelerator when the light turned green. 'Your driving hasn't improved.'

'Neither's your rudeness,' she retorted, but she was smiling. 'No police. Screw and I found it. Find Saul. Tell Saul. Trust Saul. Screw's gone.'

'That's right, it sounds like Screw was with him, but then Screw left.'

'If we can talk to him, he can tell us what they found, and that might give us some information about what happened. And where they were. How the Land Rover ended up in the river.'

'Where were the two properties?'

'That's the problem. One is Roselyon, where he went first six years ago, and the other more recent one I only have a name for, not an address. I've googled it but nothing comes up.'

Saul let go of the dashboard and folded his arms. 'Your friend didn't have an address? Maybe it was a made-up name.'

'No, she didn't, but she was going to keep trying to track it down. It's called *Kangaroo Corner*.'

'Hmm. Could be anywhere in Australia with a name like that, couldn't it?' Saul relaxed as Gemma indicated and they turned out of the southbound traffic and onto the Ross Highway. 'I've got some mates in Parks I can ask. I don't need to say why I need to know.'

'Sounds like a plan.'

Frustration filled Saul as Gemma stopped the car in front of his gate and climbed out to remove the chain. Having a gammy leg was going to be a total pain in the butt for the next few weeks. Even the small things he'd taken for granted were a chore now. He tried to push away the bad mood that was brewing as she got back in and drove through the gate, then got out and locked it again.

'Did you have a look at the new house?' he asked as she got back in.

'No. I thought that would be overstepping.'

Saul's temper blew. 'Jesus, Gemma. Overstepping? You're not some random housesitter.'

'No, I'm your friend and I was staying in your van,' she said serenely. 'I was here to look after Atty. And while I think of it, I've washed the sheets and put them back on the bed.'

'Thank you.' Saul kept his arms folded and looked at the distant mountains as she drove up the driveway.

*

After Gemma stopped behind the caravan, she got out without looking at Saul. She opened the back door on the driver's side and quickly released the two clips securing Atty in the back seat. 'You might as well have stayed home, sweetie. He barely talked to us,' she muttered under her breath.

She took Saul's keys from her pocket and marched around to the caravan. 'You come with me, Atty.' Before she unlocked the door of the caravan, she secured the dog to the wire run she'd made yesterday in anticipation of Saul's return.

'What's that for?'

She turned. Saul had followed her and was standing beside the van, propped on his crutches. 'It's so he can't knock you down. He's close enough for you to talk to him but he can't bound over and knock you over.'

'Thank you.' He sighed. 'And I'm sorry for being snappy. I've just realised how damn hard this is going to be.'

'I know it is.' She shook her head. 'I wondered if you should have been in such a hurry to get out of hospital.' Gemma walked across and stood beside him. The slump of Saul's shoulders broke her heart. 'That's why I've got a suggestion to make.'

She put one hand on his shoulder. His head lifted and the shadows beneath his eyes were dark. 'Yeah?'

'But before we talk, I think you need to get on your bed and have a bit of a rest. You're pale and sweaty.' She walked ahead of him and held the flap of the annexe up. 'Do you think you can get up the step?'

'Yes. That was one of the lessons the physio gave me in the last therapy session this morning.'

Gemma stood behind him and clipped the screen door back out of the way while he used the crutches to get up on the step. She held her breath as he teetered a little bit, ready to catch him if he fell, before he moved up the final step that took him inside the van. By the time she followed him inside, he'd taken the half dozen steps to the queen-sized bed at the back of the van, dropping crutches on the floor as he sat on the bed.

'What's that smell?' he asked. 'Something cooking?'

'I went to the apartment and brought my slow cooker over. I was going to suggest I come over some days and get a meal going for you, for when you get sick of the pre-packaged meals.'

'You were going to? What changed your mind? My grumpiness? I'm sorry.'

'No. And it's okay to be grumpy. I have a different suggestion. Seeing you here in the van, and with Atty—who I *was* going to come over and feed twice a day—has made me realise you can't be here by yourself. So, once you've had a rest and got yourself settled, I'll come back and set up the swag in the annexe and I'll sleep out there for a few nights. That way, if you need anything through the night, I'll be close by.'

'You don't have to,' he said gruffly.

'I know I don't have to. The bottom line is I'm responsible for your injury, and I want to help.' She dropped her gaze and moved away to the sink on the pretext of checking the slow cooker. 'I couldn't leave you here alone. I'd worry all day and night. And besides, it saves me driving backwards and forwards.' She gave him a sideways glance. 'And you know what an excellent driver I am. So you're stuck with me.'

She fiddled with the dial on the slow cooker, even though it didn't need changing, and waited for him to answer. After a couple of minutes when there was no response, she turned back to him. She froze, and looked away when she saw the look on his face. The way Saul had looked at her when they'd been a couple.

Naked longing.

The look that had had her falling into his arms, and eventually going away with him to Ormiston Gorge on that last weekend. She recognised it immediately because she knew that feeling so well.

Staying here was going to be hard. What she had to remember was that Saul had left her, and she wasn't going to risk her heart again. Her priority was getting him well, and then working together to find Screw.

After that, she'd decide what to do.

CHAPTER
32

Arltunga
1903

Rose sat on the hill at Joker Gorge, waiting for Bennett to finish work. At thirteen years of age, he was a big strapping lad and had gained employment in the Joker mine. Some days, she walked the three hundred yards from the Paddy's Rockhole Hotel, where she and Bennett had lived for the past ten years, to the mine site, to walk home with him. Despite his size and strength, Bennett was a sensitive soul and he was always solicitous of her wellbeing. She was very proud of the fine young man he was becoming.

Despite the constant letters from Amelia imploring them to come home to England, Rose and Bennett were settled at Arltunga. Her father had passed on, and Ashenden House had gone to his younger brother. Amelia and Edwin had a large family now, three boys and two girls, and Rose longed to meet them, as much as she longed to visit William's grave.

But Rose would never leave the red desert. She would not leave Rufus.

As she picked up her pencil and opened her diary, a black-footed rock wallaby looked at her curiously. Rose looked down at her clothes and smiled ruefully. Since moving to Arltunga, she had paid no heed to the conventions of society, and at first glance, anyone would have taken her for a man. Her face was tanned and wrinkled and the skin of her hands and arms was weathered and constantly covered with scratches. She'd learned to be satisfied with her own company, knowing her youngest son would leave her one day.

She'd worked in the gardens at the hotel and the public buildings in Arltunga since she and Bennett had moved here. It had not been an easy life. The drought of the early 1890s had seen many miners leave the area, and there had been a perpetual water shortage and Rose had soon learned what species of plants would thrive until the government had invested in sinking wells. In recent years, the increased water supply had meant that she could raise flowers from seed and the gardens around the stone buildings provided colour to the otherwise barren landscape. The large vegetable garden behind the Pearces' store gave her a good income from the miners purchasing their provisions at Arltunga.

In 1898, when the government battery and the cyanide works had begun crushing and treating the miners' ore, more prospectors came to the district and Rose's vegetable gardens doubled in size. Last year, things had looked grim when the boiler at the government battery burst, and ore could not be crushed for months, and the mining population decreased again.

Whenever she was outside, Rose coped with her situation, and she had learned to love the barren landscape that so many found inhospitable. It was home. When she was working in the fresh air, her thoughts calmed and she felt at peace.

She picked up her pencil and began to write.

Dear Amelia,

I am pleased to hear that your children are well and that Edwin has recovered from the injury he sustained at the South African war. All is well here at Arltunga, and Bennett is working at the gold mine. I have given your request that we come home and visit great consideration, and I am very appreciative that Edwin offered to pay for our berths.

I will be honest with you, dear sister. As much as I long to visit William's grave, I will not come home. I trust that you will occasionally visit his grave and leave him flowers. Talk to him for me. Tell him I am happy enough.

I am a different person to the sister you knew all those years ago. I worry that if I did come home, I would not want to return to the desert, and I cannot, I will not, leave Rufus here alone. His grave is lonely enough. I visit him each year, and travel is much easier now than it was when William and I made our journey to Ruby Gap.

Please give my love to Edwin and your family. It was wonderful to receive the photograph you sent to us and it is in pride of place in my room.

Your loving sister,

Rose

Rose was surprised when a fat tear plopped onto the paper. There was no other decision to be made.

She lifted her head and swallowed back her sadness, stood and patted her eyes with the sleeve of her work shirt as Bennett walked up the track.

He slipped his arm through hers and bent down to kiss her cheek. 'Hello, Mother.'

'Hello, my darling boy.'

CHAPTER
33

Alice Springs
Friday, 2.00 pm

'Worth a call, do you think?' Saul looked up at Gemma sitting across the table of the small dinette in the caravan. He'd spent most of the past two days inside the van because climbing up and down the two steps pulled at the wound on the top of his thigh. Painkillers helped him sleep at night, and he'd got used to Gemma being out there in the annexe and looking after Attila. There was a small bathroom in the side of his big shed, and she'd been using that while he'd used the small ensuite in the van.

Gemma only came inside to cook and to eat with him at night, and he was well aware of the distance she seemed to be trying to put between them.

'What did your mate say the property was called?' Gemma asked. Saul had managed to get a close match from one of his Parks mates in Darwin.

'Kangaroo Crossing. Just over the border in between Katherine and Victoria River.'

'On the way to Roselyon. It's probably worth a shot.' They'd had no luck with Kangaroo Corner.

'Do you mean worth a shot to call the property? I suppose even if Screw heard someone was asking after him, he's not going to take off,' Saul said.

'I disagree. Think about the tone of Ethan's warning. *He* sounded scared, and if Screw was involved in whatever it was, he might be watching his back. I mean, Pat said he hasn't been home since he left and barely stays in touch. An occasional Christmas card? That's not the Screw we knew.' Gemma had barely touched her meal. Saul had noticed how little she had eaten over the past two days. 'He knows something, and he's too scared to come back. Look how scary Mike was when we first met him. Who knows what else they came across out there?'

'True, Screw was everyone's mate, wasn't he?' Saul put his knife and fork together on the plate, reached across and put it on the sink opposite the table. 'Thank you, that was really good. When did you learn to cook so well?'

'When I was studying and couldn't afford to eat out every night.' She pushed the meat left on her plate to one side. 'I looked up some recipes online and discovered I enjoyed cooking. Mum never let us in the kitchen when we were kids. It was another part of her being a control freak.'

'Well, you've cooked us some great meals this week. I'm not much of a cook.'

'What do you usually do for meals?' She tipped her head to the side and a tendril of hair fell from the hair clip she always wore to hold her thick hair back.

'As much as I hate to admit it, I live on those pre-packaged meals you put in the freezer. A couple of times a week, I go to the Gidgeewalla Pub and have a steak and veggies.'

She rolled her eyes. 'That's terrible, Saul.'

Saul grinned. 'You're quite welcome to visit and cook a meal whenever you want to.'

'We'll see what happens when we both go back to work.' She lifted her hands, took out the clip and tucked in the recalcitrant strand of hair. Their eyes met and held.

'We've missed out on a lot of each other's lives, haven't we, Gem?'

'We have, but we're almost caught up now.' She stood up quickly and scraped the two plates before filling the small sink with hot water.

Saul suppressed a sigh. Every time he tried to turn the conversation to something personal, she managed to change the subject.

'Okay, so if we don't call the properties, what do you say about us driving up and paying them a visit?'

'Over to Western Australia?' She looked over her shoulder, incredulous. 'You with a broken leg, and your stitches?'

'I've got my check-up on Tuesday. Hopefully the stitches will come out then. My leg is healing really well; I've eased back on the painkillers too. You'd have to drive but we could take it over a few days.'

Gemma looked thoughtful. 'How far is it to Kangaroo Crossing?'

'About eleven hundred ks. And then another three hundred to Roselyon if we don't have any luck at the first property. I was thinking about a trip last night. How do you reckon you'd go towing the van?'

'I could,' she said slowly. 'I spent enough time in my teens towing the horse floats for Dad. I suppose it's not that much different.' He could see she was warming to the idea. 'And if we find Screw, he can't very well ignore us, can he? Not when we've gone so far to see him.'

He could quite easily ignore them, but Saul wasn't going to say that. 'And we're both on leave from work, so broken leg aside, this is the time to do it.'

Gemma's face brightened and she nodded. 'I like the idea. It means we're not sitting around waiting.'

'So, that's the plan?'

'What about Atty?' she asked. 'Could Rod have him?'

'I thought he could come too. We're not going through any national parks, and I've got a big cage to put on the back of the ute for him. He travels well when we drive up to Darwin.'

'Okay. I think that's a plan, then.'

'We'll have to do some shopping, get some stuff for the camping fridge. There's nowhere to shop between Katherine and the border.' He tapped his fingers on the table. 'Only problem is, we can't take fresh stuff over the border into WA, so we'll have to take some frozen meals too.'

Gemma's cheeky smile sent his blood pumping. 'If we're going on a road trip, there's no way we're taking any of those prepackaged meals. I'll have a big cook up before we leave and freeze some meals.'

'This could be—' Saul stopped. He'd been about to say this could be fun, but then remembered why they were going. His mate, Gemma's twin brother, was buried in a shallow grave and they were going away to try and find out what happened to him.

He pushed himself up from the table and reached for a tea towel. 'Do you want to watch some telly tonight? Maybe a comedy?'

Gemma looked surprised then her expression grew serious. She read him well. 'It's not a holiday, is it?'

'No, but maybe we can take a trip together another time. When all this is sorted.'

Happiness filled him as she held his gaze steadily. 'That does sound nice.'

Nice was a good start.

★

Gemma made a list of what groceries she needed to cook some meals for the trip and left Saul at the van on Sunday afternoon while she headed out to the supermarket. It was the first time she'd left the van—and Saul—since he'd come home from the hospital. The first day and night had been strange; they were in such close proximity, but that meant it was really easy for her to leave the swag in the annexe and give him his medication through the night. She was pleased she had her own bathroom. Sharing with Saul in the close confines of the van would have been too intimate.

At first, she'd been self-conscious working in the tiny kitchen area while he lay on the bed watching her, but after a few days, she'd got used to it. On Friday afternoon, when she was peeling some vegetables at the small sink, Saul had been quiet and when she'd taken a quick look across at him, she'd been surprised to see he'd drifted off to sleep. She'd looked her fill, trying to hold back the warmth that filled her as her eyes roamed his face—still strong and handsome in repose—and watched his chest rise and fall slowly as he slept.

The longer she was there, the harder it was to stay distant, but she was trying very hard to do that. Her feelings for him were still there, as strong as ever, but Gemma kept reminding herself that Saul had left her, and they'd moved on with their lives. She appreciated his help, and she would be forever grateful that he was the ranger who had discovered Ethan's vehicle, and that he had been willing to take her back out to Ruby Gap, but she had to stop these what-if thoughts. Thinking of the past was not going to change things.

She got her usual red light at the highway, and stared ahead as she thought of her twin. Ethan, who had been so full of life and hope · and joy; it was impossible for her to believe he was gone. Gemma still found it hard to accept that she hadn't known he was dead. It hadn't been the lack of contact that had reassured her. It had been the fact that she hadn't sensed something—a parting, a loss, or a dislocation of her life—the instant he had drawn his last breath.

A horn beeped behind her and she jumped as she noticed the green light ahead.

'Sorry,' she muttered as she waved to the driver behind, and drove onto the Stuart Highway and along to the supermarket a block away from the Todd Mall. After parking, she grabbed her bag and headed into the welcome air-conditioning of the supermarket.

These mundane chores of life helped her, and even the quest to find out Ethan's fate gave Gemma a renewed purpose. Usually, it was her teaching that kept her sane, but being at a school in the town so close to her past was a large part of the reason she hadn't felt up to going back yet. She was processing his loss all over again.

Gemma had lain in the swag and done a lot of thinking over the past few nights. A couple of times, when it had been too hot to go back to sleep after she'd taken Saul's painkillers and water into the van, she'd taken one of the chairs outside and sat with Atty.

She'd fallen in love with Saul's gorgeous boy. As she'd looked up at the stars, he'd laid his head in her lap, sensing she needed company. Looking up at the brilliant sky while caressing Atty's soft fur had soothed her, and Gemma knew that she would heal. Coming back to Alice had been the first step in that direction. But before that could happen, and she could come to terms with Ethan's loss, she had to know *why*. And *how*.

As she collected the trolley, she pulled out her shopping list and a pen to remind herself to get Atty some doggie treats. She couldn't help smiling as she looked at the note. Saul had obviously taken it from her bag when she was outside. He'd added some items to the bottom of the list; namely a block of chocolate, salt and vinegar chips—she shuddered—ice cream and an apple pie. At the bottom of the list, he'd taped his key card, and added his PIN to the note.

Gemma's spirits lightened as she pushed the trolley up and down the aisles. Half an hour later, she had just got back in the car, the shopping complete, when her phone rang. She glanced at the caller ID.

'Saul? Are you okay? You haven't fallen or anything, have you?'

'I'm fine. I just wanted to check that you did look at the shopping list. I thought you might be like me. I make a list and then don't look at it when I'm in the supermarket.'

'Don't worry, we have ice cream and apple pie and chocolate. But no salt and vinegar chips.'

'Excellent. I was worried you might chuck the list without seeing my card. It was probably a bit risky to put my pin number next to my card.'

'Yes, not a wise move. I didn't need your pin.'

'Gemma! I'll transfer it over to you.'

She smiled at his tone. 'No need. I split the bill. We went halves.'

'We'll talk about that when you get home. Are you on the way?'

'I'm going to swing by my place seeing I'm so close. I'll pack some stuff for our trip and I'll swap cars over.' She frowned. 'Do you think you'll be able to get up into your ute now? To go to the hospital on Tuesday?'

'I'll manage.'

'Okay, I'll do the car swap and I'll bring my backpack with the tin that we dug up. I forgot all about it after you went to hospital.'

'Okay. See you when you get back. And Gemma?'

'Yes?'

'Hurry back. It's too quiet here without you. We miss you.'

She couldn't help her smile as Saul disconnected.

CHAPTER
34

**Alice Springs
Sunday, 4.30 pm**

The first thing Gemma did when she let herself into the apartment was put her backpack on the kitchen bench, next to the car keys. As tempting as it was to open it and take a peek inside, she wanted Saul to be with her. Finding Ethan's grave, and then Saul's accident and rescue, had taken all her attention, and she hadn't given another thought to the tin they'd exhumed. GGG's letter, Ethan had said. She wondered who GGG was.

The air in the apartment was stale from being closed up, and Gemma opened the sliding door to the bedroom balcony. Dust motes hung in the last lingering rays of the sun as she packed her clothes into her duffel bag: long-sleeved shirts, T-shirts, shorts, socks. Her boots were still in the small laundry near the door. She ticked off the mental list before she went into the bathroom. Sunscreen, a new tube of moisturiser, soap, toothpaste.

Her hand hovered over the box of condoms she'd carried in her toiletries for the past few years. On the coast, there had been a few transient attractions, but no one had ever stirred her feelings as Saul had. If she'd ever had need of them—and it had been a very rare occasion that she had—Gemma always made sure she had the box on hand. Her fingers touched the top and then hesitated. She grinned; they'd probably be out of date, and she wasn't going down that track with Saul anyway. Besides, he had a broken leg. Even if things did turn in that direction, it would be difficult.

Gemma pushed that image from her mind, shook her head, and pushed the box to the back of the cupboard. She pulled a face at herself in the bathroom mirror, cross that she'd even considered packing them. Being with Saul constantly had made her so aware of him; she tried to ignore how her feelings for him had flared again.

Flared? They'd never gone away. The embers might have been cool, but they had stayed alight for six years. She closed the sliding door to the balcony with too much force, almost catching her fingers. Her head and her heart were in a mess. She needed to pull herself together; they had a goal, and once they'd found Screw and told Mum and Dad about the grave, her parents could decide what to do about telling the police. Maybe after that, she'd be in a place to see what she was going to do about Saul.

Gemma soon had her bag packed and she retrieved her boots from the laundry—still dusty from the weekend at Ruby Gap. As she picked up the backpack from the kitchen bench, it slipped from her grip and fell to the floor. The tin rattled; something inside must have dislodged. She picked it up, along with her duffel bag and boots, and headed down to the basement. It took a while to transfer the groceries to the ute then move her car back to her parking spot.

By the time she turned onto the highway, the shadows had lengthened. The mountains to the west morphed from red to blue as dusk descended and the western sky was a soft apricot. The traffic was heavy; there'd been an early season football game at Traeger Park and she got caught in a traffic jam just past the hospital. Horns blared and engines roared as the traffic ahead crawled, and Gemma closed her eyes, longing for the quiet of the bush. Saul's place was a haven and she'd got used to the serenity out there.

They'd fallen into a routine of Saul walking on his crutches around his land each afternoon. Poor Atty wasn't allowed to walk with them; although Saul was getting used to the crutches, the risk of the rambunctious dog knocking him over was too high. His howls had followed them up the driveway as they'd entered the house yard.

'It's going to be a lovely home,' Gemma had said, looking from the concrete floors to a large window looking out over the western ranges. 'You've done most of this yourself?'

Saul hadn't answered and when she'd turned around, he'd been watching her with a strange look on his face.

'Saul?'

'Sorry, what did you say?'

'I asked did you do most of this yourself?'

'Yeah, it's taken me a couple of years. I didn't get down here as much as I would have liked to when I was in Darwin.'

'And now your leg's going to hold you up. You'll curse the day you rescued me from that mad bull.'

'Never.'

She walked back across to him. 'What have you got left to do?'

'The kitchen goes in next week, then I have to paint through. I reckon I can do some of that when we get back. Then the floor coverings go down.'

'Would you let me help?' she'd asked hesitantly.

Saul's smile had been wide. 'I wouldn't say no to an offer like that.'

Once the traffic started moving again, Gemma glanced across at the cooler bag holding the frozen foods on the passenger seat and turned the air conditioner up. At the next red light, she considered ringing Saul to let him know she'd been held up, but the lights changed quickly, and the traffic started to move forward again.

Half an hour later as she turned off the Ross River Highway towards Saul's place, it was fully dark. As the headlights swept down the drive, she noticed a dark figure standing at his gate. Gemma frowned as she slowed the ute, wondering who it was; there was no car parked on the road outside. Reluctant to get out in the dark, she hesitated then moved the ute closer. The figure moved and relief—then anger—surfaced as she saw the jerky gait and the metal crutches glinting in the headlights.

Jumping out of the ute, she glared at Saul as he swung the gate open so she could drive through.

'Stay there, I've got the gate,' he called over.

'What the hell are you doing?' she demanded.

'I'm getting the gate for you. Where have you been?' His voice was as tight as hers. 'I was worried.'

'I told you I was going to go back to my place after I shopped. Why on earth did you walk all the way down to the gate? You could have fallen over. And you would have been here all by yourself!'

'I thought it would save you time. Plus, I have to get back to normal some time. Lying around on the bed all day won't help me get better.'

'Did you forget you've got a dozen stitches in your thigh and a leg in plaster?'

'No, I didn't.'

'You wait there and when I bring the ute through, I'll get out and lock the gate. Then we'll try and get you in without doing any damage.'

'Yes, ma'am,' he returned sarcastically.

'Don't be smart. It was a stupid thing to do, Saul.' Muttering under her breath, Gemma hurried back to the ute and put the cooler bag, her handbag and the backpack behind the passenger seat. The bags of groceries were in the crate on the back of the ute tray. She climbed up and drove through the gate, and to her surprise Saul was waiting where she'd told him to. She secured the gate and opened the passenger door for him, then watched as he came across on his crutches. He had learned to get around pretty well over the past few days, and could move quickly now.

'Okay, how are we going to do this?' she asked, keeping her tone even.

'You hold the crutches and I'll use my arms to swing myself up.' He was wearing a black singlet with his shorts; Gemma found it hard to look away as Saul put his back to the seat, and then pushed off on his good leg. His biceps were taut and firm as his arms took most of his body weight, and it was only seconds before he'd swung both legs into the ute and sat there with a satisfied smile.

Gemma couldn't help smiling back at him as she started the car. 'Very well done. I guess you were right. I'm sorry I snapped.'

'I'm sorry too, but I was worried. I guess we're both on edge.'

'I was late because there was a football game, and the traffic was awful.'

'Were you able to get everything on the list, and your stuff for the trip?'

'I did.'

Gemma put the headlights on high beam; there'd been a lot of kangaroos around the past few mornings as she'd walked over to the shed. Saul turned to look at her as the ute climbed the slight incline to the house yard and the caravan. She couldn't believe he'd come down that hill on his crutches. A shiver ran down her back as she thought of him falling and doing more damage to his leg.

'Gem?' She glanced across at him and waited. 'I've been thinking about the trip. Are you going to tell anyone we're going to WA?'

She thought about it for a moment. 'Sort of doesn't seem right to be travelling when we're both on sick leave, does it? If we don't say why—and I really don't want to—it looks like we're taking a holiday. It doesn't look like the right thing to do, does it?'

'Probably not, but I know how you always were about doing the right thing.'

Gemma flicked him a glance. 'And you.' She thought for a moment. 'I've avoided calling Mum this week, and being Sunday, she'll probably call tonight. I might send her a chatty text to keep her happy. Tell her I'm busy. She doesn't have to know what I'm busy doing. How long do you think we'll be away?'

'Around a week, depending on where—or if—we find Screw. And then, I guess it depends on what he has to say. I was thinking I'd give Julie a call and let her know I'll be away for a few days. Rod should get back while we're gone, and I'll let Julie know that it'll only be for a week or so, and that I'm taking Atty with me. I won't say where I'm going.'

'Yeah, being the parents of one of my students, I'd prefer they didn't know I was going with you.'

'As long as they don't think Atty's home alone.'

Gemma grinned, conscious of Saul's eyes on her as she pulled the ute to a stop. 'So, he's Atty now, is he?'

'I give in.'

'Good.' She chuckled. 'Now you stay there and I'll come around and help you down.'

Gemma reached for the cooler bag and closed the driver's side door and made her way around to his side. Saul was obedient and sat there waiting for her to come around and open the door for him.

'You ready?' She stood there, and slipped the cooler bag over her shoulder before she took the crutches he passed to her. Resting them against the side of the ute, she waited for him to turn to the side and lower his legs. One brown muscled leg and one plastered from the knee to his foot.

'I am.'

'Be careful. Do you want me to take your hand or step back out of your way?'

'I'll get my good leg onto the ground first, and then if you can take my hands, that'll help me balance.'

Gemma stood close as Saul half turned and slowly lowered his left leg to the grass. She held her hands out and waited close by until his hands reached for hers.

'Bloody awkward,' he muttered. He gripped her hands as he swung his plastered leg out of the ute. She hung on tight and took a step closer when he stumbled slightly. Finally, he was standing in front of her, his breathing loud. He took a deep breath and then let out a shaky sigh.

'You did it.'

'Well, I'm down in one piece, anyway.'

Gemma let go of his hands, but Saul didn't move away. He ran his hands along her arms and placed them loosely around her back.

She stayed where she was. 'Are you right now?' she asked, looking up at him. The moon was climbing and cast a bright glow around them, but his eyes were shadowed.

His voice was quiet. 'Maybe we could stay like this for a while? What do you think?' His head was close to hers and his breath was warm on her face. Contentment tempered with hesitation held Gemma in a tenuous grip. Saul's arms holding her felt good . . . too good. She stood perfectly still in his embrace.

'Gemma?'

His soft voice caressed the air. Oh, how she loved hearing him say her name. She looked up and found herself staring at Saul's lips. Hesitation gripped her again.

'Yes?' she whispered.

'Would it be okay . . . would you mind . . . if I kissed you?'

Gemma held her breath, her body taut in his arms. Her hands moved up to his shoulders, hard and muscled, much more so than her memories of the twenty-year-old young man she had once held close. Saul's eyes moved to hers and he moved one arm away. For a moment she thought he was going to let her go and a small, involuntary whimper left her lips.

'No,' she whispered.

'No, I can't kiss you?' His hand moved to her face and he ran his thumb over her bottom lip.

'No. I mean, no, don't let me go.' Her voice shook. 'I like you holding me.'

With a stifled groan, Saul lowered his head and took her lips in a single breath. Gemma opened her mouth to him and a shaft of desire shuddered though her body. She hadn't felt like this for a long time.

Six long years, to be exact.

Giving herself up to the moment, Gemma revelled in the feel of Saul's arms around her and his lips on hers. The feel of his skin, the warmth of his body, and the fresh soap smell that was always a part of him overwhelmed her senses, making it hard to think straight.

This was real, not in her imagination or dreams as his kisses had been so many times since he'd left her.

He'd left her. Left her with no explanation a few days after they spent the weekend together at Ormiston Gorge. Got her into bed then took off. She stiffened in his hold, and Saul lifted his head.

'What is it?'

'No, Saul.' She tried to step back but his arms held her close. 'I won't be hurt again. I've learned to stand on my own two feet these days.'

He rested his forehead on hers. 'Gemma, the last thing I want to do is hurt you. Or leave you. It's taken me a long time to come to terms with it, and I know now I shouldn't have listened to Ethan.'

She paused. 'What do you mean listened to Ethan?'

'He told me to piss off and leave you alone. On top of what you said to me that night, it just cemented my belief that I wasn't right for you. I was just a boy from the wrong side of the tracks.'

'No.' Distress took hold and she gripped Saul's shoulders with both hands. 'I never meant that. I never meant you to think that. And what did Ethan have to do with it? Is that what you meant that night in the hospital when you said he gave you a black eye?' Gemma hitched a breath as she realised that Saul had thought she'd meant he wasn't good enough for her. If only she could take back the words she'd said that night. She'd been trying to tell him he was smart enough to achieve anything he wanted to.

'Ethan told me a few home truths. The night you told me I needed to make something of myself. He'd found out you were seeing me and you hadn't told him. Screw told him everything about us.'

'Screw? What did he know? Told him everything what?' Her voice was a little bit calmer. 'Did you tell Screw about our weekend at Ormiston Gorge?'

'No, but somehow he'd found out, and told Ethan that we'd been seeing each other and that we'd been away together. Ethan went ballistic. I was too old for you, I wasn't good enough for *his* sister. He knew that, and I knew that.' Saul's eyes glinted in the moonlight as he stared at her. 'I got over it. We're both grown up and we're different people now, so forget all about that time. We're here to focus on finding Ethan. I shouldn't have kissed you.' He lowered his arms and took a jerky step back, knocking one of his crutches to the ground.

'What he said was stupid. And you took what I said the wrong way.'

'Ethan was just worried about you making a mistake. What you said that night gave me the push. Like you said, I needed to make something of myself.'

'You didn't need that, Saul. You always had dreams.'

'I did, but it took me a long time to believe in myself. That's why I went to uni, to prove to you—and your family—that I was worthy of you. That's why I've worked so hard. Even though I knew you'd left and made your own life, I wanted to build a home that would be up to your standards. Up to your family's standards.'

Gemma shook her head, thinking of the years they'd wasted. 'That's so stupid. We were nothing special.'

'What's done is done.' Saul put one hand on the ute. 'Come inside. It's crazy standing out here in the dark, rehashing the past.'

'And you shouldn't be standing for so long.' Gemma moved away from him and he reached for the one crutch leaning against the ute. She bent down and retrieved the other one. 'I have to put the cold stuff in the fridge.'

'I'll help you as best I can, and then we'll talk.' Saul lifted his hand to cup her cheek. 'Okay?'

'Okay.'

CHAPTER
35

Alice Springs
Sunday, 6.30 pm

'Are you hungry?' Gemma held up a round packet of pizza bases. 'I bought these and some stuff to put on them.'

Saul had moved the chair in the annexe close to the freezer and he was putting the frozen stuff away as Gemma unpacked. Her voice was bright and she kept smiling at him, but he'd seen the distress in her eyes when they'd been outside. Saul wondered if he had brought all of this to a head with his kiss; he should have resisted and waited until they'd sorted out this mess with Ethan's grave.

But he hadn't been able to help himself, and he didn't regret kissing Gemma.

At least she hadn't told him to take a leap.

'Whatever's easiest. It wouldn't bother me just to have a cuppa, I'm not really hungry.'

Her head flew up and she frowned at him. 'Is your leg okay? You haven't overdone it, have you? You haven't got a temperature?'

He suppressed a smile at her fussing. 'No, my leg's fine. But I'd like to talk some more. I don't want there to be any misunderstanding between us. How about we sit outside tonight?'

'Okay, once this is all away, I'll put the kettle on. Maybe some cheese on toast?'

He waved his hand as he closed the lid of the freezer and sat at the outside table. 'Whatever you feel like.'

Gemma went into the van with the last two grocery bags. He heard her fill the coffee machine and then the switch clicked on, followed by the sound of drawers opening and closing as she put the shopping away.

Was he making a stupid mistake? Was his timing wrong?

Saul put his head back against the van and closed his eyes. He had to think about what he was going to say to Gemma. How could he convince her that he loved her? That he wanted her to be a part of his life. It was a huge step for him; needing someone, wanting someone so badly it hurt. Apart from those few months when he and Gemma had been together, Saul had never depended on anyone else for his happiness. Not that there'd ever been a lot of that when he was growing up.

He'd never stopped loving her, and everything he'd done over the last six years had been done with Gemma in mind. Was this the right time or would he simply scare her off?

Even though he hadn't known where she was or what she was doing, whether she had a partner and a family, Gemma had always been his motivation. That moment he'd walked into the school last week and seen her for the first time, every minute of the last six

years had been worthwhile: the study, working two jobs and set-
tling into the career he had come to love. He'd tried to kid himself
that he wasn't for her, but the more time they spent together, he
could see how quickly Gemma had come to trust him, and the
harder he was going to try to convince her he still loved her.

At least she was talking to him.

The aroma of grilling cheese and brewing coffee drifted from
the van.

He called out. 'That smells good, and yes please, some for me
too.'

'I've already cooked enough for both of us.'

The screen door opened and Gemma stepped down with a tray
loaded with two plates of toast, two mugs of coffee and a bowl of
chopped fruit.

'Be careful, Gem.' Saul watched as she sat opposite him, and he
smiled. 'I could get used to this. You know the old saying, don't
you?'

She tipped her head to the side. 'And what would that be?'

'The way to a man's heart . . .'

Gemma propped her chin in her hand. 'Time for honesty, Saul?'

The way she was looking at him filled him with trepidation. Did
he really want to say this now?

No guts, no glory.

'I'd like to finish our conversation. I've been sitting out here trying to decide whether to let it go until after we find Screw, but the
truth is—'

Gemma held her other hand up. 'But the truth is, we're going to
be in close proximity for another week or more and it's going to be
awkward if we hedge around how we feel, and what we think? And
what we both want. I think it's time we were both honest with each
other, Saul. If what I have to say upsets you or embarrasses you, so

be it. Honesty and clearing the air is going to make for a much better road trip.'

Or a worse one.

A sweat broke out on the back of his neck, as he worried what
she wanted to be honest about. 'So, who goes first?'

'I will. If what I say bothers you too much, we'll pull the pin on
the trip.' She reached across the table and took his hand. 'I'm very
pleased you kissed me because it makes it easier for me to tell you the
truth. Losing Ethan has taught me life's too uncertain to stuff around.
You broke the proverbial ice. I've been inside trying to convince
myself that I can't do this, but then I think about not seeing you again
after we solve the mystery of Ethan, and I know I'm wrong.' She took
a deep breath. 'The night when you came out of theatre, and you
asked me to kiss you goodnight, I knew I still . . . I still had feelings
for you, Saul. Even before that . . . when the helicopter took you
away, I realised I still cared about you, and that nothing had changed.
Actually, it has changed; we were younger then and now I know
what really matters. What I want. When you left me, you broke my
heart, and then when Ethan, the other half of me, disappeared, I had
no one. I've made sure I was self-sufficient since then, relying on no
one, because everyone in my life always let me down. I thought I'd
be safer not relying on anyone. Dad took off, and Mum drives me
crazy, but when you asked me to kiss you—'

'Gemma, stop right now. Stop beating yourself up,' Saul said.
'I've never stopped caring about you. It's just taken me a long time
to sort myself out. I loved you then, and I've never stopped, and
there's not been one day when I haven't thought of you and wondered where you were, and what you were doing.' Saul put his
other hand on top of hers. 'If it wasn't for this blasted leg, I'd be on
my feet and showing you how much right now.'

'If it wasn't for that blasted leg, I'd be at my place and we wouldn't
be having this conversation.'

'Don't you doubt it.' He grinned. 'It was fate. The best part is that you've moved back home.' He lifted her hand and brought it to his lips. 'I was sure you'd have a new life. The last thing I expected was to see you come home.'

'It's my home, and where my heart's always been.' Gemma's smile was cheeky and Saul thought his heart would burst with happiness. 'And Saul Pearce, I want you to get better as fast as you can, because that plaster cast is going to make other things quite difficult too.'

He grinned back. 'The doc said when the stitches are out, he'll probably look at a moon boot. I can take it off to sleep.'

'I like the sound of that.'

'What gave me hope this week was how quickly you trusted me,' Saul said. 'I know how hard it's been for you, with what we found—'

'Oh no!' Gemma dropped his hand and jumped to her feet. 'God, I've done it again.'

Saul grabbed the edge of the table as Gemma lunged for her chair before it hit the mat. 'What's wrong? Done what?'

'The tin in my backpack. The one you dug up at the ruins. I keep forgetting about it. We haven't opened it yet and read that letter Ethan mentioned. It's still behind the seat in your ute.'

'Damn, I forgot too. You'd better get it.'

'Wait here,' she said, moving around to his side of the table. 'But first . . .' Saul closed his eyes as Gemma bent down, cupped his cheeks in her hands and pressed her mouth to his. The warmth of her lips eased the pain in his heart and he hoped that he could do the same for her.

★

Gemma's heart was light as she went out to the ute. She stopped at the dog run and crouched down, whispering to Atty, 'Things are looking up, Atty. Your master loves me too.' She ruffled his fur and scratched his tummy. 'Do you want a run before you go to bed for the night?'

He barked once and she grinned. 'I guess that's a yes. Hang on for a minute.' She stood up and hurried back to the annexe. 'Saul, I'm just letting Atty off for a while, so be prepared for a visitor.'

'Okay, thanks for the warning. And hurry up, I'm missing you already.'

Gemma smiled as she undid Atty's leash and headed for the ute. As expected, he bounded into the annexe, barking. Walking across to the ute, she opened the door and took her handbag and backpack from behind the passenger seat. Something rattled inside the tin as she lifted the bag, and she shook her head, realising how much had been on her mind. As she walked back to the caravan, she unzipped the bag and took it out. The red dirt came off on her fingers.

Holding it carefully in one hand, she held the door of the annexe open. 'Do you want me to put Atty back outside?'

'No, he's fine.'

'He's not on your foot, is he?'

'No, he obviously knows which is your chair, because he's curled up between that and the freezer.'

Gemma walked in slowly and put the dirt-encrusted tin on the table. 'Maybe I should wet a cloth and wipe it down first?'

Saul reached over and ran his hands over the outside. 'A good idea. If there's a letter or something in there, we don't want to risk getting it dirty.'

'It rattles too.' Gemma went into the van and came out with a damp sponge and a tea towel.

Saul held his hand out and she passed him the cloth. She pulled her chair back a bit to give Atty more room then sat down and watched as Saul carefully wiped the red dirt and rust from the tin. The sponge was soon completely red.

Gemma's fingers tingled with anticipation as a pattern began to appear on the outside. The rust had taken some of it off, but the outline of two children leaning against a pole began to appear.

'Look, it's a monkey sitting on a post,' Saul said.

'And in the background are church spires.' Gemma leaned forward. 'And the kids are in old-fashioned clothes. It looks like an English scene. It's not like anything that we would have had around at home for Ethan to bury. It looks really old, doesn't it? It might be an original tin from when my ancestors lived at the homestead, do you think?'

'Could be. But we know Ethan saw it. He had to have, to tell us where it was buried. Can you go back into the kitchen and get a narrow-bladed knife for me, please? I don't want to damage the tin.'

Atty snuffled as Gemma pushed her chair back. She rummaged through the utensil drawer until she found an old blunt butter knife.

Saul was looking down at the top of the tin when she came back and put the knife on the table beside him. 'The lid's really secure. I don't like our chances of getting it open without damaging it.'

Gemma shrugged. 'It's what's inside that's important, so do whatever you have to.'

'Okay. Here goes.'

Saul's forehead creased in a frown as he slipped the knife under the edge of the lid and carefully worked his way around the hexagonal shape. Gemma didn't speak; she could see the concentration in his expression. His lips were pursed and he didn't take his eyes off the tin as he slid the knife around.

'One more time around might do it. I think it's a bit looser.'

Gemma couldn't stand it anymore. She stood and moved around to Saul's side of the table and put her hand on his shoulder as she looked down at the top of the tin. The lid had the remains of a red and gold braided pattern around the six sides. 'God, the suspense is killing me.'

Saul looked up and his smile sent warmth spiralling through her. 'Almost there.'

She held her breath as the lid scraped up the side of the tin.

'I think I've got it.' As Saul spoke, the lid came off in his hand. He put it carefully on the table and Gemma leaned over. 'Do you want to do the honours?' he asked.

'No. I'm shaking too much.' She wrinkled her nose. 'What's that smell?'

'Linseed oil.' Saul carefully laid the tin on its side and slid his hand inside. 'Whatever is in there is wrapped in an oilcloth.'

'An oilcloth?'

'This is an original tin from way back. In those days, oilcloths were used to keep things waterproof.'

Saul carefully slid out a tan-coloured piece of cloth folded into a pouch. Gemma could see it was brittle and cracked. 'Be careful,' she whispered.

'Parts of the cloth have stuck together. The heat would do that to the oilskin.'

'Would it have got hot buried, in the dirt?' Gemma wondered aloud.

'Maybe not when the post was there to provide some shade. The earth would have been cooler. It's obviously got hot since the posts were washed away and that corner was in the sun most of the day.'

'We were lucky it was still there after the flood.'

Saul began to unfold the brittle cloth. 'There's paper in there.'

Gemma held her breath. 'I wonder what was rattling in the tin? He didn't mention anything else.'

'You have a look inside while I work on this.'

She reached over and carefully picked up the tin and looked inside. The rattle was louder now that the oilcloth pouch had been removed. 'There's a small leather bag in there.' She carefully removed it. 'It's got a leather tie but it's come undone, and something's fallen out in the tin. It's too dark to see.'

Gemma put the small bag on the table and started to gently tip the tin up and put her hand beneath it. She paused when Saul spoke.

'This is a letter, Gem. I can make out most of the words. It's signed by someone called William, not a GGG.'

'William Woodford,' she breathed. 'GGG could be Ethan's abbreviation of "great-great-grandfather". The ancestor who left his wife and children out here.'

Saul looked up at her. 'I don't think he left them deliberately. And I know what's in that leather bag.'

Gemma turned her attention back to the tin and tipped it up slowly. Two cold and heavy brilliant red stones fell into her open palm.

'So do I,' she said, her eyes wide.

CHAPTER
36

Ruby Gap
September 1928

For thirty-six years, on the anniversary of Rufus's death, Rose had left Arltunga alone on horseback. Drought or flood, every year, she travelled back to Ruby Gap.

The riverfront shanties had rotted away, the claims had disappeared, and there was no sign left of the hamlet that had existed there in the 1890s.

Further away from the river, the bush had encroached on the house William had built for them. Although abandoned, the structure still provided enough shelter for Rose to stay overnight.

Rose would spend the afternoon hours tending to Rufus's grave and talking to William, as though he was still there, listening to her.

'Oh, William!' Today, her voice held rare animation. In three days, she would leave Arltunga. For the past five years, Bennett had been trying to persuade her to move to the fast-growing township of Stuart, and she had finally agreed.

'The lily of the valley has finally flowered.' She sat at the head of the grave and gently touched the white spring bells sitting in the middle of bold green foliage that surrounded the cross. '*Convallaria majalis.*' Rose repeated the Latin name that Mr Marley, the grounds-keeper from Father's estate, had taught her so long ago. 'He told me they would survive in the dry shade and poor soil.'

Her life in England seemed like a dream now, as did the loss of Rufus, followed so swiftly by the news that William would never return.

'It was so long ago, William, and I was so unsure of you, but I should not have doubted, should I? You were a loving husband, and a fine father to our boys.' She looked down, surprised at the tear that plopped onto the dark leaves. She hadn't cried for many years. As a light breeze moved the flowers gently, a sweet fragrance filled the air and filled her with peace.

Rose sat in the shade as the sun moved across the sky, and when it disappeared behind the red cliffs to the west, she touched her fingers to her lips and pressed them to the earth of her son's grave.

'Goodbye, my darling boy. I will join you one day.' She pushed herself to her feet and slowly made her way to the house. Picking up the small spade and tin she had left on the step, Rose entered the dim coolness of the old homestead. She had wrapped William's rubies in an oilcloth and placed them in the biscuit tin that Rufus and Bennett had both loved so much.

'Look, Mama,' Rufus had said. 'It's me and Bennett.'

'Bennett and I,' Rose had corrected gently, smiling as she always did at their excitement. The biscuits had always been kept in that tin, the one Amelia had sent at Christmas one year.

'Look, it's a monkey sitting on a post,' Rufus had squealed, and Bennett had giggled.

'Monkey and me,' her baby had said.

It was almost dark by the time Rose finished digging the hole. Perspiration mingled with her tears. Again, she pressed her fingers to her lips. 'Goodbye, William. Wait for me.'

She placed the tin in the hole and used the spade to push the loose dirt over it. Clods of earth fell onto the lid with a thud, as they would have on William's coffin. Darkness fell as Rose lifted the flat stone into place.

This was her final farewell. She would not come here again.

CHAPTER
37

Alice Springs
Tuesday, 11.00 am

Two days later, Saul's stitches had been removed and the plaster cast had been replaced with a moon boot. He was getting used to walking in the moon boot with one crutch, learning to put his weight on his heel. He had getting in and out of the ute down pat. With the moon boot on his right leg, he reckoned he could even do some of the driving, but he hadn't broached that with Gemma yet. He didn't want to upset her; the last two days together had been good.

When Gemma wasn't in the kitchen, cooking up meals to freeze for their trip, she was researching the discovery of rubies at Ruby Gap in 1886.

Late on Tuesday morning, Saul limped into the annexe where Gemma was staring at her computer. 'Find anything new?' he asked. He leaned down and looked over her shoulder, happy when she reached up and took his hand. He'd been worried about her since they'd read William's letter together on Sunday night.

'No. I've found a stack of articles and primary documents online but nothing to hold up what William said in his letter. Listen to this.' She put one finger on the screen and read it out to him. 'This is what I've found everywhere: "In 1886, explorer David Lindsay found what he thought were rubies in the sandy bed of the Hale River. Many fossickers came to the area and sold their gems to buyers from Europe. The market was flooded and the quality of the rubies found was questioned. Two years later, when the gems were assayed in London, it was discovered that the gems were not rubies, but only high-grade garnets."'

Saul frowned. 'Read that bit from his letter again?'

Gemma carefully picked up the page that was on the table next to her computer and read it out.

Rose, I was right. Imagine his surprise when our rubies were definitively proved to be genuine. In addition, a further test was carried out, and our rubies were tested at a high temperature, and they took on the green hue of a genuine stone, and then regained their original colour on cooling. Mr Nock and I attended the testing, and he turned to me, and shook my hand. He was delighted that I persisted in my quest, and came to England to pursue the truth.

'So, his letter and the two rubies in the tin—'

'*If* they are rubies.'

'We can find out for sure when we get back from the trip.'

When Gemma looked up at him, her eyes gleamed with tears. 'But if this letter is the truth, and there really is a seam of rubies at Ruby Gap, it means that Ethan was always right.'

Saul nodded. 'And it also means that there was some shonky stuff happening back in London in the late 1880s, and that William found out the truth. And the history as recorded is false.' Saul had thought a lot about the construction works he'd seen at the river when they were out there, and now wondered if they had anything to do with a seam of precious gems.

He shook his head. 'It seems a really big leap, doesn't it? I mean, we're talking almost a hundred and fifty years since the stones were found to be garnets. And now six years after Ethan went missing, there could be mining happening out there. In a nature park where no mining is allowed? It's all a bit far-fetched.'

'Ethan leaving all that coded stuff for me and directing me to the letter and the two gems really convinces me that his death had something to do with that. Maybe he didn't die when Ruby went over the cliff. What if he read the letter and told someone about the rubies? Someone out there who . . . who . . .'

Saul put his hands on her shoulders and when she turned around to look at him, he could see the tears in her eyes. 'I know what you're saying, Gem. It's a possibility we have to face. I've been thinking about Mike and wondering what he knows and why he wanted to scare you, telling you not to come back out there. If we don't find Screw, I think Mike will get a visit from us.' Saul stared past her. He'd become more worried by the day as he'd thought about the letter and the rubies. When they told Gemma's parents about the grave—and he was sure the police would eventually be involved— Saul had no doubt that Ethan's body would be exhumed to discover the cause of his death, but he wasn't going to go there now.

With a frown, he rubbed the back of his neck. Maybe they had taken too much on, and it was time to report the discovery of Ethan's grave to the authorities. He stared at Gemma as she yawned and stretched her arms above her head. If he suggested that, she was just as likely to take off and go looking by herself. Even though they had cleared the air the other night and admitted their feelings to each other, sometimes she retreated a little from him. She'd leaned into him when he'd held her, but she hadn't initiated anything physical between them. Saul was giving her some space, something that was going to be difficult to do once they set off in the caravan tomorrow.

No annexe, no swag, one bathroom. One bed.

'The other thing I want to know is where and how Ethan found the tin,' Gemma said. 'Was it buried here all the time or did he find it somewhere else and bury it?'

Saul stood behind Gemma and put his hands on her shoulders, and began to lightly knead her tight muscles. 'There's no point second-guessing, Gem. We could go round and round in circles.'

'It's doing my head in,' she sighed. She reached up and put her hands on his. 'And I'm sorry. I know I've been a bit hard to talk to the last couple of days.'

'I understand. Why don't you pack up the computer and we'll start planning what we're going to do?' He was surprised when she closed the laptop without even shutting down.

'You're right. It's not getting us anywhere. So, we're still leaving tomorrow? Are you right to head off? Did you ask the doctor?'

'He said I could put as much weight as I could bear on my foot, and trust my body to tell me what I could do.'

She shook her head. 'So . . . that's a no?'

'That's a yes, I'm healing enough to go on a road trip. As long as you're right to drive.'

She nodded. 'I am.'

'Then there's one more thing we need to talk about.'

'Yes?' She turned back to look up at him.

'Sleeping arrangements. I can't sleep in the swag on the ground because there's no way I'll be able to get up and down with this blasted moon boot. And there's no way you're going to sleep out in the swag. Some of the areas we're going to travel through and overnight at are pretty remote and wild.'

Gemma stood and turned to face him. He was surprised when she looped her arms around his neck. 'The doctor said you could trust your body to tell you what you could do?' Her expression was coy.

'Yes,' he said slowly as she held his gaze.

'Is your body up to sharing your bed with me?'

Saul smiled at her as his blood thrummed through his body. 'Maybe . . . we should go inside and see how we fit on the bed?'

Gemma stepped out of his arms and crossed the annexe to the caravan door. She opened the door and waited for him to step up. 'I think that sounds like an excellent idea.'

★

Two hours later, Gemma's stomach gave out a huge grumble.

Saul was leaning on one elbow, looking at her in a way she never thought anyone would ever look at her. It turned out she hadn't needed to pack that box in her bathroom cupboard; Saul had been well prepared.

She smiled up at him as he twirled her hair with the fingers of his other hand.

'Hungry?' he asked.

'I think I need to eat. I've used up all my energy,' she said saucily. 'It was a very good idea of yours to see if we fit on the bed. I had no idea it would be so . . . energetic.'

Saul ran his hand down to her bare stomach, and then back up to curve around her breast. 'You're beautiful, Gem. Your skin is like silk.'

A warm shiver ran down her back and those butterflies began to flutter in her lower belly again. 'You're not so bad yourself. For a man who's incapacitated, I was very impressed.' She giggled when his fingers tweaked her nipple.

'Don't be cheeky.'

'You even look sexy with that boot on.' Gemma sat up and lifted her hair from her neck. Even with the air conditioner on in the van, it was hot. 'Seriously, though. Is your ankle okay?'

'It's fine. I didn't put any weight on it at all.'

'So I guess we've solved the bed problem?'

'It appears so.' Her stomach muscles contracted as Saul lay back and smiled at her. 'Unless you think we need to try one more time? Just to make sure?'

Her stomach gurgled again. 'I think I need to eat.' She swung her legs over the edge of the bed. 'Can I use your shower in the van?'

'Of course you can.'

Gemma looked over her shoulder and gave a sexy little sashay as she walked to the other end of the van and opened the sliding door. Saul's groan widened her smile as she turned on the shower and stood under the cool water.

Two weeks ago, she hadn't even known that Saul was in Alice Springs. Today, she had spent the afternoon with him in his bed.

Even though the next week was going to be tough, it would be easier with Saul by her side. And no matter what happened, knowing he loved her would help her through it.

When she was done, she turned the taps off and opened the door. Saul stood there, wearing nothing but his moon boot, holding out a clean towel for her to step into.

He wrapped it around her, dropped a kiss on her cheek and stepped into the shower.

Gemma wrapped the towel around herself and waited.

'Shit, I forgot the bloody moon boot.'

CHAPTER
38

Alice Springs
Wednesday, 9.30 am

Getting organised to head off on the first five-hundred-kilometre leg of the trip had sounded easy enough to Gemma, but she'd underestimated the time it would take to get the van ready. It hadn't helped that they'd both slept late on Wednesday morning—an early start had been planned but it had been well after one by the time they'd gone to sleep.

Taking the annexe down was a learning experience as Saul wouldn't let her help, insisting that he could do it himself. Gemma stood there with her hands on her hips, watching him roll the awning in with a long metal hook. He had given away the single crutch this morning and seemed to be getting around much more quickly. It would be good when they were on the road so he could have a bit of a rest.

'We don't have to put this up and down every day, do we? It'd be easier to stop in a motel.' Frustration had Gemma curling her fingers as he'd limped around on his moon boot, pulling out pegs and folding up the walls. In the end, he'd agreed for her to get the wheelbarrow from the shed to put it away. One thing she was quickly learning about Saul was that he was a perfectionist. His clothes were folded neatly, everything in the caravan had its place, and the shadow board in his big shed that held his tools was a work of art. Gemma hid a smile; things could get interesting when he discovered she was the complete opposite. No matter how hard she tried, she was never organised—or on time.

'No, the annexe stays here, but we'll use the awning when we stop. It's easy to put up and down. Plus I doubt if there'll be a motel at Kangaroo Crossing.' He looked around as she pushed the wheelbarrow down the drive towards the shed. 'Where's Atty gone?'

Gemma frowned. 'He came into the shed with me when I went across to get the wheelbarrow. Maybe he stayed there in the cool.'

She pushed open the shed door, but there was no sign of the big dog. 'He's not in here, Saul,' she yelled across the driveway. As she put the wheelbarrow away and locked the shed, Saul's whistles echoed around the gully.

'Bloody dog,' he said. 'I know exactly where he'll be. He can see us packing up, so he'll be hiding down in the creek. He does it every time. He thinks I'm going away and he has to go to Rod's.' Saul's face was flushed and perspiration was beaded on his brow.

'You haven't overdone it, have you?' Gemma asked quietly, heading into the van for a bottle of water.

He took it with a smile as she handed the cold bottle over to him. 'No, just a bit frustrated with our late start.'

'Does it matter? We could do a short trip today. It's not as though we have a date we have to be there.'

Saul tipped the water over his head and let it run down his face. 'You're right. As soon as Attila comes slinking back, we can hook the van up and hit the road.'

'*Attila?*' she echoed. 'He *is* in your bad books. I'll go and find poor Atty. You find some shade and have a rest.'

'Thanks, Gem. Sorry if I'm a grouch.'

She reached up and kissed his flushed cheek. 'You're not. We didn't get enough sleep last night.'

'And whose fault was that?' he said, grabbing her around the waist before she could move away. Gemma was soundly kissed and when she walked down to the creek, the smile stayed on her face.

Half an hour later, Atty had been brought home and the mud hosed off him, and he was secured in his cage on the back of the ute. Saul had hooked up the van but hadn't been able to get low enough to connect the power cables, and he'd shaken his head when Gemma had gestured for him to move, hooked them up and secured the chains.

'A woman of many talents. I think you're a keeper, Gem.'

Gemma was secure enough in their relationship to merely smile at his words. 'See what you think after our road trip,' she retorted.

As she drove down the driveway, getting used to the caravan behind the ute, Saul looked at his watch. 'Just after eleven. We'll take a break at Anmatjere. With a good run we'll get as far as Tennant Creek or Three Ways before dark.'

Driving Saul's ute with him in the passenger seat was nervewracking, especially when Gemma got every red light through town and was still getting used to learning to brake with the weight of the caravan behind the ute. At least there weren't horses in there swaying around. Just as they left town and hit the highway north, her mobile rang.

'Can you see who that is for me, please?' She gestured to her handbag on the seat. Sylvie had rung a couple of times last week to check up on some of the kids with special needs. Gemma had been happy to take the calls; she was still feeling a little bit guilty about taking time off.

Saul reached over and took the phone from her bag, and glanced at the screen. 'It says *Mum.*'

Gemma rolled her eyes. 'Damn, I forgot to text her on Sunday. It's a strange time for her to ring though. I hope nothing else has happened.'

'Pull over and give her a call. It's at least two and a half hours before we get to Anmatjere, and the service'll drop out soon. There's a truck parking area about five kilometres from here.'

When she pulled up a few minutes later, Saul picked up his crutch. 'I'll check on Atty, and give him a drink while you call.' He looked at her curiously as she got out of the car. 'Are you going to tell her we're on the road?'

Gemma shook her head and waited until he was out safely before she hit the return call button.

'Gemma! Where are you? You told me you weren't taking time off school. I called the school and they said you were on leave. Jeff said he was worried about you. How long are you off for? What sort of leave? With a new job, you don't want to be taking too much time off. It's always the sign of a slack staff member when they do that early in their employment. Although if you did lose your job, you could come home. Are you still on probation?'

Gemma took a fortifying breath. 'Hello, Mum. How are you? I'm fine, thank you for asking.'

'Don't be smart. Where are you?'

'I'm in Alice Springs.' Technically still true. 'What's wrong? Aren't you at school?' One thing she, Ethan and Dad had known was that you didn't ring Mum, and she didn't make personal calls when she was at work, unless it was a matter of life and death.

'Your father's looking for you. I gave him your address, but he just called and said he's been there every day for the past three days and you haven't been there. That's why I rang the school. What's going on, Gemma?'

'Nothing's going on. I've been staying with a friend who needed some help. How long's Dad in town for?' Gemma bit her lip, glancing across as Saul opened the door and hoisted himself up into the ute as Atty started howling.

'Sorry,' he mouthed and went to get out again.

Gemma shook her head and put her hand on his arm. 'No, it's okay.'

'What's that noise?' Her mother's voice was short and Gemma held back a sigh. Her muscles were tensing as she had the usual angry reaction to Mum's interrogation—a lump in her throat and a churning stomach. It never took long. Would she spend the rest of her life feeling guilty and letting her mother stress her out?

'Just a dog. How long is Dad staying?'

'I don't know, he didn't tell me.' And *that* hadn't gone down well by the tone of Mum's voice.

'Why didn't he call me?'

'Apparently, he's lost his phone, and all his numbers. You know what your father's like with technology.'

'You could have given him my number.'

'I could have, but I didn't.'

Gemma pulled a face and Saul reached over and put his hand on her arm. She met his eyes, and he smiled at her sympathetically. 'Text me his number and I'll call him when I get a chance.'

'When you get a chance? Where are you, Gemma?'

'Mum, I'm driving. I'll call him later. Okay?'

'Very well. Have you heard from the police again?'

Gemma sat up straight. 'No, I haven't heard from the police. Why? Have you or Dad?'

Saul frowned and sent her a worried glance.

'I don't know if he has, but I wondered why your father took himself off to Alice Springs. He wants to see you while he's there.'

'Okay. I'll call him when you send his number. Can you do that please, Mum?'

'I have a meeting now. I'm running late. I'll do it after that.'

'Thank you. I'll call him later then.'

'Who are you helping out, Gemma? I didn't think you knew anyone there now. Someone you know well enough to stay with, anyway.'

Gemma held Saul's gaze steadily. 'Yes, Mum. Someone I know very well. And so do you. You'd be very proud to see what a success one of your students has made of his life. He's done very well, and he's built a beautiful home on his farm. I'm sure he'd love to see you if you ever come back to Alice.'

'Who are you talking about, Gemma?'

A smile lifted Gemma's lips as Saul looked back at her and shook his head slightly.

'It's Saul, Mum. Saul Pearce.' She disconnected and threw the phone into her bag. 'Let's get this show on the road.'

They took a quick break at Anmatjere. While Saul filled up the ute, Gemma grabbed them each a cold drink and takeaway sandwich. Mum's text had dinged in as they pulled up, and while Saul saw to Atty, she called her father's number.

'Hello?' He picked up immediately. 'Gemma?'

'Hello, Dad.'

'It's good to hear your voice, love. It's been a while.'

Gemma bit her lip. What was it about her parents that always made her feel like the guilty party? 'It has. Mum said you're in Alice.'

'I was, but it looks like I missed you. I had to head north this morning. Start a new job next week.'

Gemma raised her eyebrows. 'Where are you now?'

'Heading up the Stuart Highway, just past Anmatjere. Too far to turn around and come back. I was really hoping to see you.'

Gemma thought for a minute. 'Where are you stopping for the night?'

'I'll probably pull up at the Three Ways Roadhouse. I've got my swag and I don't need a cabin.'

'Hang on a sec, Dad.' Gemma walked around to the back of the ute where Saul was giving a couple of liver treats to Atty. 'Would it be okay if we definitely planned to stop at Three Ways?'

'Sure.' He gestured to her phone. 'Problem?'

Gemma shook her head. 'No, it's worked out okay actually. Dad's on the road ahead of us and stopping there tonight.'

'If you're happy, that's fine by me.'

She lifted the phone and returned to the call. 'Dad? It's a bit of a coincidence but Saul and I are on the road not far behind you. We're just at Anmatjere now and heading for Three Ways. We could meet up tonight, if you wanted to?'

'Ah, love, that'd be great.' He sounded delighted. 'With Saul, you said? Saul Pearce?'

'Yes.'

'I'll shout you both dinner at the restaurant. They do a mean steak there.'

'Thanks, that'd be nice. We'll look forward to it. See you there.' Gemma disconnected the call and put her phone in her pocket.

'This could be interesting.' Saul flicked a glance at her.

She rolled her eyes. 'We'll have to decide what to tell him.'

'I mean, us,' he said. 'I was never sure what he thought of me hanging around with Ethan and Screw. I was terrified of your mother, but a bit uncertain about your dad.'

'How do you mean?' she said.

'He knew my dad, and he knew my background. I wasn't sure if he judged me by that.'

Gemma shook her head. 'You read him wrong. It was probably Mum's attitude reflecting off him. Dad was quiet, but he always had respect for others. He didn't judge them by what they had, and what sort of work they did.'

After they climbed back into the ute—to Gemma's dismay, Saul insisted on taking a turn at the wheel—he looked at her with a frown. 'I always thought you and your dad got on well.'

'We did. Things went a bit pear-shaped when he and Mum split. We fell out a bit. Or I did, I guess. It wasn't him; it was all me.'

Saul pulled out on the highway and they were quiet for a while. Gemma stared out the window. The Ghan railway ran parallel with the highway for a while, but there was nothing to look at apart from never-ending red dirt, straggly small trees and the whistling kites riding the thermals above. A few times, Saul slowed as one appeared on the road ahead, pecking at roadkill.

'That would have been hard for him.'

Gemma frowned. 'Who?'

'Your dad. Losing Ethan and then losing touch with you.'

Gemma turned to the window again. She did miss Dad, but the longer she'd gone without talking to him, the easier it had been to blame him for the lack of contact. She closed her eyes as memories flooded in. Dad piggybacking her around the big back lawn they had in their first house at Alice Springs. It had been a small, crap house but had had a magic garden. She and Ethan used to camp out under the stars with Dad.

'That's the Gemma star.' Dad had lain on his back beside her and pointed to the night sky.

'There's no such thing,' Ethan had piped up.

'Yes, there is, son. Its scientific name is the Alpha Coronae Borealis, and that's it over there to the north.'

They would have been about eight, still young enough for Ethan to chuck a wobbly. 'Well, where's my star?' he'd demanded, pushing his bottom lip out.

Dad had rolled over and tickled him; it didn't take much to make Ethan giggle. 'It's still being born. We'll get a telescope and I'll show you when it's up there.'

A smile tugged at Gemma's lips. Ethan hadn't forgotten that and had still been waiting for his star when they'd started high school.

They had come full circle because it had been those camping trips and talk of the past and rubies that had fired Ethan's obsession, and his belief that he would find them.

A bit like the Ethan star.

Finally, Gemma turned to Saul. 'You're right, you know. I was too lost in my own grief to think about anyone else. I pretty much wiped Dad, and that was mean. I figured it was safer not to care about anyone. I've been blaming everyone for not being able to rely on them, but I can see now that a lot of it was caused by my doubt.'

'I'm pleased you've changed your mind.' Saul reached over and squeezed her hand. 'Even though I was wary, I always liked your dad. He was a good bloke.'

'What about Mum?'

He hesitated. 'I was always scared of her. Even when I was twenty,' he chuckled.

Gemma shook her head, smiling. 'Weren't we all! Dad too, I think.'

Saul put his hand back on the steering wheel. 'How much do you want to tell your dad about what we're doing?'

Gemma shrugged. 'I don't know. Let's wait and see how things pan out.'

She wouldn't admit it, but after three years, she was nervous about seeing Dad again.

*

There was a long queue for fuel when they turned in to the road-house, and Saul parked the ute and van at the side of the small office. He looked with interest at the black RAM ute; he'd been thinking about getting one.

'Powered or unpowered?' he asked Gemma as he went to open the door.

'Huh?' The look on her face was comical, and Saul smothered a grin.

'Site. Do you need power? You know, for your hairdryer or anything?'

She raised her eyebrows. 'No hairdryer. What about coffee?' she asked.

'We can use gas.'

'Okay. I don't care. Whatever you'd usually do. This caravan stuff is new to me.'

By the time he'd climbed down out of the ute, Gemma was around the back, stroking Atty. Saul balanced on the heel of his moon boot while he put one arm around her waist. 'Thank you, Gem. You make Atty happy. And me.'

'You make me happy too.' He closed his eyes as she reached up and kissed him. Her lips lingered on his and he pulled her closer.

The bell above the office door dinged and Saul lifted his head. 'We'd better go book in so we don't miss out on a site. You're sure you're happy down the back, away from the power?'

A familiar voice interrupted them. 'There's plenty of sites left. Powered and unpowered. It's only early.'

Gemma swung around and her face lit up. 'Dad!'

'Hello, sweetheart. You're looking good. I've been watching for you.'

Saul watched as Tony held his arms open, wondering what Gemma would do. She hesitated for a moment and then with a broken cry, she flung herself into her father's arms.

As Saul turned away to give them time together, Tony caught his eye and he could see the tears glistening in her father's eyes as Gemma kept saying, 'I'm sorry, Dad. I'm so sorry.'

Saul left them, his throat tight with emotion as he headed for the office. When he walked away from the ute, Atty set up a howling; the big sook went out in sympathy with Gemma. He could sense she was upset too.

★

Gemma led her father around to the back of the vehicle, holding his hand tightly. She was still shaky and knew it wouldn't take much to bring her to tears again. 'Atty, shh. I'm okay. Dad, this is Atty, Saul's dog.'

Her father reached in and Atty moaned with pleasure as the top of his head was scratched.

Gemma held his other hand. 'It's so good to see you, Dad. It was meant to be, wasn't it? You ringing when you did, I mean. What were you doing in Alice?'

'Your Aunty Estelle wants me to sell your grandparents' house. She's right, it's getting to be a real pain having it as a rental. I'm going to give the inside a lick of paint and there's some boxes in the shed I've got to sort.' He put his head down. 'When you and your mother moved east, Ethan's stuff was stored in there. Time we cleaned it out, I suppose.'

'Is that where all the family journals and stuff is too?'

'Hell no,' Tony said. 'I donated all that to the library after . . . well,' he said, looking uncomfortable. 'Better off there than in a shed getting mouldy. Why? Are you starting to get an interest in the family history?'

Gemma smiled. 'Maybe.'

'I've missed you, love. I wanted to catch up with you to see how you were while I was there. I've been worried about you being by yourself since your mother called and told me they found Ethan's Ruby. I was disappointed when I called at your place and you weren't there.'

'How did you know where to find me?'

'Your mother gave me the address when she contacted me last week, but I didn't let on I was going down there yet. I called in about dinnertime three nights running.'

'Because you would have got a lecture from Mum about what to do and say?'

He nodded. 'And instructions to talk you into moving back to the east coast,' he said. 'I got it all when I called her.'

'Poor Mum. She never gives up.'

'And Jennifer can never be told that she's wrong.' Tony's voice held bitterness. 'Sorry, sweetheart, you don't need to hear me bitching. I have a feeling that was why you kept your distance from us both.'

'No, Dad.' She looped her arm through his. 'I've learned a lot about being honest in these past few days. I was trying to protect myself. I didn't want to depend on anyone else for my happiness.

If I did, I knew I'd be let down. I went into my shell, and I didn't go out with friends either, and I deliberately lost contact with you.'

Tony nodded, his expression understanding. 'And your mother?'

'I tried hard, but we know what she's like. That's one of the reasons I moved back here. I knew I could stay away from *everyone* out here.'

Tony raised his eyebrows. 'Saul too?'

'Saul's the one who brought me to my senses.'

'Good. I always knew he was a good kid, and I knew how you both felt about each other back then.'

'You did?' Gemma raised her eyebrows.

'I wasn't blind, love.' As he spoke, Saul came out of the office. He came over to Tony and shook his hand.

'Hello, Tony. This was good timing.'

'It's been a while, Saul.' Tony gripped Saul's hand and shook it and Gemma beamed. 'So, tell me what you pair are doing heading north. Is it school holidays?'

Saul met Gemma's gaze and she could sense his support for what she was thinking. 'It's a bit of a story, Dad, but one you probably should hear.'

Saul nodded. 'Why don't we go and get set up, then we can have a chat. They gave us the site next to you, Tony. I hope that's okay?'

Gemma leaned into her father. 'We won't cramp your style, Dad.'

Tony chuckled. 'Trust me, love, your old man doesn't have a lot of style to cramp. I'll go and have a swim and let you get settled. I'll bring a six-pack. Beer okay with you guys?'

'Sounds good,' Saul said.

Gemma walked over and put her arms around her father's waist. 'It's so good to see you, Dad. I love you,' she whispered. 'See you in a while. I'm not sure what I'm required to do with this caravan set-up stuff. This is our first night on the road.'

Before her father could comment, Saul answered, and the way he looked at her sent her tummy quivering. 'You just have to stand there and look beautiful, Gem.'

Tony shook his head and walked towards the pool. 'I'll see you pair of lovebirds later.'

CHAPTER
39

Three Ways Roadhouse, Northern Territory
Wednesday, 3.30 pm

Gemma did more than stand around. Saul discovered he was unable to balance and put the legs of the van down so with his instruction, and close supervision, Gemma learned another caravanning skill.

'Not a bad offsider,' he commented when she chocked the wheels. They'd stayed hooked up to the ute as it was only an overnight stay. Saul wanted to get as far as they could tomorrow, leaving a short trip for the last leg to Kangaroo Crossing the day after.

'What else?' she asked with her hands on her hips. 'I might as well learn.'

'I'll put the awning up, then the last job is to get the chairs and table out of the boot, and then crack a beer.' He came over and hooked his fingers at the front of her shorts. 'Unless you're tired and need a lie down.'

Gemma put her hand over her mouth and faked a yawn. 'I am tired.'

Saul waggled his eyebrows. 'You are incorrigible, woman, but I like it.' He looked behind her. 'Raincheck. Here comes your dad with those beers.'

'I think he's curious about where we're going.'

'I think so too. Are you going to tell him?'

She nodded. 'I think we should. What do you think?'

'I think yes.'

By the time Tony dropped the six-pack off, dried off with a towel beside his car and slipped a clean shirt on, the awning was down and Gemma had the chairs out. When Saul sat down, she got the small stool from the boot so he could elevate his foot.

'Thanks, Gem.' He reached across and took her hand as she sat on the camp chair beside him.

Tony cracked a beer and held it up to clink bottles with them both. 'Here's cheers, big ears.'

Gemma grinned at the look on Saul's face. Dad had been saying that for as long as she remembered, and it took her back to happier days.

All was quiet for a while as they relaxed. Finally, Gemma spoke. 'So, Dad, you're probably wondering what's happening here.'

'I do admit to a bit of curiosity. I was under the impression you'd moved to Alice to start a new job. Didn't it work out?'

'I'm on leave.' She leaned forward and put the bottle on the grass. 'So's Saul. We're going up to a station in Western Australia to track down Jed Turner. You remember him? Screw.'

Tony's face tightened and he nodded. 'I do.'

Gemma started the story but her voice had trembled when she got to the bit about the grave with Ethan's initials carved into the sun-bleached cross. Saul took over and Tony leaned forward and took her hand.

★

'I'll travel out there with you. I'll follow you out,' Tony said when they'd finished speaking. 'It's more important than any job interview. I want to know if Ethan died in that car and if he did, who buried him.'

Gemma wiped her eyes. When her dad finally looked up, his eyes were awash with tears and his wrinkles seemed to be etched more deeply into his rugged, unshaven face.

'I always knew my boy was dead,' he said. 'He would have come to me. Even if he'd been in trouble.'

'What sort of trouble do you mean, Dad?'

Tony glanced across at Saul. 'I don't know if you ever saw that side of Screw, Saul, but he was a bit of a loose cannon. I know he was in trouble at high school for drug dealing. Rob let it slip once. If I find out Jed's known all along that Ethan was dead, I'll bloody deal with him myself.'

'Pat would have known he was in trouble with the police back then too, I guess?' Gemma asked.

'I'm sure she did. Rob was on my crew when I was up at the copper mine at Tennant Creek about ten years ago. He was always talking about Jed, and how he and Pat were trying to keep him out of trouble,' Tony said. 'He was really pleased when he went up north, working on the cattle properties. Said it would keep him away from the temptation of easy money.'

'I never knew any of that.' Gemma shook her head. 'Did you, Saul?'

'I knew he liked a drink and an occasional bit of weed, but no, I didn't know he'd been in trouble with the police.'

Gemma narrowed her eyes. 'That's the other thing I don't get either. Pat told me that Screw went north *before* Ethan disappeared.'

Saul nodded. 'He did. Rob gave me a lift to Katherine when he took him over there. It was the night after Ethan clocked me.'

Gemma leaned over and took his hand. 'I'm sorry. That was the night after Saul and I had a bit of a hard talk, Dad.'

'Looks like you've sorted things out now,' Tony said calmly.

Gemma squeezed Saul's hand. 'We have.'

Saul nodded. 'I'm not going to let your daughter get away again. I hope that's all right with you, Tony.'

Tony lifted up his beer and his smile reappeared for the first time. 'That's one thing that makes me happy, mate. You hang onto her, she's a keeper, that one.'

'Thanks, Dad. I'll be seeing a lot more of you too, I promise.'

'I might even come back to Alice for a while.' Tony put his empty beer bottle on the ground. 'Gem, what did you mean when you said you didn't understand about Screw going north?'

'Well, Pat said he went, and Saul's confirmed that Screw went away before Ethan went missing, but I reckon from what Ethan said, Screw was back with him out there.'

Saul frowned. 'You could be right. He was heading out with Rob when they dropped me off, but something could have gone wrong with the job and he might have come back.'

'If Screw was there when Ethan . . . died . . . why didn't he tell anyone?' Gemma asked. 'Did he bury him and take off?'

Tony's mouth was set and his eyes glistened. 'We'll find him, Gemma, and we'll find out the truth. I don't care how long it takes.'

Gemma stood and collected the three empty bottles and took them to the bin to take time to compose herself. The images of Ethan dying and being buried in that lonely grave made her feel sick. She forced a bright tone into her voice and went over to Tony's chair. 'So, come on, Dad. Take us to this flash roadhouse. I could do with a meal.'

'Right you are,' Tony said, heaving himself up.

Gemma smiled as Saul looped his arm around her shoulders as they walked across the grass. He brushed a kiss across her cheek. 'You okay, Gem?'

'I'm hanging in there.' She nodded, despite the fresh ache lodged in her chest. Ethan might be gone, but she had Saul and Dad to share the grief.

CHAPTER
40

Kangaroo Crossing Free Camp
Friday, 8.00 am

Saul hadn't mentioned to Gemma the black RAM ute he'd noticed again when they were checked at the WA border late on Thursday afternoon. The ute had kept going but Saul kept an eye out. He'd noticed the ute at Top Springs where they'd fuelled up, then it had gone ahead as they crossed the east Tanami. He'd mentioned it to Tony when Gemma was in the shower last night, worrying that they were being followed. They'd turned off the main highway just before dark and found a camping spot by a small creek about thirty kilometres from the front gate of Kangaroo Crossing.

'I'm probably worrying too much. It's probably a coincidence, but I've seen it a few times and it's strange they're taking the same route we are.' When Tony had decided to travel with them, Saul had decided to cut across the Tanami desert; it saved them going all the way up to Katherine and it had got them to Kangaroo Crossing a day earlier.

'Maybe. There's a lot of mines out here,' Tony said thoughtfully. 'I'm pleased you're careful, Saul. It doesn't hurt to keep an eye out here in these remote areas.'

They rose early and Saul checked the oil in his ute while Gemma made the coffee. 'How will we handle this?' he asked, wiping his hands before taking the mug from Gemma.

'I reckon it'll be better if I go in by myself. If Screw's there, we don't want to scare him off, turning up like a posse on a mission,' Tony said. 'Are you both happy to wait here? Not too isolated for you?'

Saul looked across at Gemma as he and Tony exchanged a look, but she hadn't picked up on his tension. He was feeling more relaxed; no vehicles had passed their campsite since they'd arrived last night. 'Good plan, mate. You look like a stockman with that old hat on your head.' Saul put the bonnet of the ute down and hobbled around the side of the vehicle. His ankle had stopped aching, but he was still conscious of doing too much.

'I deliberately didn't shave this morning so I'd look the part,' Tony said, rubbing his chin.

'And put old work clothes on,' Gemma said, shaking her head. 'You do look the part, Dad. Very different to the man who used to head off to the mines in a shirt and tie.'

'I much prefer this life, love. I've done a bit of everything over the last six years. I found it hard to settle once Ethan was gone.'

'Fishing too, I hear.'

'Yep. A whole new me. Anyways, I'm off. If I spot Screw or hear he's working there, I'll come straight back and let you know.'

'Be careful, Dad.' Gemma reached up and kissed his cheek. He climbed into his old battered ute, and Gemma and Saul stood with Atty as her father headed along the narrow track.

'Come on, Gem. Let's get this camp set up.'

She wandered over to the boot and unlocked the door. 'I like this camping life. It'd be a nice way to live. Just travelling around. No commitments, no worries.'

Saul's teeth flashed in the morning sunlight as he grinned at her. 'No income.'

'A dream for down the track, hey?'

Once the chairs were out and Saul was sitting in the sun with Atty, Gemma pulled out her work boots. 'I can't settle. Do you mind if I go for a walk?'

'Go for it, but watch out for snakes. And you'd better take Atty with you. He'll howl if you leave him.'

'Okay.' She leaned down and kissed him. 'I'll just grab a bottle of water, and maybe his lead, do you think?'

'Yeah, if there's any cattle out there, he'll take off after them. He's a bugger sometimes.'

Gemma gasped in mock-horror. 'You're a lovely boy, aren't you, Atty?' She ruffled his fur, and they both laughed when he groaned. 'How long do you reckon Dad'll be?'

Saul looked at his watch. 'Half hour to get there, half hour back and an hour or so there maybe? He could be back before noon.'

'Okay, I'll walk for forty-five minutes then turn around.'

'You be careful out there; there's no phone service and not a lot to see.'

Gemma nodded. 'I'll be fine. I'll stay by the creek. I need the exercise after being in the ute for two days straight.'

'If we don't have any luck here, it's another three hundred k down to Roselyon.' Saul stretched and settled in the camp chair. 'I might have a nap.'

★

Gemma put Atty's lead on and he dragged her along, excited to be out in the bush. They weren't far from the eastern side of Lake Argyle and she wondered if she found a hill—looking ahead made that seem highly unlikely—if she'd see the water. Saul had told her a bit about the area as they turned onto the Lake Argyle Road. Nineteen times the size of Sydney Harbour, Lake Argyle was the second-largest artificial freshwater reservoir in Australia. She'd looked at him curiously as he'd quoted its size in megalitres, and some facts about the Ord River scheme.

'You're a walking Google.'

'Doesn't hurt to know about your country,' he'd said defensively.

As she and Atty walked along the side of the creek, there seemed to be a lot of birdlife ahead. Saul had told her about the magpie geese out here and by the racket ahead that was quickly getting Atty's attention, she assumed that's what they were. As she held firmly onto the lead, the creek wound through a lightly timbered section of bush, and she nodded as she spotted a hill ahead, a little bit away from the creek.

'Come on, Atty. We'll see if we can see this big lake. This creek might feed into it.'

He barked and hundreds of geese took off in a dark mass and headed west. By the time they reached the top, Gemma was puffing and Atty flopped on the red dirt. She took the bottle of water from her shirt pocket and drank deeply, then tipped some into her hand for Atty to drink. She screwed the cap back on and looked around.

'Oh wow, look. We can see the lake.' A huge expanse of water filled her vision, shimmering a pale blue in the morning sunlight. It was a spectacular sight. In the distance, she could see red cliffs that reminded her of Ruby Gap, but instead of timbered bush, the hills were covered with a yellowish green grass and there were no trees.

Gemma put her hand to her eyes and turned a full circle. About three kilometres behind her, she could see Saul's caravan and ute. The landscape was as isolated as the East MacDonnells and she revelled in the silence. She stood there, letting her gaze wander over the hills ahead and the flat landscape behind her. A puff of dirt to the north of their camp site caught her attention, and for a moment, she wondered if it was Dad coming back before she remembered he'd turned to the south. As she watched, the vehicle made its way along a road that ran parallel to the track that they'd taken in and then it pulled up. The sun glinted on the mirror on the passenger side, and she was just close enough to see two men get out.

Maybe it was someone working on the cattle property? Although there were no cattle to be seen. After a while, they got back in and drove towards the lake.

With a shrug, she looked at her watch and then tugged on Atty's lead. 'Come on, boy, time to go back. Dad might be on his way.'

She was almost to the bottom of the hill when another vehicle coming along the lake road from the south caught her attention. 'Quick, that might be him coming back now.'

Frustration set in as Atty dragged on the lead. The magpie geese had settled back along the edge of the creek again, and he wanted to stop and sniff every few metres.

'Come on!'

Halfway back, he decided to head into the creek and have a swim, and Gemma released the lead just in time before he pulled her into the water. Atty splashed and barked, but it wasn't until he'd chased all the birds away that she was able to entice him out of the creek.

'You'll probably catch something,' she said as he shook himself and brown and green algae flew in all directions. 'Ew, you're a stinky dawg.'

By the time the caravan came into sight ahead, the sun was high in the sky. Perspiration trailed down the back of her singlet, her hair stuck in tendrils to the side of her face, and she wished she'd tied it back. Gemma glanced at her watch again; she'd been a lot longer than she'd planned, thanks to her companion. She was almost back, so she tipped the little bit of water that was left over her head to cool her skin.

As she got closer, Gemma broke into a run, Atty loping along beside her. Dad's ute was parked behind Saul's, and she was pretty sure she could see three figures in the distance.

Or maybe not? When she reached the point where the track veered from the creek, she could only see two men. Her eyes narrowed. Dad was standing at the ute talking to someone, but as she got closer, she could see it wasn't Saul.

She reached down and let Atty off the lead and as he bounded ahead, Saul stepped down from the van, and she heard him call out. 'She's coming now.'

'Screw!' she called out as she got closer. 'Jed!'

The figure beside Dad moved away and walked towards her. As Gemma looked at the man with the long untidy hair and the full beard framing a tanned and rugged face, he took his hat off.

She ran faster, breath rasping in her throat as she ran towards him. It was like one of those dreams where your feet were stuck in something sluggish and she felt as though she wasn't getting any closer. Her knees were shaking so much she couldn't go any further. As Gemma stopped, her vision pricked with silver lights and she bent over as darkness threatened. He ran towards her, and tears were rolling down her face as he spoke.

One word. Only one.

'Gem.' His voice broke, and she wrapped her arms around her twin brother as he cried with her.

★

Gemma sat in the shade as Saul brought her another bottle of water from the camp fridge. She'd already drained one since she'd sat down, and it was the only time she'd let go of Ethan. She was having trouble speaking. Every time she went to talk, she started crying.

Finally, she took a deep breath and stared at her brother. 'You know I feel like hitting you, don't you? I won't say kill, because in the circumstances it's not the right word.'

He grinned at her, and she stared at him, unable to believe that this man with the rugged face and unkempt hair was really here holding her hand. Ethan wouldn't let go either.

'Ethan, have you got some explaining to do,' she said.

Their father came and sat in the chair on the other side of Gemma. 'Don't you worry, love, he's already copped it from me.'

Gemma shook her head. 'Did you know we thought you were dead? That Saul and I stood next to what we thought was your grave.' Ethan turned to face her and she drew in a quick breath. For the first time, she noticed the length of the scar on his face. It came from his beard, and ran along the edge of his left cheek up into his hairline, puckering his cheek.

'Oh, my God! What happened?'

Ethan's voice rasped as he spoke. 'I got shot. I can't go back there, Gem. They'll kill me.'

'What, why? Who are you talking about?' Gemma gripped his arm.

Her brother's eyes were empty. 'Screw's dead, and I killed a man.'

CHAPTER
41

Annie's Gorge
Six years ago

Cold water around his legs dragged Ethan awake. His seat belt was slicing into his neck, and he could feel the warm stickiness of blood running down his neck. He jerked as he remembered the feel of the bullet hitting the side of his head. Reaching up to touch his face, his hand encountered an open wound from his eye to his lip.

Nausea threatened, and Ethan closed his eyes as pain seared through his head. When he opened them, his vision cleared slowly and he looked across at Screw. Screw moaned, and put his hand to his head.

Ethan knew they had to get out. The water was coming up fast and Ruby would soon be underwater. If those blokes came to see if they'd survived the crash over the side of the cliff, and found them, they were goners. He didn't know how long he'd been out to it, but it would take those guys a while to come down the cliff. Their survival depended on whether they were watching from above.

'Screw, we've gotta get out.'

Screw opened his eyes. 'Jesus, Eth, you're covered in blood. But at least you're bloody conscious again.'

'What about you, mate? Were you out of it too?'

'Yeah, I banged my head on the way down. Bloody good driving in midair, hey, Eth?' He coughed a laugh.

'Fuck, mate. Don't be a smartarse. We have to get out of here, before they come looking.'

'Or before we bloody sink. My belt's stuck. Can you undo it from your side?'

Ethan's fingers fumbled as he tried to get Screw's seatbelt undone. The water was coming up faster now, and he wasn't sure if it was the water or his injuries making him feel cold and strange.

Finally, the seatbelt clicked undone and Screw turned to face him. Blood was trickling down the side of his cheek. 'Here, now I can get your belt. Brace yourself, mate.' His voice was slurred as though he'd been drinking. 'Can you move?'

'Yeah, it's only my face where that prick shot me.'

Ethan tried to keep his balance as he walked around the front of Ruby, who was nose down in the riverbed, but he slipped and his head went under. His cheek stung like a bastard, and he spluttered as he surfaced. He looked up; where they'd come down had been from a lower part of the cliff, and that had probably saved their lives. Even so, he couldn't believe they'd survived the impact.

'Come on, mate, don't drown on me now,' Screw said urgently. 'We need to get into that thick bush under the cliff face. But quick, I can hear motorbikes.'

It didn't take long, wading through the shallow water, to reach the thicket that was near the bend in the river. Screw sat down and put his hand to the side of his head. 'Jesus, that hurts.'

Ethan fell to his knees beside him then rolled over onto his back. His head was spinning. 'Tell me about it.'

'Stay completely quiet. I'll go and see what happens,' Screw said.

Ethan stared at him, but his vision blurred and cold crept into his chest. He nodded and leaned back against a tree trunk. 'Be careful.' His face had started bleeding again, and when he put his hand up, it came away covered with blood. He leaned forward and pulled his T-shirt over his head and folded it into a pad, pressing it against his cheek. They needed to get back to town quickly, to get to the hospital, but how the hell were they going to do that? He didn't want to bleed to death out here at Ruby Gap.

Ethan closed his eyes and gave in to the darkness.

When he came to again, he could hear voices and he froze. He sat up and jumped backwards as his hand touched someone. Finally, his eyes adjusted to the darkness and he realised Screw had come back while he was out to it. 'Screw,' he whispered. 'How close are they?'

Screw looked at him but didn't answer.

Ethan's blood iced as he stared at his mate's face then down to his chest. He strangled the cry that bubbled up as he put his fingers against Screw's neck, frantically looking for a pulse. Closing his eyes, he desperately moved his fingers, but there was nothing. The side of Screw's face was covered with blood; his ear had been bleeding.

He leaned over and lay his head on Screw's chest; there was no movement, no sound, no heartbeat. Ethan got up onto his haunches and disbelief and horror gripped him as he backed away.

There was a rustle in the undergrowth and then the sound of motorbikes roared up the gully. Terror filled him, and he stayed perfectly still, but the bikes went past. Gradually, the sound faded away. Ethan turned away and vomited on the grass.

He had to move Screw's body; he had to get them away. He couldn't leave his mate's body there in case it washed out into the river. Those bastards had to believe they'd both died in the truck. The way the river was rising, Ruby would be under already and would stay under until the water fell. He could be long gone before she was found.

CHAPTER
42

**Kangaroo Crossing Free Camp
Friday**

Saul kept a close eye on Gemma as Ethan told his story. She was pale, and staring ahead. Tony sat there quietly, leaning forward, looking down at the ground.

'Then what happened?' Gemma asked quietly.

'When it was dark, I carried Screw back to our camp site at the ruins. I covered him up with the old tarp we kept in the house while I dug his grave. It took me hours because where my cheek got shot started bleeding every time I started to dig. My head was aching like a bastard, and I didn't even have anything with me for the pain. I thought I was going to die too.' Ethan's voice broke and he put his hands over his face. Eventually, he looked up and his eyes were empty.

Saul felt cold.

'Keep going, Ethan,' Gemma said. 'What happened then?'

'Once I'd buried Screw, I collapsed in the old homestead. I didn't even have the energy to go to the river and get a drink. It took two days before I got down there. It rained one night and I managed to get outside and get some water in my mouth. Then I remembered we kept those packets of nuts in the old meat chest in the hut. With the cards, and the pencil and pad we used to keep score when we played. So I wrote down everything I knew about the rubies. I don't know how much sense I made because I was a bit out of it. I wanted you to know what I'd found, Gemma. So I wrote a message that only you could understand. A week later, I went back to look for Ruby. The moon was full, and I could see where she'd floated down the river and was wedged nose down against the cliff. My backpack was still in the mud behind the seats. I got out what I could, put the letter to you in the plastic bag with the rego in the glove box. Then I hiked up the back road to the community. I knew Danno'd help me and keep quiet.'

'Why didn't you try to get back to Alice, son?' Tony finally looked up. 'There would have been someone on that road eventually.'

'Yes, for the life of me, I still can't understand why you didn't go for help.' Gemma shook her head and let go of Ethan's arm.

'Because those blokes running the whole thing—the drugs, the rubies, and that warehouse—are dangerous. As far as they knew, they killed us. Shit, they shot me, Gemma. And they tried to shoot Screw too. It's not just a few no-hopers, it's a big drug syndicate out of Perth.' Ethan dropped his head and looked at the ground. 'And I killed one of them.'

'What? How the hell did you kill someone? I don't believe it, Ethan. You didn't even have a gun out there.' Gemma's words came out shrilly and Saul put his hand on hers.

'I hit him with William's axe and split his head open. It was self-defence. I saw their stash, and I saw where they were mining for the rubies. They *had* to believe that Screw and I were dead. Putting my initials on the grave was even more insurance for me. They still have to believe it.'

'Who are *they*?' Gemma persisted. 'Why can't we just go to the police?'

'Just listen to me, Gemma. Don't you think I'd come home if I could?' Ethan demanded. 'I've lost the life I knew. I've pretended to be Screw, because they knew who *I* was. The only one of them who knew Screw was the guy that I hit. And then Screw told me he was a copper. That's why I took Screw's wallet and his name and address . . . his identity. If I wanted to stay alive, I had no choice. Hell, I've even sent a bloody Christmas card to his mum to keep the pretence up. I hate working out here with the cattle and I keep to myself. It's a shit life, but I'm alive. And if they know I am, they'll come after me.'

Gemma's face lost all colour as he spoke. 'But when you come back, when we tell Pat and Rob that Screw is—'

'No!' Ethan's denial was like a gunshot.

'What do you mean no?'

'I'm not going back.' Ethan tugged at his beard on the side where the scar pouched his cheek. 'Nothing changes. Okay, you know I'm not dead, but I want you all to forget about it. You don't tell a soul. If you do, I'll disappear again.'

Tony made a strangled noise and held his hand out for a minute before he dropped it.

Gemma's voice was icy. 'You selfish little prick.'

Ethan's eyes were bleak, Gemma was pale and shaking, and Tony sat staring at the ground, still as a statue. The silence stretched out, the only sound was the wind whistling over the red dirt, and the magpie geese calling down at the creek.

Finally, Ethan spoke. 'I wanted you to know, Gem.'

Gemma stared at her twin. 'I'll give you one thing, it was clever using that code. It took me ages to decipher your message. If you felt the need for such—'

'What? You got them?' Ethan's words spilled over. 'How? Who found Ruby?'

'Luckily, and coincidentally, I did,' Saul said. 'I work for the Parks service in Alice now and the police asked us to investigate a wrecked vehicle out at Annie's Gorge a couple of weeks ago. That's when we found Ruby.'

'The letter was still in the glove box in the ziplock bag?'

'Yes. Gemma was always convinced you were alive, and that just made her more certain. It was only when we found the grave with your initials on the cross that she believed you were dead.'

'I was a coward. I carved my initials onto that wood, in case they came looking.' Ethan's eyes were bleak.

Gemma interrupted. 'I hate that and I don't get it, but if that was how you felt, why the hell did you write all that shit about trust and find Saul? Why didn't you just call us when you got away? Do you know what you put us all through? Mum and Dad split. Mum made me move to the east coast with her. Saul and I—'

Saul put his hand on Gemma's arm and shook his head. The last thing they wanted was Ethan taking off. 'Calm down, Gem. Let's all stay calm.'

'I told you, I was out of it for a while, when I wrote all that coded stuff.'

'But why did you?'

'I guess . . . I wanted to vindicate myself. Everyone used to pay out on me about the rubies, but that last trip out there when it all went to shit, I found a letter from William and two rubies buried in a tin in the ruins.'

'We know.'

'What do you mean you know?'

Saul stood quietly and went into the van to get the tin and the rubies. Along with Ethan's letter, they were safely stored in a small alcove under the table where the batteries were.

Ethan stared at him when he carried them out of the van, and then he turned to look at their father and Gemma. 'So, you know they're real? You finally believe me?'

'According to William's letter, they are,' Saul said.

'I can't understand why he buried the letter and the rubies then disappeared.'

'I guess we'll never know,' Tony finally said. 'I've read the journals he left right up until he disappeared and there's nothing. They just stop.'

'Where are they, Dad?' Gemma asked. 'The journals, I mean.'

'In the town library, in the local history room.'

'All of them?'

'Yes.' Tony nodded.

'You were never interested in the history,' Ethan said. 'And now those drug bastards are still out there; they've got a nice little side-line digging out hundreds of thousands of dollars' worth of rubies every year.'

Saul turned to Ethan. 'You know you can trust me, don't you?'

'Always could,' Ethan muttered.

'Well, I want you to trust me now. I can sort this.' Guilt rippled through Saul as he looked at Gemma. 'I know a bit about what's happening out there, and I have contacts in Darwin I can trust.'

She stared back at him, her expression confused.

'To do what?' Ethan asked gruffly.

Saul held Ethan's gaze steadily. 'To get your life back, and to make sure you're safe. I can do it, Ethan. All you have to do is trust me.'

CHAPTER
43

Kangaroo Crossing Free Camp
Sunday

They stayed at the campsite for two more days and Ethan came over for dinner each night. Gemma had been happy, but she was quieter than usual with Saul.

Tony was heading north to Darwin in the morning, and Gemma and Saul were going back to Alice Springs. As dinnertime approached, Tony took Atty for a walk up the hill, and it was the first time Gemma and Saul had been alone since Tony had gone to the cattle station to look for Screw.

Saul shook his head as he stood on the caravan step. What a rollercoaster of a couple of days. No wonder Gemma had been so quiet.

'Do you need a hand in the kitchen?' he asked as he stood in the doorway.

'No.' Her voice was short.

Saul stepped up into the van where she was chopping onions at the sink. 'I can do that for you.'

'I'm fine.'

He put his arms on her waist. 'Are you okay, Gem?'

She tensed in his hold. 'I am.'

'You've been a bit distant with me since we got here.'

She put the knife down and he stepped back as she turned to face him. 'You haven't been totally honest with me, Saul.'

He frowned, confused. 'I have.'

'I think you knew more than you told me. You must have had suspicions about those buildings and the work you saw on the river. You'd know from your work it was wrong. Why didn't you tell your boss? Or did you, and you didn't tell me what you found out?'

'I did know it was strange, but I thought you had enough to worry about with finding Ruby and Ethan's messages and then thinking we'd found his grave. I didn't want to burden you with anything that had to do with my work. I wasn't sure at that stage what was going on and I didn't want to add to your worry.'

'So you *were* looking for something?'

'My boss in Darwin had some suspicions and he asked me to keep an eye on what was happening. He's the one I can trust.'

'*We* can trust.' Gemma's arms were folded in front of her, blocking him.

'Okay, I'm sorry. *We* can trust. Max has got contacts high up, and he has integrity. He's a good bloke and I trust him implicitly. If anyone can sort this, and keep Ethan out of trouble, he can.'

'Fine.' Gemma turned back to the onions and Saul knew he'd been dismissed.

Frustration filled him as he limped outside and flopped in the camp chair. In the distance, Tony and Atty were making their way back to camp. He'd thought Gemma would understand. He'd always been a loner and had been used to working by himself, and thinking things through. But if they were going to make this relationship work, he knew that he would have to change a bit, be more open. It was hard after a lifetime of self-protection.

For a second, he thought about walking along the creek on his crutch and meeting Tony and having a talk, but then he realised that wasn't fair. If he needed to sort things out, he needed to do it with Gemma.

Saul sighed and leaned his head back. Maybe they were both too damaged to make a relationship work.

*

Gemma pushed the knife too hard and just missed cutting the top of her finger. It was hard to see what she was doing because she had tears in her eyes and they weren't from the chopped onions. She'd been right all along. Her old feelings for Saul had blinded her.

The week or so they had spent together had been good. Saul was kind, he was fun, and even with his stitches and broken ankle, he was a considerate lover. She admired the man he had become; at almost twenty-seven, he'd settled into a good solid career where he was obviously respected, and he'd built himself a beautiful home.

And he had a gorgeous dog.

So why was she feeling so let down? Because he hadn't trusted her. Technically, Saul hadn't lied, but he had withheld the truth. Maybe his motives had been good, but that still didn't mean he had trusted her or been completely honest with her. Gemma was beginning to realise she was still better off not relying on anyone.

And Ethan? The thought of the momentous lie that he had carried out still made her feel ill. How could someone who had been so close to her let her believe he had been dead for over six years? Her twin brother. If there'd been anyone he could have turned to, it should have been her, she thought. How could she trust that he would follow through with what he'd agreed to? Agreeing with Saul and Dad that he would stay at *Kangaroo Corner* while Saul talked to his trusted contacts in Darwin.

Gemma put the knife down, put the onions in a plastic container and sealed the lid with a snap. Anger pumped through her and her tears dried.

She couldn't trust anyone.

As they sat outside later that night and Tony cooked steak and sausages and the onions on the barbecue that he carried on the back of his ute, Gemma was still quiet.

'Nice salad, love,' Tony said as he put his plate back on the table.

'Thanks.' She knew Saul had been trying to catch her eye right through dinner, but she'd avoided looking in his direction. At one stage, he'd put his hand on her knee, and she'd stiffened until he'd removed it.

Then Ethan had asked how long they'd been together, and her answer had been snappish. 'Saul and I travelled here to find Screw. I have an apartment in town, and he lives at his place.'

She looked across at Saul and this time, he looked away. Ethan looked from one to the other and didn't say any more, but she did see her father give an almost imperceptible shake of his head as Ethan looked across to him.

Saul stood and turned towards the van. His voice was bright but his shoulders were stiff. 'Who'd like a Cornetto? I've got a pack in the freezer.'

'Sounds good,' Tony replied.

'Yes, please,' Ethan said.

'Gemma?'

'No. I'll do the dishes while you three have a chat. I'm sure you need to figure out what's happening so you're all on the same page. Then I'm going to have an early night.' Gemma held out her hand for their plates and went into the van after Saul came out with the ice creams. She ran the hot water, and when the sink was full, she started washing the dishes.

Someone came inside and she turned, expecting to see Saul, but it was Dad reaching for the tea towel.

'Thought you could do with some company,' he said.

'Don't you want to hear what Saul is going to do?'

'I do, but we're going to wait until you're out there too. I know when you get the shits, you get over it quickly. You always used to anyway when you were a kid.'

'I'm not a kid now,' she said hotly. 'Besides, I haven't got the shits, as you so politely put it.'

'So, what's wrong, love? Have you and Saul had a blue?'

'No. I've just been doing some thinking and I've realised we're not right for each other.'

'Do you think it's a good time to be making a decision like that? It's been a pretty torrid couple of days.'

'It has.' She ran the dishcloth over the plates.

'Saul's a good man, love. I was really happy when I saw you'd got together.'

Gemma sighed. 'I know, Dad. I was just thinking what a good man he is, but he didn't trust me enough to tell me the truth.'

'Not my business, but I think you're being hard. It's too easy to lose someone you love. And more often than not, it's too late to do something about it.' His tone held bitterness and Gemma turned to look at him.

'Do you mean Mum?'

Tony pulled a face. 'I know your mother put her career first, but she was doing it with the right motivation. She wanted a nice place to live, and she wanted the best for you and Ethan. She just got a bit lost along the way.'

Gemma was surprised. 'Do you still care about Mum?'

'Of course I do.' He smiled. 'She was my one love, and she is the mother of my children. We were happy once, but we grew apart. When Ethan went missing, it was the death knell.'

'And now she's remarried, so there's no chance.'

'Between you and me, I don't think that'll last much longer.'

Gemma stared at him. 'What makes you say that?'

'Your mum and I talk a fair bit these days, and I get the impression she's not happy.'

'Colin is an absolute sleazeball.' Gemma couldn't help her smile when her father burst out laughing.

'That's the best news I've heard for a long time.'

'Even better than Ethan being alive?'

'That wasn't news, love. That was the best *moment* of my life,' he said. 'When I parked the ute at the station, he was walking out of the main building. He looked up and saw me, and for a moment, I didn't know why this guy was running at me. And then I knew.'

Gemma brushed away the tears in her eyes. 'That's pretty special.'

'You know, he could have turned the other way and simply disappeared, but it shows that Ethan loves us.' Tony finished wiping the last dish. 'I see the way Saul looks at you, and I have no doubt how much he loves you. Think very carefully before you make any decisions, won't you?'

Her father's words were still in her mind as she said goodbye to Ethan. It was hard, but he held Gemma close. 'I promise you I won't disappear again. Trust me, Gem?'

She nodded. 'I do. And hopefully, we'll see you soon.'

'I hope so too. I'm putting a lot of faith in you, Saul.' Ethan let her go and held his hand out to Saul. 'If you get this sorted, mate, I'll owe you big time.'

'My pleasure, mate. It'll be good to have you back in Alice.'

They watched as the lights of Ethan's motorbike disappeared into the night.

'I'm going to hit the sack,' Tony said. 'I plan an early start tomorrow. I'll leave before sun-up, so I'll say my goodbyes too.'

'I'll come and see you when I'm in Darwin, Tony,' Saul said. 'If you're still there.'

'I'll be there for a few weeks, then I think I'll come back to the Alice for a while. No place like home, is there, Gem?'

She smiled as she hugged her father. 'No, Dad, there's not.'

'Home is where the heart is. You remember that, love.'

Heat rushed into Gemma's face as she caught Saul's eye. 'I will, Dad,' she said steadily. She gave Dad one last hug and he disappeared into his swag.

Saul stepped away from her and spoke quietly. 'I'm happy to sleep outside in the foldback chair if you'd prefer that.'

'Do you want to?' Gemma whispered. Dad's swag wasn't that far away.

'Do you want me too?' His face held no expression.

'I asked you first,' she said, not caring she was being childish. 'Do you really want to sleep outside?'

His lips lifted slightly at one corner. Was that a crack in the expressionless face? A hint that he still wanted her?

'It's up to you.' Saul sighed and ran a hand through his short hair. 'For about five seconds earlier, I thought you and I were both too damaged to make this work.'

'And?'

'And then I remembered how much I loved you. I'm not going to give you up without a fight, Gem. Even if you don't love me back, I'm going to work on it.'

Happiness unfurled in Gemma's chest. 'There's no point fighting for me,' she said, unable to resist teasing him. 'I love you too, you goose. I'm sorry about before. I know you were doing what you thought was best for me.'

'No more words, Gem. I'll show you.' Saul pulled her close with one arm as he balanced on that bloody moon boot. His lips came down on hers firmly and she wrapped her arms around his neck. Her whole world narrowed and only included Saul, and the sensation of his lips caressing hers, his arms holding her close.

Saul stepped back and held his hand out to her. 'Come to bed with me? We'll get an early start home tomorrow.'

Gemma let his fingers wrap around hers. 'Home?'

'Yes, home to our place. I'm hoping that I can talk you into letting that apartment go. I have a perfectly good house that's big enough for both of us. And my house is closer to the school and you won't have to run any red lights to get there every morning.'

'I think I could be persuaded,' she giggled.

'About bloody time,' came a voice from the swag.

CHAPTER

44

Alice Springs
Thursday, two weeks later

Gemma waited impatiently for the arrivals board at Alice Springs airport to be updated. Saul had been in Darwin all week, and now it seemed his flight home had been delayed by a tropical storm. She was going back to school next week and had filled in this week moving her stuff over to Saul's shed. The three-month lease she'd taken out on the apartment was almost up and she'd been able to get out of the agreement a week early as the agent had a waiting list for rentals.

Now that all her clothes were at Saul's, Gemma had pulled her favourite dress from one of the Woolies bags holding her clothes and dressed up to meet him at the airport. A cool, loose dress with a black background dotted with big bright red poppies swished around her knees, cinched to her waist with a bright red leather belt that matched her sandals. With a grin, she'd applied her one and only red lipstick; Saul probably wouldn't recognise her. She hadn't spoken to him since last night when he'd called with his flight details before dinner.

'I won't say much on the phone but there was already some intelligence about it,' he'd told her. 'They knew about the drug stuff, but the mining was news to them. A Northern Territory Joint Organised Crime Task Force operation was set up a couple of years back to investigate suspicious electronic interstate money transfers. They knew the money laundering was drug-based but they've never been able to find where the drugs were being produced.'

'And what about Ethan? What did they have to say about him?' There'd been a slight hesitation. 'Saul? Is everything okay? He hasn't taken off, has he?'

'I wasn't going to tell you until I got back, but he's actually been up here too. Once they heard what I had to say, they sent a chopper over to Kangaroo Crossing.'

'Is he all right?'

'Don't worry. Your dad met him and organised a solicitor to be there. It's going okay.'

'So how long do you think it's all going to take?'

'We're not privy to that, but the anticipation in the room was obvious today. I'd say they'll move pretty fast. They were talking about making us stay in Darwin, but we managed to talk our way into being allowed to come home.'

'I'm pleased to hear that.'

'We all had to sign documents to say we wouldn't say anything. Your dad and Ethan are driving down later in the week.'

'Okay, I know nothing. I can't wait to have you home, Saul. How's your ankle been?'

'Good. No pain, but I can't wait to get this moon boot off tomorrow.'

'Oh, I meant to text you. The plumber came today. The bathroom's all done. He's coming back to hook up the hot-water system at twelve tomorrow. We'll be back by then, won't we?'

'Easy. The flight lands at ten past nine.'

'Okay, I'll be waiting.'

Gemma looked at her watch and frowned. The flight was already two hours late and the board hadn't been updated for half an hour. She had to let the plumber into the house in just over half an hour, and it would take her fifteen minutes to get there. Hurrying across to the desk, she queried the guy on the check-in counter. 'Hi, do you have any more information about the Air North flight arrival time?'

'We're about to update the board. Sorry you've had to wait so long, it's just taken off, so ETA is just after one.'

'Thanks,' she said with a smile. 'I'll go home for a while and come back.'

He nodded and turned back to the computer. Gemma pulled her car keys out and headed outside to the car park. After being in the air-conditioning for such a long time, the heat hit her like a solid wall. As she crossed the concrete to where she'd parked her car in the shade under the sole tree on the side close to the entry, a stocky guy got out of a big black ute. As he closed the door, she was surprised to see the Parks and Wildlife logo on his shirt pocket. He looked at her and she gave him a brief nod as she walked past. It wasn't until she'd reached her car that she realised he had followed her.

'You Saul's woman?' he asked, belligerence in his voice.

Fear crawled up Gemma's spine as she saw his wild expression. She took a quick look around the car park, and her mouth dried as she realised they were the only two outside the terminal building.

'I'm sorry, do I know you?'

'I said, are you Saul's woman?' His cheeks were florid and spit flew out of his mouth. Gemma turned away and clicked the unlock button. As she reached for the door handle, a motor revved loudly next to them, and she swung around. The black ute had pulled up between her car and the terminal, blocking the view of anyone who may have come outside.

'Get in.' She gasped as something hard pressed into her side. She looked down to see a gun like something she'd seen in the movies against her dress. 'You want to see lover boy alive? Get in the fucking car. Now!'

He grabbed her arm and shoved her into the back seat. He jumped in the front passenger seat and Gemma heard the doors click.

'Get moving, Darren,' he yelled.

The ute sped out of the car park and turned north. Gemma's eyes were wide as the fat guy turned around with his hand out. 'Now, tell me where your brother's gone.'

*

Saul heaved a sigh of the relief as the 'prepare for landing' call came over the intercom. It had been a tough week, and he'd missed Gemma. Talking to her every night hadn't been enough; he'd worried about her being alone out at his place. Until this stuff was sorted, they'd be careful, especially once Ethan was back in town.

Max had shaken his hand as he'd said goodbye last night. He'd joined Saul for dinner at his motel after the last meeting had finished.

'At least we know that Parks isn't compromised. I was pretty worried about Terry being involved,' Max had said as they had a beer before dinner. 'We did a quiet audit of the Alice branch finances and he's squeaky clean.'

'Just a lazy, useless slug.'

'Confidentially, I'm going to come down and tell him he's going on a performance program.' Max had gestured to the barman for another round of drinks. 'I'd like you to think about your future there. I know what you're capable of, Saul, and I'm going to request that he puts you in charge of development of the eastern section of the district. What do you think of that?'

'Seriously?'

Max had laughed. 'Yes, seriously. You've got a great future ahead of you, Saul.'

'Great, then if you think I can do it, I'm in. I was going to call him in the morning about going back to work, but I'll flick him an email instead. Easier to stay low-key.'

The plane banked to the left as it approached the airport at Alice. Saul pressed his face to the window as they descended and smiled when he spotted Gemma's red sedan in the car park. She'd be peed off at having to wait for so long. Finally, they landed and taxied to the terminal. Saul was last off; he didn't want to hold up the passengers, and he was still a bit slow on the moon boot. Only one more day—and night—to put up with it. He was hoping that they could move into the house over the weekend. He hadn't mentioned it to Gemma yet; he wanted to see her face when he told her.

The terminal was bustling with passengers and their families, and Saul looked around for Gemma. While he was waiting for the luggage to come onto the carousel, he walked over to the door and looked outside, wondering if she was waiting in her car with the aircon on and hadn't noticed the plane land. There was a voice behind him and he turned with a smile, but it was the woman who'd sat in front of him on the plane talking to a man.

Saul waited for a couple of minutes and the carousel started up. He walked over and collected his bag, but there was still no sign of Gemma. After putting the bag down on the floor beside him, he pulled out his phone and called her, but she didn't pick up and it went to voicemail.

'I've landed, Gem.'

With a frown, he headed outside and walked across the car park. Maybe it hadn't been her car he'd seen. Maybe she was still at the house with the plumber.

He stood beside the car and looked inside, and his stomach began to churn. It was Gemma's car; Atty's spare lead was on the passenger seat beside her handbag. As he hurried back to the terminal, he tried her number again. No luck.

There was a queue at the check-in desk; the final passengers catching the departing flight were collecting boarding passes and he waited impatiently to reach the front of the queue, keeping an eye on the door of the ladies' room in case she was in there.

'Excuse me, my name's Saul Pearce and I came off the Darwin flight. I was just after some information,' he said. 'My partner was meeting me, and her car is in the car park but there's no sign of her. I've tried to call her but she's not answering.'

'What does she look like?' the clerk asked.

'Petite, slim, dark hair.'

The guy frowned. 'There was a dark-haired young woman here most of the morning. If it's the same one, she asked about the new ETA a couple of hours ago. When I told her the flight was just leaving Darwin, she said she'd go home for a while. You say the car is still in the car park?'

Saul looked around and nodded. The terminal was almost empty now. 'Yes, it's definitely hers.'

'Jill, can you go and check the ladies' room and see if there's anyone in there?'

'Sure.' The woman sitting at the desk behind the counter stood, walked across to the door, pushed it open and came straight out. 'No, it's empty.'

'Maybe a friend picked her up for a coffee or something? It was a long wait,' the guy said. 'Maybe they got delayed.'

Saul took a deep breath. 'That could be right.' He hid his fear and uncertainty. It was so unlike Gemma. Even though she was often disorganised, she was punctual. There was no way she would have left her car at the terminal, and if there'd been a problem, she would have texted him. 'Thanks for your help. I'll grab a cab home and we'll come back for the car later.' He picked up his bag and hurried across the terminal, relieved to see two taxis at the taxi rank.

He looked over at her car, but there was no one there.

CHAPTER
45

Ross Highway
Thursday, 2.00 pm

Gemma sat in the back of the ute without speaking. She'd handed her phone over, and the fat guy had taken it and put his head down. 'What's your password?'

When she'd refused to answer him, he'd simply stared at her then lifted the gun.

Her heart thudded. 'It's facial recognition,' she said.

He threw the phone back to her, and Gemma deliberately let it slip off her lap to the floor.

'I'm watching you. Don't do anything smart. Log in.'

Thinking quickly, she leaned forward and slid the mute button on as she picked the phone up. Her fingers were shaking as she lifted the phone to the front of her face, pretending to log in and quickly pressed the short-cut photo button. The camera snapped the guy holding the gun silently and she let go of her breath she'd been holding; she wasn't sure if it would click with the mute button on.

'What are you doing?'

'It won't recognise my face with my sunnies on,' she said, making her voice tremble.

'Well, take the bloody things off.'

'I'm shaking too much. Who are you? What do you want? I can give you my cards and I've got some cash.' As she tried to delay logging in, she managed to lower her covered eyes to the phone and quickly sent the photo to the first contact that came up.

Shit. It was Mum. She probably wouldn't have her phone at school and wouldn't ring straight back. The guy leaned over and Gemma held her breath as he raised his hands, yanked her sunglasses off and threw them onto the seat beside her.

She raised the phone and made her hands shake more than they already were, and managed to delete the photo as soon as she logged in. All she had to hope for was that the phone didn't ring.

She handed the phone over, her stomach roiling, and he turned away again.

After ten minutes, he threw the phone down in disgust and turned back to her. 'He's not in there.'

'Who?' the other guy he'd called Darren asked.

'Her bloody brother.' The fat guy turned around and stared at her. At least he hadn't picked the gun up again. She could think straight when he wasn't pointing it at her. 'Where is he?'

'Who, Saul? I was picking him up at the airport.'

'No, bitch. Your fucking brother.'

'Ethan?' Gemma made her voice high-pitched and scared. The scared wasn't hard to do.

'Yes, Ethan,' he parroted in a squeal.

Darren laughed.

'I don't know. I haven't seen him for six years.'

'Don't lie to me. I know you found him on that cattle station. There's a lot of people looking for him, but he seems to have disappeared again.'

'I don't know anything about that. But if he was, I'd be very happy.' Gemma leaned forward and put her hands on the back of his seat. 'Look I don't know who you are, mister, but I can tell you if my brother was alive, I wouldn't be here. I'd be up there asking him where he's been for the past six years. Why do you think he's alive? Who told you that?'

'Do you believe her, Terry?'

'Shut up, Darren.'

Gemma held back the gasp that rose in her throat. Terry? The fat guy was Saul's boss.

The car slowed and they turned into a residential street just past the truck museum. Terry lifted a remote as they turned into a driveway and the roller door of a shed at the side of the house opened. Darren drove the black ute into it, and the roller door came down.

'What are you doing?' Fear iced Gemma's blood, and her mouth dried.

Terry got out without looking at her. Gemma scrabbled along the seat to the corner away from the driver's side, unsure of what was happening. Darren got out and came around to the passenger side at the back where she was leaning against the door. He stood outside for a moment and Gemma looked around wildly. There was a dirt-covered twin cab ute parked beside them, but no one else in the shed.

Terry got in the driver's side of the car and as he looked back at her, the door she was leaning on opened and Gemma half fell out of the car. Darren grabbed for her arm, and she felt a shark prick in her wrist where he held her tightly. The last thing she was aware of was Terry saying, 'You know what to do.'

★

Saul got the taxi driver to wait while he opened the gate. It was the first time he'd spoken since he'd given him the address. 'I'll get you to drive me up to the shed and as soon I secure my dog, I'll drive down and open the gate for you.'

'Nothing worse than not being able to get around, hey mate?' the driver said. 'I had a hip replacement a couple of years back and I almost went stir-crazy.'

Saul nodded and climbed back into the taxi, looking around. The van was locked up and the front door of the house was shut. There was no sign of Gemma or the plumber.

As soon as Atty was tied to the run, Saul made sure he had water. He chucked his bag in the annexe and jumped into the ute. He opened the gate for the taxi to go out then followed him out, before securing the gate again. Sitting in the ute, he hit the steering wheel in frustration, wondering what he was doing. Where was he going to look for Gemma? Where should he go?

He had a bad feeling in his gut. There was something very wrong.

He put the phone onto speaker and dialled her again, but as he'd expected, there was no answer. Strangely, it didn't go to voicemail. The call was picked up then disconnected, and his unease grew.

Saul sat there for a while considering his options and then drove to Gemma's apartment, just in case she was there. He doubted it, but it was a stone he couldn't leave unturned.

As he expected, there was no sign of her and he knew he had to get help. Sitting in his ute outside, he scrolled through his contacts until he found the name he was looking for. The head of the task force had given him a number to call if he needed to contact them.

'Saul?' The answer was immediate.

'Yes. Dave, I have a problem and I don't know what to do. Gemma's gone missing. Her car's been abandoned at the airport and she's not taking my calls.'

'Right, leave it with me. Where are you?'

'I'll be at my property.' He reeled off the address.

'Okay, Saul. Just stay there. I've got a team working in Alice. They won't be long. And if you hear from Gemma, or anyone else, let me know immediately, no matter what is said.'

Saul hung up and rested his head on the steering wheel. If anything happened to Gemma . . . he couldn't bear to think about it. Being stressed would cloud his judgement and he needed to be on the ball.

Picking up the phone, he made the call he was dreading.

Tony picked up after a couple of rings. 'Hi Saul, back in the Alice?'

CHAPTER

46

Ruby Gap Road
Thursday, 4.00 pm

Gemma opened her eyes and tried to lift her right hand to her head. Something had just hit her and she couldn't figure out what. Saul was still in Darwin so he hadn't rolled over and clocked her. 'Atty,' she muttered, her voice strangely slurred. 'How did you get in the van?'

She opened her eyes slowly as confusion took hold. She was lying down but the bed was moving. Blinking, she tried to clear her eyes, but everything was blurred so she closed them. Her mouth was dry and her lips felt as though they were cracked when she tried to move her tongue to moisten her mouth. With a groan, she tried to roll over but her hands were stuck underneath her, and she couldn't move them.

Slowly, it all came back and her body stiffened as fear took hold. She was in the back of that twin cab ute, and she'd banged her head on the door when it had hit a bump. She lay perfectly still and quiet and the vehicle juddered again.

'No point talking. There's no one to hear you. Except me.'

Gemma rolled over onto her side and stretched her hands out. They were both numb; the pins and needles were excruciating as she flexed her fingers and the blood came rushing back. After a few minutes, she could feel them again and was able to push herself up to a sitting position. She reached up and clipped the seatbelt on.

Darren laughed when the catch clicked. 'Don't like my driving, love? It's the shit of a road, not my driving that's making it bumpy. That's what Saul said when we came out here looking at your brother's car.'

'I don't understand,' she managed to croak out. 'What are you doing? Why am I here?'

Darren reached down and passed a bottle of water over. 'Drink.'

'Thank you.' Taking it, she realised she was being polite to her kidnapper. Then again if she was co-operative, she might be able to get away.

'Not a lot to understand. You tell us where your brother is and you can go home.'

'I told you already, I don't know.'

'Really? Terry heard you had a touching reunion in WA a week or so back. Nothing's a secret in this town, you should know that.'

'Ethan's dead,' she lied. 'I can prove it to you. I can take you to his grave.'

'Terry needs to have a little talk with him, so if you won't tell us where he is, we'll have to tell him we've got you somewhere safe until he comes to pay us a visit. Terry was very unhappy to hear he was alive. Your brother's lain low for a long time. You and your family put on a good show looking for him.'

Gemma blinked and tried to clear the fuzziness in her eyes. He'd drugged her and it was still in her system. Her mouth dried and she felt like throwing up.

Maybe if she said she was going to be sick, he'd stop the car and she could make a run for it? *Stupid idea*. The way she felt, she wouldn't be able to stand up, let alone make a run for it. She unscrewed the cap, tipped the water bottle up and drank deeply. The more she drank, the more the drug he'd injected would leave her system. As she tipped her head back, she caught sight of Darren watching her in the rear-vision mirror. Another shiver of fear ran down her back as his eyes narrowed, almost as though he could hear her thoughts ticking over. She was entirely at his mercy until her strength came back. Gemma knew she'd be wise to make it look as though she was still groggy.

Gradually, her vision cleared, and she was surprised when she looked out the window; she must have been out to it for a long time. The shadows were long, and the sun was low in the sky as the mountains took on the blue haze of late afternoon. Taking notice of the surroundings, she tried to remember the road out and figure out how close they were to Ruby Gap, and whether they'd already passed Mike's skull-and-crossbones gate.

'Where are we?' she asked, thickening her words. 'My eyes are all funny. I want to go home.' If he thought she wasn't well, maybe he wouldn't watch her as closely.

'Does it matter? Or if your brother doesn't show up, would you like to know where you're going to end up?' He laughed, a nasty sound. 'It's your call whether you get to go home or not. Tell us where he is and you'll be back there.'

Sure I will. Fear crawled up Gemma's spine like one of the centipedes Atty had chased in the yard.

'I told you, Ethan's dead. You take me out to Ruby Gap and I'll prove it.' She deliberately made her voice weak and shaky then drew in a deep breath. 'I'll show you his grave.'

Darren sighed. 'Look, love. A word of advice. I mightn't agree with Terry's methods, but he's fair dinkum. You tell me where Ethan is, and I'll take you right back home.'

'I told you, he's in a grave out at Ruby Gap.'

Darren shrugged. 'Your choice, love. Your life.'

CHAPTER
47

Ross Highway
Thursday, 4.30 pm

Saul was surprised when he approached his property and two four-wheel-drive vehicles were already parked opposite the gate. No logos, no identifying marks on them, a white LandCruiser and a silver Isuzu MU-X. After the events of the past few weeks, he was wary.

He pulled up behind them, walked over to the driver's window of the LandCruiser and tapped on the glass. He looked in and didn't recognise the two men sitting in the front seats. The windows were tinted and it was hard to see in the back.

'Afternoon,' he said in a friendly tone. 'Can I help you there?'

The window opened halfway. 'Saul Pearce?'

Saul hesitated. 'Yes, and you are?'

'Detective Wayne Miller. You met my colleagues in Darwin earlier in the week. Dave called and told us to get out here. I believe
Gemma Hayden is missing?'

'Yes.' Relief came rushing in. 'Thanks for coming so quickly.'

'Is there somewhere we can discuss a few things?'

'Sure. I'll open the gate. You go through first and I'll follow you
in.'

Five minutes later, they were sitting around the barbecue table
in the big shed, and the detective had introduced Saul to the five
other members of the team. Atty was sitting beside Saul with his
head on his knee. He was quiet, and Saul rubbed his fingers on the
top of his head.

'We know she's only been missing a few hours, but Dave is sure
her disappearance is linked to the investigation,' Wayne said. 'We're
at such a delicate stage, we can't afford to go slamming in and risk
the whole operation. Because of the situation with Gemma, I've
been cleared to let you know that there is a raid out at Ruby Gap
tonight. We've received information they've got word they're being
watched and the whole operation is being dismantled tonight.
We're assuming that they'll load up and fly whatever they've got
there out tonight.'

'What do you mean a delicate stage? You mean you're not going
to do anything about Gemma?' Saul's tone was curt and laced with
frustration.

'No, I didn't say that, Saul. What I mean is we have to be very
careful. We've identified the major players in this operation, and
they're very clever. To run a drug business of that size for over seven
years in the one place shows just how careful and clever they are.
Our problem is that there's someone in our taskforce who's been
leaking information to them.'

'Shit!' Saul felt sick. 'How do you know that?'

'Because we've managed to infiltrate their operation in Perth in the transport side of the drugs, and that's how we know that they're aware we've located their lab and warehouse. We haven't been able to find out who the mole is.'

'A warehouse at Ruby Gap? Where the hell is that? I didn't see anything like that out there. Ethan said there was a small shed there six years ago with a small drug stash in it.'

'We've got the satellite footage. As the operation expanded, they've built a second shed where they manufacture the drugs. It's at the end of the road that leads out to the Atitjere community. About a kilometre further on, there's a runway in the desert. My team and Dave's are the only ones who know that, and they're all solid.'

'How can they do it? There's no power out there.'

'Solar-powered, with another shed holding the bank of batteries that provide their power.'

Saul shook his head. 'It's hard to believe we never knew. That would have been where the helicopter was going the weekend Gemma and I went out there.'

'It's a multimillion-dollar operation. It will be one of the biggest busts we've ever had in Australia. Once they leave here, the drugs go via Perth and to three locations in South-East Asia, and then they go onto container ships. It's worldwide distribution. We've been watching this for years, but we've never been able to find the lab until you guys came to our notice last week. I'm trusting you with this information, Saul, so you know the scale of what we're doing, and so you understand we just can't go blundering around, looking for Gemma. Those guys are on high alert, and they're deadly.'

Oh God, Gemma. 'I understand that, but tell me, what exactly are we going to be doing? We've already wasted half an hour sitting around here.'

'We've already got security footage from the airport. Gemma left the terminal and walked across to her car at 11.12 am. A man got out of a black RAM, and followed her. The ute drove over next to her car, blocking the view of Gemma. When the RAM left the car park, she was gone, so we assume she's in that car.'

'A bloody black RAM. One of those shadowed us all the way to Kangaroo Crossing. Did you get a numberplate?'

Wayne looked at the officer beside him. 'We can do better than that. We know who it's registered to.'

Saul jumped to his feet, and Atty gave a short sharp bark. 'Who?'

'Calm down, Saul. You want Gemma to be okay? We can't go blundering after them,' Wayne repeated. 'Max is on the afternoon flight down from Darwin, and he's going into the office on the pretext of meeting with Terry.'

'Terry? I thought he was in the clear? Is it his fucking ute?'

'No one is in the clear at this stage, but yes, that ute is registered to Terry O'Neil. We're anticipating that there'll be a call of some sort soon, to her family or to you. It depends on how public your relationship is. It seems a coincidence that Parks may be involved and it's your workplace.'

'Are you saying I'm under suspicion?'

'No—' Wayne paused as Saul's phone rang.

'It's Tony. Gemma's dad,' Saul said as he picked the phone up.

Wayne nodded and waited as Saul turned the speaker on and took the call.

'Tony? What is it?'

'I've just had a call from Jennifer. She was almost hysterical. She got a text message from Gemma four hours ago. She tried to call her and some guy answered, wanting to know where Ethan was. He told her Gemma was dead unless she told him.'

'What the fuck? What did Gemma's text say?'

'It's strange. No words . . . just a blurry photo taken inside a car.'

'Did Jennifer send it to you?

'Not yet.'

'Tony, can you ring her straight away and get us a copy of that photo. The police have a lead and that will confirm it. What did Jennifer tell him?'

'Jen gave the guy a piece of her mind and told him he was an idiot, that Ethan was dead, and to put Gemma on.'

Saul shook his head; that was Mrs Hayden for you. 'That would have gone down well.'

'Shit, yeah. I'm sick to my gut. We should have told her what was going on straight up. I didn't mention Ethan. I told her Gemma was missing. She's already on her way to Brisbane to catch a flight to Alice. She'll arrive about nine tonight.'

'Okay.'

'What's happening there, Saul? Any news?'

Wayne lifted one hand and shook his head.

Saul nodded. 'I'm meeting with the police now. I'll get back to you as soon as I know anything. Get the photo to me.'

'Okay. We're heading for the airport. We'll be out of service for a couple of hours. Ethan and I get in at six. If there's any news, text me.' Tony lowered his voice. 'Ethan's blaming himself. Reckons he should have just taken off. Tell them to find our girl, Saul.'

CHAPTER
48

Ruby Gap Road
Thursday, 5.00 pm

Gemma kept her eyes closed and let her head slump to the side as far as she could while still being able to see the landscape flashing past. Relief and a little bit of hope built as she realised that they were past Arltunga and had turned onto the Ruby Gap Road. From what she remembered, the gate to Mike's property was about three kilometres past the slight rise they were climbing. Turning her head a little to the front, but still keeping it down, she kept an eye on Darren as she reached down and slowly and quietly undid the belt of her dress. A centimetre at a time, she slowly slid it through the loops, pretending to slump forward when it got caught on the seat behind her. Her hands were low enough that he couldn't see what she was doing without leaning back and looking over into the back seat.

The belt was thin and stiff, and she looped each end around her fingers. As they approached the bend where she thought Mike's driveway was, she started to moan.

'I'm going to vomit. Stop the car.'

'Jesus,' he said. 'I'll pull over, but you stay there until I come around. No funny business.'

Gemma moaned again and forced herself to dry retch and gag.

'Oh, for fuck's sake.' The car slowed as Darren eased back on the accelerator. As he looked away, Gemma quickly leaned forward and looped the belt over his head, pulling it around his throat as tightly as she could. As his head was forced back against the headrest, he tried to yell and lifted both hands to his neck trying to pull it off. As Gemma pulled harder, the ute swerved to the side, and she kept pulling as they headed towards the rocky embankment.

Gemma lowered her head against the back of the seat in the brace position, kept her arms high, and held the belt tight as the red rock loomed ahead. Darren was tugging at the belt but it was too thin for him to get a grip.

With a loud crunch, the ute hit the embankment. Gemma flinched and let go of the belt as both front airbags deployed with a loud explosion. Her ears ringing, she undid her seatbelt and pushed the door open. Head down, she took off up the road, her flimsy sandals slipping on the rocky surface. The bend was ahead and she kept running, not game to slow down or look back, but she couldn't hear any sounds behind her. As soon as she was at the bend, she looked ahead, and the relief was sweet as she saw the skull-and-crossbones sign at the front of Mike's property.

The gate was locked but it didn't deter her. Hitching up her dress, Gemma climbed up the wire of the gate and dropped to the dirt road on the other side, hoping desperately that Mike was there.

She had no idea how far the house was from the gate. Her throat was dry and her head was starting to ache.

She jogged for half an hour until she had to take a break in the shade, but there was no sign of a dwelling. Worry stuck in her throat. Saul would know she was missing by now, and she wondered what he'd do. She sat for a while in the shade with her head in her hands then set off again. The track began to climb and her breath came in short gasps; a couple of times, she had to stop as faintness threatened.

As she climbed higher, the track wound between low red rock cliffs. At the top of the hill, she bent double, her hands on her hips, fighting for breath. A dog barked ahead; a deep and ferocious bark that sounded like a warning. Her head began to spin again, and with her eyes closed, she leaned against the smooth bark of a ghost gum growing in a gap between the cliffs.

Gradually, she became aware of the sound of an approaching vehicle. Her eyes flew open and she looked around at the landscape below as the panoramic view opened out to her. She could see the road in each direction, but there was no sign of a motorbike or a car coming from the house.

She turned slowly, and her breath caught as she looked down at a white ute coming from a stand of trees at the bend in the track. The front was smashed in and it was coming slowly towards the base of the hill. Gemma's eyes widened; she wondered how Darren was driving with the airbag deployed, and how he'd got through the locked gate. Why had he come onto Mike's property? As she watched, she realised there was a motorbike following the car.

Mike opened the gate for him.

Gemma looked around, searching for a place to hide. The dog was still kicking up a racket over at the house. Looking around desperately, she noticed a rockfall at the base of the cliff twenty metres or so away from the ghost gum. Scurrying over as quickly as she could, Gemma just reached the rockpile and squeezed behind it when she heard the ute and the bike coming up the hill.

To her horror, both vehicles stopped, and a door slammed closed. There was just enough room for her to press herself between the flat cliff face and the rockfall. Their voices were muted and she strained to hear as footsteps approached.

Please, no.

'There's binoculars in the console of the ute,' she heard Darren say. 'If she's on the road, we'll see her from up here.'

'How long ago did she take off?' It was definitely Mike's voice. 'Would she have had time to get to the house?'

'No, she was pretty groggy. I thought we'd pass her before here.'

'Are you sure she came this way?'

'Well, she didn't go back the way we came and you came from the shed, so if you didn't pass her, she either hid in the bush or climbed over your gate. I'll kill the bloody bitch when I get my hands on her. Choke the life out of her, see how she likes it. If I hadn't crashed the ute, she would have choked me.'

'If you and fucking Terry hadn't taken matters into your own hands, we could have been on our way by now.'

Gemma froze. She gulped down a breath to stop herself making a noise. No wonder Mike had warned her and Saul to stay away. He'd helped them, given first aid to Saul and taken her to the ute, but it had all been to get them away. There'd been no well-meaning in his actions.

There was the sound of a door opening and closing and then silence. Gemma closed her eyes, holding her breath and ignoring the growing pressure on her bladder.

'Where the bloody hell is she?' Darren swore again. 'There's no sign of her on your road.'

'I don't know but I can tell you this; your life won't be worth anything if she gets away. We could have dealt with her brother as soon as he showed up, but you and Terry and your bloody stupid idea have stuffed things right up. You should have told me you'd found that Hayden prick. If she gets away, she can identify you both.'

'Don't fuckin' blame me. It was Terry's idea. He was saving his own skin.'

'You go look around the creek. She must be hiding in the bush this side of the gate. I'll go back to the house in case she got further.'

Darren's voice was closer. 'She won't get far. She's still half drugged.'

'Just fucking find her. I'll be back at the house. The plane's coming in after dark and I've still got stuff to load in my ute.'

The motorbike started and when it faded away, there was silence—no voices, no birdsong, no wind in the trees.

Gemma jumped and put her hands to her mouth as Darren yelled at the top of his voice. 'I'm going to find you, and when I do, it won't be pleasant. But I'll enjoy it, bitch.' He laughed and her blood chilled.

Gemma fought the whimper rising in her chest as a rock rolled out near her. He was coming closer.

He's going to find me.

Her head shook uncontrollably as fear clamped hold on her body. She clenched her jaw and bit her bottom lip hard. The metallic taste of blood filled her mouth, but that was better than crying out.

She hid, completely still with her eyes squeezed shut, not drawing a breath until the sound of a vehicle approached. Gemma focused on her breathing. Something crawled across her leg but she kept her eyes shut and didn't make a sound.

'You forget something?' Darren said.

'Yeah. No witnesses. Sorry, mate.'

As long as she lived, Gemma would never forget the sound of Darren's hoarse scream before the single rifle shot.

The vehicle started up and headed down the hill and it was a long time before she forced herself to move.

CHAPTER
49

Alice Springs
Thursday, 5.00 pm

'It's Terry and bloody Darren,' Saul exclaimed as the text came in from Tony. 'It's them in the black RAM. I'd never seen it because Terry had a Parks ute for work.'

'Right. We won't wait for Max to arrive. That's enough to arrest them both if we can find them,' Wayne said. 'You stay here, Saul.'

'I want—'

'No. I'll keep in touch, I promise. Terry's back at the office; we've had that confirmed.'

'Where's Darren?'

'Unknown, but we'll put the heavies on your boss. Don't worry.'

'So what do I do?' Saul's voice was fierce. 'Sit here and twiddle my thumbs? Have a cup of fucking tea?'

Wayne stood and glanced at his watch. 'Max's flight lands in half an hour. If you go get him, it'll save me taking one of my team off the job. If you agree to do as we say, you can bring him to the Parks office.'

By the time Saul picked up Max and they'd driven across town, it was late afternoon, but Saul was blind to the beauty of the sunset and the mountains.

Max's phone buzzed as they pulled up outside the office. He nodded at Saul. 'You can come in with me. Terry's been arrested, and he's talking.'

Saul was out of the ute and heading for the office as fast as he could with the bloody moon boot on when Max caught up to him. 'Professionalism, Saul. I know you can do the right thing.'

'Mate, with respect, don't tell me what to do. Until Gemma's found, I'll do whatever it takes. Remember, I'm on leave. I don't have to follow work rules.'

He was met with a frown, but no comment. Max walked beside him as they went into the building, and Wayne met them in the foyer.

'Any developments?' Saul asked quickly.

'Yes. Apparently, Darren's taken Gemma out to the shed at Ruby Gap. Their plan was to keep her there until they found out where Ethan was. Terry knew nothing about the whole outfit moving out tonight. It seems he's pretty small fry in the whole set-up. So, it's good news. Gemma's kidnapping has nothing to do with the heavies in the operation.'

'Okay, let's go then.' Saul turned to the door.

Wayne shook his head. 'Sorry, Saul, you're not going anywhere. The team heading out there now has been told that Gemma could be out there, and to put her safety as a priority.'

Saul stood rigid and lifted his hand to rub the back of his neck. 'I want to be there.'

Wayne looked at Max. 'I'll agree to the two of you going as far as Arltunga and waiting there until it's over. That's the best I can offer, mate. Take it or leave it.' He switched his gaze to Saul.

'I'll agree to that.' Saul nodded jerkily. He wasn't happy, but it was better than being stuck in Alice Springs.

'When we find her, we'll only be half an hour away from you if you meet us halfway.'

Saul managed a smile. 'When you find her? I like your confidence.'

'Mate, she'll be fine. They took her so they could get to Ethan.'

'And what were their intentions then? When they found him?'

'Terry said they were going to let her go as long as Ethan was prepared to forget he ever saw Terry out there, and she agreed to forget about the kidnapping.'

'That's hard to believe.'

'Terry's caved. He was out there when Ethan and Jed Turner saw the meth shed, and he saw what happened. He's prepared to say that Ethan was defending himself when he killed that bloke. According to Terry, the guy he hit axe—the ex-cop—was one of the bosses. They got rid of his body and his death was never reported.'

Saul put his hand over his eyes. 'This is a whole new world to me. I can't believe this sort of stuff's happened out at Ruby Gap.'

Wayne nodded. 'Welcome to my world, mate. It's not pretty.'

★

The night enveloped Saul and Max in darkness as they sat in Saul's ute at Arltunga, a short distance from the turn-off to Ruby Gap. They'd followed the convoy of police four-wheel-drive vehicles this far, and then stopped when Wayne had directed them to.

'I'll stay in touch,' he radioed over the closed channel.

Frustration filled Saul; he felt absolutely useless. Gemma was out there somewhere, in the middle of the biggest drug bust in the nation's history, and he was sitting in a car, waiting. Max had tried to engage him in conversation—Saul knew it was to take his mind off Gemma—but his monosyllabic answers soon had his former boss giving up. They sat quietly, each lost in their own thoughts, the silence broken by the chirping of crickets and the occasional monkey call of the blue-winged kookaburra. His skin crawled as the eerie call of a wild dingo echoed across the gully, and Saul prayed that wherever Gemma was, she was safe. At this time of the year heading into the dry, snakes were active at night and dingoes roamed the bush, seeking food. If she was out there in the scrub, she was as much at risk from the natural world as from her kidnappers.

They both looked up as two helicopters approached from the west, and headed out towards Ruby Gap.

'Things are starting to move, mate. Not much longer,' Max said.

'Do you reckon we can start heading out there?' Every nerve ending in Saul's body was poised, ready to get moving.

'No. We wait.'

'I can't sit in here any longer.' Saul opened the door and climbed down from the ute. He leaned against the bonnet, looking ahead. The indigo blue night sky was brilliant with stars, and a small crescent moon high above them. Saul took a deep breath and put his head back. His body tensed as he spotted the navigation lights of a plane flying low in the east. He went around to Max's window.

'Shit. Their plane's just come in. I hope the police choppers were down in time.'

Max got out of the car and stood beside him. 'Almost time. She'll be right, mate.'

'I couldn't bear to lose Gemma again,' Saul said. 'This last month has made me realise what I want from life.'

'Again?'

'Long story.'

'I look forward to hearing about it when I meet—' Max paused and cocked his head to the side. 'I can hear a vehicle coming. Slowly.'

Saul frowned and looked ahead. 'So can I, but there's no headlights.'

'Move the ute to the middle of the road. It's narrow enough up ahead to stop anyone getting past.'

As Saul started the ute, he left the headlights off.

Max radioed Wayne. 'WM, MP here. There's a vehicle approaching. No lights. One of ours? Over.'

The detective's response was instant. 'No. Don't engage. Over.'

Max turned to Saul. 'Park it up there about fifty metres then we'll go bush and wait and see what happens.'

Saul moved the ute onto the Ruby Gap Road and parked it across the centre of the narrowest part of the track. Two ghost gums glowed white in the dim moonlight on each side of the road and would make it almost impossible for a vehicle to get around.

'Quick, mate, out and into the scrub. There's a bit of a rocky outcrop over there.'

Saul put both windows up, grabbed his keys and locked the ute before following Max into the scrub. A faint light showed over the crest of the hill ahead. 'Look, they've got their parking lights on. Just enough to light up the track. I hope it's enough to see my ute. Bloody hell, I don't want to be stuck out here when Wayne tells us to get out there.'

CHAPTER
50

Arltunga
Thursday, 8.00 pm

As she approached the turn-off to Arltunga, Gemma was tempted to turn the headlights on, but she resisted. She had waited two hours after hearing the gunshot, until it was pitch dark and all had been quiet for a long time. Her head had cleared and the shakiness had left her limbs, but her mouth was dry and a slight headache remained. It was a hot night, and she was thirsty.

As she'd stepped slowly and silently from her hiding place, faint moonlight reflected on the white Parks ute sitting almost at the top of the hill. Darren lay in the dirt behind it, and Gemma held back her gasp as she approached his lifeless form. She could see the pool of blood beneath his head, and she knew without going too close that there was nothing she could do. Moving across to the smashed ute, she opened the door carefully. He'd driven it this far, so she should be able to drive it out.

The white airbags had gone down and it looked like Darren had used something sharp to hasten their deflation. The one on the steering wheel had two slashes across it. Gemma reached around, feeling the dashboard, and relief was sweet as her fingers touched the keys.

She sat there for a moment, trying to find the courage to turn the key and start the engine. There'd been no sound of any vehicles after Mike had driven off. She fought off nausea as she thought of him killing Darren. No matter that Mike had helped them when Saul had been gored by the scrubber, her instinctive fear of him had been right.

Taking a deep breath, she turned the key and the engine flared to life. She'd driven slowly down the hill with the headlights off and the windows down, listening for any sound, but she'd reached the gate without incident. The gate was wide open and she switched the parking lights on, heading towards Arltunga.

It had been a slow trip, with the bull bar hanging half off the front of the vehicle and scraping on the road. As Gemma got closer to the T-intersection that went north to Hale River and south to the safety of Alice Springs, she could see something white in the middle of the road ahead. Her heart pounded. Was Mike waiting for her? Her hands gripped the steering wheel as she thought of turning around, or getting out and running, or simply risking it.

There was no sign of anyone around the ute, but it was blocking the road. She doubted she could get around it without going bush. She approached slowly, her senses on high alert, listening and watching for any sign of movement.

As she got closer, Gemma's eyes widened, and her heart kicked up a notch.

It was Saul's ute.

She flicked the headlights on to confirm it. Pulling the damaged vehicle to the side, she jumped out and hurried over. The doors were locked and there was definitely no one in it.

Gemma looked around and put her hands to her mouth. 'Saul!' she yelled as loud as she could. 'Saul, where are you?'

Desperation filled her, along with fear that Saul had been out looking for her and had encountered Mike. Fear that she'd come this far and couldn't go any further. Leaning back against his ute, she put her hands over her eyes, willing herself not to break now. A sound in the bush across the road made her tense and her eyes flew open, scanning the darkness.

'Gemma!'

Two figures emerged from the bush, one hurrying ahead, and the other limping behind.

'Saul?' she called warily, not recognising the other man.

'It's okay, Gemma. I'm Max, Saul's boss. Are you all right?' He hurried ahead of Saul, but Gemma only had eyes for the man she loved. Saul's limp turned into a jerky run and she waited for him to reach her.

'Gemma. Gemma, love.' Saul's arms went around her and he held her tightly to him. She closed her eyes and let the warmth of his body calm her. 'It's okay, sweetheart, I've got you. No one can hurt you now.'

★

When the news broke the following morning, Gemma had been discharged from hospital with no lasting effects from the sedative she had been given. Tony and Jennifer were waiting at the house when they arrived home, but Ethan was still at the police station.

Tony handed a copy of the *Centralian Advocate* to Saul.

Gemma sat quietly and listened as he read it to her.

A sixty-two-year-old man was arrested and charged yesterday after the Northern Territory JOCTF officers executed a search warrant at a remote property in the East MacDonnell Ranges. He is facing a number of charges including murder. Police seized methamphetamines, more than $500,000 in cash and financial documentation from his property and a warehouse in the nature park at Ruby Gap. The park has been closed to the public while investigations continue.

Two other Alice Springs men accused of being involved in the alleged drug-dealing network were also arrested and charged with a range of offences after search warrants were executed at their Northern Territory homes, and at a government office. A collection of rubies and other precious stones has also been seized.

Saul and Gemma's place, one month later

Gemma put the knife down on the chopping board and looked around the kitchen of *their* house. Saul had insisted that she stop calling it *his* house the week their lives had gone back to normal. The house was finished, and the barbecue area had been completed just in time for their celebration this afternoon. The stone kitchen benches were covered with a variety of salad bowls and Saul's favourite dessert—a lemon meringue pie—had just come out of the oven.

'Your mum and dad just pulled up, and it looks like Ethan's with them.' Saul wandered into the kitchen and stood behind Gemma, nuzzling her neck.

'Can you hold the fridge open while I put the salads in?'

Saul smiled and dropped a kiss on her lips before he opened the fridge. 'Have I told you how much I love having a domestic goddess in the kitchen?'

Gemma slid the potato salad into the fridge then swatted him playfully. 'Yes, several times.' She paused before she picked up the next bowl. 'Hang on, did you say Mum and Dad are in the one car?'

He smiled. 'I did.'

'I wonder?' Gemma said thoughtfully as she put the green salad on the shelf and closed the fridge door. 'Since Mum told me she threw Colin out, she's talked about Dad a lot. And she's really mellowed. I'm pleased she came over for the Easter holidays.' A car door shut and she and Saul went over to the kitchen window. Tony walked around to the front of his new car, and opened the door for Jennifer. The look on her mother's face as she looked up at her former husband made Gemma smile. 'Stranger things have happened.'

'There's certainly been a lot of that since you came back to Alice.'

'But it's all over now.' Gemma lifted her hand as Saul held the screen door open for her, and the diamond and ruby ring on her left hand caught the sunlight.

'It is. A few loose ends to tie up and then we can relax.'

Ethan was hurrying across the back lawn carrying a box. 'Hey, Gem.' He kissed her cheek and then juggled the box to one hand and shook Saul's hand. 'How are you, almost brother-in-law?'

'I'm good, thanks, mate. What have you got there?'

'Something pretty special.'

Jennifer and Tony walked over from the car; their father was carrying a brightly wrapped parcel.

'If it's an engagement present, at least you could have wrapped yours up, Eth,' Gemma said with a grin.

'Nuh, I chipped into that one.' He gestured to the parcel Tony put on the barbecue table.

When the greetings were over and everyone had a drink in front of them, Ethan skivvied Gemma along. 'Hurry up and open your present, and then I can show you this.' He tapped on the box.

Gemma did as he asked and widened her eyes when she saw the Thermomix inside. 'Oh wow, thank you! I've wanted one of those for ages.' She grinned as she looked at Ethan fidgeting in his chair. 'Now you can show us what's in that box.'

Since Ethan had been advised that there were no charges to be laid over the incident at Ruby Gap six years earlier—they'd all been relieved when the possibility of a manslaughter charge was dismissed—he was almost back to his former self. He'd had a haircut, but had kept a trimmed beard to cover up the scar on his face. None of them had been out to Ruby Gap yet, but the police had taken Pat and Rob to their son's grave. Saul, Gemma and Ethan had attended the memorial service held for Screw in town last week. Gemma had sat beside Pat and held back tears as Ethan held the older woman in his arms when she broke down as they left the hall.

Pat had reached up and touched his scarred face. 'Don't blame yourself, Ethan. I know you tried to do right by our boy.'

Ethan sat back and opened the lid of the small A4-sized box. 'The Women's Museum in town contacted Dad when they read the report in the paper.' He held up a brown-covered book. 'They've had this for a long time in their historical collection. The whole time I was researching Ruby Gap and the rubies at the library, I didn't know this was at the museum. They've loaned it to us for a month.'

'What is it?' Gemma leaned forward and looked at the book. The cover was illustrated with local flora.

Dad sat back and grinned. 'Would you believe my great-grand-mother Rose's diary?'

Ethan's smile was just as wide as their father's, and love surged through Gemma. It was still a miracle to have her twin back with them. He tapped a finger on the book. 'What's in here has tied up every loose end, and the best thing is, it's vindicated my "obsession", as you all called it.'

Tony chipped in. 'And in the back are letters from Rose's family and William that tell us exactly what happened.'

'How did it get to the museum?' Gemma asked.

'Rose moved to Alice Springs from Arltunga in the 1920s and became quite a well-known identity in the town. She was an active member of the Country Women's Association—even though she was in her seventies when the branch began—and was apparently very knowledgeable about local plants. She passed away in 1942, and her diary and letters were given to the local council, then passed on to the museum when it was established.'

'Oh, please tell us what happened. I felt as though I knew the family living out at Ruby Gap.'

Ethan looked at her, his expression sad. 'The child's grave out where we camped at the ruins was William and Rose's eldest son. He died from a snake bite in 1892. Rose and their other son, Bennett, Dad's grandfather, moved to Arltunga to wait for William. He'd gone to England, where—wait for it—he was able to prove that the rubies were the real deal. I told you all for years they were real!'

'So, he came home and they made their fortune?'

Ethan shook his head, and Dad held out a letter covered in faded spidery writing. 'The day they left the homestead was the day Rose was given the letter from her father in England advising her that William had been killed. It was so sad; he never came back to Australia.'

'And Rose would never leave here to go home to England,' Dad chipped in. 'She wouldn't leave Rufus alone.'

'Oh, how sad,' Mum said. Gemma tried not to look when Dad reached over and took Jennifer's hand, but she nudged Saul with her knee.

'Apparently, there was some suspicion around the circumstances of his death,' Ethan said. 'Anyway, in his letter to her, William told Rose not to tell anyone about what he'd discovered, and it appears she didn't. The ruby fields were abandoned as the prospectors all moved to Arltunga, where gold had been discovered.'

'And Arltunga was the first town in the Territory. I knew that,' Gemma said. 'You'd never know now driving through it. It's desolate and deserted. Like a ghost town.'

Saul shook his head and frowned. 'But there's one thing I don't get. If there weren't supposed to be rubies out there, how come those drug guys were mining under the pretext of building park infrastructure?'

Tony answered. 'There's always been fossickers out there. I guess the only thing that we can assume is one of them discovered some valuable gems, and someone out there got wind of it. They kept it quiet and just pillaged the river for their own greed. We'll never know and they're not going to say.'

'That was Terry's involvement, to make it look like park work. And he got away with it for six years,' Saul said.

'There aren't many places in the country so remote that have an abundance of solar power and the permanent waterhole at the base of the cliff,' Ethan said. 'If the flood hadn't dislodged Ruby and pushed her downstream, and if those hikers hadn't reported it—'

'And if Terry had sent anyone other than Saul in, you'd still be hiding up in the north, and we'd be none the wiser,' Tony concluded.

'And the meth lab and warehouse would still be in operation,' Saul added.

Gemma put her hand on Ethan's. 'Eth? How do you feel about not fossicking out there anymore? Seeing it's a nature park now, I mean.'

'I can if I get a permit, but I don't need to. I only ever wanted to prove that the family history was right and there were rubies out there,' Ethan said. 'What's hard is, if I'd known about this diary back then, Screw might still be alive. We wouldn't have been out there and stumbled on those crims.'

Gemma pulled the diary over to her, and carefully turned the pages. 'It's so sad. Other people's greed destroyed Rose and her family all that time ago, and it happened again to Screw. And poor Pat and Rob Turner too.'

Tony leaned across and took Gemma's hand. 'I'm sorry to say, love, greed is an inevitable part of human nature. We all have it to some extent, but it corrupts when a person will do anything to satisfy that greed, no matter who it hurts.'

Gemma turned to the last entry in the diary and tears misted her eyes as she read it. 'Have you read this, Dad? It's what you just said.'

Her father looked over her shoulder. 'No, I haven't got to the end yet. We only picked the diary up yesterday. What does it say?'

Gemma kept her voice firm as she read part of the entry. The writing was fine and faded, but the words were strong.

No matter what happens, nor what human greed takes from us, life renews and we learn to live without what we once had . . .
But my life was enriched by the love of my husband and my sons.

Saul's arm came around her as Gemma blinked back tears. She looked up and saw the anguish on her mother's face.

Jennifer stood, and her voice broke. 'As my life too was enriched by my husband and children. I'm sorry. So sorry.' She hurried away across the lawn, and Tony was quick to follow her. Ethan and

Gemma looked at each other as their parents stood close, and then Tony took Jennifer into his arms.

'I guess the path I took has had some positive outcomes too,' Ethan said with a catch in his voice.

Gemma looked up at Saul as he pulled her close. 'The best.'

EPILOGUE

Gemma wandered down to the site of the old homestead and looked around, imagining what the house would have looked like in Rose's day. She could imagine the porch where Rose had sat on the rocking chair that William had built, and she could still see the flat area of dirt where the boys had played with their wooden toys. Now that she had read Rose's diary and each of the letters inside, Gemma felt as though she knew her well. Knowing what a sad life Dad's great-grandmother had, and seeing how she had overcome the tragedy that life had thrown at her, made Gemma more determined to live a life where those she loved took priority over anything else.

The day was bright and cool and she shivered in the biting cold wind that blew up the gorge. Across the gorge gap, the rich red of the quartzite cliffs glowed in the midday sun. Ethan and Saul were putting up the small headstone that Mum and Dad had ordered to be placed out here at the homestead. Saul had sought and gained permission from Parks and Wildlife to install it where Rose and William and their two boys had lived.

Gemma sat out of the wind, leaning against the broad trunk of a towering ghost gum. She took Rose's diary from her bag, and turned to the page she had bookmarked. She had wanted to bring it to Ruby Gap today as they remembered their family who had settled here in the nineteenth century.

June 1942

Sometimes when I close my eyes, I can hear the wind whistling down the cliffs and the birds calling as they ride the air. If I listen carefully, I can hear Rufus and Bennett's laughter as they play with the wooden animals William carved for them, and the thwack of William's axe on the timber as he chops the kindling for my stove. With my eyes still closed, I put my hands out, and run them across the seeds that have sprouted in the winter sun. No matter what happens, nor what human greed takes from us, life renews, and we learn to live without what we once had.

I have no regrets for the path I chose. If I knew when I was a young woman where the direction I chose would take me, I would gladly take the same path. I have loved, and I have lost, but my life was enriched by the love of my husband and my sons. When I look at Bennett's children, I see William, and I see Rufus.

'Gemma!'

She put the diary on her lap and looked up the hill as Ethan called her.

'Are you ready?'

Gemma pushed herself to her feet and walked up the hill to Saul and Ethan. Her brother held out his hand and led her over to the old grave where they had dug the headstone into the hard dirt. She blinked as she read the words etched into the white stone.

She stood between her brother and the man she loved, and read the words.

This stone commemorates the memory of the Woodford Family

William 1858–1891

Rufus 1888–1892

Rose 1862–1942

Bennett 1890–1962

Rose Woodford was one of the early pioneers of Ruby Gap, and spent most of her life at Arltunga.

She overcame hardship and loss and had no regrets for the path she chose.

'May you all rest in peace,' she said.

As they walked back to the river, Gemma could have sworn she heard voices whispering in the wind.

ACKNOWLEDGEMENTS

At the far end of the East MacDonnells, 150 kilometres east of Alice Springs, lies Ruby Gap, an oasis sitting in a wide sandy riverbed shaded by stately white ghost gums. Now a Nature Park, Ruby Gap and Annie's Gorge are located in a stunning landscape of brilliant red quartzite cliffs under clear blue skies.

We travelled there in our four-wheel drive and caravan in 2019, intrigued by the story of the first mining rush in Central Australia. A once thriving mining hamlet is now a remote wilderness and this unique landscape with its chequered history inspired my story of the original ruby rush in the 1880s and the implications for my contemporary heroine.

A visit to the Alice Springs Public Library, and hours spent in the Alice Springs Special Collection room where I viewed publications relating to the historical, scientific and cultural heritage of Central Australia, produced gems of information just as exciting as discovering my own garnets at Ruby Gap!

Red Kangaroo Books in the Todd Mall in Alice Springs was a fabulous place to browse, and the following book purchase there provided great insight into the days at Arltunga and Ruby Gap for

Rose in the 1890s: *Man from Arltunga: Walter Smith, Australian Bushman* by R.G. Kimber (Hesperian Press, Carlisle, 1996).

As always, a huge thank you to my 'support' team: Susanne Bellamy for your thoughtful comments and ability to steer me in the right direction when I get stuck on a plot point, Roby Aiken for your pertinent comments and proofreading skills, and Kristen Woolgar for excellent proofreading!

Thank you to the whole team at HarperCollins Australia for their ongoing support, especially Rachael Donovan, Laurie Ormond, Sarana Behan and Eloise Plant. And of course, a special thank you to my awesome editor, Libby Turner, who polishes my stories until they gleam.

And to you, the reader, thank you so much for supporting me and reading my stories. I would love to hear from you. You can email me: annie@annieseaton.net

talk about it

Let's talk about books.

Join the conversation:

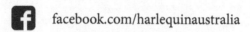 facebook.com/harlequinaustralia

 @harlequinaus

 @harlequinaus

harpercollins.com.au/hq

If you love reading and want to know about our
authors and titles, then let's talk about it.